ALSO BY JOHN J. NANCE

Fire Flight

Golden Boy

Skyhook

Turbulence

Headwind

Blackout

The Last Hostage

Medusa's Child

Pandora's Clock

Phoenix Rising

Final Approach

Scorpion Strike

What Goes Up

On Shaky Ground

Blind Trust

Splash of Colors

SAVING CASCADIA

JOHN J. NANCE

SIMON & SCHUSTER
NEW YORK LONDON TORONTO SYDNEY

SIMON & SCHUSTER
Rockefeller Center
1230 Avenue of the Americas
New York, NY 10020

SIMON & SCHUSTER and colophon are registered trademarks
of Simon & Schuster, Inc.

For information regarding special discounts for bulk purchases,
please contact Simon & Schuster Special Sales at 1-800-456-6798
or business@simonandschuster.com

Designed by Davina Mock

Manufactured in the United States of America

10 9 8 7 6 5 4 3

Library of Congress Cataloging-in-Publication Data

Nance, John J.
Saving Cascadia / John J. Nance.
p.   cm.
1. Search and rescue operations—Fiction. 2. Seattle Region (Wash.)—Fiction. 3. Natural
disasters—Fiction. 4. Islands—Fiction. 5. Hotels—Fiction. I. Title.
PS3564.A546N36 2005
813'.54—dc22   2004061603
ISBN 0-7432-5051-6

To the unsung heroes who run our emergency airevac and medical air transport services nationwide—an amazing cadre of men and women, who 24/7 balance the highest standards of aviation safety with the vital and life-saving medical mission.

And to Dr. Brian Atwater of the U.S. Geological Survey.

SAVING
CASCADIA

CHAPTER 1

Twice now on the way back from dinner Diane Lacombe had aborted the process of lighting a stale cigarette. She'd been dredging them from the depths of her purse—her emergency stash buried just in case she had to fall off the wagon some night—but once again she tossed the unlit cigarette into a street-corner trash can, pushing back her mane of auburn hair with an unsteady hand. Relaxing right now was an apparently useless quest, and the need to rummage for yet another cigarette was rising.

She calculated the number of blocks back to her Mission District apartment and dug in her purse for an emergency package of chewing gum instead. Too much agony with nicotine patches to blow it all now.

The Tonga Room had been fun, and all the more so since it was one of her dad's favorites, set amid the elegance of the grand old Fairmont Hotel. Some of her best childhood memories centered around lush, elegant dinners with her parents, the princess daughter scrubbed and dressed up and feminine, demonstrating impeccable manners and basking in family privilege and tradition. But this evening's visit to that world had felt like a hologram. She could see it, but she couldn't actually touch the old warmth of those moments, though nothing in the hotel had changed. Since she'd left for college, the childhood years were now only glimpsed through a murky lens, as if they belonged to someone else. It was an awful feeling she was determined to change.

A neighborhood tavern she'd frequented over the years was just ahead and she decided to duck in for their usually pathetic attempt at an espresso. She took the tiny cup to a dark corner like an addict, placing her laptop case by her feet where she could keep an eye on it.

Not for the first time she felt around in her coat pocket for the reassuring shape of the CD that she'd intended to hand to her father at dinner. Just the thought of committing that act was the source of her jangled nerves. It might as well have been a small nuclear device, she thought. It would have killed him just as surely. What had she been thinking?

Diane knew that California State Senator Ralph Lacombe had wondered through coffee and dessert why his beautiful, educated, twenty-seven-year-old daughter was so jumpy and distracted. Fit and distinguished in his late fifties with a large trademark smile, his full head of dark hair belying his age, the senior Lacombe had sat in patient, paternal puzzlement waiting, Diane supposed, for the explanation which never came. All the normal subjects they had once shared in open father-daughter communication seemed flat and forced—the 49ers, the latest political betrayals in Sacramento, the plans for a summer Lacombe family reunion in the wake of her mother's surrender to cancer—and nothing had reduced her jittery demeanor or ended her constant denials that anything was wrong. There she sat, elegant in a reasonably conservative, calf-length little black dress, smiling at him and lying her head off by saying none of the things that needed to be voiced. He knew his daughter was fibbing by omission, and she knew that he knew, but they played the game anyway, more like two strangers being courteous than familial confidants.

And all the while the CD had been burning a hole in her heart. The last thing she wanted was to make him a casualty of what she had to do.

How would he have reacted if she'd been foolhardy enough to hand it over? Would the most ethical man on earth fall to the level of ordinary mortal before her very eyes?

And how could he not?

How would the conversation have gone? she wondered. *Oh, here, Dad, just a little hard seismic evidence that the critics were right after all about your old friend Mick Walker's Cascadia Island project, which means that not only is Mick going to be ruined, but my engineering firm may end up like Enron's accountants, and, oh, by the way, you'll probably be publicly accused of misusing your political influence on behalf of Walker for promoting his resort.*

Was there any way a loving daughter or anyone else could expect Ralph Lacombe to say, "Sure, Honey, you go on and do what you have to. Blow the whistle. Destroy everything." Not even her father was that brave. Or foolish.

He would end up asking her not to pull the trigger, and she wouldn't be able to stand his plea or her denial.

No. It was going to be far easier to deal with the damage after the fact, even if that method was cowardly.

The island was always a time bomb, Dad, she thought. *Pity poor old Mick didn't know it in time.*

What she'd found in the seismic test data meant that Cascadia Island off the Washington coast was too dangerous an outcropping to support any human habitation or facilities, and especially not a resort hotel and convention center. There was a massive split down the middle, a hidden fault line so profoundly active that Walker's resort would end up pulled in two with any substantial earthquake. And that same data, she knew, would also be seized upon by a certain scientist in Seattle as validation of his discredited hypothesis about the entire island being some sort of sensitive seismic trigger. According to the paper he'd published, Cascadia Island's small, rocky mass was supposedly resting on the geological equivalent of a hair-trigger detonator connected to a massive fault zone deep within the Cascadia Subduction Zone. Other seismologists had loudly rejected Dr. Lam's ideas, but he continued to insist that any significant vibrations from that island could set off a chain reaction of amplified resonant vibrations and trigger a great earthquake equal to or greater than the monster that tore through Alaska in 1964.

No one disputed the fact that the Cascadia Subduction Zone was one of the world's most dangerous tectonic faults. But the idea that the pile drivers and explosives used to build Mick Walker's world-class resort could uncork three hundred years of unrelieved tectonic strain was just too far out to be real.

Diane sipped the last of the extremely bitter espresso and smiled to herself. Dr. Lam's "Theory of Resonant Amplification" was utter nonsense. If subterranean nuclear explosions were insufficient to trigger major earthquakes, a little construction activity on a coastal island had no chance of doing it. Maybe the rocks below did amplify any compression waves from a pile driver or rock blasting, but such impacts were ridiculously puny against the massive forces of nature.

Nevertheless, she was very glad for Dr. Lam and his theory. He was exactly the man she needed for the dirty work of blowing the whistle on the hidden fault her firm had apparently missed long before construction began.

Diane felt her heart accelerating. The last thing she needed was more caffeine, but if she had to have an addiction, coffee was fairly benign, especially after wrestling nicotine to the mat.

She stood to go. *I'm outta here.*

She picked up her laptop case, paid the tab, and left quickly, setting a course for her flat and trying to retain just enough situational awareness to avoid becoming a hood ornament on various passing trucks.

There were millions of dollars at stake. Maybe even a hundred million of Mick Walker's dollars. And God knew how much she was about to damage Chadwick and Noble, the globe-girdling, prestigious firm that had reached down from the heavens of architectural engineering to pluck her from the newly graduated masses. She felt another brief and distant echo of guilt over that. The chairman, Robert Nelms, was a straight shooter, or so she'd always believed. But how could he do anything but suppress, cover up, deny, and hide when he discovered what the real data said?

She recalled her first meeting with Robert Nelms so clearly. She, the Stanford graduate student shown into the elaborately decorated corner office. He, a man whose girth made him look like an amalgam of Charles Laughton, Raymond Burr, and Marlon Brando in his later years. The effect had been instant intimidation heaped on a towering platter of insecurity, even though Nelms couldn't have been nicer, rising with surprising ease and polished courtliness to take her hand and welcome her. It was clearly an interview, as she had hoped, but he made it pleasant, impressing her with the easy way he wore the mantle of power of the managing partner of such an august firm—not to mention his own impressive professional history as a brilliant engineer. She had left the office not only aching to work for Chadwick and Noble, but wanting to work for and please Robert Nelms in particular. The memory still made her feel good, eliciting an unbidden smile that quickly faded as she returned to the reality of what she was doing.

What she was doing was disloyal in the extreme, and she professed to hate disloyalty. But her mission was righteous, and if it meant she had to repay the kindnesses they'd shown her with disloyalty, so be it.

Feeling guilty about impacting Robert Nelms was one thing, but the potential effect on Jerry Schultz was entirely another.

The memory of her first serious professional interaction with Schultz, her new supervisor, was all too clear. She'd sought help with a problem involving an extremely important construction project in the Philippines and was flabbergasted to realize that he was either a poor engineer or a poorer manager with no grasp of details he should have known. It was clearly on her shoulders alone, and the only elements of her work he did seem interested in were the signatures and other means of tracking who might be responsible for mistakes. Schultz was all about covering his own tail. He was a raging incompetent, she'd told a close friend. A dangerous incompetent with delusions of adequacy.

Somehow she'd transcended Schultz during her first year and had become a guardian of the stellar reputation of Chadwick and Noble. She'd been loath to accept the reality that the firm had grown too big to maintain its quality or even its integrity, and she'd resisted the conclusion that the managers cared only about preserving their careers and paychecks.

Finally, however, those realities became unavoidable, and in the Cascadia Island fiasco, the properly constituted managers of Chadwick and Noble had wanted to hear no criticism of their prior decisions.

They had been *so* pathetically predictable! Once the firm had anointed the island as buildable, the managers were arrogantly certain that not even God would dare to second-guess their decision.

She'd had no authority to push it any further, nor any desire to do so. After all, she was an engineer, not a seismologist. That gave her an ironclad out when the truth finally exploded into the public arena. How could anyone have expected a mere engineer to know what seismic data revealed? Especially since she wasn't even supposed to *see* the data. Even if she had known, who was *she* to say the data was right, the Chadwick and Noble cognoscenti were wrong, and Cascadia Island was doomed?

But the data *was* right and the island was indeed doomed.

She wondered if an answer from Dr. Lam would be waiting for her on her computer. The anonymous e-mail she'd carefully worded and sent contained a way for him to answer through an intermediate e-mail address that would prevent her having to reveal her name—a bit of necessary cat and mouse to focus his interest without leading to her doorstep. But she could only check that intermediate site once a day, and she'd been doing so every night without results. Eventually he would have to respond, since he was sure to realize that what she was offering would be a vindication of his own discounted, discredited theory.

There would need to be a face-to-face meeting, she figured, to actually hand over the disk. But Dr. Lam could be expected to quickly trumpet the results to the geophysical world. She was sure of that. As sure as she was that if the name Diane Lacombe wasn't involved in the publicity storm that would undoubtedly envelop Chadwick and Noble, Senator Ralph Lacombe couldn't be drawn in either.

That was very important. It was not going to be pretty.

Walker may still survive, she thought. *He's worth hundreds of millions.*

Diane's right hand closed around the doorknob to her apartment as her left hand approached with the key, but the door was neither latched nor closed, and for a moment she stood in confusion, wondering if she'd left it that way hours ago.

No way! I always check it.

Maybe the manager was inside.

But he's not supposed to . . .

Perhaps her father . . .

He doesn't have a key. But Don does!

The impulse to call the police and try to have Don Brevin arrested for breaking and entering was already forming in her mind, a deserved retribution for his being a boorish ex-boyfriend and for refusing to return the key when they'd argued earlier in the day. He'd probably come back for his mea-ger belongings, she decided. He wasn't dangerous, just a slob and an ego-maniac, and she couldn't fathom why she'd ever dated him, let alone al-lowed him to move in for two very long, very unsatisfying months. Just another in a long line of toxic rebound boyfriends, and her tastes were get-ting worse.

I should have changed the locks.

She pushed open the door and stood stunned by the chaos that had been her apartment. Someone had ransacked her things, pulling out drawers, opening cabinets and spilling the contents. She stepped in, leaving the door to the hallway open in case anything moved inside and she needed to flee.

Her largest suitcase was in the corner, pulled from the back closet and opened and left at an odd angle. The sofa had been ripped open, its stuffing strewn everywhere. The recliner had also been gored. In all the mess, she couldn't tell whether anything was missing.

The new high-definition TV she couldn't afford still stood untouched where she'd left it in the corner of the living room, and she felt a momen-tary spark of relief, as if now everything would be all right.

The spark quickly died.

Diane stepped over the strewn clothes, papers, and books and moved cautiously toward her bedroom door. Inside, it appeared little or nothing had been taken, but virtually everything had been dumped and, she as-sumed, pawed through—including lingerie. She felt violated and dirty, as if she, and not her apartment, had been raped.

And she felt an old familiar rage escaping from its cage again.

But this didn't make sense. Brevin was a sideshow, and a harmless one at that. He wouldn't do such a thing. Would he?

A sudden realization chilled her. Brevin wasn't the cause. *Someone was looking for something!*

The small, toxic object in her pocket was the target. Someone was on her trail and this was a very clear message.

But how on earth could they already know? No one was supposed to know of her plans, but someone must have figured she might have the records.

And here I stand with the CD waiting for whoever did this to come back!

A crystalline memory of what she'd written in her e-mail to Dr. Lam popped into her mind. Was there anyway it could have been intercepted and tracked back to her?

No! She concluded. *I didn't even send it from my computer.* But what else could have tipped them off?

She thought about Jerry Schultz, her boss, the dithering neurotic she se-cretly called the world's only walking invertebrate, a man scared of his own shadow. Her *purported* supervisor, she'd labeled him. There was simply no way Schultz could have figured out what she'd done, let alone have been brave enough to invade her apartment. Who then?

At least I had the disk with me instead of leaving it here, Diane thought. The overall mission was intact, even if her apartment wasn't. She'd been more than naïve, but considering the money at stake, the loss was small.

Don Brevin forgotten, Diane revised her plan on the spot. She jumped like a startled cat and began rummaging quickly through the spilled contents of her top bureau drawer until her passport emerged from underneath the wild display of her costume jewelry. There was a small gym bag in the middle of the floor which used to be in the closet and she grabbed it and began scooping a supply of basics into it before dashing to the bathroom and dumping in makeup and toiletries to accompany her toothbrush and dryer. The bag was too stuffed to be zipped fully closed, but she grabbed it up anyway, holding the straps extra tight to keep the contents inside as she dashed to the door.

Distance and anonymity were the keys to success—and safety—now that someone was on her trail. She raced into the empty hallway and headed for the stairwell, focused on ways to evaporate from San Francisco.

Chapter 2

Despite all her training and instincts as a helicopter pilot, Jennifer Lindstrom did the unthinkable and took her hands off the controls.

The big commercial Chinook helicopter with twenty-six paying passengers aboard continued to fly straight and level, the breathtaking vista of mountains and clouds and blue sky staying right where it should be in the windscreen.

To compound the heresy, Jennifer moved her feet off the pedals that controlled the yawing motion of the craft.

And still it flew on, steady as a rock.

Smiling, exhilarated, and feeling otherwordly and decadent, she lifted her hands over her head and clasped them together, losing herself like a kid riding no-hands on a bicycle—a gesture no sane rotary wing pilot would ever make at the controls.

The horizon remained steady.

She closed her eyes, feeling the smile grow, her eyelids fluttering open only when a small sideways motion caught her attention.

In an instant everything changed. She was being shoved to the right, and forests and fields were appearing in the windscreen where moments before only blue skies had been. Her heart rate jumped alarmingly as her body suddenly became lighter. The big Chinook twisted to the left, its attitude dangerously nose-down now, the airspeed rising.

Jennifer's hands instinctively found the controls again, her left on the collective, her right on the cyclic between her legs, her feet on the pedals as she began nudging them back in the right direction.

But the controls were strangely reluctant.

She pulled harder, but the harder she pulled, the more the controls resisted moving—and the turning dive was becoming acute.

This isn't happening!

Panic began to seep into her like cold, rising water, overwhelming her quickly and quietly as options evaporated. Pulling was useless, the controls were somehow locked. The helicopter spun inexorably downward.

———

Waking suddenly from the nightmarish scene, Jennifer Lindstrom sat bolt upright in bed, her feet and hands tangled in the bedcovers, her heart racing.

Shakily she got to her feet and padded into the bathroom, noting when she looked in the mirror the haunted look on her face and the fear still in her eyes.

No wonder the cat won't sleep with me anymore!

This was the third time in a month, and always the same insane dream, the same place, the same helicopter. Usually she couldn't remember her dreams, but *this* one was there in living terror time after time, and it was beginning to shake her confidence as a pilot.

Why would her mind even conceive of such a suicidal act, even in a dream?

NEAR KING COUNTY INTERNATIONAL AIRPORT (BOEING FIELD)
SEATTLE, WASHINGTON
FRIDAY, NOVEMBER 25TH 5:05 P.M.

Good way to get us killed, Bub! Jennifer Lindstrom thought as she yanked her aircraft into an evasive maneuver.

The tower controller had cleared a tiny Cessna 152 to land on the long runway, 16R, while Jennifer had clearance to land her Beech Bonanza on the small, parallel runway on the left. But she recognized the complete confusion in the hesitant response of the Cessna pilot and knew exactly what he was going to do, which was to aim for the wrong runway and slide dangerously in front of her.

The agitated voice of the controller, a longtime friend, responded immediately. "Cessna Three Two Bravo, I told you, one six *right!* You just cut in front of a Bonanza!"

A shaken, almost reedy male voice came on the frequency, the enormity of the mistake settling in. "Ah . . . I'm sorry, Tower, I thought you said the left one."

"Three Two Bravo if that's you calling, use your call sign every time you transmit."

"Ah . . . Three Two . . . ah . . . Bravo, roger."

"Three Two Bravo, you're now cleared to land runway one six *left*. Bonanza Five Four Hotel, you're cleared to land on one six right. Break. Three Two Bravo, once on the ground, we'd like you to give us a landline call in the tower, sir. Ask the ground controller for the number when you're parked."

"Ah . . . roger, sir. Three Two Bravo."

Jennifer punched her transmit button. "Bonanza Five Four Hotel, one six right, roger." Undoubtedly, the Cessna driver was going to get tongue-lashed by the tower, and maybe formally violated. He deserved it.

Jennifer flared her beloved old Bonanza and touched down smoothly, taxiing back to the large hangar belonging to Nightingale Aviation.

Her company.

The momentary duel with the clueless Cessna pilot forgotten, she ran the shutdown checklist, letting her eyes stray pridefully to the line of heli-copters parked in front of the hangar door. Two were part of their separate charter operation, but the remainder formed the best, most modern fleet of emergency air evacuation helicopters on the west coast.

Sven Lindstrom had taught his daughter well, though the process had been painful. Sven had always been a screamer as an instructor pilot, more attuned to the temperament of the worst of the old-time IPs in World War II than the enlightened methods of professional airmen. But through all the berating and verbal abuse he heaped on anyone who dared be his student in either fixed or rotary wing aircraft, the end result was an ability to meld with the ma-chine, especially with helicopters. Jennifer loved flying choppers the best. She loved the feeling of not knowing where she ended and where the helicopter began, so in tune were her hands and feet with the essence of the controls. That was thanks to her father's merciless insistence on perfection—especially in the case of a daughter who insisted on trying to do a man's job.

Just for a moment she lost her place in the checklist as her discipline wa-vered and her mind flashed to Doug Lam and the evening to come. She yanked herself back to the job at hand, smiling at the ground crewmen who hadn't noticed her transitory failure to compartmentalize.

Jennifer shook her mind back to the present and climbed out of the old J-35 Bonanza, the classic V-tailed doctor killer, as the joke went, a four-seater built in 1958 and purchased for fifty thousand dollars two years before. She'd wanted her own helicopter, but there wasn't enough money in her personal accounts to handle the price or the cost of maintaining one.

She passed through the building trying not to think of business. The hour in the Bonanza had been therapeutic, but passing the charter desk of Nightingale Air Services and the entrance to the medevac operation forced her mind back to business.

The two operations were separate companies, and she served as presi-dent of both, a challenge that kept her scrambling to stay qualified and safe as a pilot. The resistance from the chief pilots of both operations to her fly-ing the line was a constant irritation, yet she had to honor their independ-ence and listen when they demanded more proficiency time or drew a line in the operational sand about attending another proficiency training course. Even the boss had to take a checkride twice a year.

Six years as an Army Reserve MAST helicopter pilot had given her the basic flight experience, but the fact that she'd continued to build flight time on her father's helicopter fleet during the six years she'd spent as a civilian nurse didn't impress her colleagues much. To them, a professional medevac helicopter pilot had too big a professional challenge on a daily basis to permit any moonlighting. It was all but inconceivable that an ordinary individual could take a decade-long diversion into medicine and come back to fly line missions. But she refused to be ordinary.

Not missions, she reminded herself. *We're not mission oriented. We're operationally oriented.* It was a small point, but significant. Mission orientation—save the patient at all costs—was a deadly philosophy responsible for many accidents and deaths across the country. It was called the "White Knight" syndrome, and it was her responsibility to keep it out of the heads of Nightingale pilots.

Four years ago a stroke had grounded Sven Lindstrom as a pilot, and to some extent it had shoved him out of the business he'd built. A lifelong practice of buying commercial real estate had made him the fortune that enabled him to start Nightingale, but helicopters, not real estate, were his real passion. He'd loved every aspect of the operations, and turning over the reins to a mere girl had been traumatic. Jennifer couldn't be sure which form of torture had been worse for her father: fighting to recover fully from the stroke, or watching her settle in as the boss.

She turned for a moment to look at the impressive sign over the entrance to Nightingale Aviation. It would have been no surprise to see her father come barreling out of that same door like an energized tiger the way he'd always done at the end of the day, his face a study of intensity.

It was getting late. She needed to get moving if she was going to be on time, but there was an unfinished matter tugging at her conscience. She couldn't just walk off and leave that poor young pilot in the crosshairs of Brad Temple's temper.

She retraced her steps into the building to pick up the nearest phone with a tie-line to the tower, pleased to hear the familiar voice of the same controller who'd just snarled at the Cessna student.

"Brad? Hi. Jennifer. Have you talked to that Cessna pilot yet?"

"He just called in on the other line. I'm letting him cool his heels for a second."

"Look, Brad, the truth is, I really had plenty of room out there, and he's obviously a newbie who'll never forget the mistake he just made."

"We can't have people pulling that sort of fool stunt without consequences, Jennifer."

"Yeah . . . and you're talking to someone who has to admit she pulled that very same fool stunt a bunch of years ago, same runway, same airport, everything."

"You get violated?"

"No. This very gruff, but gentle and wise tower controller had me come over in person. I thought he was going to yell at me and take my license and everything. He couldn't have been calmer, and the way he handled it made a huge impression. I never even got close to doing that again."

"Okay. I get the point."

"Just . . . thought I'd let you know."

"I'm not going to violate him. Just read him the riot act."

"Good."

"Gently and wisely."

Jennifer smiled before replacing the phone and heading for the parking lot. She slumped behind the wheel of her 4Runner and closed the door, aware she had little more than an hour to become as drop-dead beautiful as possible before Doug arrived at her front door.

Doug.

How could she possibly explain to him how frustrated she was? And yet, how could she not? She should have been able to just ignore the feelings of uncertainty about their relationship, but the doubts had begun to eat at her, eroding her confidence. Was she being played for a fool, or was she just being foolish? There were moments when she felt guilty in wanting so much for him to take the final step of turning his three-and-a-half-year separation into a divorce. Why he couldn't slam the door on Deborah Lam was a deepening mystery, but it was also tearing at her. Why on earth was he dragging his feet if he'd been as unhappy in the marriage as he'd claimed? He kept avoiding the subject, and that, too, was disturbing. Worse, it was now becoming a real cancer in their relationship. She could deal with a rational explanation—a real reason—but she couldn't deal with silence, and if he hadn't figured it out for himself, she was going to have to risk the relationship and just tell him.

In some ways she was as upset with herself for hesitating as she was with him for doing nothing. Her timidity was embarrassing, especially for a woman who had such a need to be in control.

But there was a lot at stake, and she had no idea how he'd respond. She'd long since fallen in love with him, and with that reality came the fear of losing him if she pushed too hard. Earlier in the week, though, she'd decided tonight was the time to bring it up as gently as possible. She owed that to herself, and to him.

But, she thought, why ruin *this* beautiful evening? Why not leave it alone and hide in his arms for another night? Just one more. Wasn't that a better thing to do? After all, there was a good reason. Tonight was the third anniversary of their first date.

Jennifer felt as confused as ever, and when uncertainty overtook her, she knew what to do. Action was the only way out of the fog. If Sven had taught her nothing else it was how to square her shoulders and wade into whatever had to be done, rather than spend her life hiding from it. "Face it. Deal with it. Square your shoulders like a man," Sven was fond of saying—knowing full well that he was addressing his daughter, who always cringed at the chauvinistic reference.

There was no son to inherit the diminutive empire Sven had built. Fate had dealt him the Henry the Eighth card and given him only a daughter, and despite all his efforts to whip her into shape, regardless of how good she was at everything she did, she was still a she, the weaker sex.

And yet she loved him endlessly, and spent far too much of herself trying to please him.

She had staged one major rebellion at least. After earning her MBA, she had suddenly changed directions and decided to go to nursing school, and Sven had hit the roof.

"A bleeding-heart *nurse?*" he'd raged to a male friend one night over brandy when he didn't know his daughter was listening in the next room. "I try to get her ready to be a doctor or lawyer or something worthwhile, and she wants to prance around with bedpans like Florence Frigging Nightingale!" The verbal sneer became an oft-repeated complaint to anyone who'd listen.

But there was delicious irony in the fact that just after Jennifer's graduation, Sven Lindstrom's young helicopter company had landed a major air medical transport service contract and one of his financial backers had suggested the name "Nightingale." His fortunes were sure to soar with the building of an exclusive network for flying patients to hospitals, and somewhere along the way his eye-rolling animus to the "Nightingale" name had disappeared.

"Great name, don't you think?" he asked Jennifer the day they filed the corporate papers. "It's a European bird, as well as the sympathy-evoking name of that famous nurse, and it instantly puts us on the side of the angels."

"Good decision, Dad," she remembered telling him as she stifled a laugh.

"Mom," she said to her mother sometime later, "maybe we should push him to expand the name and make it the 'Florence Frigging Nightingale Aviation Corporation.' "

"Or 'Bedpan Air!' " her mom replied, laughing uproariously at her husband's unsuspecting expense.

The truth was, Jennifer loved the old grouch. She just wished that it wasn't so important deep down inside to please him, since complete fulfill-ment of that dream would always be blocked by her gender.

She pulled the 4Runner into her condo parking spot, wondering if she should solve the painful discussion dilemma by just cancelling the date with Doug.

But that was the coward's way out, she thought, and she'd waffled back and forth too much as it was over the previous months. It was time to set a course and stick to it.

Jennifer unconsciously headed for the shower, turning her attention to the more practical question of whether her feet could survive an evening in the new red pumps she'd bought a month ago and hadn't had a chance to wear until now.

Chapter 3

Mick Walker had leased an entire floor of the Transamerica building long before he could afford the rent. But it was just that level of bravado and risk taking that propelled the value of his high-wire-act developments around the world, doubling and redoubling his annual profits in a success story that seemed endless. There were rumors around town that now he could not only afford a couple of floors, he could buy the entire building.

But he didn't need a building. He needed a break, and for more than three decades he'd refused to stop working long enough to take one.

He stood in front of his floor-to-ceiling office window thinking through the planned events of the next two days. The fractional business jet he'd ordered would be waiting at San Francisco International for the short flight to Seattle, and then his island.

His island! As with so many other projects, he had run roughshod over the naysayers, defeating bad science and environmentalists and political enemies to create a marvel.

The offices of Chadwick and Noble, the renowned engineering and architectural firm, had done most of the work on the amazing complex. It boasted a hotel, casino, convention center, and even ferry docks, all state-of-the-art and ready for the opening. The world headquarters of Chadwick and Noble stood two blocks away from the Transamerica building, and Mick imagined the discomfort of Robert Nelms, the managing partner, who was going to have to loft his considerable girth into a car to get to the same jet. Mick had insisted that Nelms "share" the limelight, but it was more a defensive maneuver in case technical questions were asked that the developer couldn't adequately explain. Nelms was the master architect and engineer while Mick was the master showman who orchestrated talented people into lending him money to build things no one else would attempt.

A gossamer image from long ago, a young woman with large, piercing eyes wearing a stunning blue cocktail dress at a dinner in Hong Kong, swam into his mind again. She came often in reflective moments. The daughter or girlfriend of an expatriate Westerner, she'd sat quietly through an important dinner with important men, listening to the captains of industry dance their dance, and just when he'd concluded that the lady in blue had been intimidated into silence, she'd caught his eye, and with a disturbing little smile that spoke of wisdom beyond her years, she asked if he was happy. Nothing more. Just that. "Are you happy?"

He was just getting started with his Aussie air of confidence and his ability to orchestrate wonders, and he thought he had all answers to all questions on tap. It wasn't the question that had rocked him. It was his inability to answer.

She'd excused herself and left before he could even mouth the words, "I don't really know."

And how would he answer the same question now? he wondered.

Mick smiled. The answer was still complex, but at least he had one, and it was mostly yes.

Mostly.

An electronic tone broke into his thoughts, followed by his secretary's voice.

"Mick? Sorry to interrupt. There's a gentleman from the San Francisco Police Department here to see you on an urgent matter."

Mick turned with a frown and moved back to the desk, intent on challenging the intrusion, but one of the walnut double doors to his office was already opening to admit a dark-haired man in his late thirties. His secretary was holding the door and looking worried.

"This is Detective Craig Bailey," she said, adding a mouthed, "Sorry," before retreating. Bailey held out his hand and Mick took it as he quietly assessed the detective's cheap business suit and regrettable choice of striped tie.

"What can I do for you, Detective Bailey?" he said somewhat grandly, motioning to a sitting area across the office from his desk. Bailey looked uncomfortable, which was a satisfying response.

"I'm sorry to . . . to . . ."

"Interrupt? So late in the day?"

"Yes, but . . ."

"Perfectly all right. I am on my way to the airport, but I can spare a few minutes. Please, sit down."

Bailey allowed himself to be motioned onto the couch as Mick settled into one of the custom-made mahogany wing chairs.

"Mr. Walker, we're looking for a young woman who works for Chadwick and Noble. A Mr. Robert Nelms over there suggested you might have been in touch with her lately."

"To whom are you referring?"

"A Miss Diane Lacombe."

"Diane Lacombe?" Mick felt himself involuntarily sit forward as he searched the police detective's face, his reply even and unruffled. The mention of her name brought a sparkle of apprehension he carefully suppressed. He knew the detective was watching for his reaction with a practiced eye. "She's an engineer over there, but tell me, why are you looking for her? Is this a criminal matter of some sort?"

"There is potential criminal conduct involved, but she would be the victim. We're concerned that she may have been kidnapped," Bailey said, "from her place in the Mission District. Given the wrecked state of her apartment, we also think the perpetrator was searching for something either personal or professional, and if it's professional, I thought you might be able to help us figure out what it was, and who might have wanted it."

"Diane Lacombe kidnapped? Good Lord. But I don't understand why Robert would think I might have any information. She hasn't worked on any of my projects for many months."

"I think he felt you might have had an ongoing . . . friendship with her."

"The word you're stumbling for is *relationship*, right?"

"Perhaps. Your call."

"I don't particularly appreciate the innuendo," Mick said, wondering just what the detective thought he knew about their friendship. The subject was unsettling.

"*Relationship* was your word, Mr. Walker, but no offense intended," Bailey said. "I'm just trying to gather facts."

"Well, I'm afraid I can't help you. I have no knowledge of her activities."

"But, you do know her? You have had some sort of relationship, friendship, acquaintanceship with her in the past then, haven't you?"

"As I said, she's been assigned to some of my firm's projects, and certainly I've had some professional interaction. Is that all you've got, by the way? A torn-up apartment?"

"It's enough to worry us officially. I, of course, can't discuss everything we've found."

"Of course."

"So . . . did you know Miss Lacombe socially, or personally . . . anything other than professionally."

Mick thought for a few seconds as he stared the detective in the eye.

"Well, if you must know, yes. We have had a relationship, and we still do. But not what *you're* thinking. Fact is, I've known Diane since she was toddling around in diapers, and I'm practically her uncle, since her dad's been a close friend of mine for decades. But I don't keep in touch with her, and I haven't even talked to her in many months."

"Okay."

"I'm deeply distressed that you think she's missing, or the victim of foul play."

"I actually didn't say she was the victim of foul play . . ."

"What else would you call kidnapping?"

Bailey shrugged. "It's just semantics, I suppose."

"So what else have you got? Isn't it possible she just ran off to Mexico for the week, just playing hooky, and someone burglarized her place in the meantime?"

"It's always possible. We've checked outbound flights, trains, that sort of thing. Fact is, we can't find her. Did she ever indicate she wanted to disappear?"

"No." Mick sat back slightly, letting his mind race. "Are you aware that Diane's father is State Senator Ralph Lacombe?"

"Yes. We're already in touch with her family. Her father has heard nothing from her. And I need to know when you last saw her, Mr. Walker."

"Actually, several months ago. Or longer. It was one afternoon when I dropped by Ralph's house. I haven't worked with her directly for maybe a year."

"Do you know whether she routinely kept company records at home?"

He shook his head. "How would I know that? I've never seen her apartment, and I have no idea."

"No trade secrets her firm's competitors might want?"

"Chadwick and Noble don't really have competitors, Detective. They're the gold standard."

"All right."

Mick sat forward, his voice suddenly more intense.

"Look, I'll put the entire resources of my company behind helping in any way I can. Post a reward, pay for TV ads, pay a ransom, whatever. Whatever Ralph needs. Just let me know."

"That's all premature right now. But I've got one more thing. Do you know a Don Brevin?"

"No. Should I?"

"Diane Lacombe's boyfriend?"

Mick sighed and shook his head. "Detective Bailey, let me make this really clear. I have had no participation in Diane's daily private life. I have no idea who she was seeing."

"Again, sir, there's no need to get defensive. I'm just trying to get as much background as I can, and I thought . . ."

"You thought that, since I'm a single man, maybe I was somehow involved with Diane romantically. Right?"

"Romantic or . . . sexual involvement is not normally what I think about when the male involved is the girl's godfather."

"You're aware of that?"

"Yes."

"I'm sure Ralph told you, which is fine."

"Mr. Walker, forgive my directness, but . . . is there something you need to tell me?"

The phraseology sparked another wave of worry. Fully composed, Mick laughed. "Hardly, Detective. I guess I've just been watching too many reruns of Columbo."

"Yeah," Bailey chuckled. "That can get to you. Even as a detective. You know, you begin to suspect saints and little old ladies, and even your own mother."

"Mothers can be sneaky."

They moved toward the door and Mick accepted the detective's business card. "That's my cell phone number," Bailey said. "Don't hesitate to call if there's anything you think of that could help. Anything."

"You can depend on it."

The detective's cell phone rang as he moved down the corridor, and Mick turned to his secretary. "Get Ralph Lacombe on the phone. Quickly."

MILBRAE (SAN FRANCISCO)

The fleeting shadow of someone running past a side window toward the backyard preceded a sudden rap on the front door by less than a second. Don Brevin spun around in momentary confusion, the freshly opened beer on the counter already forgotten.

"Hold on," he bellowed in the direction of the door, wondering what it would be like to have a butler to take care of such irritations. It galled him that there were eighteen-year-old actors out there with staffs and Rolls-Royces in their sixteen-car garages, and here he sat in his parents' San Francisco stucco rambler, which sported less than two thousand square feet, having to do everything for himself. Some success. Yeah, he had a Porsche and a Harley, but they were mainly owned by his bank.

Scowling at the thought, he swung the door open on a collection of cops standing behind a man in a business suit holding out a badge wallet much like the one Don had carried in his last movie. So the guy was a detective.

"Yeah?"

"Don Brevin?"

Brevin snorted, letting the crooked smile he intended to make an icon in American moviedom spread across his face. It was his James Dean fantasy.

"Should I ask who wants to know?"

"When you've got a face full of badges?" the suit replied. "I doubt it."

"Whazzup?"

"May we come in and talk to you, Mr. Brevin?"

"Hey, sure. You guys were nice to help me prep for my last flick." He stood aside as the detective and the uniforms moved into the living room, the suit's eyes obviously recording everything within as he introduced himself as Detective Craig Bailey.

"So what's going on?"

"Do you know a woman named Diane Lacombe?"

Something cold began spreading around his insides as he struggled to keep an even expression. He should have expected this.

"Yeah, sure. She's been my girlfriend for a couple of years. Or, at least, last year. I mean, we only lived together for a while, but . . . that's over, and I just got my things back."

"When?"

"Yesterday morning. Why?"

Craig Bailey studied the young man's eyes and waited. It was one of the habits that made him a better than average cop, the ability to keep his mouth shut until the silence became an uncomfortable void the subject just had to fill. Brevin was growing increasingly antsy, and Bailey let several more seconds pass before continuing.

"Where is she, Mr. Brevin?"

Brevin shrugged, his eyes flaring slightly in surprise. "Hell, I don't know. At her place, I guess. She was taking the day off."

The sound of a car door in the driveway distracted Brevin for a second and he turned, spotting the doors of his Porsche being opened by a team of uniformed officers.

"Hey!"

"Stay where you are, Mr. Brevin. We have a warrant, if you'd like to see it, although we don't need one to search your car."

"What are you looking for, man? I'm clean."

"We're not looking for drugs, Mr. Brevin. We're looking for Miss Lacombe, and you were with her yesterday. Exactly what time?"

"Hey, I didn't *memorize* the time, y'know?"

He began to pace slightly, rocking left to look at his car, then right to stare with growing agitation at Craig Bailey, his hands stuck deep in the pockets of his jeans, then just as quickly on his hips, or running through his hair and scratching his chin. He was acting like a man in desperate need of a bathroom.

"How was she when you saw her?"

"Her usual self. Angry, selfish, unpredictable, bitchy."

"And did you leave her in her apartment, or did she come with you?"

He snorted again. "Hey, what is this? Has she filed some sort of complaint? 'Cause man, I'm telling you, that was *my* damned snowboard! Okay? And . . . if she said I hit her or anything, that's a lie! She slapped *me*."

Bailey stood his ground, his eyes boring into Brevin's as the young actor turned to one of the uniformed officers with his hand out, palm up, then looked back at the detective.

"What is it? *What?*"

"Why was Miss Lacombe's apartment ransacked, Mr. Brevin?" Craig Bailey continued.

"Ransacked? It wasn't ransacked when I left."

"Did Miss Lacombe leave with you?"

"No. I mean, she swiped at me in the hallway like an angry cat and then went back in. She wouldn't give me my things. What's she saying? That I trashed her apartment?"

"She isn't saying anything, Mr. Brevin. We're having trouble finding her."

"Then, I don't understand."

"We need to find her."

"Well . . . did you check her office?"

"Yes."

"How about calling her cell phone?"

Bailey shook his head.

"Then, hell, I don't know. I mean, she could be anywhere when she's pissed."

"Why was she pissed, Mr. Brevin?"

"Who knows. We had a good thing and she got tired. Go figure. Hey, ah . . . can you excuse me a second? You know. The bathroom? I was headed there when you guys arrived."

Craig Bailey nodded and caught the eye of the policeman to his right. The uniformed officer followed Brevin into a back hallway. There was the sound of a door closing, then opening, and Brevin's voice from around the corner.

"Hey, dude . . . I've gotta snag another roll of toilet paper back here in the closet, okay?"

"Yeah, go ahead," the officer replied.

Craig let his eyes wander around the living room, taking in several pictures Brevin had hung of himself in various roles. There was a huge movie poster on the far wall, and an unpainted rack of bookshelves crammed full of DVDs in no apparent order.

An internal alarm began to sound in the detective's head. Too much time had passed without the right sounds coming from down the hallway. He turned to move in that direction just as the engine of a large motorcycle roared to life at the back of the house.

"Oh, shit!"

Bailey made it out the front door in time to see Brevin smash a Harley through a flimsy wooden gate and roar off down the street as all the uniformed officers dove for their cars.

Chapter 4

Quitting was definitely an option.

Dr. Doug Lam blew out of the Administration Building too focused on masking his anger to spot Sanjay Singh, who'd apparently been waiting at a discreet distance while warming a stone bench. Singh jumped up and gave chase.

"Doug, wait up. You okay?"

Lam stopped and turned, relaxing slightly at the sight of his assistant, a newly minted PhD seismologist and one of the sharpest students he'd ever mentored.

"What are you doing over here, Sanjay?"

"Waiting to see what a sudden summons to the head shed meant. You look really mad."

"Do I?" Doug shook his head sharply, then motioned Singh to walk with him and continued on toward the center of the sprawling campus. The broad-shouldered, six-foot-one ex-halfback was walking so fast his much shorter assistant had to scurry to keep up.

"So . . . what the heck happened back there?" Sanjay tried again.

Once more the director of the university's USGS-run seismology lab stopped and turned, his green eyes dark with anger as he shook his head and glanced back toward the source of his pain.

"They're blind, Sanjay! Plain and simple. A bunch of play-it-safe bureaucrats terrified of the slightest controversy. They're dithering because we haven't brought in any new grant money lately. Forget the fact that the United States Geological Survey pays my salary. The thinly veiled threat is: No grant money, no teaching position."

"But we've got three current grant applications out there."

"And two of them were rejected this past week."

"*What?* Why?"

"Because the lead researcher—me—is the same guy who had the unmitigated temerity to come up with that embarrassing cockamamie theory of

Resonant Amplification triggering the Cascadia Subduction Zone, and it scares the pacemakers out of their faint little hearts. They were upset enough when I named the locked area of the zone after the Quilieute tribe and ended up with all that publicity."

"Doug, frankly, your theory scares me, too."

"It also happens to be dead right. Whoa. Scares *you*? Are you doubting me, as well? Should I say, '*Et tu,* Sanjay?' "

"No . . . but you know very well that I'm skeptical. Your reasoning is sound, but it's a very bold, intuitive leap on a shaky foundation. No pun intended."

Doug chuckled and glanced around, as if looking for eavesdroppers. "Very diplomatic, Dr. Singh. Just like I taught you." He began walking back toward the seismology lab several hundred yards distant as Sanjay struggled to stay in formation.

"Doug, you don't know for a fact that the turndowns were because of your theory, do you?"

"Yes. They told me so. Flat out. Both grants failed because I've become too controversial. You know what one of them suggested? Get this! He seriously suggested that I consider retracting my paper and reversing course for the time being. *For the time being!*"

"Just to get the grants?"

"Yes! Jeez, whatever happened to academic freedom, not to mention academic courage?"

"So, we'll just write more grant apps."

"No, I'll just resign and let them sleep at night, until the coming subduction zone quake dumps their candy asses out of their safe little beds. You want to run a slightly used seismology lab? It was hardly ever operated except on Sundays."

"You're a gifted professor, Doug," Singh replied, ignoring the sarcasm. "We need you."

"Well, thanks, but I can live just fine doing hardcore USGS work."

"They haven't been too supportive either."

"Who, my guys in Menlo Park?" Doug asked, referring to the USGS Western Headquarters in California.

"Yes."

"They think I'm smoking something strange, that's true, but they *are* supportive."

"Doug, forgive me for challenging your creative memory, but they've jeered you in two conferences, insulted you in print, and essentially apologized to Washington for your stance."

"No, they apologized for my going on TV."

"Whatever. They've hardly been supportive."

"They send the green checks. That's supportive."

He changed direction and Sanjay followed, glad their new course terminated in a Starbucks just off campus, where they ordered in the Seattle dialect of lattes and breves and decaf no-whips and sat in a corner with the resulting concoctions. The conversation veered from the mundane back to the Cascadia Subduction Zone.

"You know," Doug added, his bravado and fury diminishing, "I like winning, and what hurts is that right now being right feels an awful lot like losing." He paused, uncharacteristically focusing on his cup for a while. "Why is that, Sanjay? They all want to ignore the possibility I could be right. Even as we sit here, that turkey Walker is out there pounding the crap out of his island as if no one had warned him. Like some annoying little brat harassing a dog until it reaches the breaking point and eats him."

"At least, you *think* it's a hair trigger."

"I wake up at 3 A.M., Sanjay, knowing I'm right and scared to death I'm going to be proven right. And yet, who's listening? If Walker's greed ends up triggering a hundred-billion-dollar earthquake I'll be able to sit atop the rubble and shout, 'I told you so!' but all our efforts in the meantime have been useless."

"Doug, I think you need a reality check. There was never any way you or your paper were going to generate enough credibility to stop a hundred-million-dollar project on the basis of an unproven theory that not even the USGS endorses."

"I know it. I flatly refuse to accept it, but I know it."

"Besides, most of the construction on Cascadia Island is finished. They open this weekend, and, so far, the locked part of the subduction zone is still locked."

Doug Lam nodded thoughtfully as he sipped the last of his drink. "That's true, and that's encouraging. I want to be wrong about this."

"Good."

"But I'm not."

"What are you going to do about the university's ultimatum?"

"Wasn't really a thrown gauntlet. More of a warning. I don't know." He sighed and grimaced. "I think I'd rather just spend my days in the field and teaching in a junior college than undergo the professional lobotomy they're demanding."

Sanjay checked his watch. "Sitting on a bench waiting for one's leader generates hunger. How about joining Sondra and me for dinner?"

"You know she hates last-minute invitations. She's very gracious, but I imagine you're on the couch for at least two nights afterwards."

"Three, actually, but that's all right. I'm the man of my house. I rule, and sucking up to the professor is worth it."

"Yeah, well, I'm not a real professor . . ." He checked his own watch. "Oh, jeez, I've got to pick up Jennifer for dinner in less than an hour." He stood. "Tell Sondra I appreciate her husband's invitation, but I'm taking a rain check on intruding, so she doesn't have to sleep alone tonight."

"I wish you the same delightful fate," Sanjay smiled as Doug headed for the door with a wave and walked back to get his bike. It was a short ride to his floating home on the south side of the Montlake Cut, across from the university. He wheeled into the tiny parking lot ten minutes later and paused to admire his well-polished but ancient fire-engine red Austin-Healey, which spent most of the weekdays sitting beneath a tarp. It was mechanically cantankerous, but no amount of cajoling could interest him in buying a new car, and he rather enjoyed the reverse snobbery of his chosen wheels—even if it did eat batteries and consume more money than having children.

"At least make it an Aston-Martin, like Bond," Jennifer had teased.

As soon as he'd finished a quick shower and dressed in his only business suit, Doug double-checked himself in the mirror and decided to sit and meditate a few minutes on the waterside deck of his floating house, focusing on the evening ahead. He was well prepared this time, and the small jewelry box containing the present he'd bought for Jennifer was safely stowed in his coat pocket. The thought of her reaction when she unwrapped it made him smile.

Darkness had already descended over the Seattle area and the twinkling lights and gentle reflections from the water between his floating house and the Seattle Yacht Club across the way were entrancing. He opened the sliding door and strolled outside, breathing the cool, humid air. Maybe, he thought, he should have planned to bring her here and cook dinner on the deck tonight.

No, he concluded. *The fifty-degree temperatures would have chased us inside anyway. The Space Needle is better.*

And there was the uncomfortable history of the last dinner they'd had together on his deck, a wonderful evening that had turned sour when he overreacted to a casual question about Deborah, his estranged wife, and when he planned to change his separation into a divorce. They'd smoothed it over in the following weeks, but he knew she was still upset and trying not to show it. She didn't understand, and he couldn't explain it to her. At least not yet.

Doug got to his feet and entered the living room, sliding the door closed behind him before heading for the car, hoping the subject could be avoided for at least one more night.

A small, insistent electronic alert cut through the tense quiet of the La-combe residence for at least the tenth time in the past few hours, prompting Senator Ralph Lacombe to reach for his beeper. The two police officers monitoring the recording equipment set up on the three family phone lines glanced over, but rapidly returned their attention to their magazines, trying, out of deference to the distraught family, not to look as bored as they were.

The senator got up and walked down the hall to his study, quietly shut-ting the door behind him. He quickly sat down at his computer and put on a headset, following the instructions on the screen of his beeper.

> Dad, show this to no one else for now. I'm okay and by myself but had to leave town and hide quickly. Go to a computer no one is monitoring and send a digital message to my beeper, 12345, with your headset on. I'll use the web phone to call you when I get it. D

He entered the numbers in a message form and sent it, drumming his fingers for several very long minutes until the web phone alert screen popped up.

"Diane?"

"Dad. It's me."

"My God, I've been terrified! What the hell is going on?"

She told him about discovering the break-in.

"Someone's after me, Dad, for proprietary information I took from Chadwick and Noble."

"What are you talking about? The police are all over this, your face is on all the TV channels, and I've got a duty to tell them you're okay at the very least."

There was a long hesitation on the other end. "Okay, tell them I'm not kidnapped or dead or anything."

"They've arrested that fool boyfriend of yours, thinking he killed you."

"Don?"

"Yes."

"He's my *ex*-boyfriend, Dad, but he didn't do anything. Tell them to let him go. I don't know exactly who I'm hiding from, but I do know it isn't Don."

"They'll want to talk to you. What's that noise in the background?"

"Don't ask, Dad. And, yes, they'll want to know where I am, and I can't let anyone know, even you, until I've figured this out. I'll send you a FedEx package in the morning, and in case they don't believe you, I'll include a signed statement confirming I'm alive and well and Don's innocent. I'll write part of it on tomorrow's San Fran *Chronicle,* and there will be a duplicate CD in there. Please don't show it to the police. It's just for you to keep safe for me."

"Diane, what does this involve?"

"I can't tell you, Dad. Not yet."

"I got a call earlier today from your supervisor, Jerry Schultz, wanting to know if I'd heard from you. He sounded more panicked over company materials you might have with you than whether you were okay."

"*Schultz* called?"

"Yes."

"I guess somehow I'm not surprised. Don't tell that weasel anything."

"I didn't know anything to tell him. But, Honey, is it anything I'm involved in as a senator?"

"Not directly, Dad. But you said yourself, everything in politics is a political problem. That's why I can't tell you. I wish I could."

"Okay. I'm not sure I understand that, but I do understand you don't want me to ask anything more."

"Right."

"Do you need money?"

"No."

"What can I do, then?"

"Call off the police and just trust me. I'm working this out. And if you get any other packages from me besides tomorrow's FedEx, just store them, don't open them."

"I will. When can you check in again?"

"I don't know. I've gotta go now. I love you."

Chapter 5

Jennifer watched Doug's smile evaporate as a ripple of fear shot through her. Why had she suddenly changed her mind yet again? The question she'd asked him had chilled the evening.

Her eyes were on the empty jewelry box in front of her, the stunning necklace it had contained looking elegant around her neck.

But her appreciation had been muted.

The dinner and wine and conversation had been comfortable and memorable—the shimmering Seattle nightscape orbiting steadily past the windows of the landmark revolving restaurant—until the words had burst through her previous decision to wait.

"Doug, about Deborah . . ."

"What about Deborah?" he asked, knitting his eyebrows at the intrusion of his estranged wife into their evening.

"I'm sorry, but I really need to be sure you're intending to divorce her. I mean, you're not going to let it go on like this forever, are you?"

His eyes found hers again after an unhappy sigh, his tone all but condescending, as if he'd grown very tired of explaining an obvious fact to a simple mind.

"Yes, Jennifer. The separation *will* become a divorce. I've told you that. Why is this bothering you so?"

"I guess I just don't understand the perpetual delay, you know? I love you, Doug. Very much. But I wonder if you're just stringing me along and . . . and want things to go on like this forever."

"Absolutely not! Why on earth would you say that?"

"Because I feel like your mistress at times, or worse, and I don't like that feeling."

"Honey, you're anything but a mistress. I mean, I'm legally separated for God's sake! The divorce is just a formality."

"Is it?"

"Yes. Of course!"

"You're sure you're not having . . . second thoughts?"

"No!"

"Because . . . if you are, after all those years you've spent with her, I'll back away."

He reached across the table for her hands, almost knocking his wine goblet over in the process.

"Jen, look. You have my word that the marriage is over."

"All right," she replied, trying to smile, though the answer had done nothing to assuage her fears.

"Honey," he continued, "what in the world is this really about? Your biological clock? A wedding thing? I love you, I'm totally committed to you, we're together most of the time when we're not working, so why tonight, for God's sake?"

She withdrew her hands, stung by the trite accusation, her eyes on the table. "Don't belittle my reasons, Doug."

"I'm not, but . . . but I'm frustrated with this subject."

"So am I."

"Jen, it's not like it's been five or ten years."

"No, but people who are ending their marriage eventually file for divorce. There's some reason you haven't, and I don't understand it, and frankly it scares me."

"Why? Tell me why it scares you."

"Because this is the one subject we can't discuss without your getting upset, and that's not good. And because I think you may be in a kind of marital purgatory, and I can't live there with you."

"Jennifer, this is nuts!"

She looked him in the eye for the longest time and he met her gaze with a steadiness and intensity that moved her. She fought the urge to look away. "Doug, I've been agonizing about this for months. But the truth of the matter is, we can't possibly walk into a future together until you close the door on the past, or at least explain to me why you're waiting. If you want us together and you want the family I want, with kids and Christmas and Suzuki recitals and teacher conferences . . ."

His tone was soft, but she could feel the consternation behind it. "Not just yet. But soon."

"Why, Doug? That's all I need to know. A good reason."

He was shaking his head, his eyes on the skyline and avoiding hers. "I don't want to go into it."

"See . . . that's what I mean."

"There are good reasons for going slow."

"And I can't be trusted to know what those reasons are?"

"It's not a matter of trust."

"I think it is," she said quietly. *He'll never understand this,* she thought. *I'm living with the constant presence of his wife and he's blind to it.*

A long silence stretched between them to the threshold of embarrassment.

"Okay," she said. "Let me try to explain the other part of this, the part I don't think *you* understand."

"Please do!" There was a hint of anger crossing his face like a reflection. "Apparently, you're speaking in some strange female dialect that males aren't biologically equipped to understand. So please explain it to me in English."

She ignored the barb, needing desperately for him to grasp it. "Doug, yes, you're legally separated, and you say you've got good reasons for going slow, but there are three people in this relationship. Three."

"That's ridiculous."

"No, it isn't. Deborah can still get you to jump with a single phone call. You'll drop anything and run to help her or take her somewhere, and it's harder on me every time. She's still a big part of your life and I can't even begin to guess the reason for all her calls. Are you fixing things around the house? Warming her . . ."

"No!"

"Well, how do I know? You . . . you even *measure* your world, and mine, by reference to your years with her. You've got one foot in a dead marriage and one foot in our relationship, and a girl gets tired of sharing her bed. I'm never in control. She is." Her voice was getting more forceful. Being intense always meant more volume, but controlled volume. Always controlled.

"I do not jump when she calls."

"Yes, you do, sweetheart. I know you don't see it. But when you're jumping, I'm jumping, too. Like we're both some kind of marionettes dancing on the end of a line."

"Jen . . ."

"As much as I love you, I can't spend my life like this, being jerked around." Tears were gathering like distant storm clouds, but she forced them back. "Let me give you an example. Two weekends ago when we were in the San Juans, I counted the number of times I heard Deborah's name. How many would you think?"

"Hell, I don't know," he said, the irritation openly spilling into his tone. "Five? Six?"

"Try sixty-three times in two days. Some were stories of your past, and that's completely legitimate, but most were like, 'Deborah and I went here,' or 'Deb always hated those.' Every time I've tried to *gently* get into this subject, you run from it, or give me some gift you think will dazzle me. If you really want to give me something, Doug, give me you."

"Or?" he said, his voice dead serious.

She simply shook her head without replying, tears glistening in her eyes, a fact that made her angry with herself: the ultimate female breach of composure.

"Jen . . . look, do we really have to do this tonight? Couldn't you corner me some other time when there isn't a great evening to ruin?"

"I'm truly sorry, Doug. I had decided not to bring this up tonight."

"Then why did you?"

The question chilled her. Having pushed him away with the truth, she suddenly felt desperate to pull him back, and she pulled a plastic card from her purse and slid it across the table to him as he looked at it with dawning recognition.

"Is . . . that a Breakwater card key?" he asked, his interest suddenly piqued and his tone more cautious.

She nodded, watching his expression soften with the beautiful memory of the first time they'd made love—an amazing night in the same waterfront suite at the same hotel. "I thought," she said, "that we could do an anniversary thing and just sink into a beautiful night of lovemaking with the ships and ferries gliding by, and room service in the morning."

"That sounds idyllic," he said. He hesitated, his eyes on the table for a long time before looking up at her. "Jen, I *am* listening to you. But you need to trust me. I have reasons for going slow that I'm just not ready to discuss, but they're nothing you need fear."

She sighed and tried an unconvincing smile. "I guess we should talk about it later. I'm sorry I brought it up."

"The last thing I want to do is hurt you." He took a deep breath as if arriving at a momentous decision and reached across the table to take her hands as he locked eyes with her again. "Okay, look, there is something I've wanted . . . needed to tell you for the longest time, but . . . when you're not at liberty to divulge something that affects someone else . . ."

The loud, insistent beeping of his pager interrupted. He reached for it quickly, trying to keep a look of relief off his face.

"What is it?" she asked as he scanned the tiny screen.

"It's my computer alert program. I've got to go to the lab. An earthquake has happened somewhere in the world," he said.

"Oh, Honey, no!" she replied in dismay. "Not now. Please finish what you were starting to tell me."

He looked embarrassed. "Let's wait 'til later when we have more time. Right now," he glanced back at the beeper, "with the extreme danger along our subduction zone, I need to get in there quickly."

"What extreme danger?" she asked, looking alarmed.

"The effects of the construction activity on Cascadia Island. We've been •
monitoring it carefully."

Her shoulders fell slightly. "Oh. That again."

"Yes, that again. Honey, I'm not going to argue with you about whether
the resort should have been built. I know how you and your dad feel. But the
reality is that, if my theory is right, there really *is* a heightened danger of a
major quake."

"Can't you just get Sanjay to go take a look?" she asked, defeat already in
her voice.

"No, Jen, I've got to run over to the lab myself. If it's nothing big, I can be
back here in—"

"Doug," she interrupted, her eyes on his, a faded smile on her lips. "It's
okay. Go do what you have to do as quickly as you can do it." She tossed her
head and forced a smile, raising her wine glass in a mock toast. "Here's to
the Richter Scale."

He hesitated, debating whether to correct her as she caught his eyes. "I
know, I know," she said, recognizing his professorial need to set the technical record straight. "The Richter Scale is only good in California quakes
and . . ."

"Saturates at . . ."

"Right . . . above 6.4."

"A little higher."

"Go!"

He finished extricating himself from the chair and moved to her side,
cupping her face gently to kiss her with an intensity that once again messed
with her resolve.

"I love you, Jennifer," he said when he pulled back.

"I love you, too, damnit."

"Damnit?" he chuckled. "That's the strangest expression of everlasting
love I've ever heard."

"Sometimes I don't want to love you," she said softly, still smiling.

"Really?"

"Yes, but apparently you've drugged me or hypnotized me or used something irresistible."

He laughed as he straightened up and looked at her. "I'll never tell. But I
will hurry. Maybe thirty minutes."

"Call me as soon as you're on the way back, okay? I think I'll probably go
on to the hotel and wait for you there."

He nodded and walked quickly out of the restaurant. As his fit, athletic
form receded, Jennifer watched appreciatively, relaxed in a glow of renewed
hope.

She decided to tarry for a while and ordered coffee. Meanwhile the lights of Seattle continued to pass dreamily around her, the restaurant turning almost a hundred and eighty degrees as she waited, trying to sort through a jumble of emotions as she replayed the conversation in her memory.

Doug's call came while she was still physically at the top of the Space Needle, but mentally far away.

"Jennifer, I hate this, but I have to stay here for at least a few hours."

"Oh, no. Why? Is there some immediate danger?"

"No, but there's a puzzle I need to work out."

"Can't you do it tomorrow?"

"No, Jen. I've got to stay a while. But I can join you later at the Breakwater, maybe around midnight?"

She paused, her thoughts cascading as she tried to suppress the flash of irritation at his escape back to the lab.

"No earlier than that?" she managed. "Doug, is it really so important that you just have to . . . to let it interfere?"

"Yes. I've got some calculations to make and a bunch of small hypocenters to analyze."

"Hypo-who?"

"Remember? The actual location of an earthquake within the earth is the hypocenter. The point on the surface directly over the hypocenter is the epicenter."

"I'm kidding. I know what a hypocenter is."

"Okay."

"Call me first. If it's too late, I may not stay."

As soon as she closed her flip phone, it rang again with his number on the screen.

"Jennifer, one more thing. I know you've got that Cascadia Resort inaugural tomorrow, and I really don't think you ought to go."

She could feel her stomach tightening and the muscles in the back of her neck twisting up. They'd had this discussion before.

"Why not?"

"Jen, I've explained this a hundred times . . . my paper and the theory of Resonant Amplification were on this very point. The whole island is a potential death zone."

"I think you're more concerned that Alex Jamison's going to be there. You think I'm going to take up with him again?"

"Of course not. I know Jamison hurt you badly. I'm really worried about you being on that rock, and . . . I've received some important new information which apparently validates all my suspicions about the place."

"What information?"

"An anonymous e-mail from someone saying he has a pile of seismic re-fraction data that proves I'm right, and that the island is very dangerous. But I'm having a hell of a time unmasking the sender or getting back in touch with him, and yet I absolutely have to. Quickly."

"Oh, come on, Doug. An *anonymous* e-mail and seismic data you haven't even seen? How do you know it's got any validity, if it even exists?"

"I don't, but I have a very bad feeling about this weekend, and about your being out there. Among other things, there's apparently a major fault right under all the buildings."

"Doug, they wouldn't have built over a known fault."

"Point is, according to whoever sent the e-mail, the engineering firm missed it. In any event, I've got to find out who sent it. The return address was garbled, and I'm wondering if that was on purpose, or if someone else intercepted it and monkeyed with it. For that matter it could be one of my detractors down in Menlo Park trying to bait me with tantalizing, made-up evidence just to get a reaction he can use to embarrass me."

"Honey, you're sounding paranoid. You know that?"

"I'm not paranoid. I'm just very worried. My paper generated a lot of en-emies."

"Doug, look. Have there been any earthquakes below Cascadia Island?"

"Not yet, as far as I can validate."

"Okay, then I'm having a hard time appreciating this, because obviously there's no immediate danger, and I'm scheduled to fly more than half of our charter flights between here and Cascadia Island tomorrow. Dad and I are invited guests for the evening. We're investors, as you well know."

"And I'd rather not lose you to a collapsing island or collapsing buildings if the worst occurs. I know what I'm talking about."

"So do the other scientists who've discounted your theory," she said qui-etly. "Remember the old rule? For every PhD there is an equal and opposite PhD? Honey, I respect the seriousness of your work and your incredible confidence that you're right about this, but I have a job to do tomorrow and even your own employer told you to get off that hobby horse. Doug, I love you, but on this one, I have official support in concluding that your head is full of squirrels."

She could hear the exasperation in his voice. "Jen, even if the Resonant Amplification effect turns out to be garbage, you agree that we could have that great subduction quake at any moment, don't you?"

"Well, sure, but . . ."

"Okay, and you know it's been proven before I came along that the whole coastline will drop one to two meters when that occurs?"

"Yes."

"And . . . you're aware that we have thousands of years of evidence that every time a huge subduction zone quake has hit this region, the coast gets hit with a huge tsunami. Right? You know none of that is controversial."

"Yes. I know all that, Doug. Being there is an assumed risk."

"Well, if it hits while you and Sven are there, long before you could start up and lift off, the whole island will be washed clean of people and buildings by a thirty-foot-high tsunami, and I do not want my potential future wife in danger!"

The words hung there for a few heartbeats before she could deal with them.

"Potential future wife? Is that the strangest quasi-proposal on record, or are you tantalizing me?"

There was a chuckle on the other end, as if he'd succeeded in diverting her irritation. "Let's call it a sincere statement of intent. But about staying away from there, I'm not kidding."

"Neither am I. This subject has been a rift zone between *us* for the last two years. You've been a sworn enemy of the Cascadia Resort project from the first, and—"

"Jen—"

"Let me finish! Some of the things you've pulled to stop that project I still can't believe. So this is not a balanced, rational request from an unbiased man without an agenda."

"Jennifer . . ."

"Doug, please get back to work so you can come to me sometime tonight . . . before I start searching for a new potential husband."

She refolded her phone with an unexpected grin on her face, and looked down, confused. An intricately folded napkin lay on the empty dessert plate before her.

When did I do that? she wondered, having no recollection of it. But it was refolded the way she always left linen napkins in restaurants: neat, crisp, and looking like a form of origami. As a young girl she'd developed the habit, fantasizing that the waiters would all be whispering about her talent. She was almost ten the night she was leaving a restaurant with her family and glanced back in time to see a busboy throw her creation into a slop tray without a second glance. It had hurt her feelings and registered as a small loss of innocence, but it hadn't dissuaded her from continuing the habit.

She was feeling better now, more optimistic. Maybe his unguarded blurt about being his potential wife was enough of a commitment, and a change of heart. At least she'd finally had the courage to engage him on the subject of her growing discontent.

But what had he been ready to tell her?

Jennifer drained the last of her third cup of coffee and took the elevator to the ground level to hail a cab for the short ride to the Breakwater. She tipped the cabby—despite his jerky driving and a near collision with the waterfront trolley—and made a mental note to visit a cash machine sooner rather than later as she breezed past the front desk and then turned back to order a masseuse to her room. Indulgence, she decided, was probably going to be the ticket to enjoying the solo time until he arrived. A great massage in the beauty of the suite, and maybe some chocolate. After all, that constituted what she most needed: control.

Control and chocolate, she chuckled to herself. The next best thing to sex and commitment.

The masseuse had been late and finished by 10:30 P.M. There had been no call from Doug, and Jennifer found herself unsure whether to leave or stay. The suite felt barren without him, and worse, it felt wrong, as if there were some unwritten rule that she shouldn't occupy the locus of such a sacred memory by herself.

She dressed suddenly and stood for the longest time at the window in deep thought, watching a small motor yacht sail off toward Bremerton, its wake catching the silver light of the full moon. It was a tragedy to share this only with herself, she thought. No, it was a travesty, and try as she might, there was no way to view his absence but as a seized opportunity to run from her questioning. She wasn't just disappointed, she was angry with him. It made it easier.

But they were so good together, she thought. There was a deep joy in just being with each other, and laughing and loving, traveling and even sparring at times over deep subjects. Their intellects and joy of life and libidos were equally matched, and for two strong, controlling personalities to be so sympathetically meshed was amazing.

Only Deborah's hovering presence had marred the idyllic nature of the relationship. Deborah was an acid she couldn't neutralize, and he was hiding from that reality as it ate away at her trust.

What was he about to tell me?

She should have been completely relaxed by now, Jennifer thought, but she was pacing and agitated and unsettled and acutely aware that her resolve was wavering. Jennifer the little girl wanted to run to him and apologize again for pressuring him and be hugged. Jennifer the woman wanted answers and commitment.

Or had she angered him by getting too close to the truth about wanting kids and a ring?

The real essence of who she believed herself to be stood rooted in the middle, dithering in near-paralytic confusion.

The room was now completely intolerable without him. She picked up the phone to retrieve the car that she had prepositioned at the hotel earlier in the day and began packing the things she'd brought for the evening. She knew what the lack of contact meant. When he went nose-down into his seismographs on a technical problem, he entered a different time continuum as disconnected from the rest of the world as it was from her, and it was painfully obvious he wasn't coming.

Chapter 6

Apparently the stop sign wasn't going to change.

Jennifer smiled ruefully at the depth of her distraction and accelerated into the empty intersection, aware she'd been driving aimlessly in the ten minutes since leaving the Breakwater Hotel.

Downtown Seattle was never really quiet at night anymore. The regional lifeline—Interstate 5—now flowed with vehicles twenty-four hours a day, and even at midnight the heart of the city pulsed with enough solitary energy to be quietly vibrant: cars and lone pedestrians appearing through the steam wafting from the occasional grate, as if the entire place was a carefully manicured movie set.

Habit guided a turn onto Interstate 5 before she realized she was automatically heading for her office at Boeing Field. She had a duty to get rested for the heavy schedule of charter flights in the morning, but neither her condo nor Doug's floating home beckoned. Instead, she decided to crawl into one of the crew bunks in the medevac section of her company.

Her thoughts drifted to the series of events which had so drastically altered her career path. She loved nursing, but she loved flying, too, and was continually incensed that she couldn't do both at the same time. But she had voluntarily fled nursing for the presumed Valhalla of running her dad's company and flying, convincing herself that her nursing skills would still be valuable. Perhaps, she'd thought, she could appoint herself chief flight nurse as well as serve as one of the line pilots. Sven had made it clear that she didn't have enough experience to be chief pilot, and the rest of the seasoned pros he'd brought in to build Nightingale quickly vetoed the chief nurse idea, especially after they'd attended her first briefing as president of the medevac division.

Eric Emery was the veteran and slightly crusty chief pilot, and his wife, Anita, had been the company's original chief flight nurse. They'd both followed her back to her office after that first briefing to administer a reality check.

"You not only can't be chief flight nurse *and* president, your attitude's going to have to change to fly my helicopters," Eric had said with the force of someone who knew resignation might be the price of failing to convince her.

Your helicopters? she thought, resisting the impulse to pull rank. It was good he thought of the fleet as his, she reminded herself.

"What's wrong with my attitude, Eric?"

"You're still mission oriented. You're still the savior determined to pull off the rescue, and that's how we crash machines and kill people."

It had been a disappointment that he was right. Her balloon of enthusiasm for running the two companies and flying constantly hadn't entirely burst, but it was leaking badly. She *was* used to being in the "angel of mercy" role, and it seemed hollow somehow to discover that medical evacuation helicopter operations were now even more clinical than her past life at Olympic Hospital. She'd thanked them, reassured them, and worked hard over the past few years to gain Eric's confidence—which he'd finally given her, even though somewhat grudgingly.

Jennifer pulled into her own marked parking place in time to witness the unwelcome spectacle of Tim Paretsky, the duty medevac alert pilot, being loaded into an ambulance with his flight nurse and sister Sarah Paretsky in tow. Sarah spotted the boss and shouted an explanation before the ambulance doors closed her in.

"Tim had an accident in the hangar. We're going to Olympic."

In the communications room the duty dispatcher completed the description of the large, metal case which had suddenly dislodged from the upper storage self Tim had been tugging at. He'd been in a brief freefall backward, and a concrete hangar floor had broken the fall.

"He's got at least a concussion, and he cut the hell out of himself grabbing for a handhold on the way down."

"I'd better follow them over."

"Jen, if you're legal, could you take a flight?"

She hesitated, thoroughly unprepared for the request. "We have a call-out?"

"We're on standby as of three minutes ago. I expect the call momentarily. A head-on collision on the west side of Stevens Pass with two dead at the scene, and two injured."

"Do we have nurses, with Sarah gone?"

"Sarah was off duty. Gretchen and Karen are on alert, and they're ready."

Jennifer sighed, inwardly glad to have something besides Doug to seize her focus for an hour or so.

"I'll get into my flight suit. And for the record, I had nothing alcoholic tonight."

Snow in the Cascade Mountains during any November was normal, but the flurries that had started around Stevens Pass just before midnight had been a surprise to the forecasters as well as motorists speeding along the two-lane section of the roadway. The collision had closed both lanes of the highway and left a small army of State Patrol troopers holding back the tide while the emergency medtechs triaged the horror. The call for Nightingale's services followed.

Jennifer had the EC-135 Eurocopter airborne and headed for the accident site well within the required seven minutes response time. She'd done a personal systems check and come up with the conclusion that she was safe to fly, but there was no avoiding the fact that she was emotionally tired. It wasn't like the crushing fatigue of the countless nights she'd spent working doubles on the hospital floor, nor the disorienting weight of flying the last leg home from a long medevac sequence, but she was tired, and she was less than one hundred percent, and that meant she'd have to cut wider margins around any tight situations to stay safe.

"Could you turn up the heat a bit?" Karen asked from the back.

Jennifer nodded and made the adjustment, glad she'd asked. She wondered why she'd refused to admit she was freezing, too, before Karen brought it up. The macho syndrome, she concluded. All pilots had the same problem to deal with, knowing when to admit to being human, sometimes even when no one else was around.

This flight was already demanding her undivided attention, and she could feel her concern rising in direct proportion to the rate the weather was deteriorating. The weather ahead at the intended landing zone was just above legal minimums for visibility and ceiling. The site was well into the Cascade Mountains, and she already had the location plotted on the GPS-driven moving-map display in front of her. The plan, as she'd briefed herself and the flight nurses, would be to intercept U.S. 2 near Monroe and follow it eastward into the landing zone, which was a pre-scouted meadow by the roadway a half mile from the accident scene.

Gretchen had taken the left copilot's seat and was watching her, unwilling to interrupt with questions, but Jennifer could tell she was apprehensive. There was very little visible outside other than a ribbon of taillights, and they were in and out of the snow flurries as Jennifer flew them through the turbulence of what was a relatively gentle wind. The snow was worrying her despite the ship's anti-ice systems. It wasn't severe enough yet to test the aircraft, but it demanded attention.

The ceiling had remained at roughly two thousand feet above the highway, but suddenly the layer of clouds became increasingly ragged as she flew east, forcing her down to a thousand feet above ground level. She could see the bonfire of flashing red and blue lights of the State Patrol cars and ambulances in the darkness ahead, but they seemed to be floating in a vacuum, a pulsing, exploding convention of police lights adrift in a sea of black.

They've stopped the traffic! she realized. That had been in the pre-departure information, but the significance hadn't hit her until now. Miles of red tail lights from hundreds of cars stranded by the highway closure snaked ahead of the EC-135, then stopped cold. The accident site and landing zone were miles beyond, and almost invisible further up the pass was a long line of headlights marking the stopped oncoming traffic.

Her mission, she thought, was to find the right patch of ground in the middle of that black hole without hitting trees, power lines, or the towering palisades of rock invisible on both sides of the narrowing valley.

Jennifer toggled up the frequency for the state troopers and made contact.

"We have two stabilized now and ready to transport," was the response. "But we need you right here on the roadway, and we've stopped the traffic."

"Roger, I can see," Jennifer replied, passing over the end of the uphill traffic queue and turning on the craft's landing lights. A thousand feet below she could make out a few dark shapes, but the road itself was invisible and the looming collection of flashing visibars on top of the squad cars were guaranteed to create visual landing illusion problems.

Flares had been lighted to mark the appropriate spot on the highway just short of the accident site and she slowed the 135, trying to set up her approach, acutely aware that she had nothing but black on either side of the mountain valley. Maybe, she thought, if I turn on the searchlight and slow to ten or fifteen knots, I can do this safely.

But the ceiling had forced her down another two hundred feet and it was clearly even lower over the black highway ahead. With no reference points on either side and pitch blackness masking the mountains, the negatives were piling up.

Judgment! she thought.

The information that one of the victims barely clinging to life down on the highway was a child was not something routinely passed to an inbound medevac pilot. But she had overhead enough of another transmission to know the stakes were high.

She was supposed to ignore such things. Safety first. No mission orientation.

But she already knew too much, and there were lives leaking away below and forcing her into a corner.

"No!" she said to herself out loud. Her reference points were already too murky and her emotional fatigue was pressing her to just *go ahead and do it!* Those were already the early links in a potential accident chain of causation.

She announced the go around on the interphone and immediately increased power, using the standard go around procedure to nudge the EC-135 up and, when she had enough altitude, turn it around a hundred and eighty degrees to retrace the GPS course she'd followed in. She climbed to the base of the clouds and toggled the radio to ask for the only thing that was going to work.

"Can you start the traffic moving in both directions?"

The same trooper she'd talked to moments before came back, his voice skeptical.

"Yes, but why? Don't you need the road clear?"

"I need reference lights. You're in a sea of black out there. I need tail lights and headlights flowing by. As soon as I'm stable overhead, that's when I'll need you to stop them to give me enough room. But not before."

There was a brief silence before the radioed agreement, and Jennifer flew five miles west into a wider part of the valley before turning back and orbiting slowly at a safe altitude, wondering if the advanced night vision goggles Nightingale had just ordered would have made such a request unnecessary. She'd already tried them out, and they literally turned night into day.

But tonight she had only the traditional tools, and her ability to back off. There was a little sparkle of pride that she'd broken the momentum of the approach, as well as rising apprehension that even the lifeline of the moving traffic might not be enough to allow a safe landing.

It took nearly ten minutes for the taillights to start flowing again, but this time the river of red flowed directly to the accident scene, marking the safe route of her approach as Jennifer descended, pausing in a hover some fifty feet over the roadway as the troopers once again stopped the traffic. The resulting landing zone was only a few hundred yards wide as she descended straight down at a ninety degree angle to the traffic flow, aware of the slight slope of the roadway in both directions. The Eurocopter's lights picked up the tree tops along either side of the highway. She settled the EC-135's wheels firmly on the blacktop just as a snow flurry began to get serious.

Gretchen and Karen opened the rear clamshell doors of the helicopter as one of the paramedics rushed up to brief them. The lone driver in the eastbound car had somehow escaped serious injury, but the family in the other vehicle had not been so fortunate. The parents were dead, their ten-year-old son and six-year-old daughter had been briefly trapped in the wreckage, and the boy had expired just before Jennifer touched down.

The paramedic was blood-soaked and was working hard to stabilize the little girl for transport.

"How long?" Jennifer heard Gretchen ask him.

"Five minutes."

The snowfall was increasing and Jennifer had the anti-ice system working to keep the blades and engine inlets free of ice, but it was beginning to worry her. Too often they'd sat down at a landing zone and had had to wait for what seemed an interminable period for the paramedics to stabilize a patient enough for the transport, but this couldn't be allowed to drag on for long.

"Gretchen, tell them we've got ten minutes maximum," Jennifer said, aware of the surprised look she got in response. Only twice before could she recall issuing a deadline to the paramedics.

Within three minutes, the stretcher bearing the little girl was loaded aboard, and the clamshell doors closed within seconds as Gretchen relayed the clearance to depart.

There was a light breeze blowing down the highway from the east, frigid air flowing down from Stevens Pass, and she had pivoted on landing to face that direction. Picking up the EC-135 now was a simple matter, but she carefully followed the same procedure used on rooftop heliports, lifting the twin engine helicopter straight up for a power check before committing to forward flight.

She could see the tree tops descending in her peripheral vision, but she added another fifty feet before pivoting the helicopter toward the west and nudging it forward, accelerating into the snow flurries as she gained altitude and calculated the course back to the rooftop of Olympic Hospital.

That landing would be the easy part.

UNIVERSITY OF WASHINGTON SEISMOLOGY LAB, 10:55 P.M.

The plan to make a few calculations and race back to Jennifer had begun to evaporate the moment Doug's computer located the source of the tremors that had sounded the alarm.

My God, they're coming from the Quilieute Quiet Zone!

Doug sat back in his chair, trying to calm himself, glad he'd called Sanjay to come in as he drove to the lab. The young postdoc was just coming through the door, a puzzled expression on his face as he passed the wall of seismic recording drums to reach the small desk where Doug was sitting.

"What's going on?" Sanjay asked.

"You're going to want to see this!"

Doug tapped the appropriate part of the computer display.

"And what will I be looking at?"

"We're getting microquakes right next to the Quilieute Quiet Zone. It could be coming awake."

Sanjay pulled up a rolling office chair next to Doug and scooted closer to the computer.

"That's quite a conclusion."

"You check my math and tell *me*."

"By the way," Sanjay said as he put on reading glasses and squinted at the figures on the flat-screen display, "Sondra was very appreciative that you would not let me bring you home for dinner tonight unannounced."

"That's good."

"Until you called me to come in and . . . more or less broke the mood. Now she is no longer so appreciative."

Doug smiled. "You're saying my call was badly timed?"

"You have no idea." Sanjay pointed to the screen. "Is this what you're so excited about?"

"You see the distribution of those tiny temblors?"

"I see something slightly above the level of background noise. And I recall that you were supposed to be having a wonderful evening with Jennifer while permitting me a similar delight with my lady."

"Blame these microtremors."

Sanjay nodded toward the tracings. *"These* set the program off?"

"Yes."

"You must have set the sensitivity threshold to near zero. Doug, these vibrations barely register."

"But this is how it can start, Sanjay. If I've been right all along and no one should have been sending even the smallest seismic impacts down from Cascadia Island, and if they've now pulled the trigger on three hundred years of unrelieved tectonic pressure, this sort of microquake is exactly what I'd expect to see as the seismic bomb starts to arm itself."

Sanjay looked troubled. "That would be one point of view. That would also be a very hyperbolic way to state it."

"Okay, *you* tell me where those tremors are occurring, Sanjay." Doug said, coming forward in his chair, hovering on the ragged edge of irritation. "Go ahead. Where are they coming from? Please check my math."

Singh worked the keyboard to call up the raw data and flew through some calculations before pushing back from the screen and turning to his leader.

"Well, I do see a distribution of tiny hypocenters about twenty-six kilometers down, laterally along a fifty-mile front, approximately eight microquakes within a ten-minute period, each less than 1.5 magnitude, distanced about forty miles on average west of the coastline."

"And that would be?"

"The vibrations, in magnitude terms, would be the rough equivalent of mice mating in Australia. In other words, next to nothing."

"No. They're next to what zone? Maybe even in it."

"Perhaps the twilight zone. Doug, there's really nothing here. I can't believe my exalted leader pulled the panic button for something that small."

"You *push* a panic button."

"Sorry."

"You . . . *pull* an emergency brake, and *push* a panic button."

Sanjay studied Doug's face for a few seconds. "Doug, forgive me, but you're jumping to conclusions."

"Why?"

"I know you believe firmly in your theory, and you may be right, but this isn't validation of anything yet. Do you have corroborating seismographs from other seismic networks yet?"

"No, but—"

"Then, with all due respect, this fails to alarm me."

Doug cocked his head slightly. "Remind me again," he laughed. "Whom do you work for?"

"You, your majesty, and your eternal charge to me on being hired as a postdoctoral fellow was that I should at all times maintain my scientific integrity, which includes telling you the unvarnished truth, which is what I am doing."

"Come on and say the words, Sanjay. What zone are these microquakes occurring in, or next to?"

"What *zone?*"

"You know what I'm asking. And use my terminology."

He sighed. "You want me to say they're coming from what you labeled the 'Quilieute Quiet Zone,' correct?"

"Yes, I do."

"Very well, they appear on very cursory examination to be in or adjacent to the Quiet Zone, but they may not be real, and they may not be a precursor."

"Ever see anything in that zone before? A microquake? A shadow of something? Even an indication someone unwrapped a candy bar and threw the wrapper down hard on the shore?"

"No."

"Then I rest my case. For the first time in recorded history we have microquakes along the Quilieute Quiet Zone. And this is after Walker gets through whacking the earth's surface for two straight years because no one's listening to a lone seismologist with a nutty theory trying to say you shouldn't pull on a seismic hair trigger."

"You really think these tiny rumblings could be the start sequence of the big one? The 9.5?"

"Yes. Damnit, yes."

Sanjay turned toward him with a troubled expression. "But, if that's true, why do I detect that you're *enjoying* this?"

The smile faded from Doug's face as he realized that was exactly what he'd been doing, enjoying the "I told you so" possibilities. "God, Sanjay, you're right. I'm ashamed." He looked back at the screen with a sigh. "That's really embarrassing. I just get through telling you earlier this afternoon how much I wanted to be wrong about my entire thesis, but the second I saw these, I started gloating."

"I understand. You've been the lone voice of warning for several years."

"Well . . . with this, naturally I'm now waiting for the other shoe to drop, although I take it you think it's premature to sound any public alarms, right?"

"Absolutely, it's too soon. These may not even be real quakes."

Doug shook his head and lofted a wadded-up scrap of paper across the room to a perfect landing in a trash can. "The hell of training and hiring smart people, Sanjay, is you have to listen to them occasionally."

"Thank you, I think."

"It's just that I know I'm right and I feel like the little kid confronting a naked emperor."

"That e-mail is really bugging you, right?"

Doug nodded energetically. "Like a burr under my saddle. The guy claims he's got the proof I need but his return e-mail was garbled, as I told you. I checked when I came in a bit ago and he's finally written back with a good return address, so I can finally answer, but I'm really frustrated. In fact, his timing was spooky. It's almost as if he's watching these same microquakes unfold."

"Maybe he is. Maybe he's at USGS headquarters in Menlo Park trying to prove to a room full of detractors that you'll snap at anything."

"Come on. We don't act like that. Nevertheless, I'm being careful in my replies."

"I'd bet it's a hoax. But what did he say this time?"

"That he has a collection of seismic refraction data for Cascadia Island that proves the place is extremely dangerous, but that he's got to be very careful getting it to me because there are people who don't want that known. Walker, for one, I'll bet."

"So this mystery source has read your paper?"

Doug shrugged. "Who knows? I'm not sure what he's got. But, if there is real data out there which validates any significant part of my theory, we've got to sound the alarms. Especially now."

"But if they've finished construction . . . stopped banging around on the surface and creating seismic waves . . . and nothing has happened, then the risk on Cascadia Island won't be any greater than anywhere else along the Washington coast, correct?"

"Correct."

"And right now there is really nothing indicating the zone is coming active. Right?"

"Technically, right."

"So, even if you tell everyone it's dangerous and they believe you, most of the people assembling for the resort's opening weekend will still go."

"They're taking one helluva chance!"

"Yes, but it's the doctrine of assumed risk, Doug. People always assume the risk doesn't apply to them. You can't protect everyone."

"It's not everyone I'm worried about, Sanjay. This is personal. Jennifer refuses to listen to me. She'll be there the entire weekend."

PLEASANTON, CALIFORNIA

Senator Ralph Lacombe drummed his fingers on the kitchen counter, waiting for someone to answer the ringing at the other end of his call. The house was quiet now that the police had folded their tent and departed, severely consternated over having to defer to the word of a powerful state politician that his daughter was *not* kidnapped nor the victim of any other crime. Clearly dissatisfied with the sudden end of what had become a major manhunt, they had released Diane's cretinous boyfriend and left a half dozen business cards with numbers to contact in case there were some reversal of the case and Senator Lacombe's daughter turned out to be in trouble after all.

He had been diplomatic and appreciative and apologetic, stroking their bruised egos at the same time he'd pulled rank to force them to end the case, but Diane's name was now up in lights, and in effect she was now a minor target for the San Francisco police. The department had been embarrassed, and someone needed to pay.

"Hello?"

The male voice on the other end snapped Ralph Lacombe back to the moment.

"Bill?"

"Yes. Who's this?"

"Ralph Lacombe. I know it's been a while . . ."

"*Been* a while? Jeez, Ralph, that was a previous *life*, for God's sake! How are you? I hear you're a highfalutin' state senator now?"

"Yes, and I need an off the books favor."

"Well, hell. I thought you were calling for friendship."

"I am. My little girl's in trouble, and I need some help finding out who, what, where, when, and why."

"So, you turn to an old spook?"

"Who better?" Lacombe asked, appreciative of the self-deprecating CIA reference.

"Okay. Fill me in. Who do you want me to shoot this time?"

Chapter 7

The brief flight to the Olympic Hospital heliport and the short hop to Boeing Field had been completed by midnight, but there was an injured employee in the same hospital and Jennifer had changed back into her cocktail dress and driven the brief distance to check on him. Tim Paretsky, was still in the emergency department conscious, but embarrassed and apologetic. Satisfied he was going to be okay, she started for the door, but found herself unable to resist checking on the accident victim they had just transported.

The little girl was clinging to life after a transfusion, and Jennifer watched from a distance as the battle continued and the emergency team prepped her for surgery, unprepared for the empathetic self to take over as she left the ED.

Medical professionals kept their distance and their emotions in check. She knew the routine all too well. But occasionally the trauma would leak past the personal firewall, and when the battle was over, an emotional tidal wave could hit, embarrassing the clinician with a sudden venting of all the fear and angst stored during the emergency.

Jennifer stepped into a corridor to deal with the sudden tears and then dried her eyes, glad no one had been watching. She was aware that the turbulent evening with Doug was the major contributor, and she was also suddenly in need of a comforting environment.

Jennifer found herself moving automatically to the twelfth floor and the familiarity of 12 West, the unit where she'd spent six years of her professional life as a nurse and a nurse manager. It was like coming home, something you do unconsciously.

Being back on the floor completed the feeling. She found herself gliding through a time warp into her old domain, relaxing in the normalcy and familiarity. There was a comfort about Olympic she could never define, a feeling of need and belonging and purpose—of safety and security—all of which contradicted the very real problems that had driven her out. The dreary truth of how frustrating her time at Olympic had been was something she actively suppressed. Even as a nurse manager she'd been unable to change this small part of the world where finances ruled over patient safety and staff satisfaction. It wasn't at all what she'd expected when she left nursing school with her RN degree in hand. Caring for the sick and injured had simply become an industry, and a surprisingly archaic one at that. Even faceless manufacturers in the most basic of industries understood the need for respecting and caring for their employees. But to healthcare it seemed a mystery. She had tried hard with her MBA to meld the knowledge of medicine with the realities of business and forge a common language. She'd spoken out when others kept silent, rattled cages and made friends and powerful enemies, but to no avail. There had been a flirtation with professional depression, too as she came closer and closer to burnout trying to convince everyone that they couldn't run things by financial considerations alone without killing careers and patients, if not the hospital itself. And ultimately, her respect for the system had hit bottom.

Jennifer smiled at the charge nurse on 12 West as she passed, keenly aware that the woman was staring back with suspicion at her outfit.

It was probably all the same, Jennifer thought. Indeed, so many of her friends still in practice confirmed it with every conversation. Year after year little in the American hospital changed: the nurses still burned out, doctors still felt powerless, and patients were still not as protected as they could be from mistakes fostered by the flawed process of running health care as a business. Despite her best efforts, despite the vision and enthusiasm of her team on 12W, they had never quite achieved the level of quality care they were reaching for.

Jennifer had taken each defeat personally during those years. But Sven's stroke had changed everything, and suddenly it was apparent that either the reins of Nightingale Aviation were going to be passed to an outsider, or Sven's sole heir would have to leave nursing and take over.

Her decision had taken little more than a nanosecond.

It really had been a resurrection of sorts, an instant, if dark, relief. A way of giving up while pretending to move on. The professional change had sparked renewed meaning at the same moment it had brought Doug Lam into her life, with all his energy and joy of living and exasperating work ethic.

The floor felt different somehow. Cold and antiseptic and sterile, and she wondered why. Visually, nothing seemed changed.

Doug.

As she walked past another room, Jennifer caught sight of him on the local PBS channel, a rerun of an interview on his controversial theory that had later been broadcast nationally, to the chagrin of his USGS leaders. She shook her head. She couldn't escape him if she tried. The diagrams of the

Cascadia Subduction Zone were on screen as well, including the area around Cascadia Island where she would be tomorrow night. She should think about his warning, but right now the two realities refused to intersect.

She turned into one of the rooms from which Doug's voice could be heard. The patient, an elderly woman, was engrossed in the interview. The room, Jennifer noticed, was bare of any get-well cards, and only one small vase of flowers sat on the nightstand.

"Hi," Jennifer said. "Mind if I watch with you a second?"

The woman smiled, her eyes taking in the cocktail dress.

"So, this is the new uniform?"

Jennifer sat down, laughing easily, feeling even more of her old life as a nurse taking over as she fell into conversation. The woman introduced herself as Hilda Bromberg. She was the eighty-one-year-old former owner of a local broadcast empire, sharp, feisty, and recovering well from surgery, but achingly lonely.

"I don't recall hearing your name for a long time, Miss Bromberg."

"The name is Hilda, please. And of course you wouldn't be hearing about me. I sold out fifteen years ago and everyone thinks I'm dead and living in Florida."

They talked for nearly half an hour, Jennifer relaxing at last in the grateful presence of the fascinating woman who had once been a feisty fixture in Seattle's somewhat boisterous social world. Jennifer remembered how much she had loved the process of talking with her patients when the floor was hers, touching them as human beings, finding out as much about them as possible, and trying to help on more levels than just the clinical. It was something she sorely missed in emergency medicine, and something that was apparently absent on 12W.

"Is there really someone out there?" Hilda joked. "I heard rumors of a nurse having been spotted in the lobby the other day, but I sure haven't seen one in person."

"Really?"

"Well, not a *human* nurse. These are Stepford Nurses. Must be a factory back east where they stamp them out. Wish I owned stock in it."

There was the soft squeak of a rubber sole on a polished floor and Jennifer looked up to see the charge nurse walk by for the second time. She was orbiting, undoubtedly working on the question of who the woman in the red cocktail dress was, and whether to challenge her.

Not a lot of courage, huh, Sweetie? Jennifer thought. The nurse was making the dangerous assumption that a woman moving as confidently among her patients as Jennifer had must somehow be authorized to do so.

"You see," Hilda was saying as she pointed toward the door. "That's one of them. She's been gone for hours, probably to recharge her battery pack."

"Stay here."

"I have a choice?"

"Of course. But I'll go see if she's human," Jennifer said, a finger to her lips.

The charge nurse had reappeared at the door. Jennifer moved into the hallway and introduced herself, giving a shorthand version of her years there.

The nurse was decidedly unimpressed.

"Miss Lindstrom, may I ask you a question, with no offense intended?" The tone was edgy and guarded. No offense perhaps, but no friendliness here, either, Jennifer thought.

"Sure."

"When you were the nurse manager, would you have let someone like you wander around the floor?"

Jennifer had written the rules about strangers on the floor to comply with a mind-numbing federal law called HIPPA. But then she'd quietly bent those same rules if they clashed with the need for positive human contact. And here she was simply smiling at patients and being pleasant. But, the nurse had a valid point.

"You're right. I wouldn't want someone wandering around without being challenged. And I apologize. I really should have introduced myself first."

"Yes, you should have."

"I have to go, anyway," she said, turning back toward Hilda's room. "But first, if you don't mind, I'm going to say good-bye to my new friend."

"Knock yourself out."

"I remember who she reminds me of, that one," Hilda said when Jennifer reentered the room.

"Who?" she asked, glancing back to make sure the charge nurse wasn't listening.

"Nurse Ratched from *One Flew Over the Cuckoo's Nest*," Hilda chuckled, pointing a finger at Jennifer as if sighting a pistol. "Okay, Honey, I can tell you need to go, but first you tell me what's troubling you."

"Me?"

"All over your face. I'm an experienced woman with built-in radar, re-member? And I used to boss hundreds of employees and do it well."

"No, I'm fine. Really. Just tired."

"Bull. Who is he and what did he do to you? The guy on TV you were watching?"

Jennifer smiled and adopted a puzzled look. "Hilda, why, if you perceive me to be upset about something, does it have to involve a relationship with a male?"

"First, because I don't think you're lesbian. Second, because you didn't jump in here to learn about earthquakes on TV. Third, because what else is there for a woman to be upset about? Everything but men we women can more or less wrestle into compliance."

Jennifer sat and gave her a brief synopsis of Doug's divorce anxiety.

"So," she concluded, "what do you think? Ignore my worries and stay with him, or give him an ultimatum?"

Hilda smiled at her and patted her arm. "Dear, there are 280 million people in the U.S., that we know about. About half are male, although in some cases it's arguable. But at least a tenth of that half form a reasonably eligible smorgasbord from which a gal like you can choose."

"You're working up to a point, Hilda. I can feel it."

"Damn right. Stick to your guns, that's the point."

"Were you married?"

"Three times. Never got it right and don't believe in it anymore."

"And no children?"

Sadness crossed Hilda's features like a passing cloud, and she shrugged it off. "When I get out of here, let's get together and I'll answer that question. And, in case you run into any of my kin, you didn't see me here."

"No one knows you're here?"

"No. And I have my reasons."

Jennifer exchanged numbers and bade her good-bye, leaving the floor under the baleful, if safely distant stare of the charge nurse. She descended four flights of stairs letting Doug's face swim into her thoughts once more. He was there at the lab tonight, undoubtedly immersed in his scientific world and probably alone. She wondered if it had dawned on him yet that it was past midnight, or that his lover had probably tired of waiting at the Breakwater.

I should call, she thought.

CASCADIA ISLAND HELIPORT

The unscheduled midnight charter from Boeing Field to Cascadia Island's heliport had been arranged at the last minute. Mick Walker had offered no explanation for cancelling the much cheaper reserved flight earlier in the evening, but for the Nightingale charter pilot, no explanation was needed.

"One of those urgent matters," Walker had explained with a smile as he climbed aboard and accepted an offer of the copilot's seat. The pilot,

Kevin Chapman, nodded without comment, aware that the "urgent matter" was no doubt a beautiful woman. He'd agreed to handle the pop-up
flight after returning from another charter, hoping to see again the stunning, statuesque brunette in an ermine coat and spike heels who'd met
Walker's business jet earlier in the evening. He'd watched mesmerized
from the operations center as she unfolded herself from the back of a
white stretch limo with the poise of a woman serenely secure in her
wealth and privilege. Kevin had expected to see the same car pull onto the
ramp again, but much to his disappointment, Walker had appeared alone,
climbing out of the back of a garden-variety taxi to board the charter
operation's Sikorsky S-76.

Fifty minutes after liftoff and safely around the north end of the ten-
thousand-foot peaks of the Olympic Peninsula, Kevin began his approach
to the tiny outcropping that had sparked so much controversy among environmentalists, and aligned himself with the bright rotating beacon at the
helipad.

Transitioning a helicopter from forward to vertical flight was a gradual
process that often scared fixed-wing pilots on a very primal level, and the
pilot in command of Sikorsky N344NT was watching the passenger in the
copilot's seat for that kind of reaction.

As the speed dropped, Kevin could see his passenger's feet move forward
defensively, the man's glances at airspeed becoming more frequent and his
breathing more accelerated as his fixed wing instincts began bellowing for
more speed.

Kevin was used to explaining that while speed equals life in fixed-wing
flying, the same wasn't true for helicopters, and he repeated the explanation
now.

The lights of the island were just ahead, the lighted heliport all but lost in
the sea of illumination around it. Now the speed was decreasing below fifty
knots as the pilot slowly nudged the cyclic control stick backward slightly
between his knees, diminishing the percentage of the Sikorsky's engine
power that was going to produce forward momentum, and transitioning it
into vertical lift. The collective, a floor-mounted lever with a motorcycle
throttle grip in the pilot's left hand, was being nudged steadily downward in
almost undetectable increments, lessening the engine's output at the same
time the rotor blades were being unloaded of excess lift.

The lighted pad was beneath them now and Kevin was maneuvering
around to land into the southwest wind when a large hand cupped his left
shoulder.

"Can you fly me completely around the island once?" Mick Walker
asked.

"Sure," Kevin replied, stifling the impulse to add that a full excursion around the tiny rock might take all of thirty seconds.

The circle done, he resumed his approach and worked the controls almost imperceptibly to bring forward and downward vertical speed to zero at precisely the same moment with the craft fifteen feet above the pad. Satisfied with his motionless hover, Kevin lowered them vertically to the surface.

Walker shook his head, a large smile on his face as he unlatched his seat belt and shook the pilot's hand. "I gotta learn how to do that!"

"Well, if anyone can afford it, I imagine you can."

Mick Walker nodded, his expression carefully unchanged despite the old familiar twinge of apprehension that had just twisted his stomach. Long ago he'd learned how to keep such reactions off his face, in poker and in business.

"Yeah, you're right," was all he said in response, adding his thanks as a black limo pulled up to the helipad.

Chapter 8

For some perverse reason, Diane Lacombe thought, she was almost enjoying this clandestine escape.

Almost.

And now I'm the anonymous woman in 28D.

Her soon-to-be-gone career with Chadwick and Noble had flashed through her mind twice since she'd slipped aboard Amtrak's Coast Starlight while it sat in the Oakland station Thursday night. She'd left the train with equal stealth in Sacramento in the wee hours Friday morning, darting between shadows for the nearly two dozen blocks to a friend's apartment, as if she were a downed pilot escaping from the Viet Cong.

And now she was back aboard the Coast Starlight, her plan intact, if changed.

Thank God for Debbie, Diane thought. There was very little chance of anyone connecting Debbie Hill's Sacramento flat with the name Diane Lacombe, and as luck had arranged it, Debbie was on vacation in Mex- ico—although Amtrak's records would show that it was Debbie Hill who had fled Oakland Thursday night.

A dozen times Friday, Diane had considered calling her in Puerto Vallarta just for moral support, but always pulled her hand away from the phone. The less Debbie knew, the safer Debbie was, but she was helping by just being absent.

Diane always smiled at the thought of time with Deb. She was truly her best friend, and, almost from the time they met at college, they'd shared everything from problems with boyfriends to clothes and classes and lots of laughs and tears along the way.

She shivered at the memory of the time Debbie had been stalked by an unhinged college hacker who had been able to follow her through her credit card usage, even by the hour. It was three years ago, and Debbie had ended up panicked on Diane's doorstep in San Francisco and merged into Diane's identity for several days until the stalker was caught. Ever since then they'd had a mutual-aid pact, carrying each other's apartment keys, credit cards, and carefully fabricated IDs with each name under the other's picture, all for a quick getaway if ever needed. Someday, Diane figured, marriage would probably cancel or modify the pact, but so far they were just as dedicated to it.

The real Diane snuggled a bit deeper into the coach seat, her ticket already in the conductor's possession. She'd holed up silently in Debbie's apartment all day Friday, deeply startled when she turned on the TV in the evening to find her picture all over the media and her parents horribly stressed on camera. She'd never considered the possibility the police might get involved, or that anyone would think she'd been the victim of foul play. She'd almost dialed her family's home directly, before realizing the traps the police would set for a supposed kidnapper.

Earlier in the day she'd carefully burned a duplicate CD of her files and prepared the FedEx package for her father, then intending to walk out in front of God and everyone to drop it off, never suspecting half the state was searching for her. Instead, she'd dropped it in the FedEx box in the dead of the night before boarding the train.

The thought of Don Brevin starring in a low-speed chase and being very publicly arrested was amusing. The rat deserved it, although he'd soon be off the hook—if they hadn't already released him based on her phone call. She had to laugh at the thought that the whole thing would end up helping his pathetic career and boosting his bad-boy image. She was always attracted to losers like Don. Something about them made her go slightly insane, like a cat obeying an insatiable desire to climb to the top of a tree it couldn't hope to climb down.

Over and over again.

But Don was lucky, she thought. He hadn't done anything so bad as to trigger her primal instincts for revenge. Anyone who did, she had long since decided, would pay a terrible price. And that included anyone who hurt Debbie, or Ralph Lacombe.

The train was north of Sacramento now, the windows showing only the deep black of nighttime farmland dotted by occasional rain showers. It was cold in the coach car and she pulled her jacket back on and snuggled against the sidewall forcing her mind back to the problem at hand.

After sending the e-mail to Doug Lam once more, the reply she'd been waiting for had finally come around midday Friday. It was a hesitant response which claimed her original address had been too garbled, and the overall tone was suspicion. She couldn't blame the man for that. Lam had taken enough grief for the paper he'd published, and there were plenty of crackpots out there claiming to have proof for everything from extraterrestrial visitation to antigravity devices.

But she'd dangled something irresistible in front of him, and, as she'd expected, he'd taken the bait and provided a phone number in Seattle, undoubtedly hopeful that the corroborating research she was promising would really help.

He has no idea, she mused.

She thought about the explanation she'd sent him detailing the growing worries she'd claimed to have over the hurried way the Cascadia Island seismic engineering research had been handled. Those worries, she'd written, had been eating at her for over two years, and they had finally sparked a dangerous midnight run on the company's project files just a few weeks ago. It was, she knew, a firing offense to monkey with the deep data files of the firm without proper authorization. But as she had stated it to Lam, ". . . it was a necessary chance to take, especially since I was originally responsible for supervising the team that gathered the seismic refraction data on Mick Walker's island at his specific and urgent request."

She told him how shocked she'd been to find that the firm's formal evaluation of the data had resulted in a clean bill of health for the island's geology even though she had studied seismology enough to recognize the signature of a major fault, a bombshell of a rift running through the middle of it they had somehow missed.

But there had seemed to be more. She wasn't trained in seismology, but she had read his controversial professional paper on the concept of naturally amplified resonant vibrations acting as earthquake triggers. She went back to a copy of the raw data and tried to look deep below the island. There were, she found, strange aspects of the rock formations over the subduction zone, just as he had predicted, aspects an engineering evaluation wouldn't normally be concerned about. The graphs and waveforms suggested some very strange things about the way the miles of rock beneath Cascadia Island were put together.

She had set the hook well, she thought. "Dr. Lam, I may have the actual seismic reflective proof that the rock strata beneath Cascadia Island can focus and even amplify any physical impacts on the surface which produce compression waves, just as you said. If my interpretation is correct, then, in a phrase, you were right."

The lights of a small town flashed by the window of the train, the muffled sound of grade-crossing bells passing and falling in pitch as the darkness returned, broken only by distant farm lights. She was hungry all of a sudden, but too deep in thought to do anything about it.

When the truth of what she knew was in the company's files was exposed, the firm would appear at best negligent, and at worst, engaged in a cover-up to save their client. Those who cared would think that Chadwick and Noble had simply been too pressed for time to do the deeper analysis correctly and had been sloppy in discounting Lam's theory. After all, most experts would never read into the situation what she was seeing. But once they reprocessed the data, all hell would break loose.

The shock of discovering that someone was willing to wreck her apartment to find what she possessed had altered the whole equation. But who was responsible? It was more than an unexpected complication, it was deeply worrisome, and she had to assume they were trying to find her. She'd tried to think through and anticipate all possible reactions, but this one had caught her off guard. If the firm was trying to intimidate her to silence, they were far too late. But if tearing her place apart was supposed to be a warning to be careful, it had been effective. It wasn't too much of a stretch to imagine someone killing an out-of-control female engineer if there was a billion dollars to be saved. After all, accidents happened, women disappeared with depressing regularity, and even murder could be made to look like suicide.

Every creepy movie she'd watched had been haunting her for the past twenty-four hours, and even someone as innocuous as a young soldier who'd briefly sat beside her on the train was suspect.

Diane pulled a blanket up around her, partially hiding her face like a child raising the bedsheets against monsters. There wasn't time to be scared. She had to concentrate on planning the next move.

SEATTLE

Jennifer awoke with her heart racing, slow to recall she had driven the short distance to her condo and collapsed into a deep sleep following the Stevens Pass pickup and the visit to Olympic Hospital.

She rubbed her eyes and searched for the clock, expecting to see six or seven A.M.

Two-thirty?

She'd been out less than ninety minutes, but there was no point in trying to go back to sleep when she felt so suddenly wide awake, and all she could think of was Doug.

A quick call to the lab confirmed that he and Sanjay were still there.

"Is there a big earthquake somewhere, Sanjay?"

"Let's just say we're monitoring some things that concern us," he explained, caution clearly draping his words.

"Don't tell him I'm coming over, but I'm coming over with food."

Bok Choy Takeout was a twenty-four-hour operation and was on the way to the university. Devoid of aesthetics, trees, or even a decent sign out front, it had always been one of her favorite places—though she'd never quite learned how to communicate with the woman who owned it. Thirty years in Seattle and the immigrant Chinese woman's thick accent was still all but indecipherable. Jennifer drove the short distance to the Chinatown shop, double-parking as she ordered a small feast and waited for the stuffed sacks to be slid over the stainless steel counter. Mrs. Wong was home, the young girl behind the counter told her in perfect American. "Grand-mother's been sick lately."

"Well, please tell her that Jennifer from Olympic Hospital said hello. She'll probably remember me. Tell her I hope she's feeling better soon."

"Okay."

"I don't get in here much anymore. I miss your grandma."

The girl brightened. "Yeah, she's really cool, but I can't understand her half the time."

"You don't speak Mandarin at home?"

"I don't speak Chinese at all, and my parentals are bummed about that. But, hey, I'm from Seattle, right?"

It took less than ten minutes to drive to the seismology lab. The collection of fragrant white sacks was attracting attention as she found Doug in urgent conversation and slipped a free arm through his, marveling at the way he flashed the smile that always melted her without missing a beat in the discussion. Sanjay nodded and smiled at Jennifer, his eyes on the sacks of food.

"Dude, your lady's brought a feast."

"She sure has," Doug said. "Thanks, Jennifer."

"So, Doug . . . you going to eat that all by yourself?" the postdoc added.

"No, he's not," she said. "He's going to share. Dig in."

"I'm glad you're here, Honey." He resumed his discussions and she began setting the small boxes of food on the top of an adjacent table.

Typical, she thought. She could show up at his side unexpectedly at any time and get an equally pleased and casual response. His endless acceptance of just about any change of mind she might have was slightly irritating and comforting at the same time, and a skill she couldn't emulate herself.

She finished laying out the food and faded into the background of the lab, watching him, studying the intensity of his concentration on the various tasks at hand, amused at the way he'd tried to make his crisp business suit look more university-casual with his loosened tie. There hadn't been a flicker when she touched his arm. No awareness that this night had been a difficult watershed, a turning point.

I'll never understand men and compartmentalization, Jennifer thought. *How do they do it?*

And yet she did understand it. Somewhere inside, she knew she, too, was a master at it.

An alarm of some sort suddenly blared through the room from the far end of the seismograph drum array. Doug got up and moved toward the protesting instrument as a long, significant shudder rippled beneath their feet, rattling the equipment racks and most of the people in the room.

"Uh, oh," Sanjay uttered, his hand wrapped around the edge of a metal rack.

Doug's eyes were wide with genuine shock as he turned to look for her.

"That was a big compression wave," he said. "Everyone brace yourselves!"

Chapter 9

The first tremor began twenty-six kilometers beneath the ocean floor slightly more than thirty miles from the west coast of the Olympic Peninsula. It was little more than a small shift of lightless rock, heated to temperatures of nearly five hundred degrees Fahrenheit, but the shock waves headed off in all directions, the primary compressive wave, or "P wave," traveling predictably faster than the side-to-side motion of the train of secondary "S waves" that followed. In magnitude terms it was minor, but the waves coursed through the rock and mud beneath Puget Sound from west to east and flashed underneath Seattle, dissipating slowly as they crossed the Cascade Mountains and wiggled the seismometer needles a bit above a magnitude 5.0.

Under the forest of office buildings in Seattle and the thousands of homes and lesser structures to the east, the ground shifted, undulating a tiny distance to one side and back as the surface waves passed.

QUAALATCH, WASHINGTON

The former leader of the Quaalatch Nation Tribal Council took the fresh cup of tea she'd poured and moved back to her tiny kitchen table in the predawn darkness shrouding the ocean side of the Olympic Peninsula.

The lights and the pounding noises from across the channel were riveting her attention again, as they did even in sleep. Better to sit and sip her tea and think quietly than toss and turn. She knew how to meditate, and the terrible things that had been done to the small Quaalatch island labeled Cascadia had prompted much introspection in the last two years. But four days ago her meditation had produced a vision as clear and certain as the crash of the surf and the morning coastal fog, an omen of deliverance, and the hour was drawing close.

There were very few of her tribe left now, too few to be counted together as anything but an also-ran in the list of sovereign nations of American Indians. Marta Cartwright herself was seventy-eight and very tired of the way the earth was losing its battle. To the north, the Makah and the Ozette nations were stable, if not thriving, and in Lapush, just to the south, the

Quilieutes were maintaining themselves in a stable poverty more typical of the plains nations.

But her people—the Quaalatch—were down to four hundred souls, and her own direct lineage down to one disappointing grandson named Lester.

Marta had been forced to take her Anglo name by those who had tried to assimilate her tribe in the thirties, and all attempts to change it back had led to naught. Social security numbers, medical entitlements, and just about everything else in the web of American life required her artificial Anglo name, and one day she had simply stopped fighting that battle. She would be Marta, but her heart would always be Quaalatch.

She squeezed some more lemon into her teacup and pictured her arch-rival, Sara Tulalin. Marta wondered if Sara had any idea what she'd done in leasing the island to Mick Walker. It was one thing to take over leadership of her people and their traditions, and quite another to contaminate their mea-ger land holdings with something as crass and disgusting as a casino.

The enemy knew Marta well. The builders who had eagerly dug and plowed and reshaped Cascadia Island—utterly destroying it as a bird sanctu-ary—had been unable to resist raising their middle finger to their former ad-versary in the form of the hated searchlight that revolved all through the winter night. She watched patiently as it flashed arrogant confirmation of its presence in her face every fifteen seconds, aimed maliciously and squarely, she was sure, at her seaside window.

She thought of Mick Walker as a devil, as much as her traditional beliefs would accommodate the concept Christians considered to be the devil. She didn't hate Walker, but he was clearly her enemy, a man who had not hesi-tated to bankroll her political defeat when she, as the matriarchal leader of her people, refused to lease him their island and befoul their heritage. Walker had dangled money before her people and brought in dour men who had built successful native casinos elsewhere. They promised gambling riches and a renaissance for the Quaalatch for nothing more than the price of their souls. Hopelessly seduced, they had giddily sold out, throwing their longtime matriarch out of office and, as was their tradition, choosing an-other woman, Sara, who could not wait to cash in.

But Marta's vision confirmed that Walker would find her defeat a Pyrrhic victory. That sustained her. Her vision showed clearly that sooner or later everything he had erected on the raped remains of her tribal land would be swept away.

The Quaalatch oral history told of the periodic times of cleansing when the people would be forced to take to their canoes for many months while the sea reclaimed and restored their lands. Those were accounts of the great earthquakes which hit at long intervals over the thousands of years her people had lived here, accounts it had taken modern scientists decades to confirm.

And now it was coming again, the time of cleansing. The opening round of tremors minutes before in the cold, dark night had been as welcome as fresh water to a refugee in the desert. The strange shuddering had prompted her to rise, and she sat now with great patience in her ringside seat waiting for the moment of renewal. It did not matter that the great tidal wave that would sweep Walker from the island would engulf her, too, only seconds later. The last moments of life would be sweet indeed, and her people—those that survived—would be renewed.

She recalled the old lodge owner named Harry Truman who had refused to leave the land and his home on the flanks of Mount St. Helens as the mountain prepared to explode in 1980. For a non-native, he had shown extraordinary understanding, she thought, letting the mountain sweep him and his land into history as one, his honor intact.

She would be proud to go like Mr. Truman.

The searchlight was slapping at her through a layer of fog now and periodically disappearing for minutes. In those brief periods when it was invisible, she could experience again, briefly, what the sea had looked like outside her window for so many tranquil years before. Then the light would reappear, pulsing indistinctly at first, then restored to its intrusive flash.

She got up and poured another cup of tea, doubling the lemon this time before resuming her post. It was beginning.

Soon the light would stop forever.

10 MILES SOUTHEAST OF FORKS, WASHINGTON

There was a sudden vibration in the steering column.

State Trooper Gavin Quintin muttered to himself and began slowing to stop on the shoulder as he turned on his blue and red Visibar lights. Something was very wrong with his patrol car.

It was pitch dark and foggy. He checked his rearview mirrors for oncoming trucks as he moved his hand to the door release. Not many logging trucks screamed down the Olympic Peninsula's Highway 101 anymore—certainly not as many as twenty years ago when he first put on the uniform—but they could still appear out of nowhere, careening like stampeding buffalo around a blind curve.

But tonight there were no headlights bearing down on him from either direction. He was alone on a ghostly black ribbon of road snaking through a moonless forest and trying to figure out why his cruiser had been jumping around on the road so severely. It hadn't felt exactly like a flat, more like all four tires had gone somewhat square.

He opened the door and grabbed his heavy KelLite flashlight, starting the tire inspection with the right front.

Nothing. Did I throw a weight or something and go out of balance? he wondered. *No. Far too severe for that.*

It had still been shaking as he slowed through thirty.

A distant noise caught his ear and he looked to the south, aware of the occasional star overhead through a break in the low-hanging fog. But only the soft sound of the wind answered his glance, with no hint of the gale he knew they were predicting for Saturday.

Okay, let's try it again, he sighed, reinserting himself in the car and starting south.

Once more the car began shaking, this time less severely, and he braked to a halt again.

And again he could find nothing wrong. If it happened a third time, he decided, he would just live with it until the damned wheel came off.

Damnit. This car is possessed, I've got a broken engine mount, or I really need some time off!

Once more he got behind the wheel and accelerated to the south. Other than a few irregular bumps in the road, this time the ride remained smooth, and Gavin gradually let himself relax, letting his mind drift to the lore of his Northwest native heritage, the product of a Puyallup mother and a father from the Makah tribe in Neah Bay. He didn't put much faith in the old beliefs and superstitions, but on moonless nights like these it was as if the forests were trying to talk to him and he didn't know the language. Instead, he reverted to what he did know: the police work that sustained him when it helped others, and depressed him beyond words when he couldn't make a difference.

He knew this section of highway all too well, since his worst professional memory had happened just ahead. A migrant family of nine—six children, parents, and a grandmother—driving all night to their next job in Sequim had pulled their old station wagon over along this deserted stretch of road to sleep.

The same evening a disgruntled twenty-eight-year-old trucker making less than he thought he had a right to be paid spent a couple of hours drowning his sorrows in a Port Angeles tavern before getting back behind the wheel. An hour later he fell asleep at seventy with his boot on the throttle. He never saw the disabled car.

Gavin shook his head to expunge the memory and concentrate on the road. There was a tight and dangerous left-hand curve a few miles ahead where the western shoulder had washed out many times over the years, and he made a mental note of it as the car reached sixty again. He always slowed there instinctively to check it in his headlights, especially when the rains had been heavier than normal. It was an all but unconscious gesture, carried out less than thirty miles from the Hoh Rain Forest, a patch of Olympic National Park known as the second wettest spot on earth.

Suddenly his foot was dynamiting the brakes even before his conscious mind caught up with the image. The police cruiser came to a skidding halt, the headlights stabbing the night and disappearing into a void. Gavin threw open the door and snapped on his side-mounted searchlight, then leapt behind the wheel and snapped the car into reverse, pulling it back thirty or forty feet as he activated every flashing light the cruiser had and grabbed for the radio microphone.

"Dispatch, Seventy-Three."

"Go Seventy-Three."

"We have a major washout on Highway 101 approximately 19 miles south of Forks! I'm going to need emergency road crews and a complete shutdown of the highway in both directions, and a trooper or sheriff from the south."

"Copy Seventy-Three. How big a washout? Is it impassable?"

Gavin worked to keep his voice calm. He could see the lights of a heavy truck approaching from the south and would have to figure out how to slow him down in time.

"Dispatch, there's a twenty-foot section of the entire roadway missing! It's caved in somehow. Somebody's going to get killed out here if we don't barricade it quick!"

UNIVERSITY OF WASHINGTON SEISMOLOGY LAB

"Okay, *now* I'm worried!" Sanjay Singh said as he turned from a keyboard to find Doug Lam nodding in agreement. Fewer than five minutes had elapsed since the lab had stopped shaking.

"Are we still calculating a 5.1?" Doug asked.

Sanjay nodded. "For the first one, yes. The second was four-seven. And both are dead center in the Quilieute Quiet Zone, with new microtremors spreading north and south."

"I really did not want to be right, you know," Doug said, his expression hard and serious.

Jennifer had moved to his side, watching quietly, and Doug turned to her, explaining quickly what they were tracking as phones began ringing in the background. One of two graduate students who had been summoned just past 2 A.M. swept up a receiver, punched up two lines in succession, and motioned for Doug's attention.

"It's Channel 4 on line one wanting to talk to you and send out a crew."

"Just a second."

"And . . . another channel's holding on line two. I think it's Channel 7."

The remaining line had begun ringing and Doug's cell phone chimed in as well.

"And now it begins," Doug said, grimacing to Jennifer.

"The media drill?"

He nodded as she smiled, recalling the irony of how effective he was in TV interviews at calming people down, even when trying to suggest a seismic Armageddon was at hand.

"No one handles it better, Sweetie," she told him.

5 MILES SOUTH OF QUAALATCH, WASHINGTON

Dr. Terry Griswold awoke with his heart pounding like a pile driver as he vibrated unceremoniously off the bed and tumbled onto the cold, pine floor. There were no lights burning in the rustic beachfront cabin, and for a few seconds he imagined his belly flop had been a product of some strange nightmare featuring huge vibrators or giant paint mixers, or whatever the crazy dream sequence had been.

He lay there, feeling silly and disoriented and very, very cold, the aroma of cold wood smoke from an exhausted fire perfuming the frigid air.

Another shudder shook the pine boards and with it his unclothed posterior. Terry stood quickly, patting the end of the bed in the dark for a robe before starting the hunt for a light switch.

That, he thought, *was clearly a seismic tremor of some sort.*

He'd experienced winter waves crashing onto the beach with enough force to tweak his seismometers, but no wave would wiggle things for that long.

Terry padded over to a table filled with laptops and began toggling the screens back to life one by one. His feet were blocks of ice rapidly losing nerve contact with his brain and he suspected the pilot light had gone out again on the single propane heater in the one-room cabin. If he could survive long enough to reach the stove, he could light the oven for warmth. At least he still had electrical power for the important equipment.

The full seismic array he'd installed was designed to be always on, and a series of keystrokes brought up the record of the various channels covering the past three hours. He stood in shock looking at the voluminous record of the first tremors and the small but continuous events that had followed.

Where the hell have I been? he wondered, recalling at the same moment his misgivings about the sleeping medication. He'd been exhausted from weeks of field work that had him pioneering new frontiers in sleeplessness. The prescription had made sense, but he couldn't have picked a worse evening to take it and go to bed early.

He entered more keystrokes, the freezing cold of the frigid cabin all but forgotten as he pulled in a broader array of reports to form a three-dimensional map with tiny red dots pinpointing the hypocenters generated over the previous ten hours. The picture was emerging slowly, rotating in 3-D in the middle of the screen, and he sat back in utter shock.

Under twenty kilometers depth, thirty to fifty kilometers offshore, aligned along the Cascadia Subduction North-South Axis. Jesus H. Christ!

Three long months of fine-tuning an array of seismographs to catch and catalogue tiny tremors just above the Quilieute Quiet Zone and now he had the zone itself waking up and growling at his seismic "camera." The implications were cascading in his head. The locked sections were coming unlocked, and with the massive energy stored beneath his feet, anything could happen.

This cabin had been built on the beach before such acts became federal and state violations, and sitting as it did within a few feet of the high-tide line, the floor was no more than eight feet above sea level. A fifty-foot-high tsunami would kill him where he stood, and the only thing needed to create a fifty-foot wave would be a major break at any one of the same hypocenters his screens were now showing. He was, in other words, in severe and immediate danger—for that matter, so was the entire Pacific Coast from Eureka, California, to northern Vancouver Island in Canada.

"God, why didn't someone call me?" he mumbled, well aware of the answer. His cell phone was turned off, and had spent the last few hours as dead to the world as he'd been.

Terry scrambled back to his bedside table to find the phone. With no landlines nearby, the cellular connection was the only reliable voice link with Seattle—other than a roadside phone booth five miles distant. His seismic array used a satellite connection to send its data, but he hadn't been authorized to use grant money for the extra price of voice transmission. It was cell phones or nothing.

Fumbling for the right number, he punched it in, stamping his numb feet with impatience and hugging himself for warmth as he waited for it to ring.

Another shudder, this one almost too tiny to be felt, wiggled the floorboards as Sanjay Singh came on the line to brief him.

"We've been trying to call you, Terry," he said. "Doug needs a download of your array immediately."

"It should have been transmitting already. Damnit! Okay, I'll recheck it and retransmit in just a minute. I don't know what you're seeing there, but this is incredible. Are they evacuating the coast yet? I haven't heard sirens."

"No one's evacuating anything," Sanjay replied.

"What? Jeez, this could be the so-called 'big one' announcing its presence! Doug was right. Does the governor know?"

"I think that contact is in progress."

"Well, I could be wrong, but this looks ominous to me."

Terry hurriedly inspected the satellite data connections and ordered another download of the previous hour's tracings before rushing around to pull on his clothes. His core temperature was down and he was beginning to shiver uncontrollably, but there was too much to do to just stand in front of the oven or try to relight the heater. The Land Rover was right outside, and he planned to have it loaded and ready to go in fifteen minutes.

And a tsunami could hit within five minutes of a major break, he reminded himself. The fact that the very place where he was standing was below sea level three hundred years ago impressed itself into his consciousness like never before. He fully expected the coast to drop five to seven feet as soon as the seismic waves came lashing in.

A loud beep announced the end of the download and Terry terminated the circuit and started pulling wires and plugs and throwing things in suitcases. He'd been with the U.S. Geological Survey for twenty-six years, but never had he felt such a panicked need to escape.

Chapter 10

The silent blinking of a light on the telephone console reminded Doug of the call he'd momentarily forgotten and he scooped up the receiver.

"Dr. Lam here."

"Doug, Bill Harper in Olympia."

"Bill. I was just getting ready to call you."

"I felt the shaking. What's going on?" The voice of the state's emergency services director was instantly recognizable, the gravelly rumble distinct but not unfriendly. Prematurely gray and excessively dedicated, he was almost a friend.

"I wish I could say for certain, Bill." Doug ticked off a quick rundown of the situation. "In my opinion this is vastly more serious than anything I've ever witnessed up here. The quakes are continuing, they're all in the same area, every single one is unprecedented in modern seismic history, yet it could be anywhere from ten seconds to ten years before the real bomb goes off."

"Doug, I've got to ask you this. Are we talking real seismic reality now, or is what you just said related to your theory of . . . what was that, amplified resonant motion?"

"Vibration. No, this is based on real data, Bill. Look, I know you think my theory is BS."

"That's too harsh. I just think you're wrong about the coast being too dangerous to build on. The tiny waves produced by a drilling rig or pile driver aren't even in the same galaxy with the kind of force needed to trigger a major quake. In fact, the difference is around three orders of magnitude."

"Without any amplification, yes, that's absolutely true. If the miles of rock below have the inherent ability to amplify tiny waves into big, focused waves that can move rock and break lynchpins, then wrong."

"You've got to admit the idea that a little construction work could cause a 9.5-magnitude earthquake seems very far fetched, especially now when all the construction on Cascadia Island is finished, even if you consider some sort of natural amplifier."

"Is it finished?"

"Well, they open tomorrow."

"And isn't it chilling that here, one day ahead of the opening, two years of construction may have finally pulled the trigger?"

"If that's really what's going on, yes."

"Bill, there was never any justification for drilling and pounding on that island just to pave over a bird sanctuary. You'd think the fact that I just might be right would be enough justification for cancelling the project. You know, err on the side of caution? Play it safe?"

There was momentary silence on the other end before Harper sighed.

"I was afraid of that."

"What?"

"That if we had any quakes during construction, you'd use them to validate your theory. You're getting ready to take credit for this, aren't you? If any aspect of the big quake comes, you're going to say you told us so, regardless of the truth."

"Well, aside from the fact that I'm hurt you would think such a thing, what I'm reporting to you now has nothing to do with my work, my so-called theory, or the past. We've got hypocenters we can't explain, and they may well be a precursor. Look, man, the number of lives at stake, if I'm right, is so great that I think we've got to get ready to act."

"What do you mean 'act,' Doug?"

"Well, you realize that however it starts, when the big subduction zone quake finally comes, it could trigger a series of shallow, crustal quakes all over the Puget Sound area, and that could put a host of major surface faults in motion."

"And one of them runs right underneath downtown Seattle. Yes, Doug, we're all aware of that. And you know I hate showboaters."

"I'm not showboating, Bill. I'm pointing to a naked emperor. If we get a few more minutes of this pattern, I'd start thinking about evacuation of the entire coast."

"What? Doug, get real! Even if I totally believed you—and I'm trying to—I can't ask the governor to order an evacuation of the entire coast unless we've got a genuine official prediction. I mean, do you have any remote idea how complex and difficult a total evacuation would be? God! If it was only up to *me,* I'd really consider it, but I don't have that kind of power. . . . Even though the governor knows about this as of a few hours ago, he's . . ."

"Unimpressed?"

"Yeah, well . . ."

"As unimpressed as I am with him?"

"What can I say? The people elected the man, and I answer to him."

"I know. I'll refrain from using the word *moron* this time."

"Thank you. My point is that he's going to be a hard case to convince, and he's going to insist on literal application of the guidelines we all wrote for when to evacuate. And whatever else, if I put *your* name on it, I'm sure he'll say no."

Doug sighed. "It's always nice to have such credibility. Bill, our state guidelines weren't written for this situation. We're into virgin territory here. Did you feel that opening tremor down there?"

"Yes. I heard that it rattled the capitol building. Even my cat is terrified. She's sitting here digging her claws into me . . . which I—Muff, stop it!—hate. I'm calling from my house."

"We should err on the side of caution and at least stand by to evacuate."

"Well, it is a judgment call, isn't it?"

"Damnit, no! It's the sort of thing politicians get fried for later on when the whole world asks, 'Why didn't you do something when the scientific community was warning you in such strong terms?' "

"Doug . . ."

"You want justification? Let me tell you what's almost certainly going to happen, okay?"

"Doug, you don't have to bellow at me."

"I'm not bellowing. But I *am* trying to kick some recognition of urgency into you. Here's the timetable. First we get microquakes right smack dab in the middle of a place we have never in the history of seismology experienced or even imagined microquakes. That so-called place is a zone eight hundred frigging miles long from north to south, twenty-five kilometers down, and it is, as you well know, the lynchpin holding back enough force to shake the entire Pacific Northwest with as much energy as a month's worth of hurricane-force winds, all released in five minutes as an earthquake of at least Moment Magnitude 9. So, first the microquakes, then we start unlocking the surface faults and we bring down half of downtown Seattle or Portland with massive shallow temblors perhaps as high as an M7.5 . . . a Moment Magnitude 7.5 . . . although those faults may wait for the main quake. Meanwhile, the Quilieute Quiet Zone gets noisier, and as the second or third day dawns, we start getting sympathetic volcano activity as magma begins roiling around under Mount Rainier and maybe Mount Hood or Mount Baker as well. Now the quakes in the Quiet Zone begin to hit a magnitude of 4, and they become almost constant, triggering some major deep-focus quakes like the 2001 Olympia temblor that almost leveled the state capitol building. And finally, for just a few heartbeats or a few hours, it all goes completely quiet, the calm before the storm. We'll sit here holding our collective breaths in frozen horror watching the drums and the flat tracings and wondering, is it over, or is it coming?' and suddenly, Bill, with your disbelieving boss sitting out on that rock in his last few minutes of life, it will all give way, just like in the year 1700. The lynchpin disintegrates over an eight-hundred-mile front all at the same time, and all the energy comes roaring out with far greater force than all the nuclear arsenals we've ever built. The whole region begins to undulate, slowly at first, then back and forth with huge, mammoth seismic surface waves 1.5 seconds in period, the coastal areas suddenly yanked downward five to eight feet, the seismic waves vibrating buildings between five and fifteen stories until they resonate and begin to shake themselves apart. With landslides all over the place, bridges along I-5 begin to drop, some on occupied cars, each collapse cutting our north-south lifeline. Stadiums collapse. Gas lines are shut down, power goes down, reservoirs break and spill, runways split and fragment, chimneys and masonry buildings collapse, and all the cranes and facilities in Vancouver, Seattle, Tacoma, Portland, and all the smaller coastal ports begin to sink as the saturated land below undergoes liquefaction and becomes quicksand. When the shaking finally stops some five minutes later, fifty miles out at sea the backwash tsunami begins charging eastward, building as it approaches the coast, until the monster rises over thirty feet high, roaring in and over all the coastal land areas that were less than eight feet above sea level and are now at sea level. The wave, hundreds of miles long, blasts all buildings and cars and people away, leaving no survivors as it flows inward on a wave of debris and bodies and sand, leaving the detritus as far as ten miles inland. And when it's over, my friend, we will be not only without a governor and his family, we'll be without an economy, ports, and perhaps as many as two thousand of our citizens in Washington alone. And you want to *wait* to notify that fool?"

At last he fell silent, and Bill Harper spoke quietly.

"Are you through, Doug?"

"No, man, I'm an angry Paul Revere with a fresh horse and a megaphone, and I'm just getting warmed up."

There was a long sigh from Olympia.

"You know, if it wasn't for your passion and sincerity, I'd be mightily offended to have just been lectured on a scenario I know so well. But the truth is, I'm in your corner, Doug. But *you* have simply *got* to understand that there are things at stake from a political perspective that are incomprehensible to a scientist. But people like me *have* to consider that aspect!" Harper's voice was rising, too, though only slightly. "For instance, do you have any concept of how much monetary loss and potential liability the state will incur if we chase everyone away from the coastline and nothing happens?

SAVING CASCADIA

That's the first question the governor is going to ask. And can you guarantee him it won't be a false alarm?"

"Of course not."

"Neither can I, and God doesn't seem to be in on our hotline tonight."

Doug shook his head and rolled his eyes, grateful that videophones were not commonplace. They'd played these parts before, the subordinate bureaucrat officially resisting the worried scientist and requiring a level of certainty designed primarily to shift potential blame. He had no respect for such cover-your-ass political games, or for the weasels who played them.

Not that Bill Harper was a weasel. He was a good man working for a clueless governor and an even more ignorant staff. Despite the state law against surreptitious taping, Doug imagined the director had a recorder going unannounced on the other end, just in case.

"Bill, I'm sorry, but I'm strongly advising you to wake up the governor and recommend evacuation of the coast. We could lose thousands of people, and I mean any minute."

"You're really and truly that spooked? This isn't practice for the cameras?"

"Yes, damnit! I mean, no and yes. This isn't theater, it's real."

"Officially, the price tag for a gubernatorial wake-up call is simply a prediction from the USGS. It doesn't have to be fancy. Just please tell me we're going to shake badly and I'll do my best to convince him. But I just cannot act unilaterally and hope to keep my professional head."

"And I can't make a short-term, official prediction for the USGS, Bill. You know that!"

"Then, sadly, we're at an impasse—for the moment."

"I could call the State Patrol and have them wake the man up," Doug replied.

"You could, yes. And please be my guest. I need to remind you, though, of the level of skepticism you'll be dealing with. And he knows you, Doug, and he thinks he knows this subject and he does not believe your theory. For him, it's always black and white. No prediction, no eviction."

"God, not another bad poet."

"Excuse me?"

"Nothing. Look, could you at least alert your network of police and fire and rescue forces in those counties that we're hovering on the edge of a prediction and they might want to lock and load?"

"Yeah, that I can do."

Doug rubbed his forehead, unconsciously searching for the release mechanism to the steel band that seemed to be tightening around his cranium. Aside from the scientific realities he could see, there was rising alarm in his gut that those left on the coast the next day were very likely to die.

"Bill, you understand the prime reason we can't make a hard prediction is that we've never ever seen patterns of tremors like this before. We have no precedent, only guesswork. But that doesn't mean I'm wrong. And I'm guessing the balloon has really gone up. After all, have I ever given you a false alarm?"

"Not before today, if then," Harper replied. "I'm sitting here genuinely worried, too." There was a weary sigh from Olympia. "Doug, when you're scared enough to issue a formal warning, call me back and I'll shove my opinions into the lion's den. I am listening."

Not well enough. Doug thanked him and replaced the receiver, aware of a gentle hand on his shoulder and he turned with a start to find Jennifer standing behind him, her coat on and her hair back in place. There was a faraway, hunted look in her eyes.

"You okay?" he asked her.

"Yes, but I have a 7:45 A.M. takeoff and I've got to get some sleep. I'm going to bed down in my office." She leaned over to give him a quick kiss.

Before he could protest she'd turned and dashed out the door, leaving a sudden void he had no time to deal with.

"Our careers are on the line, aren't they?" Sanjay had asked an hour earlier. "Damned if we do and damned if we don't predict a disaster. If we're wrong, we're the disaster."

More information was cascading in from the seismograph networks than even the computers could crunch, but they were far from having the justification for a USGS alert. It would take a smoking gun—either a big enough foreshock or some new bombshell information supporting his theories—before Menlo Park would take the risk.

Sanjay was right, Doug thought. If they were the cause of a formal prediction of the big one and nothing happened, or worse, if they failed to convince their superiors in California in time to issue an alert and then lost the Pacific Northwest and tens of thousands of people, they would become an embarrassment to the seismological community and the USGS. No matter that the science wasn't mature enough to provide a hard and fast prediction or a warning beyond enlightened guesswork. The career risk couldn't be greater.

Doug found himself wishing he knew a good, genuine psychic he could consult, but for a serious scientist that was also unthinkable.

NIGHTINGALE AVIATION OPERATIONS, BOEING FIELD, SEATTLE

Sleepy at last, Jennifer closed the door to her small office bedroom just before 4 A.M., stripped down to an oversized T-shirt, and dropped onto the hed, achieving REM sleep almost immediately. An interminable period seemed to drift by before she awakened, her eyes on the dispatcher who was leaning in the opened door spilling light into the windowless room.

"Jennifer?"

"Did I oversleep?"

"What?"

"I'll be out in a minute. Why didn't you wake me at 7?"

"Jen, it's 6:45," Dan Zalinsky replied as he snapped on the overhead fixture. Jennifer squinted hard against the assault of light.

She sat speechless for a few seconds before looking at her watch.

"A.M.?"

"Yes."

"I . . . could have sworn I've been sleeping all day."

"Are you rested?"

She got up and slipped on a robe. "Yes. Strangely."

"I woke you early because we've got a situation. The whole area is getting rattled with small earthquakes and we're going to need to make some plans if things get worse."

"We had a pretty good one just before 3 A.M. while I was at the lab with Doug."

"Well, they're continuing. He's been on TV this morning, too, and called several times to convince me that none of our ships should go to Cascadia today. Especially not you and Sven."

"Okay. Give me ten minutes."

"Coffee's on your desk."

"Thanks, Dan."

He closed the door as she struggled to remember the last shards of a long, involved dream that had now evaporated. The room seemed to undulate for a second. Was that her sleepy state or another quake? Her gyros were still wobbling too much to be sure.

The bathroom off the other side of her office had a small shower and all the toiletries she needed, and she rushed the process while downing the coffee and made herself reasonably presentable in fifteen minutes. Her hair was slightly uncooperative but not fatal to the professional appearance she was determined to maintain, and she decided not to let it bug her.

On the way to the charter operations desk, an unquestionable tremor rattled the building with not enough force to move objects off desks, but enough to prompt Dan Zalinsky to point downward as she approached.

"Like that one, for instance. I'm surprised you slept through them."

"I am, too. Fill me in."

Dan ran down the list of charter shuttle flights, the special mission to

Cascadia carrying Mick Walker the night before, and the locations of the Nightingale Medevac fleet of EC-135 Eurocopters positioned across the Pacific Northwest.

"Your dad's inbound, too."

"Why? Never mind. I'll find out."

She poured another cup of coffee, feeling the cobwebs slowly clear as she looked around the interior of the main reception area.

Despite Sven Lindstrom's lifelong frugality, the offices of Nightingale Aviation spoke of understated wealth and good taste. It was evidence of a surprising passion of the near-penurious founder, who thought that the way a company's headquarters looked determined the level of trust of the clients. Most of Nightingale's Medevac clients were unconscious people barely clinging to life on the way to some hospital helipad, but the sister company—Nightingale Air Services—had become successful in no small measure because Sven had maintained a customer-service point of view through the years of building the company.

The philosophy had covered chairs and sofas in elegant leathers, spread expensive oak through the furniture selection, and turned the operations section into an impressive and comfortable combination of mission control and corporate boardroom. With such elegant offices, Sven's driving to work every morning before retirement in a ratty 1974 Volvo had been an embarrassing contradiction.

Jennifer caught a glimpse of Sven's new gray Cadillac on one of the TV security monitors and began walking to the front. She pushed through the door to find him standing by the car and for just a second she felt her stomach tighten up as if she had been called to the principal's office.

Dad, what are you doing here? she thought.

His eyes were on a faraway target, and he was apparently trying to gauge the base of the fog that lay like a cool, damp blanket over Seattle.

"Dad, hi."

"Hey, Honey. Rotten morning. And these earthquakes! You awake?"

She nodded and hugged him. "I'm tired but I got a few hours of sleep."

"Here? I know you weren't home."

"Yes. Here," she said. There was no point in going into details that would trigger a lesson on crew fatigue.

"When a dad doesn't know where his daughter is sleeping, it's worrisome."

"This daughter is way too grown for you to worry about that."

In truth, she thought, the question didn't bother her. She was used to his bursts of sudden curiosity, and his predictable irritation at being unable to instantly reach anyone he called. But despite his mania for instant contact, he had a thing about calling her cell phone. It was as if calling her at home at 3 A.M. was more humane somehow than risking a midnight cellular call. She had yet to figure out his logic.

"I thought I'd come in and give you some moral support with these earthquakes. Your boyfriend's been on TV making some worrisome noises."

They pushed through the doors together and into the reception room.

"I just heard he'd been on. Was he saying anything about Cascadia?"

"The subduction zone, not the island. Yeah. Saying we might need to evacuate the coast. For a scientist the boy's pretty brave." Sven moved to the counter and picked up a clipboard. "So what's the charter plan, with or without earthquake problems?"

Jennifer glanced outside at the gray morning. The bottom of the fog layer was barely a hundred feet above the runway and the entire shroud only two hundred feet thick. It was effectively hiding the distant Olympic Mountains, the top half of the airport's control tower—and a clear path to keeping Nightingale on schedule.

"Let's go take a look, Dad. Even if that's the last of the earthquake tremors it's going to be a banner day—provided the fog doesn't shut us down."

"Not that bad," he said, dismissing the possibility with an air of authority that invited no uncertainty. If Sven said it was going to be good enough to fly, it would be. The weather wouldn't dare challenge him.

The distant sound of an arriving airliner caught Jennifer's ears, triggering memories of the first time she'd witnessed the Space Needle sitting all alone on a cloud. Seattle's foggy mornings were surreal to arriving passengers, the top twenty floors of the city's tallest buildings along with the iconic Space Needle appearing as disembodied alien structures floating on an endless field of aerial cotton, a vision more attuned to science fiction than real life. The mysterious image of the city in the sky would float magically past the windows as the airliner extended flaps and landing gear and slowed for a southbound touchdown at Sea-Tac Airport, daring the witness to believe it existed. Within minutes, the gritty task of surviving a modern air terminal would enfold the traveler's mind, yet the image of a suspended city would continue to float in memory—a very personal experience of momentary transcendence.

Her own plentiful memories of such moments brought a smile. From the ground—especially in the eye of an aviator surveying what was little more than a low-hanging cloud—fog carried a different dynamic beauty, a disorienting dichotomy ranging from soft, misty diffusion best viewed in a bathrobe with coffee and a lover, to the professional challenge of dealing with low visibility in a fast-moving air machine.

She glanced at her father as he stood at the operations counter and read the schedule. At his side she had learned to evaluate the seductive visual confection that difficult weather could present, and how to appreciate it even as she worked to defeat the challenges it could throw at an airman. Sven Lindstrom, it had turned out, may have been properly described as difficult, but her old man had the heart of a poet who secretly saw the world as beautiful and could seldom openly admit it.

"So, what do you think, Dad?" she asked.

"I think I need an IV of Starbucks' goopiest espresso," Sven answered. "And since you're a nurse, you can hook it up for me."

It was the first time he'd referred to her other profession since the night of his collapse, and Jennifer felt a small flag go up in her mind. Why now?

"Are you getting enough sleep yourself, Dad?" she asked.

"Well . . . the older your mother gets, the louder her snoring."

"As if you didn't snore like a buzz saw yourself."

"Scandalous rumor," he smiled. "Jen, Doug Lam looked completely spooked a while ago."

"Really?" The mention of Doug's name triggered a surge of desire to confide in her father the frustrations she was having with their relationship and her attempts to talk to Doug about it. She knew better, but the urge was there, first as a warmth and then the hollow realization that he was incapable of giving his daughter sympathetic advice on such matters.

"Doug thinks we should cancel this whole Cascadia thing and stay away from the island," she said, suppressing the other thoughts.

Sven snorted. "Yeah, give up nearly a quarter million dollars in revenue, not to mention a really fun evening in a plush hotel."

"It does sound like fun, provided we don't get washed out to sea."

"Is Mr. Wizard going, too?"

Finally, she thought, his real feelings about Doug had returned.

"I'm going alone, Dad. Lucky me."

"Well," he snorted, "it's hardly a surprise that he isn't taking you to the hated opening of the hated resort."

"I wouldn't say 'hated.'"

"I would. I'm well aware that Dr. Lam wants to keep the island safe for gull droppings, but he's going to have to get over it, especially if he's thinking of marrying my daughter."

Jennifer decided to ignore the marital reference.

"Actually, Dad, today he's got a legitimate point. We're in real danger of a major quake, and I'm going to have to brief everyone to keep the rotor rpm's up and lift off instantly if anything out there starts rocking and rolling."

"Yeah, whatever."

"You . . . don't think it's a danger?"

"I don't like scientists trying to scare the hell out of us to get more re-search money."

She closed her eyes, her palm to her forehead. "Oh, shit!"

"What?"

"I mean, damn. I . . . forgot something I need for this evening."

"What is it?"

Your birthday present, Dad, she thought. *Stop being so nosy.*

"Just a thing."

"So, where'd you leave whatever it is?"

She shook her head in dismissal as she calculated the distance to Doug's floating home. He'd helped her design the custom-made bronze plaque commemorating Sven Lindstrom's pioneering development of Pacific Northwest Emergency Medical Service helicopters and together they had arm-twisted the directors of the Seattle-based Museum of Flight to hang it there permanently. Tonight's gala was the perfect showcase to present it.

"It's okay," she said. "I'll get it later."

With a monthly company meeting scheduled, a steady stream of Nightingale personnel had been flowing through the door and waving to Sven and Jennifer. Now, as father and daughter pushed into the conference room, a total of twenty-one employees from both the medevac and charter operations were arrayed around the table as last-minute tweaks were made to the charter battle plan glowing on the large liquid crystal flat screen covering most of the wall at one end of the room.

Six ground crew, four flight nurses, five control room dispatchers, secre-taries, and coordinators, plus the six pilots assigned to the Cascadia charter missions and four others standing medevac alert were present. On the ramp outside, more than 41 million dollars' worth of state-of-the-art helicopters sat fueled and ready, with sixteen more scattered around the four-state area served by Nightingale.

In the early days of Sven's fledgling helicopter operation, he had tried to incorporate a military-style operational briefing each morning, but his pi-lots had hooted the idea down. Too many of them were military veterans whose memories of the real thing generated no desire for a civilian ver-sion. Worse, other EMS helicopter company owners were aghast at his at-tempt to reignite the "mission-oriented" mindset, and Sven was forced to back off.

The architecture, though, was another matter.

As a Marine Corps aviator, Sven had flown F-4 Phantoms off carriers during Vietnam long before discovering helicopters, and according to his squadron mates, the endless months aboard ship had apparently warped his sense of reality. Now that he was running his own company, Sven insisted on calling his conference room a "ready room," and only at the last minute—faced with another pilot revolt—could he be talked out of bolting rows of surplus Navy bucket seats to the floor to make it even more authentic.

The podium, blackboard, and squadron patches around the walls remained, however, giving the old man the desired flashbacks whenever he swept in to watch his brainchild in action.

"This will be our most important revenue-producing day of the year, thanks to the opening of Cascadia Resort," Jennifer began. "Everyone has last month's operations results, I hope. This morning we're just going to focus on the next forty-eight hours. I know you have no tolerance for OPs briefings, but I'm worried about what we're obligated to do this weekend. So, bear with me. The earthquake activity could vastly complicate things. You know we're all flying a heavy schedule with very tight turnarounds. Any significant maintenance problem or other disruption could have a cascade effect."

"No pun intended," Gail Grisham chuckled from the front row. Gail was also a former Navy pilot and one of Jennifer's favorites, principally due to a rapier-sharp wit she rarely sheathed.

Jennifer motioned Norm Bryarly, their chief dispatcher, over to brief the weather, which was anything but ideal. He triggered a series of PowerPoint graphics on the screen, moving around in front of the map like a TV weatherman, which, indeed, he'd been very briefly many years ago when TV weathermen had to write in the L's and H's manually across the map with a grease pencil.

The fog would be lifting within a few hours, Norm briefed, and a significant winter storm was marching across the last few hundred miles of the eastern Pacific with Seattle in its crosshairs. The prospect for uninterrupted late-night operations was not good.

"The overture will be this afternoon and evening with rising winds due to a very sharp pressure differential because of the oncoming low. Around midnight, the chorus of rising winds should herald the second movement until they're out of limits for our operation—above thirty-five to forty knots—with a coda of high overcast as a counterpoint."

"You just can't resist the symphonic metaphor, can you Norm?" Joe Clarkson, one of the newer pilots, needled.

"Life *is* a symphony, my son," Bryarly said, lifting his bushy eyebrows for emphasis. "Now, if there are no more gratuitous and incredibly rude interruptions, the general will continue."

"You wish! General, indeed," Clarkson muttered with a grin.

"All right. The real storm begins after midnight, and there's a lot of moisture in this system, so expect high winds and torrential rains along the coast . . . and no more flying until past noon on Sunday, at the earliest."

"You sure of those times, Norm?" another of the pilots asked.

"I'm never sure of those times. Stay sharp on the radios for any updates I transmit, and do *not* assume the winds are within limits unless you're personally certain the windsock over there doesn't look like a horizontal metal cone. I understand we'll have two choppers on the ground overnight, Jennifer?" he said, turning to her.

"Yes. That was the plan."

"You might want to rethink that plan, boss lady. You're going to have to lash those birds down for a gale, and we're going to get salt spray all over them."

Bryarly returned to the sidelines and Jennifer stood to continue the briefing.

"Look, one more thing, and it's important. Is everyone fully aware of the earthquake threat we're under right now?"

There were nods around the room but serious expressions on no more than half. A bad sign, Jennifer thought.

"I felt something shaking this morning, but I didn't turn on the TV," one of the mechanics said, looking around to see if he'd failed some implicit test of current knowledge.

There was no time to repeat the myriad seismology lessons she'd absorbed from Doug in order to convince the unconvinced of the seriousness of the threat, but she did her best with a miniature version.

Gail raised her hand. "Wait, Jennifer, you're saying that at any minute we could get hit as bad as Anchorage got mauled in '64?"

"That's what I'm saying."

Gail Grisham was silent for a few beats. "My mother slid halfway to Turnigan Arm in the wreckage of her house in that quake. She was four months pregnant with me, and she said she thought it was the end of the world because the shaking went on for almost five minutes."

"Really?"

Gail nodded. "Five minutes! That's forever in an earthquake. My dad was in Seward," she said quietly. "He didn't make it."

Jennifer felt the uncomfortable silence in the room. The words on her lips were "That's how serious *this* could be," but the message was obvious and she squelched the impulse to say it, opting only for a soft "I'm very sorry to hear that," to Gail.

There was an accusatory clock on the back wall reminding her they were already running late. Jennifer marshaled them through the remaining items and was in the process of dismissing everyone when the room shuddered. Worried glances were exchanged as the surface waves arrived seconds later and the building began to sway, gently but distinctly.

Chapter 11

For a thousand years a massive, unrecorded fault line had lain buried below several miles of sediment in northwestern Washington.

No one knew that it ran from west to east and was an integral flaw in the rocky foundation of the port town of Bellingham, nor that it was associated somehow with the Darrington-Devil's Mountain fault zone to the south.

The tortured twisting and turning of the rocks, pushed and shoved by the inexorable movement of the entire North American tectonic plate, had long used the ancient shear zone as a kind of geologic battery, storing an impressive amount of seismic energy dangerously close to the surface. The fault line was a hundred miles inland from the Pacific coast and far above the Benioff Zone, and potentially deadly if sustained seismic shaking from a major Cascadia Subduction Zone earthquake ever rattled it enough to pull its trigger.

The first waves from the multiple small quakes along the subduction zone had passed through the trigger point Friday night without harm, but hour by hour the additional seismic waves had jiggled and nudged and excited the same area, slowly working loose whatever lynchpin had been keeping the fault locked and quiet for so long.

And at thirty minutes past 7 on Saturday morning, one surface wave too many shuddered through the rocks and pulled the pin.

A cold predawn darkness laced with low clouds and ground fog enfolded the port city of Bellingham as the residents were jolted awake by the massive upthrust. The compression wave from the sudden break four miles below moved straight up, pushing their homes and bedrooms and highways—along with the stately buildings of Western Washington University—essentially into the air with a so-called "acceleration" of just over one gravity.

The homes of Bellingham, built like most northwestern houses on wood frames, slammed back down precisely where they started, but brittle structures of brick and unreinforced masonry reacted very differently. Chimneys, stucco, brick facades, and concrete slabs cascaded from hundreds of structures as the S waves arrived seconds later to shake the city back and forth. Early morning drivers yanked their cars to the side of the road fearing that their wheels were coming off, and unstable structures that had come through relatively intact from the compression wave now began to disassemble themselves in the side-to-side motion. On the waterfront, wet, saturated soil began to liquify as concrete foundations sitting on them literally began to capsize and sink, accompanied by the bizarre sight of giant cargo cranes rocking back and forth and threatening to topple.

And on the university campus, fifty-year-old buildings constructed to withstand much smaller quakes began to fail, the walls of Old Main bulging outward seconds before the floors began crashing down in pancake fashion, instantly crushing the six people inside. Hundreds of students crossing the campus on their way to morning classes hit the deck, watching the disaster with disbelieving eyes.

A tenth of a mile from the geology department, the dean of geophysics sank to the ground to ride it out, recognizing the waves as a major, shallow earthquake, watching the very thing he had long taught could never occur: visible earthquake waves moving across the ground shaking trees and poles and buildings as they wobbled the foundation of the campus.

Thirty-eight seconds later it was over. Power was out, clouds of dust were rising from wrecked structures, and an eerie silence prevailed. Minutes passed before sirens began wailing and shaken emergency crews ran on wobbly legs to vehicles that had not been damaged or crushed. Slowly, like an injured animal rising shakily and regaining control of its muscles, the community began to come alive in the rubble, as those who were unhurt put aside their stunned reactions and disbelief to come to the rescue of the hundreds of trapped and injured.

The first broadcast reports were aired in Denver, a thousand miles distant, when the key USGS monitoring station in nearby Golden recorded the seismic signature of what would be measured as a 6.4-magnitude event. Within minutes the telephone computers routing calls to and from Bellingham were overwhelmed and cellular phone towers reached saturation levels with the number of frantic calls flashing back and forth.

In Olympia, all lines on the bedside phone of Governor Frank O'Brien lit up simultaneously.

NIGHTINGALE AVIATION OPERATIONS, BOEING FIELD

Disorientation, Jennifer Lindstrom decided, could be a good thing at times. It was working now like an anesthetic, dulling her senses to the severity of the problems they were dealing with. With two TVs blasting the latest news emerging from the shattered community of Bellingham and the medevac side suddenly called to action, her head was swimming.

She poured a third cup of coffee and stood back for a few moments, watching her people with admiration. Dan Zalinsky had padded in from the break room where he'd gone for a ten-minute micronap. He looked exhausted after his all-night shift, but he was refusing her order to go home as long as there was a crisis in progress.

"What's our medevac status?" he asked.

She patted him on the shoulder and leaned down slightly to engage him eye to eye.

"You okay?"

"Yeah, yeah. I'm fine. How are we?"

"Well, I just checked with our medevac operations. Emery and Jackson are both orbiting the Bellingham airport, but the visibility up there is almost zero-zero," she said. "Emery made two approaches without seeing anything. He's sitting on a hillside right now above the fog, waiting it out. Jackson should be setting down there, too. We'll probably send the ambulances up the hill to them unless the fog lifts."

"Are we the only airborne responders?" Dan asked.

Jennifer shook her head no as she nibbled on her lower lip, a habit she'd tried to break since childhood. She nibbled when nervous, but internalized pure panic.

"Are you aware Interstate 5 is cut in three places south of Bellingham?" she asked Dan, who was busy rubbing his eyes.

"No, I wasn't."

"Two major bridges are down south of Bellingham and a lot of emergency equipment is coming south from Vancouver, and Army helicopters from Fort Lewis are orbiting around up there with us in three Chinooks and two Black Hawks, but they can't find a safe way down either. The fog's much thicker there than here."

"Wonderful. Say, aren't you supposed to launch for a Sea-Tac pickup?" he asked.

"I shuffled the schedule. Dan, what makes you think they're going to go ahead with the Cascadia inaugural?"

"I talked with Walker's assistant about a half hour ago. He knows about Bellingham and the weekend plans are still full speed ahead."

"Well, guaranteed the governor won't be there," she said.

"Frank O'Brien? Are you kidding? Jennifer, if there's a party and money involved for his next campaign, not to mention TV cameras, O'Brien would ignore a nuclear blast and an outbreak of smallpox to be there." Norm Bryarly, the medevac dispatcher, materialized at their side, a clipboard in hand.

"Jackson made it on the ground at Bellingham Airport, Emery is on approach now. The ceiling is too low to let them fly underneath it anywhere, so the ambulances are coming to them from the university."

"How bad is it up there, Norm?" Jennifer asked.

"What, the weather?"

"No, the human damage. And how is this going to affect us?"

Norm hesitated. Jennifer had inherited him as a senior employee when Sven had suffered his stroke, and he'd known her for years, but there were times for Norm when standing before Jennifer with Sven anywhere in the building was uncomfortable, like having two bosses and being unsure at any moment who was giving the orders.

But she was expecting a response.

"It's nowhere near what we all feared, Jennifer. Maybe a few deaths on the campus where they lost Old Main, their oldest structure. But other than a mess of minor injuries, several fires, and one or two unaccounteds, it may turn out to be a lot less disastrous than we first thought. One Army Chinook is going to follow our birds in, but the others are already headed back to Fort Lewis."

Norm returned to the desk as Jennifer nodded with relief. If they could keep everything on the medevac side flying and avoid any charter cancellations, there would be no loss of money, and less of a chance that her golden opportunity for dazzling her father with a stellar financial year would be screwed up. It wasn't her first priority, but it was vying for second place. If the figures on the bottom line worked out the way she'd predicted, he would be forced to congratulate her, not just growl that the year had been okay.

Jennifer walked after Norm, catching his attention as he sat down again behind the charter desk.

"Yeah?"

"I've got an urgent errand to run. Be back in twenty minutes."

He looked startled. "Sure. Okay."

"Hold the fort. There's something I have to have with me tonight."

"You want me to find someone else to get . . . whatever it is?" he asked.

She shook her head as she scooped up her purse, being careful to maintain the facade of business as usual, as if she always dashed across town thirty minutes prior to every mission. Better that, she thought, than admit to the embarrassment of poor planning.

ON APPROACH, BELLINGHAM INTERNATIONAL AIRPORT

Knowing the other Nightingale EC-135 Eurocopter had broken out of the fog was reassuring. Jenny Jackson had been on the instrument landing system approach—the ILS—before reaching legal minimums, but as chief pilot Eric Emery reached the same decision height in his EC-135 two hundred feet above the surface, there was absolutely nothing but gray fog ahead of him.

Eric increased his blade pitch and engine speed of the twin-engine helicopter and began the go-around, his suspicions blooming into anger as he thought about Jenny's apparent success minutes before. Jackson's tendency to press the limits had raised his concerns before. This time she'd pushed too far for anyone's good and obviously brought her helicopter down in almost zero-zero conditions.

She probably didn't see the runway until she bounced on it, he thought, aware his teeth were grinding. Worse, she had enticed him to try it as if it was completely clear below 250 feet. The possibility he might have to fire her was already distracting his mind.

Linda Bennett, one of the two flight nurses, was in the left seat. She looked puzzled at his stern expression. With the radio frequency back on Bellingham Approach, Eric declared the missed approach, listening carefully to the instructions at the same moment he lifted clear of the fog into sunshine, and noticed a thin patch of fog on the left.

"Ah, Approach, helicopter Two Four Bravo, let me go VFR on top for right now . . . I think it may be lifting south of the field."

He noted the controller's approval of his request as he banked the Eurocopter left toward what he knew was the mauled campus of Western Washington University, which sat on a hillside perhaps 150 feet above sea level.

Sure enough, the fog had thinned sufficiently to clear a grassy area next to a parking lot on the south end of the campus, and he pointed it out to Linda with a bob of his head as he switched frequencies again and made contact with the State Patrol dispatcher, redirecting any ambulances which might otherwise be heading for the airport.

"Okay, we can make this happen!" he said. "Tell Seattle."

Linda used the state EM Repeater System to call Nightingale dispatch as Eric turned into the wind, slowing and descending through the danger zone below two hundred feet, where an engine failure would leave them largely unable to recover. Linda had turned to get Eric's attention as she triggered the interphone.

"What?"

"Norm wants you to go sit back down on the hillside and let them send the ambulances to us."

"Tell him I've got a perfectly good clearing ahead."

She leaned over in conversation as Eric resisted the urge to flick on that channel and listen.

Linda was looking up again. "He says not to try for any sucker holes."

"This isn't a sucker hole, Linda! The fog is moving away. We can do this."

If Jackson can make it into a zero-zero airport, he thought, *the chief pilot can sure as hell land in a clear patch that big.*

The intended landing zone was clear now, the fog retreating as if a steady downdraft were widening the circle of visibility.

Someone had run onto the parking lot and into the line of vision ahead, motioning where he wanted the oncoming chopper to set down. There were tall light poles at intervals in the parking lot with enough space between them for the rotors, but it would be tight. Eric checked his forward speed, now down to fifteen knots, the turbine engines at a rather high power setting as he made the subtle adjustments and watched his target get closer.

Fifty feet, he thought to himself, the forward and vertical speeds now down to a fast walk. He slowed to a dead-stop hover and began descending, automatically adjusting for a sudden zephyr from the left, unaware that the breeze was bringing the fog back with it. The sudden influx caught him completely off guard until a gray curtain moved across his windscreen. Suddenly, at less than ten feet in the air, between metal light poles, everything was gone!

He hadn't been on his instruments but suddenly he had to transition to them without changing anything but vertical speed. There was a world of impenetrable gray enfolding them at the worst possible moment.

Eric transitioned his eyes quickly to the attitude indicator and began smoothly increasing power, pitch, lift, and speed, but his inner ear was protesting that he had suddenly entered a left bank, an intense and urgent physical message. He fought to stay on course straight ahead, the unspoken words crackling back and forth, yet somewhat disconnected from the uncertain control inputs.

Left rudder, NO . . . right . . . what's my heading? Where the hell is the heading! Altitude . . . airspeed . . . pitch . . . oh God, I'm losing it!

The proprioceptive "voice" of his inner ear was screaming at a level he couldn't ignore, bypassing his conscious control and wiring itself directly to his feet and hands, which suddenly complied with an order to jerk the helicopter to the right and push forward to avoid the uncontrollable climb his middle ear was convinced it was tracking. A part of him "yelled" back that it was the wrong way and too much, but the resultant confusion froze his hands just long enough for the main rotor to find the top ten feet of a metal light pole, the impact snapping off the outer third of the blades in instant succession, the bone-shattering impacts leaving the massively unbalanced rotor shaking the fuselage and his eyeballs badly enough to obliterate further coherent vision. Nosed over and shaking itself apart, the Eurocopter struck the surface of the parking lot at less than twenty knots of airspeed, flipping over, the assaulted blades departing the helicopter's mast and flying like missiles in two directions as the cabin split open.

UNIVERSITY OF WASHINGTON SEISMOLOGY LAB

Rubbing his eyes against the residual image of the television lights, Doug loosened his tie and pushed his way back into the now-crowded seismograph room, spotting Sanjay, who was looking as fatigued as Doug felt. There were telephones ringing constantly in the background and an undercurrent of conversations raising the noise level in the room and only adding to the confusion following the Bellingham disaster. He needed some coffee and probably a couple of aspirin, but both would have to wait. There seemed to be a dozen people at once pulling at him for attention, most of them with cameras, microphones, and notebooks.

It grabbed at his gut how serious this was. Clearly the stakes were getting higher by the minute as the periodic vibrations rattled more and more of the Pacific Northwest, even if the temblors damaged little more than nerves before the Bellingham break. But now, in addition to the emerging reports from Bellingham, rumors of injuries from weakened structures around the Seattle area were flooding in, boosting the public need for information and reassurance to unprecedented levels, a service Doug Lam had always been exceedingly good at providing.

This time, however, reassurance was what he felt least equipped to give. If the Cascadia Subduction Zone was waking up, this was just the beginning, and getting the right message to as many people as possible to get away from the coast was both an awesome responsibility, and an urgent one. Yet whipping up a panic would help no one. He couldn't let the unblinking eye of the cameras see just how convinced he was that Mick Walker's project had set off a timer, and the big one was mere hours—or less—away.

Usually he relished the opportunities to face the cameras—not so much for the fun of being an occasional local star as for the chance to walk a difficult tightrope and do it well. But even if his apprehension hadn't been so high, the cacophony of the media attention alone was threatening to overwhelm him, putting to the test the very real duty of the seismic lab's director to translate the science and put a calming human face on a complicated and dangerous subject.

"What's the latest?" Doug asked Sanjay. "Any aftershocks in Bellingham?"

"Yes. Predictable ones near the surface. It's probably the offshore tremors that have been triggering them, though that might be a scientific stretch. But the frequency and magnitudes in the Quilieute Quiet Zone are slowly increasing. It's fitting the model you predicted, Boss."

"Thank you for acknowledging that. It is, almost exactly. I tried to tell Harper this was coming."

An exceedingly tall man wearing a heavy turtleneck and carrying a small notebook had followed Doug in from the last interview. He'd waited quietly a few steps away, previously unnoticed. Now he leaned almost over Doug Lam's shoulder and spoke, causing Doug to jerk his head around in surprise.

"Excuse me?"

"May I ask, what are the 'Benioff Zone' and the 'Quilieute Quiet Zone?' You were talking about both in those interviews you just did."

"May I ask who you are?" Doug replied, a bit sharply.

"Sorry to startle you, Dr. Lam." The man held out his hand. "I'm George Landry with the *Seattle Times*. We met a few years ago."

Doug shook Landry's hand.

"I especially don't know what the 'Benioff Zone' means," Landry added apologetically.

"All right. Look, George, give me a few minutes and then I'll explain it to you."

"Sure. Take your time."

Doug turned his attention back to the seismograph drums, concentrating on the vertical acceleration readings. The pen in his hand was gyrating back and forth between his index and middle fingers, as if at any second he would start twirling it like a miniature baton. The habit was a direct barometer of the level of his agitation, even when he succeeded in maintaining a glacial exterior. "Do we have the data piped into the computer?" he asked Sanjay, whose eyes were on the pen and gauging the frequency of its movements, knowing well Doug's nervous habit and its meaning.

"We do. And as I was saying, every one of the new hypocenters is in the Cascadia thrust zone, and I like the explanation you just gave on the camera."

"Which one?" Doug asked.

"That the thrust zone is where the ocean floor is being thrust under the advancing continental tectonic plate."

Doug's pen began moving even faster.

Nearly a dozen people had pressed into the crowded seismograph room now with more coming, most of them geophysics students whose instincts were to gravitate to the lab at the first hint of serious seismic activity. Most were peering at the various recording drums, and all of them were puzzling over the meaning of what was happening. Doug knew they'd be expecting immediate answers from him, and the pressure was building, a human micro-version of the immense tectonic pressures beneath the coast now approaching the break point.

Am I brave enough to go ahead and tell everyone what's about to happen? he wondered. *And for that matter, am I really, really sure?* He thought back quickly over the broadcast statements he'd made during the previous hours. Even if he got it exactly right every time, there were trip wires and professional dangers in all directions, including the inevitable jealousy of other members of the scientific community who viewed the habit of speaking to the media as occupying a moral stratum only slightly above prostitution.

Doug looked at his pen for a moment, then replaced it in his shirt pocket before turning to Landry. "Would you excuse us a moment? We need to consult, way off the record."

"You need to figure how much to tell me?" Landry asked with a knowing smile.

Doug shook his head. "No. I need to make sure that I really know what I think I really know."

"I almost understood that," Landry laughed, stepping back. He bent over and pretended to read the drums as Doug took Sanjay by the elbow and moved a few yards away between a rack of electronics.

"Did you hear my last interview out there?"

"Yes. Watched it in here live."

"Okay. I need your input. Am I going too far, or not far enough? I mean, I can't let this get out of hand, but I'm so used to being . . . well . . ."

"Reassuring?"

"Yeah. You know, calm down, the world's not ending. Earthquakes don't kill people, collapsing buildings are the danger, et cetera."

"You're the best at it, man."

"Yes, but shouldn't I pull the emergency cord a little harder, Sanjay? You've been a good conscience for me on this, but you see it, too, don't you? The zone coming alive?"

Sanjay nodded gravely. "All kidding aside?"

"I would hope."

"I've been wondering how to apologize to you, Doug, for not being a true believer."

"So . . . I should be more forceful about what's going on and the possible need to evacuate?"

"A little more. Not total. Not yet. You've been getting it right so far, Doug, as far as I can tell. You said we didn't really know for certain this was the beginning of a major subduction zone break. But you might want to explain the zone a bit more. If people understand how loaded with pent-up energy it is . . ."

"It makes the dangers more clear. Good point. I just don't want to pander to my theory, or say I told you so."

Sanjay shook his head. "You haven't been. You're probably entitled to do so, but you shouldn't. At least not yet."

Doug nodded thoughtfully.

"Okay, let me make sure I understand your mind on this. You're as convinced as I am that, while we can't be certain, this looks for all the world like a windup to the main break?"

"Yes."

"And, maybe yes, maybe no, about the role of Cascadia Island's construction in triggering it?"

"Maybe yes. More likely than not yes. When we're talking hypocenters in the Quiet Zone, at a depth of twenty kilometers or less some forty miles west of the coastline, I'd say that's a precursor to a major break, Doug, and all this began right under the island. Please tell me I'm wrong."

"I can't. But I also can't formally get ahead of the USGS."

"Have you seen the 3-D view I did?"

Doug shook his head. "Show me."

They moved toward one of the computer terminals and two students got up wordlessly to clear the way. Sanjay slipped into one of the chairs, running his fingers over the keyboard in a series of commands that brought up a simulated three-dimensional picture of the Cascadia Subduction Zone and input in the first half hour of quakes.

Doug felt his jaw drop as he took in the pattern.

"Holy shit," he muttered. "Look at the consistency north and south, right along the same plane, and less than twenty kilometers down."

"Right. That's what convinced me." Sanjay gestured to the door and to Landry, who was watching them closely from a few yards away while a new TV crew set up outside in the hallway. The pen was out of Doug's pocket again and gyrating.

"Okay. I'm going to follow the plan," Doug said, as much to himself as to Sanjay. "We're going to need to shove Menlo Park hard to issue the appropriate warning. Then, to get a full alert and evacuation going, we'll need the recommendation of the Department of Emergency Services, the governor's approval, and maybe even the Federal Emergency Management people."

"What else can I do for you, Doug?"

"Let's go to the precautionary mode and check data from the rest of the seismograph networks around the country, then put FEMA on standby and locate the state emergency director. He can brief the governor."

"I'm all over it," Sanjay said, turning for the nearest phone.

Doug walked quickly over to George Landry, who was watching but pretending to consult his notebook. Doug crossed his arms and leaned against an adjacent electronics rack and smiled as best he could at the reporter.

"Okay, George, fire away."

"Thanks. Okay, I've been told that you're seeing little earthquakes where there's been no movement recorded since seismographic records were created, and I understand it involves the subduction zone where the North American continent is colliding with the Pacific oceanic plate and shoving it down."

"You mean the Juan de Fuca plate, not the Pacific plate. The Juan de Fuca plate probably isn't being shoved down as such by the advancing North American plate as much as it's sinking of its own accord. We call it 'slab pull.'"

"But what is the Benioff Zone, and what does all this mean?"

"First, the place where no movement has ever been recorded in modern times is what you overheard us referring to as the 'Quilieute Quiet Zone,' which is an area within the overall Cascadia Subduction Zone. Second, the Wadati-Benioff Zone was named for seismologists Kiyoo Wadati and Hugo Benioff of Caltech," Doug began, his mind running the explanation by rote. "It's basically the zone of crushed rock which forms the sloping, horizontal plane along which two tectonic plates slide past each other."

"Okay. So why are you guys so wide-eyed?"

Doug smiled as wryly as he could. It was a perfect opening for what he needed to get across. "We're wide-eyed?"

"Seriously spooked would be another phrase."

"Well," Doug chuckled, "first, understand that while we can't formally say that any of this is a precursor for a major subduction zone earthquake—"

"Yeah, I understand. You can't say it, but you're very, very worried."

"That's a fair interpretation."

"What do you think of the fact that Cascadia Island Resort is getting ready to open and here we go with unprecedented earthquake activity in the same area, just like you predicted?"

"You mean, do I see hard evidence of a connection yet?"

"Yes. You're the guy who came out a couple of years ago and said that any deep drilling or heavy blasting activity along the coast could set off a major subduction zone earthquake."

"I sure did. And I appreciate your bringing that up. My paper of three

years ago triggered a major controversy, and it happened again in the Cascadia Island hearings. Almost all my colleagues disagreed with me, but I
firmly believe I'm correct. What we're seeing right now is major, unprecedented activity that may be the overture to a major subduction zone
quake. True, we don't have *any* hard evidence yet that there's a connection
to the Cascadia Island construction, but that's *not* the important question."

"But you've got tons of circumstantial evidence."

"Perhaps, but right now we need to just deal with the possibility of an impending great quake and what people need to do to protect themselves. Forget all the hooh-hah about whether my theory is right or wrong. That's a
sideshow."

"So, no 'I told you so's'?"

"That would be completely self-serving and nonproductive right now."

"But, you *did* tell us so, right?"

"George, again, we don't know if there's a connection. Until we do, any
talk about my paper is inappropriate."

"Okay."

"I mean, off the record, yeah, I damn well told you so, but on the record,
what's important is that we've recorded plenty of earthquake hypocenters
over the years in the Benioff Zone down around thirty to forty miles beneath Puget Sound and Seattle. What's important is that we've never, *ever*
confirmed a hypocenter along what I dubbed the Quilieute Quiet Zone located some twenty miles west of the coastline."

"You came up with the name?"

"Yes. That's where the plates are locked with over three hundred years of
pressure. Now, it's no hotter down there than about 350 degrees centigrade
at a twenty-kilometer depth, and that's not hot enough to melt the rocks or
make them sufficiently elastic, so they can snag and lock the zone, as they
have. But they can also break all at once. In other words, in that zone, the
earth can store an amazing amount of energy before the inevitable break
occurs, and we wouldn't necessarily see that break coming. Think of the
Quilieute Quiet Zone as a huge lynchpin which can be overwhelmed and
shattered if enough force builds up. And someday, without question,
enough force will build to break it."

"And that someday is now?"

"Could be. Maybe. We should all prepare just in case it is."

"And you said three hundred years of pent-up, unrelieved energy?"

"God, it's hard to articulate how much energy that is. There's a twelve-
meter slip deficit out there. The tectonic plate that all of North America
rides on and the remains of the Juan de Fuca tectonic plate should have

moved twelve meters laterally past each other in the last three hundred years since the last great earthquake, the oceanic plate sliding down at an angle beneath the North American plate. But they haven't moved past each other at all. Meanwhile, the entire North American continent has been pushing harder and harder from the east to the west against that locked section along the coast, and the process has been warping the Washington and Oregon coastlines upward, maybe as much as six or seven feet, and storing the immense energy that way. The calculations of how much stored energy has built up aren't terribly complex, but they're very impressive."

"And . . . it could all be released at once in a gigantic quake? I want to make sure I've got that straight. Not little quakes, but one monster quake releasing all that stored pressure, or energy? Today or tomorrow?"

"Well, we're studying a phenomenon we call 'silent earthquakes,' which might relieve some stress every thirteen months or so, but we know how much energy is still there, and that it equals a monstrous, great earthquake. We know the precise date and even the time of the last gigantic quake, thanks to very good records kept by seventeenth-century Japanese scribes who recorded a strange tsunami with an unknown origin from the east. It was on January 26 of the year 1700 at about 9 P.M. We also know from recent, separate studies that the entire zone released all its energy at once, and that squares with an extensive record in the actual muds and layers along the coast which shows irrefutable evidence of periodic great tsunamis. It's a heck of a detective story."

"And . . . that could be as large as the 7.1-magnitude quake in 1949?"

"7 . . . ?" Doug studied the reporter's face for a few seconds, trying to decide how graphically to describe the monster that could be awakening off the coast.

"George, try over a hundred times greater than that. Maybe as much as a 9.5 on the Moment Magnitude Scale, bigger than the great M9.2 Alaskan quake of 1964, which shook Alaska for nearly five minutes."

"Good Lord!"

"It could also, in the extreme, mean that large sections of the northwestern seacoast could drop in altitude by as much as eight feet and then almost certainly be hit by a thirty-foot-high tsunami going up to ten miles inland."

"That's possible?"

"It's all but a certainty. Now, again, we don't *know* that the zone is really going to let go right now, but that's why I look a bit spooked."

"Oh, by the way, are you going to go do more TV interviews?" Landry asked.

"Absolutely."

"Then . . . you're very good at it, Doc, but could I make a recommendation, off the record?"

"Sure. What?"

"Phrases like '9.5 magnitude' and 'five minutes of shaking' all sound like Armageddon to the average person. I'd be a bit more gentle, or at least explain that it doesn't mean the earth is going to collapse. Just that we're going to shake horribly."

"Thanks. Good advice. I'll keep that in mind."

Landry shook his hand and turned to walk away. Doug stood rooted to the same spot for a moment before chasing after him.

"Hey, Landry. George. One more thing."

The reporter turned back.

"If I turn out to have been right all along, the only 'I told you so' I'd like to indulge in is a cautionary warning to the scientific and governmental community to be more open-minded in the future. I tried very hard to get people to understand there could be a real danger in thwacking the bejesus out of Cascadia Island for two years, but no one wanted to listen."

"I'll do a big follow-up if it turns out that way," Landry said. "But—forgive me—isn't that also a big swipe at your employer, the USGS?"

Doug cocked his head in thought for a second and smiled as he shrugged his shoulders. "If the shoe fits, I guess. Some of my colleagues are very quick to reject new ideas."

"Apparently."

"But, in fairness, that's the essence of the scientific method."

Landry turned to leave again as Sanjay touched Doug's arm.

"Channel 5 needs you outside. I'll keep watch in here. I've got the calls started to the state authorities. Oh, and should I send someone to Starbucks?"

"Yes! I'd kill for a grande nonfat no-whip mocha."

"Really?" Sanjay asked, stepping back slightly for show. "In that case, it's on me."

"No, no. Use my credit card," Doug replied, handing over his American Express. "Take orders for all our people. Good morale is fueled by good caffeine."

Chapter 12

Frank O'Brien had really wanted to be president of the United States, but he knew it wasn't going to happen. Too many compromises and barely concealed encounters with women who ended up talking. The governorship was the best he could hope for.

But he'd had one hell of a great time in politics. A lot more so than if he'd remained in the banking business, which was boring as a grave and not much more profitable.

The state patrol and his aides knew better than to disturb him on a weekend unless it was a genuine emergency. From the reports unfolding from Bellingham, he had decisions to make.

"Okay, James," he said, sitting at the dining room table, "fill me in on the latest."

The death toll was far less than he'd feared—four people, all victims of the campus building collapse. It was an instant political problem, of course, since Western was a state university. He made a mental note to check who had been governor when the building was built to unrealistic seismic standards. Eighteen were seriously injured, and a medevac helicopter accident had added two more to the injured list. Property damage in the Bellingham area would probably approach $2 billion or more, James was saying, but from experience the governor knew it would accelerate, and that, too, would be a political football bringing calls for reform of any aspect of state aid that didn't work exactly right.

Not that human disaster was *only* a political problem. He wasn't without sympathy. But as governor he felt entitled to a clinical detachment. He could openly mourn and commiserate, but it was better to keep his real emotions securely walled off in order to make better decisions, both politically and personally.

James droned on, consulting the pad in his hand, and the governor kept nodding at what seemed the right places as his mind appropriately pigeon-holed the earthquake problem and drifted back to what he was most interested in, the big picture of the life of O'Brien.

Fourteen years had gone by since he'd sold his stock and left the chairmanship of the Tacoma-area bank he'd started, leaving it to crash when the market turned bad and the legal but risky investments he'd encouraged over his junior executive's signatures had failed. The lesser men and women he'd left in charge and holding the bag had been befuddled by the legacy of wheeling and dealing, and the woman who took over as chairman had made a myriad of bad decisions, almost putting herself and her senior executives in prison with a series of panicked, dishonest moves against loan customers as the bank tried to call in all the cash, cover their losses, and prepare to sell out—the very thing they'd promised Tacoma would never happen. By then, Frank O'Brien had been elected to Congress and discovered that he had an incredible talent for spin. It was Continental Puget Bank's fault that they had to fire-sale themselves to an eastern megabank, he said, and the public bought the explanation, having little interest in the boring esoterica of the truth.

Six feet four, square-shouldered, and dignified at fifty-one, his eyes were too blue and his smile too big for anyone to believe otherwise. And, as a Democrat in a state occasionally liberal enough to scare its Russian immigrants, he could get pretty much whatever he wanted as long as he stroked the teachers union and the AFL-CIO, made the right noises to the Teamsters, tendered to the longshoremen's union, and took the right campaign endorsements. They all loved him for reasons that even few of his supporters could link to any definite achievements.

"Sir, did you hear me?" James was asking.

"Yeah," the governor said, removing his fist from under his chin and sitting up a bit. He adopted a puzzled look his aide well recognized. "I was just evaluating something you said earlier. Repeat that, please."

"Ah, what part?"

"The part about the recovery efforts. Wasn't that what you just asked me?"

James's eyes had all but glazed over, which was precisely the response O'Brien had intended to trigger.

"Aw, that's okay," he said, adopting a magnanimous tone. "We'll get back to it when you can remember."

"Sorry, sir."

"Hey, it's understandable you'd forget where you were in an intense briefing like that. Good job, by the way."

The figures and facts began to flow again, and once more he drifted to the much more pleasant retrospective.

Life as a congressman had been, quite simply, beneath his dignity. Nowhere near enough power or perks, and after one term he'd railroaded his way into the Senate, winning a second term before deciding to come home to Tacoma to plot a takeover of the statehouse.

The years in the Senate had been good. Publicity, perks, and as many skirts as he wanted. Women were amazingly stupid, he thought, attracted like mosquitoes when someone with a little power blew past them. He'd cut a wide swath through the field of feminine charms, following in the tradition of John Kennedy, Bill Clinton, and a former senator from Washington who was accused of using a date-rape drug on women otherwise unwilling. Frank O'Brien would never stoop so low, he thought. He didn't need to. His campaign offices always featured at least one teary-eyed woman, the morning-after sexual conquest devastated because the senator suddenly couldn't remember her name. But such women were always consenting adults, and he was proud of that.

The other side of the table had grown quiet, and the governor realized the briefing was over.

"So? Options?" he said with a smile, noting from the look on his aide's face that options had been precisely what he'd been presenting. "I mean, which of the ones you covered should we attack first?" he continued without missing a beat.

"Ah, there's the matter of disaster declarations and—"

"Wait a second. I need to decide about the Cascadia Resort opening tonight. I'm scheduled to chopper out there with the family in a few hours and ride over on their new ferry."

"I know. I wouldn't advise it, sir."

"Aw, you just told me that Bellingham's not that bad. And it'll be a good party."

"Sir, our emergency services director has been relaying word to me that this Bellingham quake may just be the beginning. He says—"

Frank waved him off. "Don't start with that seismic nonsense again. It's the same foolishness as the global warming mythology. Something vibrates down there and immediately we're going to have Armageddon. You should see the last budget request Harper had the audacity to present to me."

"I did, sir."

"Well, forget his scare tactics."

"Governor—"

"James, are you aware that I carefully studied this whole issue two years ago?"

"I . . . no. I guess I didn't recall that."

"Well, I did. My hostility to the Chicken Little voices doesn't come from lack of interest or lack of understanding, it's from lack of respect. I'm not being blasé—or *cavalier* is a better word—at all. There are a lot of scientists out there with too much time and grant money on their hands always looking for more research opportunities, and if they can scare us a little bit more, they can perpetuate their jobs. Sometimes it's an honest enterprise, but all this hooh-hah about the Cascadia Subduction Zone flies in the face of the eminent seismologists who say it could well be another three hundred years before it corks off."

"There are competing opinions, I know . . ."

"Well, they're not competing for my attention and unless the USGS makes the flat-out statement that I need to worry, I'm not worrying."

"But, sir, if the naysayers are right, and they could be, you could be putting yourself and your family in harm's way."

O'Brien was already on his feet. "James, let me make this really clear to you. When and only when the USGS issues a formal, no-foolin', warning or prediction, I'll cancel. Otherwise, I don't want to be bothered about this again. It's all a ploy for more funding."

Frank O'Brien swept around the corner, and James Bollinger sighed as he gathered his notebook and wondered how to duck Bill Harper the rest of the day. If O'Brien wouldn't even consider his trip to Cascadia Island unsafe, the chances of a coastal evacuation were virtually nonexistent.

QUAALATCH, WASHINGTON

Marta Cartwright awoke with a start, surprised that she'd slept through dawn still sitting in her chair beneath the warmth of her favorite afghan. The fog had thickened now and she couldn't see the island or the light. Small comfort.

She glanced at the clock, reading a few minutes before 9, aware that part of her mind had been tracking continuous earth tremors as she slept. As she rubbed her eyes, another tiny shudder vibrated through her consciousness, too trivial in intensity to rattle the cups in her cabinet, but enough to reassure her.

Something disturbing had been stalking her since just before she awoke from her dream time. A troubling feeling of pain and fright from somewhere distant, but not so distant. There were seldom any distinct images accompanying such moments of clairvoyance, but she was a modern shaman who knew well what to do when such feelings coalesced in her mind: turn on her TV.

She reached for the remote, filling the screen with the images from Bellingham of fallen buildings and frantic rescues. It was at once settling to confirm the premonition, and disturbing to realize many innocent lives would be lost paying for Mick Walker's sins against the planet. Cleansing at the hands of nature was something she well understood. It was the same balance as death being the ultimate affirmation of life.

Gravel crunched in the small driveway behind the cottage. Too early for her circuit-riding postman, she thought, realizing with a small grin that she was resorting to logic instead of instinct to figure out who might be visiting.

The voice and slamming car door erased the mystery. She waited in the entryway for Lester Brown, her grandson, to round the corner of the cottage with his two boisterous friends, young Quaalatch males and a pair of losers she knew all too well and thoroughly distrusted. Lester had a chance at life, but they were helping him destroy it.

All three of them were very excited about something.

"Grandmother!" Lester exclaimed, throwing open his arms to embrace her.

"I see you've brought Bull and Jimmy," she said without pleasure, hugging him back with some reserve as she eyed the other two.

"Yeah. We've got something we've got to go take care of, but we wanted to come by and pay our respects to our leader."

She shook her head. "I am just your grandmother now, Lester, and only that. Sara is your leader."

"No she's not!" Bull barked, his fist jammed in the air. "We recognize only you! Right guys? Woo, woo, woo!"

The intensity of his words and the utter absence of any phrase even remotely Quaalatch disgusted her. But the mindless nodding of Jimmy—the younger, simpler member of the trio—was just too much to take.

Lester leaned forward, his hand out to the others as he looked her in the eyes.

"You all right, Grandmother?"

"Yes."

"You look upset."

She shook her head. "Worried, Lester. Not upset." She took a quick breath and forced a smile.

"Well, we hafta go, y'know?"

"Where are you three going?"

Bull smiled conspiratorially while Jimmy started to speak. Lester cuffed him, ignored the resulting curse, and answered for all of them.

"Just a little mission we gotta do. Bye, Grandmother."

They rounded the cottage and piled into the car, throwing gravel as they sped off to the south.

Mission indeed, she thought. All three of them had police records, and

Bull had done hard time in a Washington state prison for theft. Bull was dangerous, a walking time bomb of barely contained anger inside a muscular body. And Jimmy, she thought somewhat guiltily, was a barely functional idiot.

Her grandson, by contrast, was smart, but completely misguided, wishing for the chance to experience some sort of mythological glamour as a Quaalatch brave and ready to go fight off the majority of white society—provided he had enough money for liquor and gas.

Marta served herself a fresh cup of tea and sat down, trying to pick through the warning signs for clues about their mission. Undoubtedly she would hear of it later, and it was unlikely to make her happy. Lester was on a collision course, his own disaster simply searching for the right place to happen. And even she was helpless to intervene on the path chosen.

UNION STATION, PORTLAND, OREGON

He is watching me!

Diane Lacombe picked up her bag and headed for the front drive, keeping track of the tall, expressionless male she'd spotted working hard to be inconspicuous. His eyes had never left her body since she'd entered the station, and at the very least she resented it. The restoration of Union Station had been an unqualified success, with the ceilings and frescos paying homage to a simpler time of architectural elegance. She wanted to take a few minutes and enjoy it, but if she was being tracked, there was no time.

With one eye on the station door, she selected a cab and launched herself into the back seat with her bag, snapping at the startled driver.

"Just drive! Go! Now!"

The station began receding from view as she twisted around to peer out of the rear window.

And just as she'd suspected, the same tall man stepped through the door and stood watching the departing taxi and, she figured, memorizing the cab's registration number.

"To the airport, please."

The driver partially turned, a grin on his face.

"You just in a hurry or are you running from someone?"

The question froze her for a second until she realized his joke and remembered to smile.

"No, no! Just always in a hurry. Got to catch a flight to California."

She could lose herself in the terminal and loop back to the car rental counter, where once again Debbie's driver's license and credit cards would hide her presence.

There would be approximately two hundred miles to drive, and a needle to find in a haystack.

MONTLAKE CUT, SEATTLE

Jennifer let herself back into Doug's house, all thoughts of the previous evening safely stored away in a less practical side of her mind. The pilot in her was on a mission that had little to do with flying, but everything to do with pleasing her father. It was pro forma—one foot in front of the other to accomplish a given task.

She glanced around almost absently at the comfortable, familiar interior of the floating home, more the abode of some academic bookworm than a dynamic geophysicist—or perhaps her stereotypes needed massive adjustment. The place, in short, could use a better housekeeper than he employed.

Jennifer closed the door behind her and winced to think she'd been too distracted last night to remember her father's plaque. She moved into the main room of the home, well aware that she was visible from a half dozen windows in adjacent floating homes across a tiny waterway. For reasons she never understood, Doug refused to hang curtains in the living room, and it had always made her feel a bit decadent, even in the dark, when she had a midnight occasion to dash naked between his bedroom and the kitchen. He'd teased her about being a closet exhibitionist, and she'd countered with feigned seriousness that it was a premeditated act of charity for the four retired men living across the way, two of whom were fighting long-term illnesses. Surely an occasional flash of the female form would improve their recovery rates.

He kept a large rolltop desk in the corner and she began with the bottom drawer as the most likely storage spot, working her way up without success and glancing impatiently at her watch. This was already taking too long, but she didn't want to distract Doug with a phone call in the middle of the media storm he was handling. She knew the house well enough to find anything, and he'd already told her the plaque had arrived and looked great.

She moved to the hall closet and unfolded a small stepladder to stand on, rummaging through the upper shelf where he tended to toss incoming boxes he wasn't ready to open. A pile of FedEx and UPS boxes finally yielded the right one and she pulled it off the shelf, catapulting a small manila envelope to the floor in the process.

Damn!

Jennifer placed the shipping box containing her father's plaque on a chair and knelt to pick up the spilled envelope, which was unsealed. According to the postmark, it had come several months ago from a major cruise ship line, and out of idle curiosity she slid the pair of 8 x 10 photos halfway out of the envelope.

Deborah Lam, Doug's estranged wife, smiled back in Kodachromatic glory from the sundrenched deck of a cruise ship obviously plying the Alaska route. There were glaciers in the background and a date in the corner indicating the shot had been taken in August, three months before, and she pulled the photo the rest of the way out, wondering who Deborah had sailed with.

Maybe, Jennifer caught herself thinking, *Mrs. Lam has a new boyfriend and she's finally ready to let Doug go.*

There was another figure in the picture, a handsome male in his thirties looking slightly sheepish, as if he hadn't welcomed the photographer's attention, and had been even less interested in posing with his arm around Deborah. Jennifer felt a cloud of confusion envelop her as she stared at the picture. The man with Deborah Lam was Doug.

How in the world . . .

Her hand was shaking slightly as she pulled the photo closer and scrutinized the date. She fumbled in her purse for a pen and on the back of the first business card she could grab she wrote it down: August 23.

Her PDA was in the same purse and she yanked it out now, punching the keys too rapidly at first, finally bringing up the schedule for August.

I was in town most of August. And Doug . . .

She blinked at the multiple days blocked out on the tiny calendar screen. From August 16 through August 30 Doug Lam had been in Menlo Park, California, the western headquarters of the U.S. Geological Survey, on business.

Or so he'd said.

Yet, he'd posed for a picture on a cruise ship in Alaska at the same time.

If he had ever lied to her before, she couldn't recall when, but here was cold, hard evidence of purposeful deception. He'd even called her several nights during that time, supposedly from Menlo Park, although each time he was on his cell phone, which meant no strange area codes would have shown up on her screen.

Jennifer sat down hard on the floor, her head swimming with conflicting thoughts. The need to get back to Boeing Field fought the need to confront him. She'd found the shots by accident, but it was while pawing through his things. Could she even admit that? The reality that he'd lied about something he knew would be a very big deal to her meant she could no longer trust him. And worse, he had apparently sneaked off for a week or two with the very woman he was supposed to be divorcing, with whom he was supposed to be through.

He was cheating with his wife! God! And here sits stupid, vulnerable, trusting little Jennifer waiting for Godot.

Fleetingly she wondered if he was even separated. But no, she'd seen those papers. That was real enough.

Somehow she'd lost control of their relationship, and last night she'd tried to regain it. Now, one way or another, she was going to have to seize control again—rip it away from him or anyone else who might redirect her life in ways she didn't want.

You are so busted! she thought, trying to let the words have a comedic ring.

But there was nothing at all funny about what she'd found.

Chapter 13

"Skipper, what the hell is that, over?"

The pilot of the Coast Guard Black Hawk using the call sign Angel Twelve glanced to his left at his helmeted crewmember leaning over the center pedestal. His copilot was leaning forward and looking in the same direction. Both pointed to something in the water below and the pilot banked left in response.

"What are you guys seeing?"

"That rock just ahead . . . there's something big on top of it."

A tiny archipelago of stony outcroppings too small to be called islands studded an area a half mile offshore, most of them home to only birds and the occasional sea lion.

"Which one, Davis?"

"Third on the left. The larger one."

The pilot latched his eyes onto the correct one, spotting the same anomaly. He lowered the collective and slowed as they descended, his mind searching through the database of familiar shapes for anything matching the large, gray cylindrical mass bisecting the rock and barely contained within its confines. There was always a small rush in discovering out-of-the-ordinary sightings on routine patrols, and he felt his level of interest spiking.

The sea fog that had obscured the coast from Neah Bay south had mostly dissipated now, but there were still patches here and there, and such pockets of fog could do strange things to visibility. But there was definitely something there, and, considering the fact that they were still a half mile away and descending through a thousand feet, it was large.

Not a ship, the pilot thought to himself. *It looks more like a . . . a deflated blimp.*

The last few hours had brought one of the oddest series of alerts and calls for help he could recall from a dozen years of service. An inbound

Russian freighter captain had stopped engines and called a mayday in the middle of the Strait of Juan de Fuca only to find out that the frightening clanging and banging sounds he and his crew had heard throughout the ship were caused by seismic waves transmitted through the water. It had taken the Coast Guard cutter *Point Glass* an hour to convince the captain that his ship wasn't falling apart. Other captains and boaters were jamming the VHF channels with worried questions relating to the tremors. Commercial fishing boats off Westport were reporting a wide variety of problems, and the mood was one of jumpy apprehension.

And now this.

The target ahead just would not resolve itself into something familiar, and the pilot brought the Black Hawk in fast and low, circling around into the wind from the east before what he was seeing finally clicked.

"My God, that's a whale!" Davis exclaimed.

"You're kidding? On a *rock*?"

The crewman and the copilot were nodding excitedly.

"That's a gray."

"No, it's a humpback. Or not."

They were within a few hundred feet now and there was no mistaking it.

"Where's the tide?" the pilot asked.

"It's a rising tide, and it doesn't hit high tide for another five hours."

"Meaning," the copilot added, "that this fellow had to have lodged himself there over six or eight hours ago."

"But how?" the pilot asked, slowly changing their visual perspective as he rotated the Black Hawk from one end of the creature to the other.

"Only way he could have done it is breach and fall on it," the copilot responded.

"Not by accident, then?" the pilot asked.

The copilot and the crewman were both shaking their heads.

"No," the copilot said. "I've studied a lot of whales and I've never even heard of this. He's thirty tons if he's a pound, and that rock would have been "visible" to his built-in sonar in the equivalent of living color. No, he meant to put himself right where he is . . . and die there."

"So he's dead, you think?"

The copilot shook his head. "I don't know, but we need to alert a bunch of agencies before he washes onto the beach."

The crewman had produced a tiny digital camera and was snapping a series of shots when the copilot triggered his microphone again.

"My God in heaven," he said almost reverentially. "That's a blue! That, gentlemen, is a hundred-foot-long member of the largest mammalian species on earth."

Every property Mick Walker built had a fabulous owner's suite, and Cascadia's was spectacular. In Mick's view, it was never the expense of the furnishings or even the ample electronics that made his suites so desirable, it was the view—and how effectively he could use such magnificent vistas to wow those from whom he might want favors, or reward those who had already provided them. A weekend in this beauty, Mick thought, would soften up a judge. Of course, such suites worked well with women, too, as he'd proven on many delightful occasions.

Mick sipped his coffee and searched the southwest horizon for evidence of the oncoming weather. Two hours of REM sleep, routinely induced by self-hypnosis, had been just enough to get him through the day; he was marshaling energy for what he was determined would be a memorable, wonderful celebration. He planned to turn every glitch or adversity into an asset. There was a storm coming, of course, but by his definition it would allow a marvelous and unique opportunity for his guests to see how beautiful the coast could be in a winter gale. There might be service problems, but, if so, he'd label them staged pre-opening exercises. Lemons into lemonade. There was no one better at it.

He took a look at himself in the mirrored wall which lined the side of the living room opposite the floor-to-ceiling windows. Mick never bothered with clothes in his own environment when he was alone, and part of the price for such indulgence was keeping himself fit and trim. Flat stomach, moderately hairy chest, muscular shoulders, and a head still full of brown hair was a satisfying image. He patted his stomach and turned in both directions in a combination of admiration and systems check. No strange sores, no splotches, no growing love handles, and a naturally rough-hewn face that wasn't showing too many wrinkles as yet—thanks in part to his ability to sleep fast.

He'd learned the brutally demanding mental gymnastics of self-hypnosis thirty years ago from a professional hypnotist as a way of getting the jump on his competition by working longer and seeming to be indefatigable. There was a small legend going around about Mick Walker never needing sleep, and he encouraged it because it frightened his adversaries. The secret, he knew, was to make incredibly good use of the time you had by avoiding the normal slow descent into the lower stages of sleep. He simply forced himself to drop instantly into REM. It had taken a year of practice before he got the hang of it, but the advantages it had brought him over the years were incalculable.

Mick smiled as he walked through the bedroom and stepped into the gleaming, glassed-in shower stall in the spacious bathroom. His "ritual shower" was as vital to the process of being Mick as his sleeping technique. Fifteen minutes of focus and meditation and five of washing and he was ready to tackle almost anything—provided it wasn't someone else's reality. Mick had always engineered his own success by refusing to believe in anyone else's assessments of the art of the possible. He had learned early that the way to escape the hardscrabble life of a sheep station in the northern Australian outback was to be not only better than everyone else, but to wear his opponents down with unshakable confidence.

As he adjusted the stream of water to exactly the right temperature, Mick reflected on his promotional prowess, pleased that it wasn't just hype. He *was* a great salesman, and maybe even a great con artist— though he didn't victimize or cheat people. He preferred to be known as a slightly dangerous but thoroughly ethical scoundrel whose worst vice in business was the occasional tendency to select the most useful version of reality.

Mick relished hearing the many stories about him, and especially the one that had all but become legend. He'd tired one day of a group of Japanese investors and decided to convince them that it was raining despite a completely cloudless afternoon. "The downpour is there," he told them. "You just can't see the drops in this sun angle." He had his secretary hand them complimentary umbrellas on the way out and phoned his limo driver to turn on the windshield wipers, then watched with immense pleasure from the executive suite as all six of them ran to the limo with their umbrellas open.

His eyes closed and his mind cleared as the white noise of the shower drowned out all other sound. He stood in deep contemplation for nearly fifteen minutes before emerging to the sound of a ringing phone.

"Yes?"

"Is this Mick Walker?"

"It is. And who is this?"

"Dr. Douglas Lam of the U.S. Geological Survey."

Mick's mood darkened as he nodded unseen. "Oh, yes, Doctor. I remember you all too well. How'd you get this number?"

"From Nightingale Operations."

"I see. Don't tell me I left you off my invitation list for this weekend?"

There was a brief pause on the other end.

"Look, I know we've clashed in the past over your resort—"

"Oh, I'd hardly call it a clash, mate," Mick said, feeling the need to swing at Lam and be cautious at the same time. "As I recall, you made it abundantly clear this resort shouldn't be built, for some very novel reasons no one else agreed with, and you tried to use your scientific status to overwhelm all opposition. Thank God you failed miserably to convince even your own colleagues, or I'd be standing here in the cold on nothing but a wet rock covered with gull shit. I've never calculated the cost of the delays you helped create with your oppositions."

"Look, for the record, I never did believe you really were out to rape the planet."

"Really? Meaning you once thought I was?" Mick asked.

"No, I never thought or said that, but some of the, ah, environmental people did."

"Ah, yes. The environmental people. Your basic tree hugging ecoterrorists."

"Just . . . environmental groups, some less responsible than others. And for the record, I'm not a member of any of them."

"Not even the Sierra Club?"

"Not even."

"Pity. I am."

"I . . . didn't know that."

"Quite a few things you don't know about me, Dr. Lam." He paused, trying to keep the acid out of his tone. "Fair enough. So if you don't want to come join our little soiree, to what do I owe the pleasure of this conversation?"

"Mr. Walker, are you aware of the earthquake swarm we're having right now out there, or the damaging surficial quake that just happened in Bellingham?"

"I wasn't aware Bellingham had had one, but I felt a few shudders this morning and did some checking. I'm sure you're going to give me your expert point of view without my having to request it, right?"

Doug quickly explained the unprecedented nature of the Quilieute Quiet Zone epicenters they'd been observing all night. "That's why I have to ask you in the most respectful terms—"

"Respectful?" Mick snorted, recalling several of the permit hearings at both county and state levels when the prime scientific opposition had been from Doug Lam. "Since when does a sustained attempt to wreck a man's life work for the purpose of saving a mangy flock of common sparrows on a water-soaked rock and espousing a lunatic theory about tiny vibrations setting off earthquakes constitute being respectful?"

"Your pile drivers out there have hardly been gentle with the bedrock."

"Whatever. In any event . . . I have to admit in fairness, Doctor, that you do have a point. A twisted and somewhat distasteful one, to be sure, but that was a gratuitous snarl for which I apologize. Please continue."

"Please, despite the cost and the inconvenience, would you at least consider postponing your opening for a while until we know for sure what's happening? I am very, very worried where this current seismic activity is going, and that is an honest, science-based statement that has nothing to do with any bias about the resort."

"Are you making a formal prediction then, Doctor Lam?"

"I can't. Not yet. We don't have enough certainty. I'm just telling you what my best guess is, but I don't have enough to formalize it."

"Has the state's emergency director made such a recommendation or prediction?"

"No."

"Governor O'Brien?"

"I haven't been able to discuss it with him."

"So, no one else is canceling events or emptying hotels along the coast?"

"No."

"Yet you want me to trash a few million dollars of investment in this inaugural, screw up plans a year in the making, run off nearly three hundred guests, and scrub a few hundred thousand of advertising, just in case?"

"In a word, yes."

"Then in a word, no. I will respond well to a certainty, Doctor, but in the meantime, I'm comfortable with my calculated risks."

There was a frustrated sigh from Seattle.

"You knew I was going to say that, right?" Mick asked with a chuckle.

"Yes. I figured as much, but I'd hoped for better."

"But you just had to try. In fact, I do honestly appreciate your candor."

"Mr. Walker—"

"Oh for pity's sake, call me Mick."

"In that case, let me use just a little more candor, Mick. In fact, what I'd like to say to you is this: Goddamnit, pull your head out of your wallet long enough to understand that you're putting people in grave danger this weekend!"

There was another chuckle from Mick Walker's end. "My head's in my wallet? Well, you could have used a rougher reference, I suppose."

"Look, here's the deal. If our great subduction zone quake hits while you're entertaining, all of you are going to die. Period. Don't you understand the certainty of that?"

"Of course. World ends, film at eleven. I expect my estate might even get sued."

"Damnit, I'm serious here! How about a little respect for your responsibility to other lives?"

"You're taking this very personally, aren't you?"

"Well, if you must know, it so happens I have a personal concern about some of the people who are going to be there."

"Bloody shame that doesn't include me, but I'm resigned to it."

"Mick, please listen! Please! I'm dead serious about this, and I'm not trying to hurt your interests. And this isn't about my theory. This is about a real series of quakes already happening right now which may well be and probably are leading up to the so-called big one. It doesn't matter whether your construction project had anything to do with starting this or not. The fact is, the zone is coming alive and you're in the crosshairs."

There was an angry, determined tone in the seismologist's voice and Mick felt himself shift to a different tactical plan. Lam would never be an ally, but he was a seismic expert, and something seismic was clearly happening beneath his resort.

"Oh, very well, I'll stop swatting at you. I do understand you're serious . . . ah, Doug, is it?"

"Yes."

"All right, Doug. I do share your concerns, and I *am* seriously concerned with the safety of my guests. But the only element of real vulnerability for my complex out here is the tsunami potential, and if that does appear about to happen, I'll immediately evacuate."

"That would be too late! You might have less than five minutes until the nearest wave hits after the main quake occurs."

Mick hesitated, a cold rivulet of doubt leaking past his resolve. "These are well-built buildings on this rock, and I had them engineered to withstand exactly what you've described."

"How about a loss of five feet in altitude of the whole island?"

"That, too, would be survivable I think. You wouldn't believe what I spent on the engineering just to be certain. You've heard of Chadwick and Noble, right?"

"Yes, of course. I think they probably built the pyramids in Egypt. But what will it take to convince you that the danger fully justifies cancellation of the weekend?"

"A prediction, as I said. In fact, I'll let you in on a little legal secret. If you, in the form of the USGS, issue a formal prediction or warning or whatever you call it, then I'm against a wall. I can't ignore it without being guilty of gross negligence, and that means being exposed to ruinous recoveries. Any chance you'll do that?"

"Yes. A chance. I have superiors and a process to satisfy, though."

Mick passed a phone number to him. "That's the cell phone on my belt, and it's with me at all times. If you issue that alert, call the governor first and me second. I won't argue further."

"Okay."

"And if you can't reach Governor O'Brien, call me anyway, because that's where he and his family will be. With me."

"Understood," Lam said. "I'm going to hold you to that promise."

"Not to worry. I honor my promises. Oh, and if you change your mind and want to come out, don't hesitate. I'm serious. I'd love to show you *why* I'm so confident about this place."

"I wish I had the time. I hope we all have the time."

"Doug, remember that hearing about two years ago that was held in Port Angeles regarding the permits for my island?"

"Of course."

"You remember that, after you presented a very eloquent, but what I consider essentially misguided, analysis of the earthquake threat and told everyone how tapping pilings into the mud or drilling wells was going to set off the entire subduction zone—and, therefore, I shouldn't build there—I quoted from one of your own papers in your own words that the great subduction quake you were expecting might not happen for one to three hundred years more?"

"Yes, Mick, I remember it well. You kind of beat me up with it, and you're right. No one knows for sure when it will happen. But, we've also never in the history of recorded seismograph readings seen any activity like these constant rumblings. That means the greatest possibility is a massive, impending break, right under your island, and we've been given the blessing of an early warning."

"Well, I told you I had the same philosophy as Wally Hickel, the former Alaska governor who built a hotel on a slide area in Anchorage after the great '64 quake."

"Yeah. The Captain Cook. Nice place. Someday, it's going to be involuntarily relocated by the next great quake."

"Possibly. And Wally knew that. But he made the right point. He said, 'If it doesn't start sliding for a hundred years, why not use the land in the meantime, especially if you build something strong enough to protect the occupants.' In other words, the only loser if it hits sooner is the owner."

"I just don't think that's a wise policy."

"And I do. Ain't this country great? Come out and join us. Really. If you're truly nervous, I'll even provide a free life preserver."

Mick ended the call and stood in contemplative silence for a few seconds, forcing the doubts back in their compartments. He toggled up a new line to reach Sherry.

"Yes, exalted signer of my paychecks."

"Sherry, where do you suppose Robert Nelms is at the moment?"

"Leaving Boeing Field. I just received a call from Nightingale confirming that."

"Good. He tried to get out of coming at all. So what's his ETA?"

"It's a hundred and ten miles at a hundred knots, so about an hour from now."

"I was planning to meet him, wasn't I?"

"Yes, you were."

"And was I happy about that?"

"Let me check . . . Why yes, despite his standing you up and costing you an additional eight thousand dollars of private jet time, you were ecstatic. I've left the briefing notes on the dining room table, and a copy on your e-mail."

"Any notes in our file about Robert and this weekend? You know, what I should talk about, what I should avoid?"

"There is one thing. He weighs almost three hundred pounds."

"I know, I've known him for years. We hired a cargo helicopter."

"We're talking Orson Welles, here."

"I'm sure he's heard all the cruel jokes, including the one about having his own zip code. But be charitable, Sherry. We all come in different packages."

"His secretary warned me he's in a rotten mood."

"You mean, like me, having to wait for you to get to the point?"

"Worse."

"Why?"

"Unlike you and your buff frame, Mick, Mr. Nelms has been trying some severe regimens to lose weight, all without success. Stomach staples are next. So she says whatever you do, please don't mention diets."

"Okay. No diets. And I suppose I owe you a bonus for that buff comment, right?"

"You know it. I'll collect."

Chapter 14

SEATTLE AIR ROUTE TRAFFIC CONTROL CENTER,
AUBURN, WASHINGTON

There was no time to get to the control room and plug into the appropriate position. The shift supervisor placed the incoming call from Mount Rainier National Park Headquarters on hold and punched up the tie-line to the sector controller.

"This is an emergency involving Mount Rainier. Who do you have flying right now in your sector who might divert and take a look at the west and southwest faces?"

"Ah . . . for what? An *eruption?*"

"No, no! We're looking for any significant landslide of glacier ice. An avalanche. They just had an earthquake and a slide alarm."

"Okay . . . I've got several air carriers and a King Air . . . and a C-17 inbound to McChord."

"Any helicopters?"

"Negative. Standby."

The supervisor reached over and toggled up the appropriate frequency at his desk to listen in as the words of the Chief Ranger at Rainier rang in his mind. A sudden shedding of glacial ice—called a lahar—accelerating down the northwest face of the fourteen-thousand foot high stratovolcano would have catastrophic impact on anyone, or anything, in its path. And there were a lot of homes, businesses, and highways between the mountain and Puget Sound, where any lahar would finally play itself out. Millions of tons of ice would pick up equal amounts of mud and debris accelerating down the valleys cut by previous ancient lahars in a raging wall of mud destined to bulldoze through the rich Puyallup River valley, potentially wiping out the city of Puyallup and four smaller communities. Several teams of rangers had been ordered off the mountain in the past few minutes, he'd been told, and the Park Service was asking for Army helicopters from Fort Lewis to stand by to evacuate climbers too far up the mountain's flanks.

The voice of his controller brought him back to the moment.

"King Air November Two Hundred Romeo Mike, Center, do you have enough fuel reserve to do us a favor?"

"We're good, Center, provided it doesn't involve going to Hawaii."

"Can you see Rainier clearly?"

"Ah, roger . . . there is a cloud layer down around, maybe nine thousand, but it's broken around the mountain. Why?"

"I need you to divert over to take a look at the western through northern faces for any evidence of cascading, ah . . . ice."

"Jeez, you mean a *lahar*?"

"Possibly. They've got detectors going off."

"We're cleared now?"

"Roger. Your choice on heading and altitude."

"We're turning and accelerating. Stand by."

NIGHTINGALE ONE, AIRBORNE

Jennifer wrestled her attention back to the cockpit, startled at how distracted she'd been.

There were the familiar flight instruments in front of her, the comfort of trusty controls in her hands, a three-hundred-pound passenger headed for Cascadia Island by himself in the passenger compartment behind her, and a cloudy sky ahead that was getting darker. But all she could think of was Alaska cruise ships and the picture of Doug and his not-so-estranged wife.

She had dutifully tried to stuff the emotional upheaval into a pigeonhole and slam an angst-tight door on it, but the effort was failing, and she was angry with herself.

Of all the things she could have stumbled over, cold evidence that he'd been with Deborah and lied about it had never even been a remote possibility. Another woman, a secretly fathered child, even a lie to cover some sinister criminal past would have made more sense and been less upsetting.

And, it was the lie she couldn't get over—that and the phone calls he'd made to her, which were now clearly from Alaska and not California.

No, she thought, maybe it was just the sense of betrayal. She'd let herself get so close to him, sharing so much, letting him into places in her psyche she'd never opened up before, knowing all along how dangerous that could be. Even her ultimatum to divorce Deborah or lose her had been made against a presumption of continued intimacy and trust. She could see that now, and felt exceedingly stupid.

Something was vying for her attention, and she realized belatedly the Seattle departure controller had called, how many seconds ago she wasn't sure.

"Departure, helicopter Five Seven November, were you calling?"

"Several times, Five Seven November," the irritated voice replied. "Either maintain a better listening watch, ma'am, or I'll have to cancel flight-following services."

"I apologize, sir."

"I was going to call out traffic at your eleven o'clock, but you're clear of him now."

"Sorry."

She took a deep breath and checked back over her shoulder, expecting the VIP from San Francisco to be sleeping. Instead, he had his nose pressed to the Plexiglas and an odd color about him. He'd looked somewhat pasty alighting from Mick Walker's Gulfstream thirty minutes ago, but he was looking progressively less compatible with the idea of being airborne.

The Bellingham helicopter accident loomed suddenly in her thinking, and she toggled the company radio frequency to get Norm Bryarly's attention.

"Dispatch, One-Six. What's the status on our Bellingham crew?"

"I'm happy to report that all three are okay. The machine is probably to-taled, Linda has a mild concussion but no broken bones, Jamie's just bruised, and Eric is going to be in a couple of leg casts for a while and very embarrassed. He got banged up quite a bit being thrown out of the cockpit, but they'll all live and keep all their parts."

"Thank God. When did you hear?"

"Just before you called."

The frequency fell silent and she tried to refocus, knowing what her dad would say if he could see her level of upset over her deteriorating relationship with Doug, and how she was letting it interfere. He was a hypocrite on the subject, of course. She'd seen him equally distracted, though not over a lover. Her parents had been together for nearly forty years and if either of them had ever strayed, she had no inkling of it. But news of the accident in Bellingham had barely reached their ears before Sven had grabbed one of the relief pilots and jumped in the one available helicopter to head north. Jennifer knew he wasn't about to take no for an answer, so she quieted Norm Bryarly's attempt to countermand the flight and let him go.

Sven Lindstrom still owned 75 percent of the company to Jennifer's 25, and he was still the chairman. But like so many other things he did around the company, his need to be directly involved at unpredictable times was continuously unsettling. Jennifer could feel her stomach tightening just thinking about the agonies of having the father she loved so much looking over her shoulder the way he did. Sometimes, he would compliment her on how well she was doing with the operation, yet she always suspected that he came to the office more to second-guess her decisions than to visit. It was as if he were expecting her to fail and was standing by to jump in when she did. That was something she couldn't imagine his doing if she were his son, instead of his daughter.

She sighed in exasperation. There would undoubtedly be some long conversations between them after he got back, and she suspected he'd eventually find some way to blame the disaster on her.

UNIVERSITY OF WASHINGTON SEISMOLOGY LAB

"Oh, no! Not Mount Rainier, too."

Sanjay had bent over, then knelt in front of one of the seismograph drums, measuring and calculating the squiggles that had just marked an event beneath the premier northwestern volcano as he talked to the instrument. A shudder betraying excitement and apprehension swept through his middle as he beckoned one of the graduate students over and sent him in search of Doug Lam. He was searching the tracings for the telltale beginnings of harmonic tremors under Mount Rainier, the unmistakable signature of moving molten magma—liquid rock—flowing somewhere beneath one of the world's largest and most dangerous dormant volcanoes.

And it looked as if they were there—faint and uncertain and perhaps very deep beneath the volcano—but there.

Maybe.

A host of media phone calls had already lit up all available lines before Doug made it back in the door for a rapid briefing from Sanjay.

"We've played with this question before, haven't we, Doug?"

"Linkage, you mean?"

"We'll probably never prove the offshore quakes are triggering this, but can I have a show of hands of who thinks this is a disconnected, spontaneous event?"

"No hands up in this corner," Doug replied quietly. He felt his neck muscles tightening, his pen already out and gyrating unconsciously between his fingers, the frequency increasing.

This is like drinking from a fire hose, he thought. *We can't even analyze one phenomenon before we're hip deep in the next.*

The decision to call Bill Harper was a no-brainer, the result predictable.

"So, what do you want us to do now, Doug? Evacuate the western side of the state?"

"Cute. I'm trying to tell you we need the governor to engage the population and tell them this is potentially very serious."

The sigh from the other end was pathetic, Doug thought, and he actually felt sorry for the man.

"This is Frank O'Brien we're talking about, Doug. He could be airborne in the middle of a tornado and he'd deny it was windy. This won't impress him at all."

"How about if the mountain erupts, or if there's a real lahar coming?"

"Then he'll respond like he always does, too little, too late. Remember, this guy is all about emergency *response,* not preparation or mitigation."

"Bill, damnit, I've got to talk to him."

"As I said earlier, be my guest. Here's his cell phone number." Harper read the restricted number and paused. "Prepare yourself for an explosion, though. Frank thinks he understands this subject well enough to know that we're all wrong. We're all alarmists. I mean he truly thinks that. And so he gets really angry if I call him and no one's dead."

"Someone already is. In Bellingham," Doug snapped, aware of the terminating click on the other end.

Chapter 15

Robert Nelms was relieved to be back on the ground, even if facing Mick Walker was the price.

Walker was waiting for him at the heliport, his stern expression speaking volumes. Once the handshakes and apology for canceling out on the first flight were out of the way, Nelms let himself be ushered into the back of a brand-new limousine for the ridiculously short drive to the main resort complex. When they got there Mick made no move to open the door of the limo.

"Before we go any further, I've got some serious questions to ask."

Nelms looked at him with a poker face. "Yes?"

"I know you're aware of the series of earthquakes along the subduction zone, and you probably know I've been getting my teeth rattled out here since they started, and I've had to spend some time calming my staff."

"That's understandable—"

Mick stopped him. "Yeah . . . but I had a conversation a while ago with our favorite naysaying seismologist, Dr. Lam, and right or wrong, the man brings up some very serious questions."

"And you need some engineering reassurance?"

"You bet your ass I do. We'll have just under 450 people on this rock tonight, employees and guests included, and while I invoked the Wally Hickel defense, part of me was wondering if there was any chink in my armor."

"What did you tell them?"

"That my island and every damn thing on it is built well enough so that if we get the worst-case scenario, all the people aboard will survive uninjured. That's what you told me. But what happens if we get the following things tonight: First, a monstrous subduction zone earthquake lasting up to five minutes and registering more than 9.5 on the Moment Magnitude Scale; second, the subsidence of my island by as much as five feet within minutes during the main quake; and third, a backwash tsunami—my term, not his—

which could give us a massive thirty-foot wall of water over this place within five minutes of the quake."

"You can't be serious?" Nelms replied, working hard to keep his eyes from popping out at the scope of the potential seismic disaster just outlined.

"Well, if Lam's serious, then I'm serious."

"Good heavens, man, is someone predicting all that?"

"Not yet, but don't you dare beat around the bush. I've paid you and your firm a king's ransom to make sure I didn't have to lose any sleep on this very issue, and now I'm losing sleep. Are we okay?"

Robert Nelms smiled and shifted around in the spacious backseat. "Mick, God himself couldn't build a structure to withstand virtually all you described with any degree of certainty."

"To heck with what God can build. What did *you* build?"

Nelms paused. "All your structures have been built to meet and exceed a zone-four seismic standard, as you should remember. That means that yes, everyone inside should be safe in even the monstrous quake you described, even with ground accelerations in excess of one gravity. Neither the building code we followed nor logic would guarantee that any of the buildings will be salvageable or capable of occupancy afterwards, but they won't collapse from the shaking."

"All right."

"As for the subsidence question, even if your foundation drops ten feet and has seawater running around the main floor, same answer. Occupants 100 percent, buildings may be a loss."

"And the tsunami? I told Lam we were designed to withstand a tsunami."

Robert Nelms stared at Mick Walker for an uncomfortable delay before taking an inordinately loud breath and answering.

"Where, Mick, did you get the idea that we were designing tsunami resistance into this complex?"

"*What?* How about when I said to study every damn geologic and seismic hazard and make sure we were covered?"

"The buildings are all very strong, but they have windows and walls, and the pressure of a tsunami, especially a major tsunami, involves gargantuan forces of nature. I could have built you a concrete fortress for six times the price which would have been aesthetically revolting but tsunami-survivable, but what we did build . . . well, it's vulnerable if something like that hits."

"It's *vulnerable?*"

"Yes."

"And specifically that would mean?"

Nelms shrugged, liking this conversation less and less and fervently wishing he was taping it for future protection. There was nothing as infuriating as a "he said, she said" contest after the fact.

"But if we had a thirty- or forty-footer inbound and we rushed everyone into the main buildings?"

The feeling of perspiration popping out on Nelms's brow was an indication he was beginning to panic. So much for the poker face, he thought.

"No one can guarantee whether the buildings would survive, or the people in them."

"Shit! Robert, screw you and your fancy firm! I told you to build me a fortress, and now, on the very day I have a boatload of people coming out here trusting nothing bad can happen to them, you tell me I hired the Kmart of engineering firms?"

"I . . . Mick, this is gross overreaction."

"The hell it is! I've got Lam out there and God knows who else saying we ought to cancel this inaugural and get everyone off this island just in case, and now I find out from you they may be right? Hell, I'm even starting to wonder if his *theory* is right."

"His theory?" Robert Nelms looked genuinely puzzled, then broke into derisive laughter. "You're talking about his resonant vibration thing?"

"Yeah, that's it . . . I think."

"It's fantasy! It's stupid. I'm supposed to believe there are three specific points above the subduction zone capable of transmitting, and *amplifying* the vibrations from something as geophysically puny as a pile driver, and that such vibrations might somehow trigger a release of three hundred years of stored seismic energy? Might as well blame it on space aliens. Hell, Mick, find out what the man was drinking when he thought that one up and order me a case."

"You're dead sure it's a loony theory?"

"Yes, but now's a hell of a time to ask," Nelms laughed.

"Isn't it. The man predicts that if we bang around enough out here on the island we'll set off movement in an area locked for three hundred years. So, we banged around for two and a half years, and guess what?"

Mick glanced out of the limo's privacy glass, feeling his heart accelerating along with his breathing. A doorman was waiting respectfully for the limo's occupants, and somehow that tiny added amount of pressure seemed unbearable. He struggled to control the rising tide of panic and looked back as Nelms broke the silence.

"Mick, even if the whole subduction zone goes at once, you didn't cause it. Remember the testimony of one of his supervisors from Menlo Park? He said even a 150-megaton nuclear weapon set off *inside* the locked part of the zone would be between two to four orders of magnitude too puny to get anything moving."

"I remember. I'm just a bit nervous right now, and one theory sounds as plausible as the next. You know, does it take a nuclear bomb or a ballpeen hammer?"

Nelms snorted. "You're nervous? Mister Ice-Water-For-Blood Mick Walker? Mick, you don't know the meaning of the word."

"So I've heard."

"Now—on the other issue—I've studied these types of threats, and there is no certainty that even if there was a great quake, a tsunami would follow."

"Lam says it is a certainty. He's done research on that very issue. So have some other USGS scientists, chief among them the geologist who kind of discovered the threat to begin with."

"You mean Dr. Atwater?"

"Yes. He found layers of sand in meadows around here that couldn't have come in without a tsunami!"

"Oh for cripes sake. Then why didn't you hire Lam and Atwater instead of me?"

"Lam came too cheap, and he wouldn't have let me build here."

A cloud passed over Robert Nelms's face. "I . . . we did not 'let' you build on this island, Mick. We gave you the data and you made your own decisions."

Mick waved it off. "Of course. Bad phraseology."

"And remember it may well be three hundred years before the next great quake-and-tsunami combination happens."

A silence grew between them, and Nelms's uneasiness was showing. "Mick, if you're that panicked, then cancel the weekend."

"Are you volunteering to fund my losses?"

"What? Good heavens, no! We did our job very well. And I thought I was here as a guest to celebrate, not get berated."

"Wait . . . just a minute. A minute ago you said the buildings wouldn't collapse from shaking. What *would* collapse them?"

"Well, we established that a big enough tsunami would mean that all survivability bets are off."

"And?"

Robert shrugged. "All the engineering studies were predicated on our profile of this island and its characteristics, and there are always assumptions made about bedrock, and locality of shaking, et cetera. You've seen every scrap of data that I've seen."

"I'm sure that's true," Mick said, looking away. "So what does all that mean, Robert?"

Nelms sighed and shifted forward. "It means, Mick, that you, and we, have done everything science and engineering can do at this juncture for an affordable price to uphold the public trust."

"Okay."

"So what are you going to do?"

"I don't know. Monitor the situation closely, and if these rumblings get any more ominous, maybe we'll load everyone back on the ferry this evening and abandon ship."

"Get part of the gala in, in other words?"

"Yeah. Maybe. Sure wish I had some idea when great earthquakes like to strike."

"If I knew that, Mick, I'd be a very wealthy man."

"You *are* a very wealthy man, Robert," Mick Walker said, forcing a socially acceptable smile as he stepped out of the car.

UNIVERSITY OF WASHINGTON SEISMOLOGY LAB

Doug Lam was running out of options in his quest to do the right thing.

"He's blocking my calls, Sanjay," Doug said as he replaced the receiver with an exhausted sigh. A stack of hand calculations on a legal pad sat next to his laptop, the detritus of hours of number crunching of the continuous tremors, all of which had resulted in a feeling somewhere between sick and exhilarated. The so-called big one seemed inevitable. The small quakes were getting larger, and eventually the main rupture would occur, releasing more than three hundred years of seismic energy.

"You were trying to reach Bill Harper again?"

"No. The governor. Harper's gone to Cascadia Island after him. He's finally convinced we could be as close as hours away from the main event. I mean, what does it take to convince O'Brien how many thousands of people are going to die if the whole subduction zone breaks at once?"

"It's too outlandish, Doug. People don't want to believe such things can happen. Figures like 9.5 magnitude are just numbers."

"Maybe, but I've got to get out there."

"Where? Cascadia?"

"Yes. Governor O'Brien's on the way, Walker's already there, and he invited me, so why not?"

"How? It's a long drive."

Doug had already thought through the method for getting to Cascadia, and it was inevitably going to involve Jennifer and her company's airlift services. He startled himself by reaching for the phone and punching in her cell number without any further consideration.

Her voice-mail message came up instead, and he punched it off quickly, consulting his PDA for the Nightingale Dispatch number. A dispatcher he'd met answered.

"Jennifer is probably leaving Cascadia Island right now, Dr. Lam."

"But she is going back out? Right? You're running shuttles all day?"

"Yes, sir, but they're all . . . ah . . . VIP-type flights, you know."

"Mick Walker invited me and said I should call you to make arrangements."

"In that case, hang on." There was brief pause with papers being shuffled and computer keys being punched in the background. "Well, can you get out here in the next twenty minutes?"

"Yes. Absolutely."

"Then I've got a single spare seat. We'll have to make other arrangements to get you back."

"No problem. I'm on my way."

"I'll let Jennifer know."

"No, don't," Doug heard himself say, not knowing why. "I'd like to surprise her."

"Understood."

PLEASANTON, CALIFORNIA

"Ralph, she's on an Amtrak train headed north to Portland right now, and to the best of my research, if anyone's looking for her, they're not professionals."

"What does that mean, Bill?" Ralph Lacombe asked.

"What it means is that no one's got a contract out on her, the Company's not looking for her, there are no wants or warrants anywhere in the U.S., including Homeland Security, and why she's running I have absolutely no idea."

"She was seriously spooked, Bill."

"No doubt. But it wasn't by any of *our* spooks, if you understand what I mean. She's off the radar of anything serious, Ralph, and my hunch is that this is something involving Chadwick and Noble internally. I mean, this guy Jerry Schultz who called you and she reacted to in one of your conversations is a low-level supervisor, wholly unable to mount any sort of sophisticated pursuit of your daughter."

"Bill, she's a double cum laude Stanford grad. Diane is no idiot. If she says someone's chasing her, someone's chasing her."

"Well, whoever it is, I can't turn it up."

"Okay."

"Ralph, the bottom line is, relax. This isn't something super serious. In fact, she may have inflated the seriousness in her own mind."

Ralph Lacombe rubbed his forehead and sighed, remembering the last few years of warning signs that not all was right with his precious daughter's view of the world.

"That's exactly what I'm afraid of."

Chapter 16

The master of the Motor Vessel *Quaalatch* was frightened.

There was no use kidding himself, Reilly Shelton concluded. With the winds above fifteen knots and rising, and the seas between the peninsula and Cascadia Island now roiled by waves as high as ten feet, docking on both sides was going to be dicey, and it was scaring him. Worse, he had five more scheduled runs before he was supposed to tie up the new ferry for the night. By then, the winds were predicted to be near forty, and much too high for safe operation.

And then there was the rising feeling in his gut that something was very wrong, a feeling that had gnawed at him from the first moment he heard about—and then felt—the swarm of little earthquakes, and what they might mean. Several scientists interviewed on television had used the word *tsunami*, and he knew exactly what a tsunami was.

Yet Mick Walker had made it very clear the schedule was to be followed.

Reilly took a long pull at the Diet Coke he'd been nursing and watched the passengers coming aboard. He preferred passengers to cargo or fish, and now that he looked the part of a senior ship captain with an expanding belly to match, it was fun to take his four-stripe shoulder boards downstairs and show himself off as if he were the master of a thousand-foot cruise ship.

He'd made a career of tugboats, launches, and work boats for thirty years, and now he was commanding a very special, very expensive ferry. Exercising his sixth sense about when to back off was part of his responsibility, and that sixth sense was currently yelling at him.

Yet, this was the opening day of the resort whose presence made the ferry, and his job, necessary. Somehow he'd have to make the schedule work, but if the winds really did get above thirty-five, he'd have to suck it up and talk to Mr. Walker and ask permission to cut out the last runs, and he knew what the reaction would be. The prospect of a job-threatening confrontation was already messing with his stomach and giving him a hearty headache.

An unruly forelock of silver hair migrated in front of his eyes again and he pawed it back, regretting the lack of a hat. The wind had done a number on his hair, and he hated that.

The last of the 105 passengers scheduled for this particular run were filing aboard two decks below through the luxurious airline-style jetway that the company had built into the dock on the peninsula side of the channel. What was greeting them on entry were rich fabrics and leather, comfortable captain chairs and couches, sparkling bars with well-attired waitresses from the casino and hotel restaurants, and tonight, even a jazz combo playing away in the corner.

Being proud of the MV *Quaalatch* was easy. It was great fun to show off his modern bridge, which glowed impressively at night with state-of-the-art electronics, GPS systems, radar, and chrome engine controls alongside the classic wooden ship's wheel. Even the well-designed car deck was a showpiece. It could accommodate ten cars and three tractor-trailer rigs for island resupply in a clever system of overlapping tunnels.

There had been a number of used ferries on the market in various parts of the world when Reilly was hired to plan the sea bridge to and from the island, but fortunately Mick Walker had insisted on building something new and impressive, and that's precisely what Reilly now had under his command—even if the scope of his "voyages" was only a mile in either direction.

Reilly checked the wind speed again. Part of his mind was already trying to work out the next approach to the island's newly commissioned ferry slip. Mick Walker's engineers couldn't have put it in a worse spot, right at the juncture of a small channel where an intense tidal rip always seemed to be active either in or out. At least the lead-in pilings were new, strong, and well padded with heavy black rubber. He was going to need them. In most of the proving runs he'd been forced to nudge the blunt bow of the twin diesel boat against one or the other of the pilings and shove her in with the brute force of the engines. The shipyard had equipped her with a bow thruster to move the front of the ship left or right with the turn of a small keylike control, but the current at the island slip was simply too much for the thruster, which meant he wouldn't be using it much. It was false security.

He needed to go below before they departed, and Dennis, his first mate, swung back into the wheelhouse, as if reading his mind.

"So, you want me to take over while you go schmooze the passengers, skipper?" the twenty-eight-year-old asked.

"What do you think?" Shelton replied.

"Well, seeing as how you have on your impressive captain's coat there, you might as well show it off before things get messy down there. We're issuing the barf bags."

"Really?"

"You're not worried about these crossings?"

Reilly snorted at the idea. "Me? Son, I've sailed through waves bigger than that island over there."

"Yeah, right, Captain. I happen to know you spent your career in Puget Sound in a tugboat on glassy waters."

"Hey, not true. I've got plenty of blue-water experience."

"Which blue water? Lake Washington in the summer?"

"Such rancid disrespect for your elders. You've got the controls, Mr. Christian. I'll be back to keelhaul you in a few minutes."

"By the way, Captain Shelton, sir . . . check out the incredible chick in the deck-length white coat while you're down there."

"Oh?"

"Blonde, heart-attack sexy, miniskirt barely long enough to be legal."

Reilly cocked his head. "Is she the one who came aboard with a man and woman and two other guys hanging back?"

"Yeah! You saw her?"

"They give me binoculars up here. First of all, she's jailbait. Secondly, that 'chick' is Miss Lindy O'Brien, the governor's daughter."

"She's sixteen. I read about her."

"Hands off."

"Okay, okay."

"And I'm going down to welcome the governor," Reilly said, as he headed for the circular stairway leading from the bridge to the main deck. "If he can make a point of helicoptering out just to ride our ferry, I can say hello and protect his daughter from my crew."

Instead, he continued below the level of the passenger lounge to the car deck, emerging close to the bow. There were no vehicles on this run and no crewmen on the car deck to watch him walk to the side of the ferry and stare long and hard at the wave state. The crests were already higher than he'd figured, and much more impressive than they'd looked from the bridge. With the tide coming in, the current around Cascadia Island was going to be brutal.

Once again a strange, cold feeling of dread grabbed him deep inside.

Mick Walker had made sure there was a VIP lounge aboard his ferry that would please even an Arabian potentate. It was the perfect place for Lindy O'Brien and her important parents. Sixteen, beautiful, spoiled rotten and proud of it, Lindy knew her mother was watching her closely, but there was no way either her parents or the plainclothes state troopers who watched after them could keep up with her. As usual, careful preplanning had set up the whole evening, and she was looking forward to executing the plan as soon as they reached their suite. Getting the room and getting her friends invited and in place ahead of time as a cover had been another triumph of sweet-talking and chicanery, and she was as proud of the success of her clandestine operation as she was excited about spending the night with Jeff.

Lindy accepted a Diet Coke and sat on one of the plush leather chairs, uncrossing her legs slowly and recrossing them with her eyes on a good-looking young waiter who was more than aware of what she was doing and trying hard not to react. Her mother was glaring at her, and the governor, as usual, was on the phone and oblivious to what his daughter was up to.

She felt the boat swaying as it rocked with its prow in the ferry slip, the significant waves making their presence known even before the ferry headed across the narrow channel.

Her special weekend had started, and this was going to be fun!

One deck below in the main passenger area, Priscilla Ranne from Ames, Iowa, squeezed her husband Tony's arm again and smiled as she looked around the crowded room—which was already swaying and moving in some disturbing patterns. She felt elegant in her cocktail dress and proud of Tony, looking so young and vital in his business suit. There was an eclectic mix of humanity all around her, she noticed, feeling very cosmopolitan in such a crowd. Several of the men were in tuxedos, but the styles ran the gamut from formal all the way down to the three men by one of the corner windows looking exceedingly uncomfortable in jeans, white shirts, and jackets.

Just like home, she thought, having gone to so many social functions around Ames as she was growing up. There were always a few good old boys off the farm who simply weren't comfortable off a tractor and out of overalls. She knew the look and smiled at the memories. It had always been fun to go ask one of them to dance and watch the overly scrubbed boy blush, but later be so appreciative of her attention.

"Baby, aren't you glad I entered us in the contest?" she asked Tony suddenly, squeezing his arm again for emphasis. He'd been making small talk with another couple and she wanted to share the excitement she was feeling, not talk politics, or whatever the subject had been.

"Honey," he said, looking around at her, "you ask me that about every hour on the hour." There was a chuckle in his voice as he showed his usual gentle tolerance of her silliness, and he smiled at her as he snaked an arm around her waist. "But I am glad, yes. You can win as many trips for us as you want."

"I just *love* this!" she giggled. "It's like being in New York or something."

Tony turned back to the other couple, who were also contest winners, but who had hauled along their three brats, where Priscilla had been smart enough to arrange for Tony's mother to keep their two little girls. The chance to have Tony all to herself in a plush hotel room for two free nights was not going to be subjected to the competition of children, she had decided. Besides, maybe it was time to get number three cooking.

For some reason, she glanced back at the three men in the corner, studying their faces a bit more and wondering if they were Native, or American Indians, or whatever the politically correct description was. She'd heard of all sorts of strange tribes in the Washington area, and some of the names sounded funny. Pew-allup, snow-home-ish, sue-quah-mish, lum-me as in tummy, and a town with the darkly risqué name of Humptulips.

Whoever those three were, she thought, it was obvious they were going to have to do a better job of enjoying themselves. All three were frowning.

One hundred yards distant in the parking lot of the Cascadia Island ferry departure terminal an old car pulled around the corner and slipped into a space indicated by a parking attendant, followed by a cloud of bluish smoke memorializing the deteriorating state of the engine. Mary Willis turned off her engine, startled at the relative silence as the cacophony of the sputtering engine ceased. She emerged from her battered Ford, straightened the dress she'd purchased for the occasion, and began checking her purse for her invitation, too absorbed to note a young woman with auburn hair who materialized from a row of cars in front of her.

"Hi," the younger woman said. "May I talk to you for a moment?"

"Sure," Mary replied.

The woman looked nervously toward the ferry dock and wiped a tear from the corner of her eye, then looked at Mary and tried to smile.

"I'm . . . so sorry to bother you, but, I've got a big, big problem."

"What, Dear? Can I help?"

"My husband is already on the island, in our room and waiting for me, and he gets very upset if I screw things up. He's got quite a temper . . . and I'm supposed to be over there, but I lost my invitation and now they won't let me on. They say I'm not on the list."

"That's too bad. How can I help? Do you need to borrow a cell phone and call him?"

The young woman dabbed at her eyes again and shook her head. "I tried.

He's not answering. But—here's the thing. Is there any way you would consider letting me buy your invitation?"

"You want to pay me—just for my tickets?"

"I know it would mean giving up the weekend, and your room, but I'll pay you three hundred. It's worth that much to me not to get him angry again."

Mary chewed her lip, trying to weigh the sudden proposition against the fun she was expecting to have with her twenty-five-dollar gambling stake and her free room. Only a handful of tribal council members had been invited, but three hundred could buy a lot of groceries.

"Does he beat you, Dear?" Mary asked.

She looked startled. "No. Just . . . he's got a bad temper."

"Well, I had been planning on this weekend for some time."

"Please," the young woman begged. "My marriage may hang in the balance here. How about four hundred?"

"Well . . . it's not just the money, you see."

"Okay . . . all I have, all right? Five hundred cash. Please?"

Mary sighed and finally nodded, handing over the invitation envelope and taking the money, then watching the young woman's broad smile as she hugged her.

"What's your name?" the woman asked.

"Mary Willis. And yours?"

"Cynthia," she said, waving as she bounded off toward the waiting ferry. "Thank you so much!"

Mary sighed and sat back down behind the wheel of her battered Ford feeling deflated, despite the money. It was obviously too late to reconsider, and maybe she'd saved a marriage, but losing the weekend was going to hurt, and she felt lonely already.

She started the engine after the third try, the engine wheezing to life as an image materialized in her head of the young woman's left hand.

There had been no wedding ring.

Wait a minute. If her husband is already there, why does she need my room?

Mary turned to look in the direction of the ferry. Cynthia had already disappeared inside, and she could see a deck hand on the bow preparing to throw off the ropes.

But the ferry would be back within the hour for the next load of guests, and, unlike Cynthia, the name Mary Willis was on the invitation list. And Mary Willis had more than enough photo ID cards to prove who she was.

No. I'll wait. I'm five hundred dollars richer and I'm still going!

Suddenly the weekend looked bright again.

———

When the MV *Quaalatch* was safely away from the slip and westbound, the captain picked up the PA microphone and summoned his best, calmest, deepest voice.

"Folks, this is Captain Shelton. The passage ahead is a little rough, and although we'll be there in only fifteen minutes, I would appreciate your taking your seats now while we—"

A large swell pushed the boat to starboard, almost rolling the deck out from under his feet.

"—while we prepare for our landing on the island's new ferry slip. It's wonderful to have you with us on our very first day of operation."

He replaced the PA as another roller caught the port bow, heeling the ship slightly as the first officer tightened his grip on the edge of the forward dash panel and Reilly tried to calm his rising apprehension. The *Quaalatch* displaced nearly five hundred thousand pounds. Even a low-speed impact with that kind of weight could do substantial damage.

But it wasn't the prospect of hitting something that was eating away at him, rather the worry that in front of the boss and all the guests, he might not be able to get her landed on the island.

Worse, he thought, what if the wave state got too high to bring her back even to the peninsula side? What would he do? Where could he take them? Eighty miles south through mountainous waves to find a safe harbor at Hoquiam? The professional embarrassment alone would be total, and Walker would surely fire him.

It was cold on the bridge and the first officer had already zipped up his coat, but Reilly was too busy wiping a bead of perspiration from his forehead to notice.

BOEING FIELD, SEATTLE

The high-speed dash from the lab to Nightingale's hangar took less time than Doug had figured. He parked his Austin-Healey in one of the spaces reserved for company executives and scrambled into the building, catching the eye of the dispatcher as he approached the desk.

"Dr. Lam, I presume?" the dispatcher asked, not waiting for a response beyond a slight nod. "The third helicopter out there on the line, the Sikorsky S-76. They're waiting for you. Take the left, front copilot's seat, please. Keep your head down as you approach, and approach only from the side. Our line guy will escort you."

The pilot was a woman he noticed as he climbed into the seat. "Glad to meet you at last, Dr. Lam," she said.

"At last?"

"We're all kind of aware of our boss lady's significant other." Her eyes were on the horizon as the helicopter accelerated and banked to the west, overflying the north side of the control tower. "I'm Gloria Andrews, by the way."

"Nice to meet you," Doug replied. "And thanks for ferrying me out there."

"My pleasure."

"You're the military pilot Jennifer has told me about, right?"

"One of them. I flew Black Hawks in the Army. But two wars and God knows how many skirmishes were enough. I like this a lot better."

"I imagine."

"May I ask *you* a question, since you're a seismologist?"

"Sure."

"My parents live in Ocean Shores. They're retired, and they don't think there's any seismic danger there because its basically a big sandbar."

"They're there now?"

"Yes."

"You have a cell phone aboard?"

"Why?" Gloria replied, her expression darkening.

"Once you get in cruise, I'd highly recommend you call them and get them out of there for the next few days."

"It's that bad? Their house is one story and it's on a slab foundation. There's no masonry either."

"It's not the shaking, Gloria," he said, holding the intercom transmit down steadily. "It's the thirty- to forty-foot-high tsunami that's going to roar over the entire Ocean Shores peninsula within a few minutes of any great subduction quake. In addition, the whole Ocean Shores spit will probably be yanked down four to six feet, and that puts most areas at or below sea level."

There was momentary silence from the right seat as she spoke to a Seattle departure controller about other inbound traffic, then turned back to him.

"You're scaring me, Doctor."

"I mean to. You'll almost certainly lose them if the big one does hit us."

They were passing Bremerton by the time she was able to make the call, lowering the phone a minute later.

"Technically I can't use a cell phone in flight. The FAA thinks it might interfere with the instruments, but with the digitals, that's so much B.S."

"Are your folks going to leave?"

She shook her head. "Not yet. It will take at least three calls. My parents are very hardheaded."

They skimmed some low-lying stratus clouds hanging over the northeast shoulder of the Olympic Peninsula and threaded their way along the north edge of the national park before turning south just short of Forks on the final run to the island.

Doug couldn't suppress a low whistle as the outline of the buildings became distinct several miles ahead. It seemed as if every inch of the rock called Cascadia Island had sprouted something large and built of steel and concrete, and the effect was astounding.

Doug watched Gloria, carefully assessing her degree of concentration, concerned about distracting her.

"Have you been out here before?" Doug asked.

"Three times today already," Gloria replied.

"It looks like a battleship, or . . . maybe a carrier."

"It is bristling, isn't it?"

"The hotel alone is huge."

"Yeah. And beautiful. See the helipad just to the right there?"

He nodded as she worked the controls, slowing and descending smoothly as she adjusted the approach into the wind, her expert, subtle movements almost undetectable as the S-76 she had melded with appeared to be obeying her very thoughts, settling authoritatively onto the concrete pad.

"Have a great time, Doctor."

"Thanks," he said, deciding there was no point in puzzling her with a diatribe about how there should be nothing but seabirds where they were sitting.

Doug pulled off the headset and climbed out, concentrating on the very disturbing realization that he was already impressed by what he'd seen of Mick Walker's creation.

Chapter 17

The sun was barely visible through the distant storm clouds, appearing just long enough to confirm its descent into the murky western horizon.

The winds were rising steadily out of the southwest and threatening to blow the sheet music away from the brass band that had begun playing the MV *Quaalatch* into the dock as it approached. The band members were too busy trying to stay on rhythm to notice the pitched battle the ferry crew was having with the current and the winds, and Mick Walker himself had turned toward land, concentrating only on a phone call.

On the third attempt, accompanied by several groaning impacts with the breakwater, the captain finally shoved the boat's steel prow into the right position alongside the leeward pilings. With the powerful engines churning forward, the craft slowly squealed her way along the rubber bumpers and creosote timbers to move into position, close enough for the ropes to be secured and the covered ramp to be mated with the side door.

On the bridge, Reilly Shelton heaved a sigh of relief and set the throttles to maintain forward pressure against the dock. He gave the radio signal to tie her fast and open the doors, then sat heavily, not even caring that his young first officer was looking at him with something less than glowing admiration.

On the dock below it was showtime, and Mick was ready.

As the watertight door on the ship end of the passenger bridge opened, the promoter-developer was waiting with an expansive greeting for Governor Frank O'Brien and his wife. He took Lindy O'Brien's hand as well, trying not to notice the provocative outfit being flaunted by the first daughter, or the fact that she purposefully bent forward to tease him with her well-displayed cleavage.

Mick quickly ushered the three of them, along with the mayor of Seattle and his wife, into a plush minibus and climbed in himself, gesturing the driver into motion as he picked up the PA microphone and began a glowing chronicle of the new Cascadia Resort complex. They moved around the tiny island counter-clockwise, beginning with the soaring architecture of the main casino, a stressed-concrete structure covered with copper tiles and wooden trim to achieve a wild blend of rustic and space-age ambience. He explained the difficulty Jack Nicklaus and his company had encountered building the 9-hole golf course on such a small island, and took them past the heliport and state-of-the-art convention center to the western end of the island where the pounding Pacific surf had been forced by concrete and engineering to forgo its erosive nature and put on a spectacular twenty-four-hour show instead, each wave hitting a massive concrete diversion barrier specially shaped to cause massive vertical sprays of seawater, the rumble and vibrations of wave impact distributed along a 150-foot structure. The governor and mayor stood outside the bus for a few seconds with their host, profoundly impressed with the deep, low-throated sounds made by the barrier. Even Lindy O'Brien lowered her cell phone to appear momentarily interested.

The entrance to the expansive courtyard of the two-hundred-room hotel was the pièce de résistance, and Mick had set up a grand welcome with a string quartet and the majority of the staff arrayed at attention.

"This building was the part I spent the most time working on," Mick was saying as he ushered them to the buttressed, seaside edge of the structure that perched on the southern point of the tiny island.

"I stayed in a hotel in Acapulco once that intrigued me," he continued grandly. "I think it was called the La Palapa. Each room had a balcony engineered so beautifully as to be completely private. If your neighbor on any side, above or below, tried to peer around at your balcony, he'd fall to his death. You and anyone with you could enjoy the balmy air any way you wanted, without clothes or loss of privacy, and I've reproduced the same thing here. Only a voyeur in a helicopter could see in, and we've got precautions against that happening."

"Mick, I hate to be the bearer of bad tidings," the governor began, "but it's not very often described as balmy up here."

"Which is why each balcony is heated with a combination of state-of-the-art infrared and a blanket of warm air so effective you can spend a twenty-degree night lying in your beach chair."

"Without clothes," O'Brien prompted.

"Easily."

"I'm beginning to detect a nudist theme here, Walker," the governor quipped as Mick continued unfazed. The mayor laughed.

"Each suite also has a specially designed fireplace. It's gas-fired, no wood, but it sends tiny amounts of fragrant wood smoke into each room to complete the illusion."

"Really?" O'Brien asked. "Who designed that?"

"I did. I own the patent. I can't stand having a fire without the aroma. And it's perfectly safe."

They walked into the main lobby beneath a soaring, cantilevered entryway and Mick raised his voice slightly to cover the shudder of yet another earth tremor, one which rumbled on for what seemed an embarrassing eternity.

"Sorry about the vibrations," he said, rolling his eyes as if the construction crews were impossibly stupid. "We've still got some heavy machinery operating on the last-minute stuff we couldn't get done in time."

"That felt like an earthquake, Mick," the governor said.

"Ah, I doubt it. I mean I know we've been having some, but I'm pretty sure that's our machinery."

"What, a pile driver?"

"Yes, that and some drilling."

Over their heads was a six-ton structure made of hammered brass over steel, and Mick forced himself not to look up at it as he casually ushered the group away and over toward the elevators. The hotel manager appeared behind a large smile and handed the governor a packet of key cards, and a second packet to the mayor.

"Jim will show you to your suites, and I'll see all of you to dinner at 7, if that's satisfactory. I'll come to your rooms."

The sound of an arriving helicopter straying from its normal approach path washed out the good-byes momentarily, as Mick excused himself and headed for the front drive, where the minibus and two of his key employees were waiting, both with ashen expressions.

Mick smiled at a group of passing guests and climbed in, shutting the door, his eyes on Ron Garcia, his operations manager.

"What's wrong, Ron?"

"First, Captain Shelton is on the mainland side and loading up and he's begging for permission to make this his last run."

"What?"

"I know, I know. I told him there was no way we could leave half the guests back there, and he told me he wasn't moving until I spoke to you."

"What's his problem?"

"He says the winds are approaching out-of-limit stage and the waves and current are too dangerous for safe landings."

"Bullshit! Did I hire a bloody coward instead of a captain?"

"Mick, I don't know, but it is getting very rough out there, and he did have trouble landing when the governor came in. I mean, maybe he isn't up to this, but we probably shouldn't just dismiss his worries, you know, for safety reasons."

"There are no safety reasons, okay? I paid a princely sum for that stupid boat. It's got all the bells and whistles on it, including a bow thruster, and we paid millions for the slips. You could nose a damn battleship into one of those slips and not damage anything! You tell that bastard he'll make every one of his runs as scheduled or he can get off and let the first officer take over."

"That . . . would not be a good idea. The kid's licensed, but he's pretty green."

"Then threaten him, insult him, blackmail him, whatever. Every single run as scheduled, got it?"

"Yes, Mick. I'll tell him."

"What else? Something simple?"

"I . . . don't know. Hopefully. But, we've got a strange split in the floor of the convention hall's main entrance."

"What do you mean, 'split'?"

"Ah . . . I mean there's a crack in the floor, and it appeared to be widening even as we were watching it."

"The *floor*?"

"Yeah."

"What, a foot long?"

"No, Mick. At least sixty feet long. The entire expanse of the entrance. Right through the marble."

Mick glanced at the driver. "Get over there. Now, please."

The bus began to pick up speed as Mick turned back to Garcia. "Can we patch it quickly?"

"If it doesn't get any bigger, but what's worrying me is, I can see some pressure lines in the walls on either end corresponding to the crack. Right at the bottom."

"English, Ron. Speak English."

"I mean . . . damnit, it looks like one side is being pulled one way, and the other the other, like we built the building right across the San Andreas Fault. Except that fault moves slowly. This one is moving very quickly, and we've got the aesthetic problem if the guests see it, and the second problem, which is worse, is whether something awful is about to happen to our center. Like, is it about to be torn in half?"

"Has everyone gone mad? This isn't an earthquake thing, is it?"

"Mick, hell, I don't know. I'm just reporting what I'm dealing with. You'll see for yourself in a minute."

The driver stopped quickly in front of the convention center entrance and they piled out and into the building. The crack in the expensive Italian marble floor was wall to wall, and at least a half inch in width, intersecting on each end with a corresponding vertical warp in the twenty-foot-high atrium walls, just as Garcia had described. Mick Walker moved quickly from one side to the other, peering at the rift as if his eyes alone could weld it back together. He could solve almost any problem, but with hours left before the hall was to be teeming with mightily impressed guests, this was bordering on a disaster.

There were a few moments of additional shaking as more tremors coursed through the island, but this time the tremors were accompanied by a frighteningly loud crack which echoed through the entrance hall. Mick turned, watching in disbelief as the eastern wall—a two-story slab of marble-covered stressed concrete—split from floor to ceiling as the entire building shuddered. The crack on the floor had grown larger as well, and the jog made by the veins in the marble where they crossed the crack told the tale of the two sides being pulled laterally past each other by as much as an inch.

"Bloody hell!" Mick worked to mask a sudden feeling of genuine fear. He turned to Garcia in a state of barely controlled agitation.

"Ron? Jesus, man, get someone over to the hotel and grab Nelms. I don't care if you have to pull him out of the shower, I need his read on this. We've got the banquet scheduled in here in two hours."

"Should we relocate, Mick? We can probably set up everything in time in the ballroom of the casino."

Mick thought about it for all of a second before nodding energetically. It was sensible recovery.

"Yes. Yes, do it. God, I don't believe this!"

Garcia started to leave, then turned back. "One other thing. That Dr. Lam, the seismologist, just showed up on one of the helicopters and said you invited him by phone just this morning, and he needs to speak to you urgently."

Mick exhaled, shaking his head. "Christ. Yes, I did. Never thought he'd . . . okay, give him a great room, and a fruit basket, and keep him the hell away from me and from this convention hall until I tell you otherwise."

"Mick, he wants to see you *and* the governor. He says it's a dire emergency."

"No! Absolutely not. Keep him away from O'Brien, too! Give him anything else within reason, but he is *not* to go bleeding all over the governor about these tremors."

"You got it."

Mick stood with his hands on his hips looking at the incredible rift in the expensive marble. He was feeling dizzy and flushed and he could feel his heart pounding as he hurried back to the van, determined to intercept Robert Nelms in person.

UNIVERSITY OF WASHINGTON SEISMOLOGY LAB

Sanjay Singh disconnected from the USGS conference call and immediately punched up Doug Lam's cell phone, relieved that he answered almost immediately.

"Yes?"

"Doug, where are you?"

"On the island, trying to find Walker and O'Brien. I think they're hiding from me and I'm getting really ticked."

"That conference call you wanted? We had it. Nelson and Sellers in Menlo Park, three of us up here, a total of eight . . . and they had all seen the data."

"So, what's the consensus, or is there one?"

"You're not going to believe this. They agreed that all this activity is completely unprecedented in recorded seismic history."

"That's painfully obvious, but I'm glad they concur."

"The main thing, Doug, is that they all agree, even Dr. Nelson, that there's such a significant localization of the hypocenters of these quakes, and the same steady acceleration of magnitude, that—let me read the exact words— quote, 'it raises a valid question of whether we should depart from our normal cautions and issue what amounts to a prediction.' He said this is the same position the Chinese found themselves in back in 1976 just before they saved a million lives by ordering people out into a freezing winter's night."

"Well, that is a breakthrough."

"Isn't it?"

"How soon? If I can get a prediction in hand, I can force Walker and O'Brien to comply."

"They're going to study it over the next twelve hours. I've set up a real-time hookup for all our data array."

"Sanjay, they do understand, don't they, that we may not have twelve hours?"

"Yes. I pushed that point as far as I could."

"Can I announce that a prediction is imminent?"

"No, Doug. Not honestly. Only that they're strongly considering the issuance of one. Nelson will crucify you if you overstate the case."

"I know it. I won't. But has there been any big change in the pattern of the quakes?"

"It's like watching a slow obstetric delivery where the contractions are getting closer over a matter of days, not hours. The steady rhythm is there, but when it's going to deliver is anyone's guess."

"Wouldn't it be something," Doug asked absently, "if we could somehow find the safety pin and stick it back in the grenade in time?"

"Excuse me?"

"Nothing. Wishful thinking."

"If . . . you said what I thought you said, remember that to reverse a process, you have to first have some idea what started that process, and . . ."

"That's okay, Sanjay. I was just muttering. Look, I'll check back with you when I've gotten to Mick Walker and Governor O'Brien. Meantime, try to get hold of Terry at Lake Quinault Lodge; tell him to get hold of himself and get back out to his array. We need that data streaming real-time and it's useless as long as he's cowering twenty miles inland."

"I will, Doug. But I'm not going to accuse Terry of cowering. He's got good reason to be scared."

NIGHTINGALE ONE, ON DESCENT INTO CASCADIA ISLAND HELIPORT

Jennifer squinted at the heliport lights five miles ahead, trying to make the fuzziness disappear. It was probably the fatigue, she decided; that and the black-hole effect of having so many blazing lights in the middle of a completely dark patch of water.

Thank God this is the last flight of the evening for me!

She glanced over at her father in the left seat of the Bell 412, wondering what he was thinking. He had seen her shove the door of the operations office open an hour ago and walk out on the ramp to decompress and shed some tears in private, but she hadn't really wanted to admit that Doug was the cause—or more precisely, that his cajoling a ride to Cascadia Island on the very night she needed to be as far away from him as possible had prompted her outburst.

As usual, Sven had tried to pry the details out of her, embarrassing her even more. A silly girl who got emotional over a semi-unfaithful lover shouldn't be running a company or commanding an aircraft. Not that he'd ever said anything close to those words, but she knew inside how he felt, and the words were merely her own acknowledgment of the truth.

It had taken Herculean effort to paste on a convincing smile and maintain that she'd been furious with Norm Bryarly for giving Doug the ride more than with anything Doug had done.

And she'd left out the part about his cheating with his wife. She knew her father too well. He'd simply find that ironic and hilarious.

She had looked forward to this evening, all but ignoring the seismic threats. Now she had to deal with Doug, or not. He would be there, somewhere, and she had to decide to find him and confront him or purposely ignore and avoid him, and either choice was going to be upsetting.

"How're you doing?" Sven asked over the headset.

"I'm tired, Dad, but functioning. I wish I could invite you to fly this approach." Even though he'd lost his FAA medical, she was an instructor and under certain circumstances could let him fly, and he was still the master.

But the old airman was shaking his head. "Naw, thanks for the thought, Honey, but technically I'm supposed to be rusty and this is a windy, nighttime approach, and the fact is, I trust you more than I do me."

She turned and smiled at him. "Really?"

"Yeah. Really. I taught you well."

"You did that, Dad. Your instructional style was a bit on the side of Attila the Hun, but all in all you're a master." Her throat tightened.

"Attila was a pilot?" he asked, pleased that she laughed in response.

Passing over the main buildings ablaze with light, they slowed steadily as Jennifer had done a half dozen times earlier in the day. The winds were kicking them around even with the added weight of the heavy Bell 412, the twin-engine civilian equivalent of the venerable Huey helicopter, and she was almost fighting the controls at times to keep on a safe approach path.

One other helicopter was lashed to the deck of the heliport, also one of theirs, the crew presumably already checked into the hotel.

Two ground crewmen were waiting, shielding their eyes against the serious glare of the landing lights, the 412's blades kicking up an additional miniature hurricane as they supported the ship's weight in a momentary hover as she descended straight down. Jennifer all but slammed the skids in place on the concrete pad to preclude any more up-and-down or sideways gyrations, and flashed a thumbs-up to the two men as they ran forward to attach tiedown chains to her skids.

"Nice job," Sven beamed. "Now let's go do some serious celebrating."

He opened the door and swung his leg over the side just as the helicopter and the island it was sitting on lurched to the right. Jennifer looked over but Sven was gone from view and she heard a dull thud as he fell the relatively short distance to the ramp on his side.

"Damnit!" could be heard quite clearly over the wind. In a second he popped up in the doorway, brushing himself off and looking angry.

"Something on that goddamned doorsill caught my foot."

"Dad . . ."

"You need to have maintenance check it out when we get back. Damn thing's dangerous."

It was easier to agree at moments like this and she nodded and changed the subject. "Did you feel that tremor?"

"When?"

"Just when you were tumbling out."

"No."

"That's one of those that Doug's been . . ." She paused, alarmed at how easily his name had slipped out.

"Doug's been what?"

"The ones he's been warning about. What we discussed earlier."

"Oh, that. We're always having little quakes up here. Trust a seismologist to get excited each time a heavy truck rumbles by."

Jennifer stepped to the ramp, feeling a deep, distant rumbling every few seconds and a faint noise on the wind she'd never heard before.

"What *is* that, Dad? That sound?"

He stopped and listened, pointing to the west. "Whatever it is, it's coming from over there. Some sort of heavy shuddering. Feels like really heavy surf."

Chapter 18

Right on schedule, Lindy O'Brien acquired her carefully planned migraine.

Her acting out of the onset of the pain and the reported visual disruptions were dramatic enough for an Academy Award nomination and it instantly won her the right to be left alone in her room all evening.

Governor Frank O'Brien was used to his daughter's histrionics, and sometimes secretly proud of her masterful levels of manipulation, even when he had to be openly disapproving. What neither he nor her mother had any use for were what he called her "hooker costumes," some of which she loved to bring secretly in a slightly oversize purse, arriving at some official function with the first family conservatively attired only to emerge from the ladies' room in mid-reception looking like a slutty teenage rock star in a tit tube and a leather micromini over a thong. The fact that it embarrassed her parents was clearly understood to be her goal, but despite the first family's attempts to ignore such stunts, she kept on pulling them—to the delight of the media.

But tonight she had planned a good escape to be with friends who had convinced their parents to let them come along.

One of the state troopers accompanied the governor and his wife when Mick Walker appeared at the door of the suite to escort them downstairs. The other trooper was issued strict instructions to guard the door and keep the first tart—as the troopers privately called her—safely inside.

"For tonight, young lady," Mrs. O'Brien said, "consider this room to be a nunnery."

"Whatever, Mom," she'd said, eyes closed in mock pain beneath a hot towel. "I'm in no shape to party, anyway."

Precisely twenty minutes later an unexpected room service order arrived, delivered by a crisply dressed young waiter who almost looked too young to be working at a casino hotel. The trooper, being an experienced cop, considered checking the young man's ID, but this was, after all, an opening night, and he decided to let it ride. The governor was not fond of disruptions, and arresting an underage kid would cause a large one. He

carefully checked the contents of the cart and frisked the young waiter before knocking on the door to confirm Lindy had ordered the meal. Her muffled voice swore at him, directing the waiter to set the table, and the young
man hurriedly pushed his service cart inside and started transferring everything to the large banquet table in the sitting room of the suite. Satisfied all
was safe, the trooper resumed his post in the hallway, leaving the door open
and watching carefully as the waiter pushed the empty cart past him a few
minutes later on his way to the service elevator. The trooper resecured the
door and resumed his post, unaware of the extra effort it was taking for the
waiter to push the cart down the corridor.

Once in the elevator with the doors closed, the young man let out a small
victory whoop and the tablecloth started giggling. Lindy O'Brien yanked
the linen covering aside with a large grin and pulled herself out with his help
as the elevator stopped on the fourth floor, as planned.

"Everyone's there, Lindy," he told her. She threw her arms around him
and gave him a quick, probing kiss he hadn't expected. "You were really
great, Davie! Thanks. This is gonna be a way cool evening."

Behind her on the sixth floor, the door to her room was closed, the requisite pillows subbing for her body were under the covers, but she knew it
wasn't needed. Her parents knew her moods, and she knew theirs. The like-
lihood of their even entering the room after an evening of partying was mi-
nuscule.

CASCADIA CONVENTION CENTER

Doug pulled up the collar of his overcoat against the twenty-five-knot
winds and glanced around to make sure no one was following. Slipping
away from the employee Walker had apparently assigned to keep him at
bay had been a relatively simple process of heading for the men's room
and turning through a side door unobserved. But he hadn't been fully prepared for the long walk in forty-degree temperatures and the resulting
windchill.

The printed program he'd seen pegged the opening VIP dinner at 7 in the
convention center, and the prideful maps of the island posted everywhere
had made that building easy to find. But for the location of a major event in
a half hour, the place was strangely quiet, with only a couple of service cars
parked in front and two men wandering around the lobby area.

There was a small building with a convenient overhang at one end of the
convention center plaza, and Doug molded himself into the lee of an alcove
to answer an incoming call. Sanjay was on the other end.

"Doug, Terry is back in position already, on his own, and the data he's transmitting is frightening. There are microquakes now that you won't feel there and the frequency is becoming almost predictable."

"What are you saying?"

"It's going to break, Doug. Either that part of the subduction zone or the whole thing. We can't be more than a few hours away."

"Anything from Menlo Park?"

"No. I've sent them everything. They're thinking and they're worried, but we're told to stand pat and wait. Have you gotten to the governor yet?"

"No. I'm still trying. Have you heard from Harper?"

"No."

"You have his cell phone number?"

Sanjay passed the digits and Doug forced them into his short-term memory.

"Okay. I'll call you back."

He punched in the number, expecting nothing, but Bill Harper's voice responded, low and tense.

"Bill, Doug Lam. Thank God. Where are you?"

"Waiting for the ferry to Cascadia Island. I'm headed over to find the governor. You still in the lab?"

"No, I'm already on the island trying to do the same thing. Mick Walker is trying to keep me away from himself and the governor. When will you be over here?"

"I don't know. The ferry is here and the crew had one hell of a time landing it. The first officer briefed everyone a minute ago that we'll all have to stay seated on the passage, and the captain walked by looking ashen, so I'm not even sure I can get there."

"Bill, please listen. I just got a briefing from the lab. With or without O'Brien, you're the emergency services director, and you can issue an alert."

"Doug, we've been over this—"

"Listen, man! This is deadly serious." He passed the latest information on the progression of the microquakes and the progressive change in frequency and magnitude. "Remember the sequence we went over much earlier? It's following the blueprint. Like labor pains, they're coming faster now and delivery is imminent. Our guy Terry even suspects there may have been some subsidence on the coast already."

"What?"

"He says he saw waves hitting above where they should be on his tide tables, just thirty minutes ago. Bill, *please!* I . . . must not overstate what my superiors in Menlo Park are going to do, but they are strongly, at this moment, considering issuing a prediction and warning. But we can't wait!"

There was a long silence from Harper's side.

"You know what scares me, Doug, maybe even more than the possibility of the main subduction quake?"

"What?"

"You saying that it could set off a host of the surface faults we've found all over the Northwest. I agree any of them could be devastating, and especially that one right through downtown Seattle."

"That's where Bellingham came from, Bill."

"I think you're probably right."

"Bill, be brave. Issue something. Save a few thousand lives. You'll sleep better."

"I'll call you back."

Doug refolded the cell phone and stepped out of the alcove, setting his sights on the convention center lobby. Usually he loved any sort of field work away from the lab, but this was shaping up to be perhaps the strangest night of his career, and he was angry with himself over the lack of a precise plan to follow.

The two men he'd noticed in the lobby were looking at something on the floor, and Doug's curiosity took over, momentarily subverting his anxiety over Bill Harper's decision. He stepped onto the walkway and headed toward them, figuring they wouldn't have been briefed on keeping a lone, wandering guest at bay.

CASCADIA ISLAND HOTEL

Jennifer replaced the house phone in frustration. Sven had already headed for his suite and she was clutching the key card for her room with the intention to get there as quickly as possible and change. But the need to confront Doug was too acute to wait, and now he wasn't answering.

The banquet was to begin in an hour and the location, they'd been told by the desk clerk, had been changed to the casino, which somehow seemed odd. But her thoughts were centered on Doug, and he would undoubtedly be there—although precisely what he was doing on the island to begin with was puzzling. He'd told her dispatcher he'd been invited by Walker himself, but she wondered about that explanation. Even though Doug's carefully ordered approach to things wasn't the hallmark of someone who could change directions and plans quickly, he was capable of thinking on his feet, and the excuse he'd given her pilot could have been a lie. He probably intended to confront Mick Walker about the earthquakes, but whatever his reason, it took a distant second place to her determination to hear how a

week of lies while he was cruising with his estranged wife could spell anything but the end of their relationship.

Or maybe she just wanted to scream at him from pent-up frustration
over his reluctance to commit to her. Letting events control her had been a
lifelong phobia. Logic dictated caution, but her emotions were holding
logic hostage, and the only certainty she could fish from the whirlpool of
her thoughts was that finding and confronting him would somehow be a
means of regaining control of her future. Either they were going to be committed lovers eternally honest with each other, or they were going to be history.

He'll be at the banquet, she concluded, and there was just enough time to
get dressed and meet the shuttle at the hotel entrance. Her mission refined
and targeted, she hurried to the elevators.

EASTERN END OF CASCADIA ISLAND

Lester Brown motioned his two compatriots out of the shadows where
they'd been crouching and waiting for his signal. Jimmy, his twenty-three-
year-old cousin, was strong as an ox but more than a bit dense, and Bull, his
longtime friend, was keeping Jimmy under tight control.

Jimmy and Bull ran across the service road and slid into place behind the
small concrete structure which Lester had been examining.

"Is this the right one?" Bull asked.

"I think so," Lester replied. "It's in the right place, but we've got to get inside to be sure."

Jimmy started to move and Bull pulled him down. "Not yet. Lester is running this."

Jimmy looked embarrassed, the contrite expression visible even in the
poorly reflected light of a distant street lamp. "Sorry, guys." He pulled out
his package of chewing tobacco and cut off a disgustingly large slice, a habit
Lester detested. But now was not the time for a debate on the merits of tobacco, Lester thought, and if the kid needed his comforts to stay calm, so
much the better.

"All right," Lester said. "First, we make sure this is the right thing. I'll
need that crowbar to break the lock."

Bull handed it over, knowing he'd eventually end up having Jimmy do
most of the work if it didn't pop off quickly.

"How about alarms, Lester?" Bull asked. "Any chance this thing has bur-
glar alarms?"

Lester grinned. "That's why having nearly a hundred members of our tribe employed over here helped a lot. One of the guys who built this thing is married to my sister. Took me a bottle of tequila, but he confirmed there are no alarms."

Only Lester had handled explosives before, and while Bull was nervous, Jimmy was both terrified and excited. That made him dangerous. Bull had strict instructions on when to pull Jimmy a safe distance away while Lester finished the first of the jobs they were there to conclude, but he was already worried about the wisdom of bringing him.

PLEASANTON, CALIFORNIA

"Ralph? She's headed to Washington state. I don't know why, but I had a friend in Portland watch her on arrival, and she did a very professional job of ditching him. He found her trail later on, however. She rented a car and he got a tracking device on it before she got across the bridge. She's near Centralia headed north on I-5."

"Is she alone?"

"Yes. You want me to keep on this? I assume you do?"

"Yes, Bill. I'll handle any expenses."

"You kidding, man? What you did for me in '81 pays for this, okay?"

"You were wrongly accused, Bill."

"Yeah, but mister hotshot lawyer was too softhearted to send the poor traumatized spook a bill for saving his career."

"I never believed you were working for the KGB."

"I wasn't. Their pay was far too lousy."

Chapter 19

Reilly Shelton polished off another Diet Coke and crumpled the can. He tossed it into the wastebasket as he stood and shook himself, loosening up, like a prizefighter preparing to enter the ring.

He gave the castoff order and went through his checklist to make sure all doors were showing green and watertight, then waited for the all-clear from each station before pulling the engines to idle and taking the transmissions to neutral, then reverse. With only one wheelhouse on one end of the boat, nosing in and backing out from each slip was standard, and he slipped the levers into reverse now and throttled up, feeling the boat respond as the stern poked deeper into the turbulent waves on the other side of the break-water. Already rolling and yawing, he pulled back a tenth of a mile before putting the engines in forward and powering around toward the island, knowing the wind would be trying to blow him back toward the peninsula slip.

The channel was even more brutal than before and he kept the engines at full throttle to minimize the time the passengers had to be subjected to such stomach-roiling gyrations, yet it seemed to take forever before the island slip was just ahead of him.

"How're you going to do this one?" his first officer asked.

Reilly glanced at him, too worried to toss off any sharp retorts or play the all-knowing captain.

"I'm . . . going to power us in as fast as possible and then full-reverse her once we're in the more protected area of the lead-in pilings."

"Okay."

The drift angles were alarming, he thought, the wind so stiff from the southwest that he was having to steer almost west to move northwest.

The two lines of lead-in pilings sat like a welcoming Y leading into the more narrow set of pilings firmed up by concrete stanchions that led to the actual snug-harbor protection of the slot into which the bow of the MV *Quaalatch* was designed to fit. His mistake the last time in had been to undercorrect for the wind and drift too far to the right. Each time, with Mick

Walker and everyone presumably watching, he'd had to back the ferry up and start again, making it on the third try. This time he was going to nail it on the first try.

"A bit fast, aren't we?" the first mate, Dennis, asked as the GPS screen showed them moving at twelve knots within the hundred-yard arc of the dock.

"I'm not worried about wake," Reilly said, not understanding the cautionary question.

Okay, steer more left, point her right at the concrete stanchion, and at the last second I'll come twenty degrees right and go into full reverse.

It was working. This time the rows of pilings and the ultimate destination were remaining right where he wanted them to stay in the perspective of the bridge windows, even if the boat was rolling fifteen degrees left and right with every major wave. The howling of the twenty-five-knot, or better, steady wind and the shudder of an occasional thirty-five-knot gust had long since rattled him and become expected complications, but there was a new sound now, and he recognized the rhythmic banging as a louder form of what he'd been hearing back at the dock and even earlier in the day.

Only this time it was disturbingly loud and sustained, and actually vibrating the entire boat.

"What the hell is that?" Dennis asked, his voice rising with alarm. "Have we run aground?"

Concentrate! Almost at the turn point, Reilly told himself, ignoring the cry of alarm and the disturbing vibrations as he counted down to the appropriate moment to turn the wheel to the right.

"Skipper, I think we're scraping the bottom!"

"No we're not! It's an earthquake. Be quiet!"

It was a tight maneuver only if it was delayed. All thoughts about the warnings the boatbuilder had included in the operations manual about the maximum vibrations various systems could take before knocking computerized controls offline had been read and forgotten.

Ten seconds more.

The shaking and banging reached a crescendo just as a loud buzzer sounded and a red light illuminated on the dash panel. No, he thought, it was two—no, three—alarms, and more red lights. He glanced down and back up again too quickly, not taking enough time to read which lights were involved and what they were trying to tell him. He didn't have time. He was too busy getting ready to execute a tight maneuver.

It was time. Reilly spun the wheel to the right sharply as he gathered the throttles in hand and pulled them to idle, preparing to reverse engines and power up.

Nothing happened.

The boat wasn't turning, and the engines were continuing at high power in forward, and none of that made sense. It was like a veteran conductor giving a downbeat to his orchestra and hearing nothing in response.

Reilly looked in disbelief, finally reading the words on one of the red lights: "Hydraulic Steering."

I've lost steering?

The concrete buttress he'd aimed for was less than a hundred feet ahead of them now, the boat moving at twelve knots straight for it. The emergency steering system would take several seconds to engage, and he reached for that emergency panel while still turning the wheel further right, aware the boat was neither responding nor likely to.

But it wasn't just the steering.

Damnit! The engines!

Once again he tried to pull the throttles to idle, realizing with a sick feeling that even if they responded, it was too late. Somehow the huge diesels had disconnected from the electronic controls and were still propelling the boat forward, and he'd lost precious seconds in stopping them. He lunged for the emergency engine-stop buttons and came down hard on them simultaneously, feeling the engines suddenly wind down to zero, the propellers slowing and even providing a little drag. He could feel the boat begin to lose momentum.

But it was going to be too little, too late.

The rudder was still commanding straight ahead, and the concrete piling was only fifty feet away, dead on.

The emergency rudder-control system suddenly came on line, a green light illuminating in front of him. He could feel the rudder's sudden swing to the right, shoving the stern of the boat left.

Slowly, the concrete piling began to move left in the bridge windows as they closed on it.

There was a crash alarm on the bridge, a large red button that would sound an alarm no passenger had been briefed to interpret, and he smashed it down now with the palm of his hand as he kept turning the wheel to the right, watching the nightmare unfold as the steel hull closed on the concrete, catching the edge of it at the forward left quarter of the bow section, a spot never designed to touch a dock or anything else. Suddenly pieces of concrete and metal were flying through the sky; metal groaned and ripped as the amazing momentum of the vessel kept it moving forward. The buttress peeled away the steel skin of the ferry like a giant can opener, exposing watertight compartments to the sea, rending the left forward side of the ship from below the car deck up through the VIP level. The progress of the disintegration was cutting deeply into the side, far enough to reach the hull where it sloped inward down to the waterline.

The first mate had tried to brace himself, but he was thrown forward into the dash panel while Reilly hung on to the wheel, the klaxon alarm blaring in the background. Reilly could see the frightened expressions on the faces of the dock crew as they watched helplessly in the distance, and when the boat's forward momentum had been spent in the act of fatally splitting the left forward hull, he realized they were being swept eastward, away from the dock.

The flood alarms were going off progressively on the left forward side of the boat as a pronounced list in the same direction confirmed they were taking on water at a frightening rate.

"Oh, God! What happened?" the first mate wanted to know. "I don't understand what happened!"

Reilly looked to the right, expecting the drift of the stricken boat to be stopped against the outboard right row of pilings, but there was a backwash current pushing them outward from the island, and they were going to miss that barrier and be swept toward the open channel, where the current would take them northbound. The water was forty-six degrees Fahrenheit and the depth several hundred feet by the rocky coastline. Chances of survival for anyone not in a boat would be very poor.

"We're in danger of capsizing, skipper!" the first mate said, his voice shrill.

"I know it." Reilly began punching at the engine controls, trying to restart either of the two diesels, but they weren't responding.

"What are your orders?" the first mate was asking. "Tell me what you want me to do!"

"Ah . . . we . . . ah . . . launch the . . . no, we call a mayday, and . . . ah . . . launch the lifeboats. Fast."

Reilly felt completely overwhelmed, drowning in the horror of the moment and all but paralyzed. The first mate was looking at him for wisdom and reassurance and salvation the same way he, Reilly, had always looked at the captains he'd sailed under.

"Okay, go down to the main deck, get everyone in their life jackets, get the other hands and start launching the boats. I'll call the mayday. Report back . . . ah, take the handheld. Keep me posted. I need a damage report."

"Damage report? We're listing ten degrees left and bow down twelve.

Can't you see that? The board right here says we've breached and flooded three compartments. The other ones appear to be holding and tight, but— look at the damned deck angle!"

"Yeah, damnit, I can see it."

"You aren't ordering me to open the flooded compartments and go in, are you?"

"No! Just . . . report back. Get moving!"

Dennis grabbed a radio and disappeared down the circular stairway as Reilly reached with a badly shaking hand for the marine radio and punched up channel 16.

"*Mayday, mayday, mayday,* this is the Motor Vessel *Quaalatch* just south-east of Cascadia Island. We've collided with an object and are taking on water. All available vessels please respond. We have one hundred twenty souls on board, including crew. *Mayday, mayday, mayday!*"

The automatic emergency GPS locator transmitter was on his left and he punched it on. He waited for a radio response from the mayday call, but it didn't come until his third try, just as the first mate called back on his handheld.

"Skipper, we're getting everyone in life jackets. At least a few of the passengers were hurt when the lounge was ripped open. Badly. I don't know how many, but there are at least a few terrible injuries . . ." Reilly could hear the first mate's voice catch and hear screaming voices in the background. "I'm gonna launch lifeboats one and two on the starboard side first before it gets too high. Is anyone coming?"

This is all my fault! Reilly thought, the words chilling him toward paralysis even more. He was hyperventilating, his legs shaking. The Coast Guard had called and were coming, weren't they? He didn't catch how far away. And the island had called. They had seen everything as he destroyed the dock and were trying to launch boats, or something. He couldn't quite recall.

He punched the radio button to reply to the first mate. "Yeah, someone's coming," he said, wondering how he had ever had the stupidity to think he was qualified to be the master of such a vessel.

CASCADIA ISLAND

Nearly five minutes after another, stronger earthquake had rumbled through the island, three cars pulled up in front of the mostly empty convention center. One of them quickly disgorged just the man Doug Lam had been waiting for.

Mick Walker was unmistakable even from the distance of the alcove where Doug had been taking shelter from the rain. The worried men he had talked to had told him the boss was on his way back.

The rain was intermittent now, but chilling nonetheless as Doug walked back across the drive, his mind flashing to Jennifer. She had left several strangely terse messages on his cell phone, and he'd started to worry about her tone, but there was too much else in limbo to focus on what he assumed was a continuation of her campaign to press him on their relationship. He called back anyway, but she didn't answer either her cell phone or room phone, and he left a message on her cell.

> Hi, Honey. I'm on the island, as you probably know. Walker invited me but I'm not here for the festivities, I'm here to speak with the governor. Please call me when you can. I know you and your dad are going to the opening dinner.

But something continued to nag at him. Something in her voice he'd never heard before.

Mick Walker was inside now with a very portly older man in a rumpled business suit and both were tracing the alarming split in the floor Doug had seen a few minutes earlier. Doug stopped momentarily at the curb, watching unseen as the two men exchanged animated conversation, pointing to the floor, then the wall. Walker was obviously upset, his face red and his gestures angry, and his portly companion appeared to be on the defensive.

If that guy had anything to do with designing this place, he's in deep trouble, Doug thought, the anonymous e-mail's contents playing in his mind. The chilling evidence that the e-mailer was right was at their feet, although there could be a less catastrophic explanation. But the split Doug had seen went from wall to wall and across the floor in a brand-new building, and the cause could easily be a major surface fault. If so, the convention center was toast.

And Walker still might not know.

Or maybe he'd known all along.

Doug wondered if the portly man was from the engineering firm, and whether he knew. He searched his own memory of the basic geology studies he'd seen before the construction had started, cursory summaries not based on actual seismic refraction data. It hadn't been the possibility of faults running through the rock that had chilled him, it was the cold, certain fact that someday a monstrous tsunami was going to sweep everything away while the island itself sank five to seven feet into the sea. Whether the place was a trigger point or not, someday the subduction quake would generate a tsunami that would wash away anything built on its surface.

Doug took a deep breath and pushed open the door, catching Mick Walker's attention almost immediately. A skunk waddling in would have triggered approximately the same look.

"Mick? Doug Lam," he said as he walked toward them. He could see Mick Walker mumble something to himself and then paste on an artificial smile, and he noticed the big developer was suddenly looking at anything but the gap at his feet.

"Well, Dr. Lam! I'm glad you took me up on the offer and came out." He reached out to shake Doug's hand, making no attempt to introduce the other man. "I'm quite busy at the moment. Why don't you let my driver take you over to the hotel, and—"

"Mick, I need to speak with you very, very urgently, and I need to speak to the governor, too."

Walker stopped, looking him in the eye and assessing the chances of getting rid of the interruption. They were obviously not good. He sighed and gave a quick nod. "Very well, let me introduce you to the master builder who designed this amazing complex," Mick said, with a touch of sarcasm in his tone. He announced Robert Nelms and watched him shake the seismologist's hand with the eagerness of a beaten dog taking a treat.

"I see you've got a serious foundation problem," Doug said, noting a quick, angry glance from Walker to Nelms.

Nelms nodded. Walker answered.

"Apparently," Mick said, trying unsuccessfully to sound unconcerned. "We've apparently had a construction insufficiency in the subfloor, which is what we were just discussing."

For a split second Doug considered revealing what he knew about the fault, but what *did* he know? At that point, very little, and ultimately Walker might be right. It might be just a subfloor issue—though the vertical rift in each wall all but ruled that out.

No, Doug cautioned himself. *Don't let them know you know until we're sure what's going on.*

But ignoring the obviously silly explanation was beyond him.

"That's a lot more than a subfloor problem," Doug said. "It's anything from a sudden washout of the underpinning ground beneath the foundation, or you've found a small, hopefully localized fault that's started moving with these earth tremors."

"Right," Mick answered, glowering at him. "I didn't realize you were also a soil engineer and an experienced builder, Dr. Lam, but I doubt you walked over here in the rain to analyze my construction problems."

"No," Doug replied evenly, "I came over here to tell you the latest seismological facts and beg you—and I do mean beg—to reconsider evacuating this island, despite the expense. The USGS is probably only minutes away from issuing that alert you demanded, and I can fill you in on why they're changing their minds."

There was a moment of silence between them in which Doug could almost sense the resistance in Mick Walker beginning to waver.

"All right, Doctor. You've got three minutes."

A cell phone rang at the same instant and Mick motioned for him to wait as he flipped it open and acknowledged what was apparently one of his people on the other end. Doug could see the blood drain from Mick's face as he straightened up slightly and swallowed, his eyes darting involuntarily in the direction of the hotel and the ferry landing.

"When? How?"

Robert Nelms moved closer to him, his curiosity piqued. "What is it?"

Mick raised a hand to silence him. "Jesus, what are we doing to get to them?"

Doug could hear the tense voice from the other end as it echoed into the deserted entry hall.

Mick's hand was over his eyes and rubbing his forehead. "Call the Coast Guard immediately, and get whatever rescue helicopters they have in the air." He snapped the phone closed and stood with his eyes on nothing, calculating the next move.

"What the hell was that, Mick?" Nelms insisted.

"My ferry. With a hundred of our guests aboard."

"What about it?"

"The bloody thing is sinking."

Mick turned and darted for the waiting car.

CASCADIA ISLAND HOTEL

Jennifer had been balancing on one leg and pulling on her pantyhose when an impressive tremor shook the hotel. She suppressed a momentary flurry of fear and grabbed at the bed for stability as she sat down, finishing the job of getting dressed after the shaking stopped. She was putting on the finishing touches when the room phone rang.

The tremor was a distant priority. She expected to hear Doug's voice on the other end, especially after leaving a dragnet of messages for him, and she felt her stomach tighten and her heart rate increase as she prepared to deal with him.

Instead, a man from Cascadia Operations was in her ear.

"Are you one of the helicopter pilots?"

His voice was tense, and there was a blare of radios and telephones in the background. The possibility that something bad had happened to one of their helicopters flashed through her mind as she answered.

"Yes . . . this is Jennifer Lindstrom, the president of Nightingale, the company that owns the two choppers on your helipad."

"We need you, now! Our ferry is sinking with over a hundred people on board, and they need help."

"What?"

He repeated the chilling message and she was almost too stunned to remember that she had no medical crewmembers with her, although her other crew had the usual pilot and nurses. She'd copied down their room numbers on arrival just in case, and she hung up now to call them with no success. A call to her father's room also went unanswered.

She stood for a second, trying to decide whether to change clothes or run out the door in yet another cocktail dress.

There was no time to change back. Jennifer grabbed her tote bag, stuffed her purse in, and pulled on her coat, bypassing the heels she'd planned to wear and slipping on the shoes she had worn in the cockpit. She cleared the door and ran down the corridor to the elevators, pulling out her cell phone and punching off the message alert she hadn't noticed, to clear the line for an immediate call to Norm Bryarly back in Seattle. He needed to be tearing up the phone lines looking for the other crew and Sven.

There was a limo at the front of the hotel waiting for someone else and she tumbled inside and commandeered the driver to take her to the heliport. The driver recognized her orders as too crisp and unyielding to brook an argument, and they were under way within seconds.

The helipad was all but deserted. She was the only crewmember present, and there was only one ground crewman and two of the company's helicopters, the Bell 412 and a 3-month-old AS 365 Dauphin. The Dauphin was the only one with an external hoist, and this would be a rescue. There was no time to refuel, but she calculated the Dauphin should have enough fuel for two hours in the air, although less if she had a lot of time at hover. The problem was the lack of a rescue crew to work the winch and take care of any injured. She had no idea what the ferry looked like, or whether there was room to safely set down on top of it, but she had to assume any rescue would be with a line and a basket, and she couldn't do it alone.

She stuck her head back in the limo, out of the stiff, cold wind.

"Get back to the hotel, please, and the second any of my crewmembers come out, bring them here! Also, call your operations and tell them I need several ground crewmen or I can't take off."

He nodded and burned away as soon as she had the door closed.

There were safety tethers holding each end of the rotor blades and she quickly removed and stowed them before sliding into the command seat and running the start sequence. Even sitting idle with the blades not in motion, the Dauphin was being shoved and jerked around by the high winds, and she knew well that taking off safely was not guaranteed in such conditions.

Her phone rang again with Norm on the other end and the news that the other pilot and one of the nurses were on the way out, but Sven wasn't answering the hotel room or cell phone.

"Norm, call Cascadia Operations, have them give you everything I need in the way of location and what's happening. We can't pluck a hundred people off a sinking ship, but maybe I can find a way to get the worst injured off. They did tell me there were serious injuries. And find out what the Coast Guard is sending."

They rang off and she concentrated on the preflight checklist as the lights of the limo came into view again and Gail Grisham tumbled out with her flight nurse, Ben Marcus. They started sprinting for the Dauphin.

"I need you both with me."

"Okay. Where? Copilot seat?" Gail asked.

Jennifer nodded. "Depending on what we find out there, I may need both of you to handle the hoist. We're going to have to make this up as we go along."

Gail was already climbing in and Ben had started throwing compartments open in the rear, searching out the lines and buckles he would need for a hoisted pickup. With all Nightingale's flight nurses trained in parajumper duties, he had everything from the emergency kit in place within two minutes and slid the door shut as he buckled himself in. Jennifer pulled the start trigger on the collective and waited for the first engine's rpm's to wind up. When both power plants were on line and the rotors at speed, she verified they had an aggressive thumbs-up signal from the ground crewman before turning her full attention to getting the helicopter off the ground without crashing.

Chapter 20

Bill Harper, director of emergency services for the state of Washington, realized the ferry was probably going to capsize.

He looked up from his kneeling position next to a gravely injured woman and tried to focus. He'd pulled on a life vest, but he knew it would be all but useless if he or anyone on the boat ended up in the water for more than a half hour. Hypothermia—a slow descent into unconsciousness and eventual death from dropping body temperature—was inevitable in forty-degree waters, even if they could swim clear of the wreckage.

The deck angle was getting steeper to the left and forward where the boat had slammed into the pilings, and a very small number of crewmembers were dashing back and forth and beginning the process of loading the lifeboats and launching them. Two boats were safely away carrying over forty people each, one of the lifeboats had been destroyed in the collision, and the last boat could carry the remainder of the passengers if everyone could walk.

But there were at least a half dozen too seriously injured to move on their own.

The physician kneeling on the other side of the woman was working as fast as he could to stop the severe bleeding from her mangled left leg. She was in shock, and he could tell at least four others were in similar condition.

There had been a beautiful couch in the forward left side area of the passenger deck and it had been full of guests when flying shards of disintegrating metal began cutting through the hull ripping the couch to shreds.

One of the crewmen—a young man who was wearing first-officer stripes—was bellowing at everyone to get aboard the last lifeboat. The physician Bill Harper was helping looked up and fixed the young man with an angry stare.

"Hey! You! Get over here!"

The young officer complied.

"Yes, sir?"

"Are you out of your mind? Look how many serious injuries we have in here. They can't walk to the goddamn boat, can they?"

"I . . . I'm just trying to save as many as . . ." His voice trailed off as the meaning crystallized in all their minds.

The doctor swallowed hard and nodded. "Okay, get the able-bodied loaded, but don't leave us until we've brought you as many as we can transport. Are there any other rafts?"

"Yes, sir. Several of them. And if I don't launch this last boat before we capsize, it'll be too late."

The first officer moved quickly toward the raised rear of the sinking vessel as the sound of a helicopter began to make itself known over the sounds of wind and confusion.

From the cockpit of the Dauphin, the sight of the mangled ferry heeled over on its port bow and drifting northward was sickening. Even if the boat had been level and in calm seas there wasn't enough room to land on the upper deck, but now, with its right stern sticking partially out of the water and a deck angle of fifteen degrees, Jennifer was going to have a battle getting close enough to pull anyone off.

She could see the remaining lifeboat on the ferry, and she could see people boarding it.

Whatever they did was going to be dangerous. Nighttime sea rescues were always treacherous, even for veteran helicopter pilots, but the black-hole effect could kill. There were enough lights, however, along the coastal highway and the communities there to form a horizon, and the lights from Cascadia Island were bright as well. Between the two of them—as long as she kept pointing south—there was enough of a horizon line to prevent spatial disorientation.

She turned to Ben, who was standing just behind and between the pilot seats.

"Can you go down on the sling and triage the situation?" He nodded without hesitation.

"I'll take the basket. If there's no one who needs it, I'll ride it back up. Can you hold her steady?"

"We'll be gyrating and it won't be a pretty hover."

He waved it away, knowing what he had to do trumped any fear. "Let me get ready. Two minutes, and I'll use the remote control from the basket to let myself down."

Gail was already climbing out of the left seat. "I'll back you up on the winch controls. You have your handheld and headset?"

"In place," Ben replied, tapping his helmet. Jennifer switched on the intercom and verified they could talk to each other.

He made the final adjustments before climbing into the basket and belting himself in place. Gail helped him swing the pivoted winch arm out far enough to clear the body of the helicopter, and he started motoring himself downward.

In the cockpit, Jennifer set up her hover by reference to the horizon, using her peripheral vision to track the pitching ferry below. She held the Dauphin into the wind as she approached from the right side of the boat.

The winds had to be nearly forty knots, and Ben and the basket were being blown out partially behind the Dauphin and twisting slightly. But it was steady enough, and as he descended almost to deck height, she moved him in over the edge of the rear deck and felt the winch whine once again as he plopped the basket aboard, grounding it before clambering out and quickly releasing the hook. Gail motored the line part-way back in while Jennifer took the Dauphin backward, downwind, gaining a few feet of altitude and waiting. She'd lost awareness of the fact that her hands and feet were in constant motion adjusting the controls. It was simply a part of her, and the biggest problem was simply seeing where she wanted the machine to stay, not keeping it there. Flying into a stiff wind was actually simpler than hovering in still air. It was as if she were flying in formation with the boat below.

On the sloping, slippery deck below, Ben raced inside with the young officer who'd been waving them in. He went from victim to victim, spoke quickly to the physician, and then punched his radio.

"Okay, we've got six critical injuries, two of whom appear unstable . . . at least two . . ." He echoed the physician's warning. "I'm going to start strapping the first one in and send her up. They're telling me the Coast Guard can't send any helicopters. I think we're on our own."

"I hadn't heard," Jennifer replied, feeling the increase in pressure. They were the only game in town. "Let's get these two unstable ones to shore and come back for the others. They're supposed to have the ambulance ready back at the helipad."

With the officer's help, Ben lifted the worst of the injured into the basket, strapping her down as tightly as he dared. They retraced their steps to the tilted upper deck, Ben losing his footing twice before getting the basket positioned and punching his transmit button.

They had the line winched in and the patient aboard within two minutes as Ben disappeared inside for the next litter.

Jennifer glanced over her left shoulder, aware of Gail using the training they'd all received as emergency medics. She had started oxygen and was hanging an IV and administering morphine, but it was obvious the victim needed a surgeon's immediate attention.

With Ben in position with the second patient, Jennifer held the Dauphin as steady as possible as Gail began winching the basket up. The winds had been mostly steady and her control of the helicopter had been aided by that, but a patch of turbulence had begun to roil the air the Dauphin was flying in and Jennifer's control movements became more pronounced and sporadic as she fought to stay in the same position relative to the pitching deck of the crippled boat below.

Ben was holding on to the rescue litter as it rose, trying to minimize its tendency to twist and turn, but the boat suddenly fell out from beneath his feet in a wave trough and instinct caused him to hold on to the basket a second too long. He let go and dropped about two feet to the slippery, angled deck, but his feet slid out from under him and he began flailing toward the edge of the boat. Gail watched him hang for a split second as he grabbed at the ferry's rail, but his grip faltered and he went over the side.

"Shit! Jennifer, Ben's overboard!"

"Where? Do you see him?"

"Not yet. Let me get this patient in . . ."

Jennifer moved the Dauphin aft of the ship, working the Night Sun searchlight around toward the stern. The high waves and spray were difficult to see through, and she had to keep raising her head to reestablish where the horizon was to keep from flying into the ship or the water, but finally a head appeared and she could see Ben on the surface, behind the ferry, bobbing in what were now nearly twenty-five-foot seas.

"I see him," she called. "Ben, can you hear me?"

There was no reply for a few seconds and she wondered if the new radios weren't waterproof after all, but the transmitter was keyed and Ben's strained voice came over the frequency.

"I'm here! I'm here . . . behind the ship."

"We see you. Hang on. We'll get the patient in and lower the basket."

"I'm here behind the boat," he said again. "I say again . . . I'm here behind the boat."

"I don't think he hears you, Jen," Gail said. The sound of the winch was audible through her headset and Jennifer dared a quick glance around to see Gail struggling to pull the basket inside. Within a minute the basket was free and out of the cabin again and on its way down, but without the weight of a person inside, it was swinging wildly.

"Drop it in and drag it to him. I'll guide you!" Gail said.

"Roger."

"I have him . . . don't worry. Stay on this heading, keep coming forward slowly. The basket's almost down. Okay, it's in the water, keep coming . . . you're twenty feet away from him . . . right twenty degrees now and keep coming . . . fifteen feet to go . . . keep coming . . . ten feet . . . Ben, if you can hear me, *turn around! The basket is behind you!*"

"Does he see it coming?"

"I don't think so . . . five feet, slow down, Jen."

"How's my altitude?"

"Fine but slow your forward speed. Slow down! Oh, Christ, we hit him."

"What do you mean?" Jennifer called. *"What do you mean?"*

"The basket hit him from behind. God, he's facedown. I've gotta go in."

"Gail, no!"

"He's unconscious. Get me lower!"

"I'm coming down . . . I'll take us to wave top."

"I'm bringing the basket up. I'm going to ride the line down to get him."

Moving faster than she ever thought she could, Gail yanked the empty rescue basket in and unsnapped it, substituting the hook on the harness she'd wiggled into. She snapped an empty harness to the same hook and pushed away from the helicopter.

"Okay, Jen, use the cockpit winch control and take me down."

The wave tops were barely five feet beneath them and she took the first crest head-on, her helmet filling with water as she fought to see where Ben had gone.

"Gail? Status?" Jennifer was calling.

"That's good right there! Now, lift the whole chopper a few feet and come forward. I can't see him!"

"I'm coming up ten feet," Jennifer said, frightened of the disorienting effect of being at wave height with the powerful searchlight bouncing off every wave. She desperately needed to see the horizon line to maintain contact with the lights on shore and on the island. Otherwise it would be too easy to roll off and dig the rotor into the water, killing them all.

In still air, pivoting a helicopter around 360 degrees was a small challenge, but doing the same thing in the teeth of a forty-five-mile-an-hour gale and sitting a few feet above a mountainous sea state was impossible. She'd have to back up.

"*There!* There he is, at our nine o'clock . . . our nine o'clock . . . sidestep left!"

"I'm doing it."

"*Stop!* I'm there . . . winch me down three feet or so."

Gail plunked into the water and reached for Ben, grabbing enough of his jacket to pull him to her. His harness was secure and she snapped the safety line to hers and tried to keep his head out of the water, but every other wave seemed mountainous and she was swallowing a lot of seawater involuntarily.

"I've got him!" she managed to say. "Bring us up."

Jennifer brought the Dauphin up slowly, moving her left hand from the collective to the winch and back as fast as possible, until the welcome news reached her that they were aboard.

"How is he?"

"He's waking up! I think he'll be okay."

"And the patients?"

"Don't know. I'm working on it."

"We're headed back to the island, Gail. There's supposed to be an emergency team waiting."

She heard the big doors being closed in the rear, and the roar of the rotor blades and the sea subsided. The lights of the island and even the beacon on the heliport were clearly visible some two miles away and she made the inbound radio call as she pitched the Dauphin forward smartly and accelerated.

CASCADIA ISLAND CASINO

Nothing quite irritated Frank O'Brien like a state trooper handing him a cell phone he didn't care to answer. There was a party about to start with a lot of people looking forward to fawning over him and the last thing he needed was some bureaucratic distraction. He rather fancied himself a chairman of the board of the corporation called Washington, and chairmen hired chief operating officers to take care of the minutiae.

Usually the men who guarded the governor went to great lengths to avoid the ass-chewing that always followed an unwanted call, but this time it was clearly unavoidable, since the voice on the other end belonged to the chief of the State Patrol.

O'Brien rolled his eyes as he gave in and took the proffered handset. He barked a none-too-friendly hello while the first lady pretended not to hear.

"What the hell is it, Tom?"

"Governor, I've got to get your approval on a few things for this Stage Two alert you ordered."

"What alert?"

"The . . . message I just got from the Emergency Communications Center that we've activated a Stage Two alert for all coastal areas of Washington and may go to a Stage One evacuation, because of an impending great quake."

"*What?* I didn't order any alert!"

"Well . . . it's an official communication . . ."

"From whom, for God's sake?"

"I told you, sir. The Emergency Communications Center, which would mean the director, Bill Harper. I mean, I'm assuming it came from him."

"And you assumed I ordered it?"

"Yes, sir. That's part of the plan."

"Well, you assumed wrong, Tom. I didn't order a damned alert. In fact, I am completely unconvinced we've got an emergency here."

"Sir, we've had big damage in Bellingham, as you know, and moderate damage in Port Angeles about thirty minutes ago, and my troopers are working a wild array of accidents all over western Washington that we strongly suspect resulted from the roads shaking. We've got roads out in a few places and I'm already calling in some of my reserves. We've also got a suspect bridge on I-5 near Fort Lewis that may have to be closed, shutting all north-south traffic down. So if there's a chance in hell a big one could hit, I've got a major battle plan to put together and I'd rather err on the side of caution and start now."

"Jesus, Tom! Are you sure you're not overreacting?"

"Yes, sir, I'm sure."

"Okay, go ahead and do whatever you think you need to while I track down Harper and fire his ass."

"So, are we at a Stage Two, then?"

"Hell, I don't know. I'm only the goddamned governor, and apparently I don't have a need to know, or a right to dissent. Ask Harper."

He refolded the phone and lateraled it back to the worried-looking trooper, pulled out his own cell phone, then thought better of it and put it away. The problem could sort itself out. He'd chew out Harper later.

One of Mick Walker's staff had been waiting patiently, a shapely brunette with a lovely smile in a white dress. He'd paid as much attention to

her as he could with Mrs. O'Brien nearby, but the first lady had now been escorted to the head table in the ballroom ahead and he was free to charm at
will.

"Penny, was it?"

"Yes, Governor. Are you ready to come in?"

He looked around conspiratorially, resisting the temptation to counter
with a bawdy affirmation. *Am I ready to come in? Indeed I am, young lady!* he
thought, keeping his canary-eating smile under control.

"Well, tell you what. This has already been a difficult evening and there
are a lot of serious decisions weighing on me, and it gets really . . . hard
sometimes," he said, rubbing his forehead. "I don't mean to burden you
with my troubles . . ."

"No, no! That's perfectly all right. Is there anything I can bring you, or do
for you?"

"Well . . . I'd really rather not go to the head table just yet. I don't know
how much time you have to spend babysitting me . . ."

"I'm all yours, Governor," Penny said, causing another unseen bite of his
tongue. "What would you like?"

You, naked on a fuzzy rug! he thought, keeping his expression pained and
serious and keeping his eyes off her cleavage.

He sighed. "Penny, would it be an imposition to ask if you could please
save me from the chitchat for a short while?"

She looked surprised, but recovered quickly. "You mean, in there?"

"Yes. The head table thing. Everyone assumes I need to be chatted up."

"Of course, Governor."

"Is there a—I don't know, maybe a private area where we could go so I
could relax for a few minutes? Maybe a skybox or something?"

"A . . . skybox?"

"You know, like in a football stadium?" He laughed as engagingly as he
could. "No, I guess not. Bad analogy."

She looked around, whether to see if anyone was listening or to figure
out an answer to his question, he couldn't be sure. She looked back and
smiled suddenly. "Wait! I know a room I think you'll like."

"I know I'll like it if you're in it," he said, still rubbing his forehead but
watching her reaction. She was blushing, right on cue, but she didn't back
away. Instead, she cleared her throat and started again. "Governor, we have
a brand-new—well, everything's brand new of course—but our VIP lounge
is just around the corner."

"Great. Let's go. Can we get some wine there?"

"I'm sure we can, sir. Of course, they'll be ready to serve dinner in maybe
ten minutes."

"That's okay. Politicians are supposed to be importantly late."

She led and he followed, admiring the way her hips were swaying and pleased that she'd caught a glimpse of his interest in the hallway mirror.

"By the way, Penny," he said.

She turned and smiled over her shoulder, "Yes, sir?"

"Please call me Frank."

Chapter 21

The explanation that Mary Willis, one of the last guests to check in, had lost her ID was good enough for the front-desk manager. This was, after all, their opening night, and she had apparently arrived on the last successful ferry run and taken the bus tour before appearing with her invitation packet. And, he thought, he was carefully trained to make judgment calls, even if the Patriot Act did require a photo ID of every hotel guest. Besides, far too much was already going wrong to stress out over something so insignificant, especially where a lovely young woman was concerned.

And she had smiled at all the right moments and did not seem nervous, so she passed.

"We're delighted to have you with us, Ms. Willis," he said without missing a beat. He knew better than say anything about their sinking ferry. "We have you in the west wing, and here are your key cards and your information packet, and the opening dinner will be starting just a few minutes from now next door at the Casino Ballroom. We have people posted along the way to guide you over."

"Thank you." She started to turn away, then turned back. "One other thing . . . could you tell me if a Dr. Douglas Lam is in the hotel yet?" It was a long shot, she thought, but worth a try. He'd left his lab in Seattle, and his staff thought he might be headed to the island. The information had changed her plans.

The manager entered a few keystrokes in the computer and nodded. "Dr. Lam checked in just a while ago. If you'd like to pick up one of the house phones, the operator will connect you."

"Thank you," she replied, smiling at him.

A voice was calling someone from across the lobby, and with a start she heard her name.

"Diane!" a man bellowed. "How *are* you?"

She jumped slightly but forced herself not to turn and look, bending instead to pick up her bag as another woman answered the shout from somewhere behind her.

Diane Lacombe suppressed the flutter of fright in her stomach and walked as calmly as she could toward the elevators, reminding herself of her assumed identity. The possibility that someone on the island would recognize her had crossed her mind very briefly, but the urgent pursuit of Douglas Lam had forced all other worries aside—including the possibility that one of Mick Walker's people—or Mick himself—might spot her.

Or someone less friendly, she thought suddenly, a rush of realization sweeping over her like a dizzy spell.

She rode quietly and stepped from the elevator onto her floor, hearing her heart pound and grateful the corridor was empty.

The door to her plush room was two doors down and she opened it quickly, stepped inside, and shut it behind her, standing still and breathing hard as her thoughts reconnected with a reality she'd shoved aside. She'd dropped out of sight in a panic, leaving a mess behind her with even her family thinking she was dead, all to get away from whoever was searching for what she had. All the way from San Francisco she'd alternated theories. Mick Walker might be responsible, she'd concluded at first, and, if so, her escape had been silly. He'd never harm her, and, in fact, only her apartment had been touched. But what if it was someone who'd invested in the island, or the worst possibility, what if it was her own employer? Whoever had tossed her apartment, if she'd wanted to let them find her as quickly as possible, the best method would have been to do exactly what she'd just done: blunder onto Cascadia Island.

The dark probability that Chadwick and Noble was involved was bubbling to the top of her cauldron of theories. And what if it went all the way to the top, and Robert Nelms was here? Was she walking into a trap she'd set for herself?

No, she concluded, unsuccessfully trying to lower her pulse rate with logic. *No one could know I was going to come here. I didn't even know myself until I reached Portland!*

Nevertheless, she still had the CD, and going to the formal dinner would be a foolhardy idea. Better to get on the phone and search for Doug Lam, or look for him carefully from the shadows.

It's almost seven. He'll be at the dinner, and even if I could find him without being recognized, I can't just go pull him out of there. She felt deflated to have come all this way only to have to sit around and wait for hours. This was a frustration she hadn't expected.

You didn't think this through! she chided herself. *This is the worst possible place to be telling Dr. Lam what you've found.*

There had been a bus tour of the island for everyone arriving on the ferry, and it had been startling to see how the barren rock she had thumped and searched and charted had been transformed into such a stunning resort. Not to mention some of the stranger aspects, like the massive concrete breakwater on the western end that had apparently just gone into operation in the past few days when a dam system holding back the surf was removed. It made the strangest noise.

Diane plunked herself on the bed and got up just as fast. She pulled up the phone and asked for Lam's room once again, and again there was no answer. She picked up the TV remote and sat, absently flipping on the set and punching through the channels until reaching a local newscast reporting the breaking news about a sinking private ferry and helicopter rescue in progress in the midst of a Pacific storm, the same ferry on which she'd just crossed the channel an hour before.

For no reason she could pinpoint, waiting was suddenly no longer an option, and she gathered her coat and purse and headed for the elevator.

CASCADIA ISLAND HELIPORT

Mick Walker was at the pilot-side of the Dauphin as soon as the doors began sliding open.

"Jennifer Lindstrom?" he said, shouting against the noise and the wind.

"Yes," she shouted back, nodding as well while she kept her eye on the instruments and looked around to verify that the patients were being unloaded into the waiting ambulance.

He extended his hand. "Thank you for rushing into service!"

"No problem. Can your clinic handle these people? They're critical!"

"I have two docs and more among my guests and we have a full operating room."

"What? Sorry."

"An operating room," he repeated into cupped hands.

She nodded. "We have to get back out there. There are four more injuries."

"I need to go with you and see the situation."

She was shaking her head before he finished the statement.

"No way! We don't have enough power for one more person and what we're doing is very dangerous."

"Look, I—"

She held up a hand to quiet him as she turned back to Gail.

"You have a dry flight suit in the 412?"

"Yes. Your dad is here . . . he's getting it."

"Okay. Keep that blanket on."

"Jen, Ben wants to stay with us."

"No!"

"He's insisting it was just a bump. I can go down and he could run the winch."

"He may have a concussion."

"Yeah, but who else is trained to do it?"

Jennifer saw her father pop up in the left door of the Dauphin and hand dry flight suits to Gail and Ben as she was answering. He looked at Jennifer, who was shaking her head no, fully aware of what he was thinking.

"What choice do we have, Honey?" he mouthed to Jennifer. "Ben's hurt and I'm not."

He was already climbing aboard as he looked at her again. "And I'm still the goddamned chairman, okay?"

"Dad—"

"Don't start. Gail can do the PJ work and I'll run the winch."

"We need a flight nurse!"

"And I'm not trained enough?" he said. "I pioneered this business. I'm probably a better emergency room doc than half of the licensed ones."

Mick Walker broke in again, hesitantly, and Jennifer turned to him.

"Mr. Walker, I'm sorry to be blunt but I'm in command and you can't go. Subject closed. What I do need you to do is get more rescue medevac helicopters on the way. Call Fort Lewis and ask for the MAST unit, call the Coast Guard, call the Air Force Reserve in Portland, and check with Nightingale Operations to see if there's anything more we can send. We need more help quickly."

He nodded, giving up the fight. "Okay." He let her reclose the pilot's door and backed away with his head down as he moved out of the range of the rotor blades. Jennifer looked around to see Gail strip off the last of her soaked underwear as Sven helped her into the dry flight suit and Ben waved from the sidelines where he'd been forcibly banished. She checked the fuel state again, verifying they had enough reserves, and motioned to the ground crew to clear everyone else away.

Once more the challenge was to match the forward tilt of the blades to the intense headwind so that the Dauphin wouldn't be blown backward or tilt over as soon as she had enough torque to lift off. It was an unconscious process in which the controls were in constant motion. She repositioned them approximately where they'd been on touchdown, and the helicopter leapt up from the pad, tilting dangerously to the left for a moment as she righted it and shot forward into the rain and darkness once more.

The master of the *Quaalatch* had taken one look at the damage to the passenger deck and all but folded up. With his first mate dashing back and forth among the four remaining injured, and the last of the remaining deck crew already gone in the third lifeboat, only seven remained aboard, including a man in a stained and wrinkled business suit who had looked up in puzzlement to see the captain standing in the doorway too stunned to speak.

There were two inflatable Zodiacs left, and the first mate had planned to use one for the final abandon-ship escape after all the injured were airlifted off. But Reilly hadn't formally approved the plan, or done much of anything besides make the initial call for help.

There was no question his job was gone. And there was no question the Coast Guard would crucify him for continuing the operation in the teeth of a storm, and for God knew what other violations. He would need a new line of work after all these years, since no one would trust him ever again on the bridge of a ship.

He had slipped back to the circular stairway and returned to the badly tilting bridge, noting on the electronic status board that the number of flooded compartments had not increased. The boat was heeled over to the left and toward the bow, but the angle wasn't getting worse, and there was a slim possibility that they might not sink after all.

Not that he cared if it did. Or more precisely, not that he cared whether he survived it. Wasn't a captain supposed to go down with his ship? He thought he understood why. It would be easier than a lifetime of guilt.

A Coast Guard station had been calling, hailing the MV *Quaalatch* by name, but for a few seconds he hadn't answered. Sitting in a self-pitying daze was easier.

The stunned paralysis had suddenly ended, however, and a part of his mind watched himself cross the bridge and scoop up the microphone to confirm their condition to an inbound cutter.

And, just as quickly, he was in motion back down the stairway, carrying a handheld radio and finding the first mate, moving to ready the Zodiac and double-checking the condition of the car deck. The battery-powered lights were beginning to fade, and he returned to the bridge to begin working on the engines, realizing belatedly that the emergency stop switches had never been reset. He went through the procedure and brought first the left, then the right engines to life, checking the transmission controls and finding them responsive. He slipped both engines in reverse, wondering if the screws were still in the water, and discovered that the boat was moving backward under its own power.

There were emergency pumps as well that had been forgotten, and he selected the appropriate valves now and began sucking at the water in the least damaged forward compartments as he formed a plan. With luck, he might be able to not only hold position, but maybe even power the crippled ferry back to the peninsula-side dock where a crane could keep it from sinking further.

There was no future in trying to go forward and forcing more water in. Reverse was the only option, and he got on the handheld to tell the first mate his plan just as the sound of the helicopter returned overhead.

CASCADIA ISLAND HELIPORT

By the time the Nightingale Dauphin had lifted off without him, Mick Walker was already in motion.

Talking quickly on the walkie-talkie function of his cell phone, he directed the driver first to the casino, then countermanded himself and headed for the ferry slip and the incomplete marina where the first of the lifeboats was supposed to be coming in. He climbed out of the car and took a quick look at the ashen face of the man he'd hired to manage the dockside facilities and the ferry slip. If he'd had time, he would have felt sorry for him.

"Where are they?"

The port master shook his head, uneasy being the bearer of bad news.

"They had to head for the peninsula side."

"What? Why?"

"There's no place to land them here, after the accident."

"What are you talking about?" Mick snapped. "We've got one dock completed in the yacht basin over there."

The port master swallowed hard, meeting his boss's irritated glare.

"The collision sank it, Mr. Walker."

"Really?"

He nodded.

"Well, then we're going to be dependent on the slip, I guess, which means we'll have to rent or lease another ferry, something from the Washington state fleet, perhaps. I'll need you to get on that instantly."

"Mr. Walker . . ." The man was looking almost panicked.

"I know it'll take a while to get it here, but if we can conclude the deal tonight and get a crew, we can have it here by tomorrow afternoon."

"Sir? Please!"

"What?"

"That won't work."

"Why not?"

"The . . . the impact dragged the outside pilings down and pulled up the cross braces, and then—"

"Get to the point!"

The port master winced and swallowed hard, meeting his boss's irritated glance as if he were going to be vaporized on the spot. "The ferry slip is unusable, too. In fact, it's completely blocked and destroyed. It wasn't the initial collision, it was when the boat floated backwards still tangled up with the broken pilings. It pulled everything along with it and just . . . ruined it all. We'll have to dredge the entry before any other boat could safely approach. The concrete barriers are lying across the entry, and since that main piling was also the lynchpin of the yacht dock, it pulled it apart as well and sank it."

"Bloody hell! How do we get a boat ashore? The island's entire perimeter is dangerously rocky!"

"I know it."

Mick shifted his weight, looked toward the dangling remains of the approach to his million-dollar ferry slip. "One more time. You're not telling me that we can't even get a rowboat landed here, are you?"

"Yes, I am. Not even a dinghy. The slips are destroyed and the coastline is far too dangerous. I mean, we can rebuild all the facilities . . ."

"But in the meantime, everyone's *stuck* on my island? Is that what you're saying?"

"Yes, sir. I'm sorry. Since we don't have an approachable beach, I'm afraid the only way on or off is going to be the heliport."

Mick Walker shook his head. "For God's sake, don't tell anyone. Not yet, at least."

U.S. GEOLOGICAL SURVEY WESTERN HEADQUARTERS
MENLO PARK, CALIFORNIA

The highly unusual emergency meeting in one of the somewhat Spartan conference rooms had been called in late afternoon, bringing a reluctant but alarmed group of scientists and administrators in from their homes on a Saturday. The mood was somber, the conference room connected by a conference call and speakerphone to the USGS monitoring station in Golden, Colorado, and their offices in Washington, D.C. Dr. Peter Nelson, the director of USGS seismology programs and a member of the National Academy of Sciences for his pioneering work on plate, block, and flake tectonics, was at the head of the table, his trademark understated style a magnet for respect and calm assessment.

But even Pete Nelson's patience was fraying around the edges as the associate director for geology speaking from USGS headquarters in Reston, Virginia, asked the same set of questions for the third time, obviously more worried about the political implications of issuing an earthquake warning than the potential to save lives.

Nelson cut him off.

"Jake, excuse me for being intrusive, but I think all of us out here at Menlo, and our group at Caltech, and certainly our regional director in Seattle, are trying to tell you the very same thing: the penalty ethically, morally, and politically for failing to act if we're right will grossly exceed the penalties for acting if we're wrong."

"Look, Pete, I'm just trying to get it right, okay?"

"Yes, sir, we all are, and I know the burden you have to carry with this pragmatic and somewhat anti-science White House. But the bottom line, as they love to say in business, is simply this: the Cascadia Subduction Zone has never given us a warning of an impending break before, and now it is. The warning is unclear as to the specifics of how big and when a great earthquake or quakes will maul us, but the intermediate warning it's giving is crystal clear. With three hundred years of pent-up energy behind a crumbling dam, it's time to sound the alarm. And that, our citizenry will say after the fact, is one of our jobs."

There was an aggrieved sigh from Reston.

"All right, I'll take it to the president's science advisor within the hour."

"With all due respect," Nelson pressed, "I think we should consider issuing the warning first and merely informing the advisor of it."

"Which is why I'm the political protector for geologic science back here in the Beltway, Pete. No. We get permission first."

Another voice cut in, the sound quality identifying the speaker as also being somewhere else than Menlo Park. "It's beginning to sound like we're reading a NASA script, only the ostriches at NASA were trying to ignore the danger to just six or seven astronauts. We're trying to ignore the mortal danger to thousands."

"Who the hell said that?" Jake Berg asked from Reston, but Pete Nelson cut in.

"It doesn't matter, Jake. We're all of an equal mind out here. We think delay is a huge mistake, but we recognize your authority. Please hurry."

"I don't like insubordinate employees. You all got that?"

"They do, Jake. And we're going to shut down the link out here first, okay?"

"Yeah. I'll call as soon as I know anything."

There was an aggressive click from the Beltway.

Chapter 22

The decision to continue the dinner was simple, Mick thought. People had to eat and there was no way off the island now even if he'd wanted to evacuate.

The absence of over a hundred people, of course, was a problem he couldn't ignore, especially since they were all headed back to the mainland in lifeboats and would miss the weekend festivities.

He swept into the ballroom after leaving his driver at the curb, his head still reeling from the news that a million dollars' worth of dock facilities would have to be rebuilt. There had been no time to check insurance coverage, but he was pretty certain they were protected.

We'd better be, Mick thought. *The liability for the injuries alone is going to be horrific.*

There were still groups of guests standing and talking as he entered and he worked the room like a master politician, smiling and greeting everyone as if nothing untoward had happened.

Sherry, his secretary, had been in tight formation with him as she normally was in social or business situations. She had developed an uncanny ability he considered the next thing to ventriloquism, a way of smiling and not moving her lips at the same time she was throwing a name or other information right in his ear. Somehow others never caught on, and she made him look brilliant.

"Sherry, where's O'Brien?" Mick asked as they were working their way toward the head table.

"We're looking," she said. "Penny was assigned to keep him under control."

Mick stopped and looked at her. "Penny? Oh, Christ."

"What?"

"*Never* send a pretty woman to deal with Frank O'Brien."

She was chuckling. "Mick, you never hire the other kind."

"Find them," he said, eyebrows raised. "Quickly. For her sake as well as his."

"Where?"

"Any private room nearby. You'll find him there trying a fast seduction."

Mick reached the head table and paused, noting the continued absence of the governor and Robert Nelms, and gathering his thoughts. Six people had been seriously injured and the chances any of them had relatives or friends in the audience was small, but unknown. To tell the whole story would ruin the evening. To make it sound like a mechanical problem would be far better, even though most would discover the truth later on. He could always say that he, too, hadn't been informed of the full extent. In any event, the show must go on, and he was a great showman.

Mick took the microphone and cleared his throat.

CASCADIA ISLAND HOTEL

"I don't care who you have to call into work."

Robert Nelms shifted the receiver to his other ear and tried to get control of his breathing before continuing. "And I don't care that it's a Saturday night. We've got a very serious problem out here and I need to know if we missed something. Anyone who doesn't want to come in and crunch the data is fired. Period."

He replaced the phone and sat back in the large chair in his suite, feeling exhausted, the crack in the marble floor and walls of the convention center vivid in his apocalyptic thinking. Cracks like that didn't occur because of bad materials, they occurred because of bad foundations, and providing good foundations had been their job. What on earth could have gone wrong?

The possibility that the repeated earthquakes were responsible had more than once crossed his mind, but without a flawed substratum—without some major fault or soil incongruity underneath the building that they should have found—no such cracking could have occurred just because the ground shook. Besides, Walker had paid them millions for extra seismic studies. It wasn't a seismic problem. Somehow they had missed a soil problem, and it could mean having to rebuild the entire structure.

At the same moment, Doug Lam closed the door of his room behind him and sat on the bed as he prepared to punch a number into his cell phone.

It rang instead, with Terry Griswold on the other end, his voice urgent and excited.

"What's up, Terry?"

"No, it's what's down, Doug. I've just completed a laser reading over here about four miles northeast of where you are on the island."

"And?"

"It has dropped! Doug, I don't know if there's any chance the main pressure release could end up being slow and nondamaging, but the coast and that island have dropped at least twelve inches from my last measurement last Monday a week."

"A *foot?*"

"Yes! No question. I repeated the ranging six times and it came out the same every time within instrument tolerances."

"How about the tremors? I haven't felt anything for the last half hour or so."

"I checked with Sanjay not ten minutes ago. Same pattern, same locations, still continuing."

The impact of a large P wave shuddered through the room, chattering the contents of a decorative shelf and knocking over a lamp.

"Hold it! We've got a quake coming in . . . and it's still going. Whoa!"

"Yeah, I just started feeling it . . . Wow, this one is big!"

"Here come the S waves! *Jeez*, Terry! Hang on!"

"My seismograph is going nuts . . . wait, wait . . ." There was the sound of crashing glass in the background and in the bathroom of the suite as the room began to sway sickeningly, the motion ramping up as Doug checked his watch, figuring ten seconds had already elapsed. In the corner, a big-screen television apparently not tied to the wall was threatening to fall over, and the bed was shaking itself into a new position as the building boomed and screeched.

Less than a tenth of a mile away at the Cascadia Convention Center, the same three employees who'd been standing watch several hours before had stepped outside. Some sort of aurora on the horizon had attracted their attention simultaneously, but as soon as they looked, it was gone. The concept of "earthquake lights" was unknown to all of them, but the light that had struck their retinas had been very real, and generated by yet another sudden movement of rock miles below.

The deep shudder of the first P wave got their immediate attention and all three instinctively moved out farther onto the circular drive and away from the large, stressed-concrete overhang. The S waves began to shake the building then, the oscillations becoming greater and greater until an ear-splitting bang assaulted them. In what seemed like a slow-motion sequence, the expensive new building in front of them split in two, the divided components shuddering in place for an instant before the walls began to cascade down in a boiling cloud of concrete dust and rubble.

When the shaking stopped, nothing of the convention center was standing.

One of the three Cascadia employees reached with a shaking hand for his radio. It took four tries before his finger could find the transmit button.

As the S waves died out, Doug relaxed his grip on the bed frame. The illusion that the room was still shaking was strong, and he concluded he was shaking internally.

He raised the cell phone back to his ear.

"Terry? You still there?"

"Yeah. God, that was big!"

"What do you think?"

"I don't know. Probably a 7. But either it was a deep one, or the epicenter's farther away. It had to be at least a 6.8. I'll have the initial analysis on screen in a minute."

"Any damage there?"

"Naw. Just my nerves. I'm . . . in this log cabin on the beach. It's indestructible until the tsunami comes."

"That was too small for a tsunami."

"I was kidding, Doug. Hold on . . . yeah. 7.1."

"And the location?"

He heard a low whistle. "Oh, God. We'd better get on the phone."

"Why?"

"This was a surficial quake, very shallow. Big and shallow and dangerous, and it looks to me like it just mauled Olympia."

In the Casino Ballroom, Governor Frank O'Brien had reluctantly abandoned his private pursuit of Mick's female employee to join his wife at the head table. When the first waves arrived, he glanced in confusion at his host, and when the S waves began in earnest, the governor dove under the table, leaving the first lady to follow.

"Stay calm, everyone. We've been having a few quakes lately," Mick said into the podium microphone, feeling somewhat smug for having the courage to make a calm announcement even though the shaking was scaring him profoundly. "If you'd like, just get under the tables."

Fat lot of good that will do, he thought as he watched the majority of his guests diving under the relatively lightweight banquet tables. The chandeliers overhead were wobbling and dancing.

"Okay, it's stopping now," Mick added, feeling the waves beginning to

subside and wondering why the heavy rumbling noises had been punctuated with a much larger roar from outside that was there for a moment,
then gone.

At last the room wasn't moving.

"All right, folks, it's all over. I could say that was just a planned demon-
stration of the fact that we're in earthquake country, but . . . somehow I
don't think you'd believe me. At any rate, everyone can come out now."

He could see someone racing in from a side door and glanced over. It was
Sherry, a phone to her ear and a horrified expression on her face as she ran
to his side and spoke directly in his ear.

"Mick, the convention center just collapsed!"

"What do you mean, 'collapsed'?"

"The whole thing. It's just gone. A pile of rubble."

EASTERN END OF CASCADIA ISLAND

Sliding the blasting cap into the puttylike cake of C-4 was the easy part, Lester
thought. Having the guts to connect the two wires with wire nuts to the waiting leads from the electronic timer was the real test. He checked his hands to
see how badly they were shaking, pleased to find them steady. It was his stomach that was shaking—a reaction not only to the earthquake that had hit just
as he was finishing the assembly of the bomb, but also to the actual ground
movement. Bull had pulled Jimmy away as planned, but Lester could hear
him yelp in surprise a hundred feet distant as the earthquake started.

Carefully, he connected the first wire, screwed the plastic wire nut in
place, then touched the two wires together for the second lead. Satisfied he
was still alive, he secured that one as well.

The tiny LED screen had an embedded light and he flipped it on, reading
the circuit continuity indicator as 100 percent. He checked his electronic
watch, verified the time, selected radio control and entered the eight-digit
command password, double-checked the frequency, then killed the light
and closed the case.

It was ready.

All that remained was to nestle the box in the small mound of grass he'd
prepared to conceal it.

He reached Bull's side a minute later and touched Jimmy's elbow.

"What?"

"You've got to be more quiet, Jimmy."

"I am quiet."

"You're a frigging Indian, son! We're supposed to be able to pass silently
through a forest. You? You sound like a locomotive."

"A what?"

"A train."

"Oh, bullshit."

"Just be very quiet."

"All right, what's next?" Bull asked, watching Lester unfold the map.

"We go here, here, and here," Lester said. "Then we can retreat and light 'em up."

"I want to punch the button," Jimmy said.

"The button?" Lester replied, momentarily confused.

"Yeah. When the time comes, I want to punch the button."

The sophisticated radio-controlled, digitally encoded master detonator did not have a button. It had a keyboard, but with Jimmy it was just safer to say yes and leave it at that.

"Sure, Jim. You can punch the button."

"Can I see it?"

Lester sighed and pulled out a key ring with a car remote on the end. "This is it."

"But, doesn't that unlock your car?" Jimmy said.

"Yes, but after what I just put together, it also blows up the explosive."

"Oh. Man, be careful."

"I will. But when the time comes, you can punch it."

"Cool."

Chapter 23

The decision at KOMO-TV to preempt the early-evening programming had already been under discussion before the state's capital city of Olympia started shaking. Now, with reports of massive damage to the capitol building and several other government structures, fires raging out of control in six locations, and a reported collapsed bridge on the main highway to the Pacific Coast, it was time.

Dan Lewis and Kathy Goertzen slid into their seats behind the anchor desk, aware that the station's helicopter was en route, but still fifteen minutes away from broadcasting live pictures. Reports of damage were pouring in from other parts of the South Sound as well, none of them as catastrophic as Olympia's situation, but enough to rivet the attention of a population that one night before had been more interested in staged reality shows than the reality of a potential earthquake.

But now it was getting personal.

Dan Lewis took the floor director's cue.

> Good evening. We're preempting regular programming this evening to bring you continuous Team 4 coverage of the growing earthquake activity in our area. First, a significant earthquake this evening centered under Olympia has severely damaged the state capitol building for the second time in a decade, this, following this morning's extensive impact in Bellingham from a similar earthquake. And, at the hour, perhaps an even more important story is the growing possibility that the Cascadia Subduction Zone, which provides the largest earthquake threat to the Pacific Northwest, may be on the verge of causing what's known in seismic terms as a great earthquake. KOMO has learned that the U.S. Geological Survey is very close to doing something they almost never do: issue a specific earthquake warning which would cover a three-state area. Kathy?

NIGHTINGALE ONE, AIRBORNE

The MV *Quaalatch* was not where Jennifer had left it, but that fact wasn't half the irritant her father had become.

Twenty minutes before, she'd brought the helicopter down to a fifteen-foot hover over the pitching aft deck of the crippled ferry and had been proud of her prowess at holding the Dauphin Eurocopter reasonably steady. Gail rode the hook down and prepped and lifted two patients while Sven worked the winch.

But the helicopter hadn't been low enough for him, and he'd carped at her several times about getting lower, flying more steadily, and had made half a dozen other micromanaging comments that she hadn't expected and did not appreciate. She knew she was a superlative pilot, but having the master throw barbs at her didn't prevent her self-confidence from partially deflating.

Now on the third run Jennifer had been forced to circle twice before realizing that the ferry was actually moving under its own power, half crabbing, half churning backward toward the peninsula ferry slip. Regardless of how the crew was doing it, the ship was listing no further—which meant there was a possibility that it might not sink after all.

The winds had steadied out around forty miles per hour, and she'd planned the approach to come in around thirty feet above deck level, then inch down again to the same fifteen feet to keep the helicopter safe from any sudden downdrafts or upward pitching of the aft deck in the massive swells. Gail was already in her harness and ready to go down for the last two injured people. They were down to broken ankles and legs now, nothing life-threatening as with the first two, but the adrenaline that had been propelling Jennifer was beginning to give way to a deep fatigue.

This is where fatal mistakes are made, Jennifer reminded herself, as she mentally reached for whatever reservoir of energy remained.

"Talk me in, Gail," Jennifer said.

"I'll do it," her father replied. "Bring her down to ten feet this time. The deck's steady. You've got fifteen to go."

"I'm going to hold fifteen feet, Dad. Ten is unsafe."

"Bullshit! Bring it down! You're making things tougher on Gail than they oughta be."

She could hear Gail begin to reply, then stop herself, unwilling to get between the two of them.

"Steady, Jennifer! Steady . . . right there. Come on down. You're too damned high."

"Dad, cut it out! Gail, are you good to go?"

Once more Sven cut her off, this time with a wave toward Gail as he looked at his daughter in the right seat.

"Jennifer, can you hold this machine steady or not?"

"Of course. I *am* holding it steady!"

"Then you don't have any goddamned excuse for being so high. Get down to ten feet!"

"Dad . . ."

"We're too high! *Get down!*"

"No! Damnit, *no!* I'm in command of this ship, and I say it's unsafe below fifteen."

"Yeah? And who the hell taught you how to hover over a boat?"

"You also taught me to be safety-conscious."

"Yeah, safety-conscious, but not a coward."

"Damnit, Dad, I'm not a coward, but ten feet is too low, and we're wasting time with this stupid debate!"

"Staying above fifteen feet is a coward's altitude!"

"I am not going to be bullied into doing something unsafe."

"Goddamnit, how did I end up with such a pussy?"

Jennifer's head jerked around, her eyes full of shock and hurt as she hung on to the controls and watched her father angrily pushing himself away from the open door and unsnapping his safety harness. For a split second she wondered if he was planning to hit her or drag her out of the seat, but instead he launched his body past the center console and into the empty copilot's seat, his hands and feet finding the controls and shaking them against the constant control motions she was making.

"I've got it, goddamnit! You get back there and run the winch and I'll show you how a real . . . pilot does it!"

"You don't mean 'pilot,' do you, Dad? You're going to show me how a 'real *man*' does it, right?" she asked through gritted teeth.

He turned toward her, his eyes red with fury. "Get on the winch! Now! We can talk about this on the ground."

Jennifer unsnapped her seat belt, her face crimson with embarrassment and anger and disappointment. She could see the alarm on Gail's face in her peripheral vision, but she was too crushed to look her in the eye as she took the silently offered safety harness and snapped it around her, giving a thumbs-up as Gail tested her weight again on the winch and swung out the door.

The helicopter was down below ten feet, Sven's determination to show up his daughter's timidity forcing him down to five feet, down to a range dangerous enough that one mistake could send the rotors into the ferry's superstructure, killing anyone in their way and flipping the body of the helicopter into the sea.

But even without a medical certificate, Sven was still an instinctive master, and the Dauphin steadied out in a rock-solid hover still enough to suggest it might be welded somehow to the deck.

Gail motored down the small distance and unhooked, racing inside again for the last two patients as Jennifer sat by the door holding the winch controls, tears burning her eyes and cascading around her face as the rotorwash blasted everyone below.

Her father made no more attempts to communicate from the left seat.

An emotional numbness was creeping up her spine, distorting time and insulating her from the outrageousness of the moment. Gail was back, the first patient came up, the basket went back down for the second patient, and then Gail came aboard.

"The captain and first mate are going to try to get the ferry back to the dock, Jen," Gail reported. "I'm secure. Let's go"

"Jennifer, get back up here and take over," Sven was saying. "I shouldn't be seen flying."

She stood behind her right seat, the empty command chair, and looked at her father, a barrage of conflicting emotions pinging off the walls of her resolve. She wanted to yell at him. She wanted to yank him out of the copilot's seat. She wanted to open the door and push him out. She wanted to run far, far away.

But the inner voice that scared her most of all was the one urging her to somehow apologize once again.

Only a few seconds had passed while her internal debate raged unchecked, but she found herself in motion and back in the right seat, her jaw set, her face hardened against any attempt to ameliorate the man she'd just glimpsed once more, the resentful, uncaring father she'd always tried to deny existed. She knew now she could no longer deny the reality of his true feelings toward her.

"I've got it," she said, her voice flat and professional.

His hands were off the controls now, but he was hesitating in the left seat, his eyes burning a hole in her left cheek.

Jennifer nosed the helicopter forward and brought in the collective and the power, climbing into the gloom and turning once more for Cascadia, letting the previous radio exchange with Norm Bryarly back at Boeing Field replay in her head, blocking other, more disturbing, thoughts.

There had been another large earthquake, Norm had said, and every helicopter Nightingale had, both medevac and charter, were being pressed into service for critical injury pickups, most in the Olympia area. Worse, the first two patients they had pulled off the ferry were only partially stabilized and were in desperate need of transport to a major Seattle hospital, and while she'd immediately offered to fly them, Norm had overruled her, as she'd given him the authority to do.

"You're far too exhausted, Jennifer. Gail's fresher, and Ben's back on his feet and waiting with the ambulance and the patients. So let Gail and Ben bring the Dauphin back here. You and Sven can fly the 412 out tomorrow, after you've had some sleep."

"I'm too tired to argue," she'd said, vaguely aware that her father had turned toward her from the left seat.

"Hey, Honey, I'm sorry about taking over, but you just weren't cutting it."

She said nothing, her eyes on the approaching heliport lights, and he refused to take the hint.

"Jennifer, damnit, the job comes first. But I . . . I am sorry about that remark. You know, the pussy thing."

A wave of bile engulfed her as the import of it all once again washed away the wishful thinking that she could ever measure up.

"So am I, Dad. So am I."

CASCADIA CASINO BALLROOM

The ballroom once again seemed safe and still, and Governor Frank O'Brien was reveling in what he did best: charming his constituents.

Especially female constituents.

Mick Walker had introduced the governor of Washington substantially ahead of schedule and then raced out of the room, which was just fine with Frank O'Brien. In his opinion, developers always tended to talk too long about their accomplishments during groundbreakings or opening ceremonies. Better to leave it to a master politician to strike just the right note, using a mix of humor and the force of a governor's presence to leave the audience with the idea that they'd just experienced one of the greater celebrations of recent history.

Right on cue he'd left the podium and exhorted them to enjoy dinner, then moved off the platform. Totally in his element, O'Brien began working the room, greeting a few old friends and allies, embarrassing one political enemy in a humorous way, and paying careful attention to any pretty female, wife, mother, daughter or otherwise. Lately he'd been overjoyed to see his poll numbers climbing again among Washington women. Maybe they'd forgiven him.

The governor could see the waiters holding his main course at the head table, and he turned to shake one more hand. The man looked familiar, but then there were so many people parading past him every day, there was no way he could remember them all.

"Governor? I need to speak with you immediately."

"Well, apparently you already are. Your name?"

"Dr. Douglas Lam, of the U.S. Geological Survey and the University of Washington Seismology Lab."

Frank cautioned himself to remain polite, even though he wanted to release Lam's hand and turn away. The scientist had been a thorn in the side of some of his supporters, especially Mick Walker. What the hell was he doing here, of all places?

"Well, Dr. Lam. What happened? You decide you like this project after all?"

"Governor, if you'll give me five minutes, I have a huge growing body of scientific evidence that we're about to have a monstrous subduction zone earthquake that could—"

O'Brien's hand was already up. "Okay, that's what I figured. You go find my emergency services director."

"Governor, I chased you down over here because we're out of time, and I can't find Harper. You have to issue an evacuation order for the—"

"Hey, calm down! Okay?" Frank placed his hand on Lam's shoulder, leaning down slightly to look him in the eye like a worried teacher trying to get through to a dense student. "Let me tell you this plain and simple. I'm well aware of the earthquakes we've been having, I'm well aware of the damage in Bellingham, and I know we just had a quake here a few minutes ago. But I'm not evacuating anything until I've got sufficient scientific proof, and that means—as I told Bill Harper a while ago when I cancelled the premature alert he tried to trigger without proper authority—when the USGS, your agency, issues a genuine earthquake warning, I'll act. Not until then. As leader, that is the appropriate thing for me to do."

"Governor, are you aware the state capitol building has partially collapsed?"

Frank O'Brien dropped his hand and took a half step back, his head cocked in an expression of pity.

"What are you talking about? That was years ago, and we merely got cracks in the dome."

"Well, sir, this time the dome came down. Three people are dead as of twenty minutes ago. You mean no one's called you?"

A dark cloud of uncertainty crossed the governor's face, his smug smile fading rapidly. "That's Harper's job."

"Harper was on the last ferry. It was sinking, and everyone had to abandon ship in lifeboats, from what I'm told. I don't even know if he made it to shore."

Frank glanced around, looking for his state trooper bodyguard, but the man was nowhere to be found. The governor turned back to Doug. "If you're making this up, Lam, I'll have your ass in a sling."

"I'm giving you the absolute truth as I heard it about the capitol, Governor, and I'm waiting for printed confirmation of our USGS warning. It isn't completely official until I get the—"

The trooper appeared through the doorway of the room and raced to the governor's side, a cell phone in his hand.

"Where the hell have you been?" O'Brien growled.

"I . . . had a bad signal in here, sir," the trooper explained. "And—"

O'Brien cut him off. "You haven't heard any nonsense about the capitol collapsing, have you Sam?"

"Yes, sir. I have the command post on the line for you right now."

O'Brien looked momentarily stunned, then recovered and snatched the cell phone from the trooper's hand, his eyes on the floor as someone on the other end transmitted the same grim information. He finished and snapped the phone shut, handing it back to the trooper as Doug waved for his attention.

"Governor, *please* let me explain what's happening about twenty-five kilometers below our feet."

"Okay, look, Doctor. I know all about your little theory, and I also know none of your colleagues agreed with you. Furthermore, I don't appreciate at all the way you dogged my friend, Mick Walker, and made his life miserable because you wanted this island kept untouched."

"You're misinterpreting my entire stance, sir."

"Am I? Am I misinterpreting the fact that you stated this island should not be built upon?"

"No, but—"

"How about your public pronouncements that people like Walker were subverting the process of environmental protection?"

"Yes, when he uses his fortune to tie up any opposition in the courts."

"That's not what they're for? The courts? To fairly resolve disputes?"

"That's not how he used them."

"I really don't like your tactics any more than I like rabid, wild-eyed tree huggers who'd rather launch all humans off the planet and keep it pristine for animal life."

"That is *not* my philosophy!"

"Really? Then who was it who tried to stop this project by ramming his discredited, so-called theory down our throats in order to block the project, despite the tax revenues it raises for the state?"

"Sir, this has nothing to do with my theory."

"What, then?"

"Please forget any question of why the subduction zone is rumbling and just give me a few seconds to tell you what is happening down there."

Frank O'Brien studied him for a moment in thought.

"Okay, against my better judgment, I'll give you two minutes, Doctor. This is too important a subject not to hear you out for the umpteenth time."

Doug took a deep breath and compressed a half-hour explanation into a headline as Frank O'Brien stood and listened.

"In a nutshell, Governor, we have a massive series of quakes proving the zone is doing something we've never seen before, and if it breaks, there will be no time to evacuate before a tsunami wipes out a huge number of citizens. Those are scientific certainties."

"Why do these little quakes have to equate to a huge one?" O'Brien asked.

I'm reaching him! Doug thought.

"We don't know whether they're an inevitable prelude to the big one or some other phenomenon that *doesn't* end with a huge quake. But what we're seeing has never happened before in modern history, and the only conservative, safe action is to evacuate the coastal areas, if it's not already too late."

"And that includes this island, I assume?"

"Yes."

"Does your employer concur? Are they ready to issue the alert I'm still going to demand?"

"They just did," Doug said, feeling his blood run cold at the enormity of the lie. There was no justification for saying such a thing, but O'Brien's antagonism was simply too much to bear.

"Really? And you found out when?"

"Just as I walked in here," he added to the lie.

O'Brien was standing in thought. "Okay. Thank you, Doctor. We'll take it from here." He glanced at the trooper and inclined his head toward Doug as he turned to walk away. The trooper anticipated Doug's trajectory and stepped in front of him. "Sir, do not follow the governor. Understand?"

"I was just—"

The trooper's hand moved to the butt of his holstered gun. "Stop!"

Doug raised both hands and backed away a few feet to wait. The trooper's expression was angry and he turned suddenly to follow O'Brien out of the hall with a determined Doug Lam right behind. At the doorway the trooper turned and blocked his way. "Come one step closer and I'll put you in cuffs, understood?"

"I'm trying to warn the governor of my state of a public hazard, and I'm violating no laws. *You* back off!" Doug snapped, surprised at the anger in his response.

Frank O'Brien sighed, stopped, and turned. "Down, Billy. Dr. Lam, stay by your phone."

"Do you have my number?"

"I . . . Billy?" he said to the trooper. "Write down Dr. Lam's cell number and then follow me."

Doug repeated his number and the trooper turned to follow his boss, who was just sailing out of the room, his voice raised a touch too loud for Doug not to overhear a question about retrieving the first lady.

CASCADIA ISLAND

It didn't require more than climbing out of the car for Mick to confirm Sherry's report. The Cascadia Island Convention Center—all twenty million dollars' worth of it—was now a pile of rubble, as if a controlled-demolition company had carefully planted the necessary explosives to flatten it.

Sherry had accompanied him and was standing by the car, but he waved her back, not wanting her to see the pure, unadulterated panic on his face. His knees felt weak and a large part of him wanted to just sink to the ground and roll up in a fetal position, or maybe take a long walk off the shortest pier he could find.

Not that Mick Walker hadn't lived through bad times before. There had been plenty of them, starting with a mean childhood in the Australian outback with a drunk, abusive father. The fact that he'd ended up with any money at all instead of being sentenced to prison in his wild youth was in itself a small miracle. But even after he'd become successful and wealthy, he'd never felt secure. He was sure the establishment he'd conquered and pretended to join was always looking for the opportunity to send him packing back to the poor, hardscrabble life that had spawned him. There had been transitory moments of professional panic before. But this time was different. This time his life, fortune, and self-worth were all inextricably intertwined with the resort. If it collapsed, so would he.

And never had he felt so vulnerable before, all his chips on one table against a loaded roulette wheel.

Sherry Thomas had worked for Mick for more than twelve years, and other than a brief affair in their first years together, they had, by mutual agreement, kept the lines clearly drawn between them. They were friends and colleagues—a boss and his employee—and while the mutual sexual attraction had never been completely slaked, they'd kept it well contained.

But Mick knew she'd probably been in love with him for all those years, and maybe he loved her, too, but he'd never let himself admit it.

He sat now slowly on the remains of a concrete post, emotional fatigue enveloping him, unsurprised when Sherry materialized at his side. He quietly longed for the reassuring touch of her hand on his shoulder.

"It'll work out, Mick," she said. "We'll rebuild."

"Maybe."

"No, we will. You've got the financial strength to weather this or anything else."

Sherry was studying him now, leaning forward, completely off balance to see his face glistening with tears.

"Mick, hey. Let's be thankful no one was hurt here."

"There were people hurt on our ferry."

"True, but no one was killed."

She heard a long, heavy sigh. "Sherry, this may be it."

She sat beside him, her arm moving around him. "What do you mean?"

"That financial strength you mentioned?"

"Yes?"

He shook his head sadly. "It's gone, Sherry. If this goes, all I have goes with it."

"I'm not following you, Mick. We're well insured. In fact, we're extremely well insured, including earthquake coverage."

He looked at her, his face reflecting the years that usually hid behind his enthusiasm and his broad smile.

"You recall when the financial backers wanted an emergency meeting just before they were ready to fund?"

"Yes."

"I never told you, because I was too ashamed of buckling, but they would have pulled the whole package and collapsed all those years of work on the spot if I hadn't signed."

"Signed what?"

He sighed again, this time a sound of resignation, or maybe it was defeat. Should he even tell her the truth? If he lost it all, she'd know soon enough. But being miserable alone was simply too much.

"Sherry, the backers demanded I pledge virtually everything I owned. All my stock, all my cash and accounts, all my real estate, and all goodwill. Everything, even down to that silly patent on the wood-smoke generator."

"You pledged . . . Mick, I had no idea."

"If this place goes into receivership, the first thing they'll do is take my back teeth and throw me out. And you, I'm afraid, will be out of a job for sticking with a loser."

She reached up and smoothed the hair back from his forehead. "Mick, I'll always work for you, with you, even if you can't pay me. You've made me a millionaire, remember? They can't touch that."

"No, they can't," he agreed.

"So, is that your worst fear?"

He laughed ruefully. "That's a pretty bad one, don't you think?"

"Yes, but . . . if that's the worst case, face it. We don't have debtor's prisons, and they can't take your expertise. You'll rise again!"

"God, Sherry, I'm too old to rise again. I'm sixty-one. And I'm getting tired."

She was breathing hard beside him, holding his hand and struggling with her own panic.

"Okay, we're staring the devil in the teeth, but you've got people depending on you, and we still have a hotel and a casino, and survivors of a maritime accident. All is not lost."

"It may be," he said, getting up after squeezing her hand.

"I refuse to pencil 'give up' into your calendar! Whatever comes, you can handle it. And I'll be right beside you."

"You know something young lady?" he said, trying to smile lightheartedly and failing. "I don't deserve you. Never did."

"Shut up and look here," she said, guiding his face to hers and kissing him deeply as his arms slowly encircled her and held her tightly for a few moments.

The kiss ended and she smiled at him as he tried to speak.

"Sherry, I should have said . . . a long time ago . . . I mean . . ."

She put a finger over his lips.

"I know, Mick. I've always known. But right now we have work to do."

Chapter 24

"Lester, only you could get busted in a damn golf cart," Bull said under his breath as a Cascadia Security car came up a few feet behind the electric cart.

"Shut up, and let me do the talking. Jimmy? You, too. You under-stand?"

"Yeah. Are we gonna have more of those shakers, you think?"

"Probably. We'll talk about it later."

Lester brought the electric utility cart to a halt and set the hand brake, wondering what sort of paranoid mentality would buy squad cars with red and blue Visibars for an island barely the size of a barge. With the same hideously bright spotlight used by the state patrol blinding him from be-hind, he couldn't tell whether the man climbing out of the car was a rent-a-cop or a real trooper, but whoever it was obviously got off by turning on enough flashing lights to alert the upper West Coast.

Yeah, it's a rent-a-cop.

"Sir, who are you, and why are you in a company cart?"

Lester looked up at the uniform.

"If you'll take that flashlight outta the face of one of your boss's honored guests, I'll tell you."

"Sorry?"

"Hey, I know you're just being cautious, but I doubt Mick Walker would appreciate you hassling us." He flashed the formal invitation bearing his name in gold leaf. "We're here for the weekend."

"I'm sure you are, sir, but this cart is for employee official use only."

"Tell Mr. Walker that. He told us since we were too late for the tour to take one on our own."

That did it, Lester thought. Doubt. He'd instilled enough of it to make the man think, and when rent-a-cops weren't sure of themselves, there was a window of opportunity. Lester could see he was studying their damp, di-sheveled clothes.

"I mean, we really wanted to see the place, but . . . with what happened after we caught the last ferry . . ."

The guard's expression changed to one of shock.

"Oh, wow! You were on that run? I didn't know any of the guests made it to the island after the collision."

What the hell does that mean? Lester wondered, deciding to go with the flow anyway. "Yeah, well, it wasn't easy but we managed. We really wanted to be here."

"God, how'd you land? I mean, the dock is toast."

"Well, there was a small boat, and we're used to coming ashore in rocky places."

"You had one of the inflatable lifeboats, right? A Zodiac? Okay. I thought they'd probably launched more than just the main lifeboats. Sure glad you guys made it."

Lester smiled at him. "Yeah, so are we."

"Please," the guard said, "go ahead. Just leave the cart back in the drive at the hotel when you're finished. We've got all sorts of problems this evening with the earthquakes and we need all of them."

"Thanks, we will."

The guard started to turn away, but the sight of the rubberized black duffel bag sitting by Jimmy caused him to hesitate. He inclined his head toward the bag.

"You . . . had time to save your gear, too? With the ship going down and all?"

Lester could sense Bull's hand sliding silently into his pocket in search of the small .25 caliber Browning automatic he'd insisted on carrying.

"No, we didn't," Lester said quickly. "But one of them popped up in the surf next to us and we pulled it out and put it in one of the survival bags. You need to check it?"

The hesitation was transitory but suddenly he was shaking his head. "Naw. Glad you salvaged it. Have a great weekend, fellows. And . . . thanks for your patience. Oh, and please don't go anywhere near the wreckage of the convention center."

"Wreckage?"

"I'm afraid it collapsed in that last earthquake."

"That's awful, man. We felt it."

The man got back in his car as Bull snickered. "This is gonna be a real bang-up of a weekend, all right," he said, smiling at his double meaning as Lester kicked him hard in the ankle. They began moving smoothly away from the curb.

The first of the emergency diesel generators was just ahead, and they would need to make sure they weren't followed.

"You weren't really thinking of shooting that guy while we were carrying enough C-4 to blow the island into next week, were you, Bull?"

"If he'd gotten too nosy, I would have."

CASCADIA ISLAND HELIPORT

To Jennifer, relinquishing control of the Dauphin to Gail was a welcome anesthesia. They finished loading the two critically injured patients aboard for the flight back to Seattle, and in what seemed the blink of an eye the helicopter had disappeared into the gloom, leaving her standing in awkward silence next to her father.

Sven tried to put an arm around her but she shrugged it off and stepped ahead of him, roughly aiming her steps toward the waiting car.

"Jennifer," he began, but she waved him away, careful not to turn back, unwilling to trust anything that might burst from her mouth. But when she reached the car she turned to him, barely under control. "You take the limo. I'm going to walk."

"Oh, bullshit, Jennifer! If you hate me that much, *I'll* walk to save you having to ride with me."

She lowered her head, chewing her lip, a cacophony of competing reactions fighting for voice. But all that emerged was a strange little sound that at first seemed to belong to someone else.

"I don't hate you."

"Well, then get in, for God's sake."

Still she stood rooted, unable to make her muscles obey the conflicting orders emanating from the civil war in her head.

"Oh for Pete's sake, *say* something, Jen! Tell me to go to hell or . . . or tell me why you're mad, or something. You know I hate the silent treatment."

You can dish it out, but you can't take it, huh, Dad? she thought. Maybe she should stay silent. Maybe she should yell. He'd had a stroke. Could he take an argument? His blood pressure had to have gone through the roof when he'd ripped the controls away from her.

As had hers.

He looked away in disgust and snorted, then looked back. "Now you're acting just like your mother!"

That did it. She locked eyes with him.

"You're right, Dad! A real child of yours would *never* act emotional like your wife, because that would make her female. God forbid!"

"What?"

She turned away, shaking with rage, needing so desperately to cry but not willing to do so in front of him.

"Jen . . . Honey, look . . ."

She whirled on him. "No, *you* look Sven Lindstrom! Forget the fact I'm your daughter and not the son you wanted. I happen to be president of your company, and if you think I can't cut it, I'll resign, and you can go out and adopt someone with an MBA *and* a penis. Okay?"

"Jennifer, for chrissake! What is this gender stuff? I apologized back there for taking over. What more do you want?"

"For what did you apologize, Dad? For demeaning me in front of an employee? For making me look incompetent? For calling me a coward? For illegally flying a commercial helicopter and risking everyone's lives? What are you sorry for?"

"Well, all those things, since you've decided to be so sensitive all of a sudden that you've got to go and get this upset."

"Oh, no, Dad! No, no! The truth came out back there. Didn't it?"

"What the hell are you talking about?"

"In front of Gail, in the middle of a dangerous mission, you turned to me, the pilot in command of the aircraft, and snarled"—she lowered her voice, emulating his rumbling tones—" 'How did I end up with such a pussy?' You said it! And it doesn't really matter whether you meant, 'How did I end up with a girl when I wanted a boy?' or whether you meant, 'You're too timid, Jennifer, for my daredevil tastes.' It all comes down to the same thing. I can't ever please you!"

"That's not true . . ."

"*Yes it is!* I can never please you and it's killing me, and I'm not going to be blindsided like this by you ever again! Do you hear me?"

What contrition he might have imagined himself to be showing had clearly not worked, and the frustration at losing control boiled over.

"Oh, shit! I'm getting pretty sick of this emotional garbage, young lady!"

She smiled ruefully, hands on hips as she straightened up and shook her head in disgust. "Oh, right, Dad. Good strategy. 'Now I'll try to shame her with the Young Lady epithet.' Make me feel guilty again for being female, like I always have."

"Jennifer, you're twisting everything I say."

"No, Dad. I'm just finally waking up to the real meaning of everything you say. And this is the end of the line."

"What's that mean?"

"The end. I'm finished! I quit."

"What?"

"It's simple. I'm obviously not matched with your expectations so you can take back the helm and run Nightingale all by yourself. I fucking quit! Okay? Is that a masculine enough way to say it?"

His eyes were flaring again in defiance. "Damnit, you can't quit! You're the president, part owner, a board member . . ."

"*I quit!* It doesn't matter what I am. The price is too high! You'll have my formal written resignation as fast as I can find a piece of paper to write it on."

"Jennifer, pull yourself together!"

"Oh, I'm more together right now than I've ever been before, Father."

He was moving toward her, the anger suddenly changing to alarm as the implication of what she was threatening sank in.

"Hey, Jennifer, wait just a minute. This is stupid. I need you . . ."

"Yeah, *you* need me? For what? As a whipping boy? I'm done with that."

"No, seriously. I can't run Nightingale by myself and we don't have anyone else who can."

She was looking off to sea, struggling to hold in the seething emotions as he tried again.

"Jennifer, look . . . tell me what I need to do to make this right? Okay? You know, so you'll . . . stop this and . . . and stay on."

She snorted as loudly as she could manage. "You want me to stay?"

"Of course."

She turned to him. "Dad, I am going to gain control of this situation with you or else. I'm tired . . . I'm desperately tired of never being good enough. So you want me to keep on as president?"

"Of course! You've been doing a good job."

"What's that? *Praise?*"

"Yes. I've praised you a lot."

"Only grudgingly, and never when and where it counts, Dad. Not ever in front of others. But in the heat of the moment you slip and reveal what you really think."

He sighed and hung his head in silence and she reached out to raise his chin and lock eyes again, as she'd been taught so many times.

Look me in the eyes, young lady! he'd roar. Now it was her turn, but that phrase wouldn't come, and there was no feeling of victory in turning the tables.

"Okay, Dad. The price for my continuing to be part of this company? You will never again question my judgment or my capabilities in front of my people. That's number one."

"All right," he said quietly.

"And number two? You will *never* speak to me or write to me or communicate with me in any way that uses that sneering, eye-rolling tone of fatherly disappointment I've seen and heard all my life that says that I'm not good enough because I'm a girl."

"I . . . come across that way?"

"Yes, damnit! And you know it, too."

He sighed. "Not really."

"Promise, or I'm gone."

"Okay, okay. I promise."

She let go of his chin, but he kept his eyes on hers.

"You never were the perfect pilot or the perfect businessman you always pretended to be, any more than I am."

"I know that."

"And, if you remember, I was the one who quadrupled the company's size and profits."

"I know that, Jen. I'm sorry."

His image grew indistinct through a quiet cascade of tears as the emotional dam broke at last, despite her best efforts to hold it together. She turned to hide her face, incredulous at the words she'd spoken, but even more shaken by the image of her father as she turned away: ashen, old, defeated, and at long last confronted. Where was the feeling of triumph? She felt only a dark emptiness, as if somehow the pain of his disapproval had been a life vest holding her afloat, and now it was gone and she was foundering.

She brushed away the tears with her sleeve and turned back to him, forcing herself to replace the truth of what she'd seen in his face with the image she'd always cherished: a strong, proud, imperfect man capable of slaying dragons. Suddenly she was the little girl again begging for acceptance, and the words rolled out of her mouth unbidden and unauthorized, punctuated by sobs.

"I'm so sorry, Dad."

He awkwardly opened his arms and pulled her into an uncharacteristic hug. His arms closed slowly around her, as if gingerly asking for permission to do so, then tightened, until his muscles were shaking against the pressure.

"No, Jennifer. I . . . I'm sorry."

There was more he wanted to say and she could feel it. His vulnerability was an untraveled road, and she was stunned by the unexpected gift. But his unspoken words were stuck somewhere between his heart and his pride, and she settled for that much for now, wondering what it would have been like to have been hugged that way as a child. Somewhere inside, she felt the warmth of compassion leaking in around the dam of her previous anger.

And then the moment passed and she pulled away gently, unconsciously patting his arm, suddenly worried about the damage she might have done to him.

"Dad, we need to get some rest."

He nodded, without speaking, as he opened the door to the car and waited for her to get in.

PLEASANTON, CALIFORNIA

"You're sure that's a direct cellular number?"

Ralph Lacombe checked that he'd copied the relayed phone number correctly before ending the call with the California governor's protocol officer. The comprehensive listing of the hotline numbers for every governor in the nation was at the man's fingertips, and a state senator with Lacombe's seniority and clout could get any one of them.

He paused before dialing the number, going over the latest information relayed from his ex-CIA friend. Undoubtedly Diane was on a mission regarding the seismic dangers to Mick Walker's island, and equally certain was the fact that someone from Chadwick and Noble was chasing after her to prevent her from handing over to Mick, and perhaps Washington's governor, some sort of work product from her firm. The conclusion might have been bizarre for others, but it was entirely consistent with his daughter's crusading nature. The FedEx package had arrived, and he'd opened it and viewed the contents of the CD, recognizing enough to know that it was seismic data somehow related to their old friend Walker's project. So that was her quest, he decided. The firm had suppressed the data, and she was going to reveal it.

He punched in the number, listening to it ring before a Washington state trooper answered and listened suspiciously to his request.

"You want to speak to Governor O'Brien?"

"That's the idea."

"Well, sir, he's giving a speech in a few minutes. Can I take a message?"

"Yes. Tell him Senator Ralph Lacombe called. Tell him my daughter is apparently headed to Cascadia Island to give him some very important information. If she arrives, it would be a personal favor to me if he'd give her a few minutes of his time."

He left a number with an invitation to call and ended the connection. O'Brien was an old acquaintance, but a skirt-chasing, narcissistic fool. Even if he listened, that wasn't enough.

Ralph picked up the phone and dialed Mick Walker's direct number.

Chapter 25

The governor of Washington was obviously not going to listen to anything Doug Lam had to say.

Doug stood for a second calculating the futility of running after him and still appalled that he'd lied about Menlo Park issuing the alert. The alert was obviously the key to getting O'Brien's cooperation, but even that news hadn't impressed him.

Or perhaps the governor just refused to reverse course in public. The way he'd acted meant he considered Doug Lam an enemy.

Doug's stomach was making obscene noises and he decided to eat something of the food on the table while deciding what to do next.

The mood in the large hall was anything but the gala atmosphere Mick Walker had intended. Only half the expected crowd was on hand, most of them worried by the continuous earth tremors and the growing rumors about some sort of problem with the ferry carrying friends and acquaintances expected for the weekend. Colorful pictures that few were watching were flashing on a large screen, professional shots carefully taken of the Cascadia project's most impressive features. How many of the guests, Doug wondered, were aware that the sparkling white marble front of the convention hall as shown on the screen was no longer even standing?

He found a place at one of the tables where an entrée was waiting and ate quickly. The others at the table were engaged in conversation and made no introductions. He opted to be anonymous and antisocial.

The young woman who slipped into the empty place next to him did so without fanfare, and he hardly noticed her at first. She waved away a waiter who tried to fill the void in front of her with a salad and sat staring at him.

Doug looked around, recording a mane of auburn hair framing the soft contours of a lovely face.

"Hello," he said, extending his right hand as the orchestra raised the volume with an upbeat piece designed to entice people to a dance floor no one was using.

"Hi," she said, her eyes on his for only an instant. She was looking around the room as if afraid a jealous husband might be watching for any hint of contact with the opposite sex. But then she took his hand with surprising aggressiveness.

"I'm, ah, Doug Lam," he said, thoroughly off balance and unsure whether to withdraw his hand. The contact was becoming intimate and embarrassing.

"Yes, I know," she replied, dropping her eyes to the table.

"And you are?" he tried.

"Ah . . . Mary. Mary Willis."

"Nice to meet you, Mary. Is everything all right?"

"Can we talk somewhere private?"

"Sure. What's wrong?"

"I sent you an e-mail. About seismic data?"

Doug felt his eyebrows go up in surprise. "That's *you*?"

She nodded. "There are some empty meeting rooms off the main corridor."

"Lead the way."

She got up quickly and he followed, replaying the e-mail in his memory and trying not to be mindful of her shapely form as she led him out into the main foyer and into a side room. She closed and locked the door behind them before sitting across from him at the diminutive boardroom table.

"First, my name is not Mary."

"I gathered that."

She nodded, a shallow reflective smile on her face as her eyes darted around the room before landing on his. "Let me get to the point. We're in a lot of danger just sitting here."

Doug smiled and cocked his head. "What . . . kind of danger?"

"Seismic."

"Oh."

"What did you think I meant?"

"Not important. Yes, clearly we're in seismic danger. I've been trying for a long time to tell everyone just that. Did you see what happened to the convention center?"

"I heard. That's the surface fault I told you about."

"Your note said you had information that validated my research. What data could possibly do that? It was only a theory, and a roundly dismissed one, at that."

She nodded. "I'm an engineer, not a seismologist, Doctor, but what I understood you to be saying in your paper is that there are three spots along the Cascadia Subduction Zone that you feel are like fulcrums, sensitive areas where any substantial impacts on the surface might be transmitted intact as they move down in the rock strata, and that such jolts might be enough to set off, or trigger, a great earthquake."

"Well, that's a colorful and somewhat cursory way of describing it, but essentially that's right. It was a trigger theory."

"So, those spots—and we're sitting on one of them—are like the business end of a mousetrap, where you put the cheese. Twang it hard enough, and all hell breaks loose? Please explain it to me before I tell you the rest of my story."

"All right. Simply put, I studied years of seismographs and began to see a pattern. I thought there was enough evidence in the way seismic energy reflects through this area—and those other two locales—to make me think there was a direct line of transmission between the surface and the locked area of the Cascadia Subduction Zone, what I call the 'Quilieute Quiet Zone.' That would mean that any construction activity on those spots, especially pile driving or dynamite explosions to excavate rock, would be dangerous. Almost no one in the geophysical community agreed with me, of course, as you kind of pointed out. My colleagues thought I'd slipped a cog, and the industrial side accused me of making it all up just to oppose their destruction of a perfectly good bird sanctuary . . . a sanctuary, by the way, that wasn't here three hundred years ago because it was below sea level, as it will be again."

"I don't think you made it up." She pulled out the CD and held it up. "I think your theory was a stroke of genius."

"Who are you, exactly?"

"Diane Lacombe. I was the project engineer from Chadwick and Noble who came here two years ago to do the last-chance structural geologic and seismic evaluation of the island, a study demanded specifically by the developer, Mick Walker. We worked hard and fast and I transmitted all the data to San Francisco and went home after a week of thumping the island with an oil-field truck we had ferried over. Another team prepared the report, and for the longest time I couldn't get a copy. I even have a copy of a memo written by my boss, Jerry Schultz, telling me to stop asking. I thought that was strange. And when I finally wheedled it out of them almost eight months later, I have to tell you I was aghast. It was almost cursory . . . alarming in its lack of depth. Like it had been rushed out to fit a predetermined conclusion. So, I started trying to get my hands on the core data in order to be sure we, as a firm, hadn't screwed up the evaluation. I was worried that we might have failed to find something that Mick—Mick Walker—needed to know about before committing these incredible sums."

"But, you were told to sit down and shut up, right?"

She studied his eyes for several moments before answering.

"Yes. How'd you know?"

He shrugged. "I'm familiar with the standard operating approach to bad news within most large organizations. Shut up and drink your Kool-Aid."

"Well, they clearly didn't want me spending time on it. Exactly why, I don't know."

"But you didn't obey, did you?"

She shook her head. "Oh, I did for a while, since it was my supervisor and then one of the partners who told me essentially to butt out. But it kept bugging me, even after construction started, and it seriously worried me that Walker, who's a longtime friend of my father and my family, might have been misled by my firm's sloppiness. So I kept on probing around until I secured the original data tapes we'd made of all the impact echoes. And I started redoing the whole evaluation, which is what led to my e-mailing you. I mean, by the time I found what I've found, this resort was already built, but I figured that only an eminent seismologist could stand a chance of convincing anyone what to do."

"I'm not sure I'm following this, and I'm anything but eminent."

"Doctor, do you have a laptop here?"

"Of course. But back in my room."

"With a DVD drive?"

He nodded.

"Then, let me show you, rather than just tell you."

"The suspense is killing me, Miss Lacombe."

"Diane, please."

"Can you at least tell me the bottom line, Diane?"

She was already on her feet. "I'd prefer we go get to your laptop. I don't know how much time we have."

She unlocked the door and cracked it open, carefully surveying the foyer before stepping out with Doug following. They were halfway across the courtyard between the casino and the hotel when a downburst of pelting rain found them, soaking them both as they sprinted for the hotel entrance. Doug's shoes were squishing as they got off the elevator and entered his room.

He got towels for both of them from the bathroom and toweled his hair down before opening the laptop. Diane Lacombe sat beside him at the desk and pulled out the CD.

"The bottom line, Doctor, is this. Our data showed sloping rock strata that clearly can transmit seismic energy from the surface of this island to the Benioff Zone, just as you postulated in your paper."

"Which area?"

"The one you labeled 'the Quilieute Quiet Zone,' the one, according to your paper, that could be the most dangerously locked and brittle trigger area in the entire subduction zone, somewhere around a depth of twenty-five kilometers, and essentially aligned with this island."

"In other words, when Walker began building here . . ."

She was nodding solemnly. "That's right. When he started building, blasting, and banging, they were sending seismic waves squarely into the mousetrap's release button."

Doug took a deep breath and shook his head. "I know you're aware of these big tremors, but are you aware of the current swarm of Benioff Zone earthquakes we've been having?"

She nodded. "I am now. But not until I got off the train in Portland."

"Excuse me, the train?"

"Someone wanted this CD bad enough to wreck my apartment in San Francisco looking for it. When I figured that out, I ran to find you. The train was the most anonymous way."

"Someone was chasing you? Do you have any idea who, or why?"

"No. Well . . . that's not entirely true. I have suspicions I don't want to discuss yet."

She put the disk in the slot and triggered the appropriate buttons, waiting for the drive to spin up before working through a series of commands, then turned the computer screen around for him to see.

"My dad is a state senator and a lawyer. He's always used a Latin phrase that means, 'Let the thing speak for itself.' "

"Res ipsa loquitur?"

She nodded. "This diagram should make its own point."

A three-dimensional representation of the entire subduction zone—a cross-section presented as if a gargantuan block had been neatly sliced from the continent carrying the entirety of the Puget Sound region on its top, its sides showing the inner structure of the earth down to fifty kilometers—now revolved on the screen. She worked more keystrokes and the picture zoomed in toward Cascadia Island at the top, with the locked portion of the Benioff Zone clearly marked below. Suddenly, the picture zoomed in further, overlaying the data she had developed and showing a corrugated series of sloping lines leading from the Cascadia Island area through the crustal rock and terminating at the twenty-one-kilometer level.

"So what do you think of that?" she asked, her expression still grim, her voice tight and contained.

"My God, this is real data?"

"Yes. Not just the reflected data from distant quakes I suspect you used, but the type of oil-field exploration data designed to reveal the different layers."

He whistled to himself, a low and intense sound. "You see it, too, don't you?" he asked at last.

"I . . . see vertical, diving strata. Am I missing more?"

Doug was nodding excitedly. "Yes! I've never seen real images of anything like this. See how the layers form a conduit that gets smaller and more concentrated as the depth increases?"

"Yes."

"I suggested such a thing might be proven someday, but this is amazing."

Doug put his finger on the screen just below the island and traced the lines downward to their termination point.

"Notice how the strata converge toward the bottom? At the top it may cover fifty square miles. At the bottom, perhaps one. That's what I called a static amplification formation, a diving, converging series of faults or breaks which compress and significantly increase—amplify—the intensity or, at the very least, the amplitude of any vibrations from the surface. It's like when a shallowing ocean bottom along a coastline will increase the amplitude of an inbound tsunami wave until the resulting wave that hits the shore is gigantic. This can take a vibration and increase its impact down below."

"You mean, like using a magnifying glass to concentrate sunlight and roast ants?"

"Similar concept. But that would be concentration, and what I'm seeing in your data is amplification."

"But your theory was only about resonant motion, wasn't it?"

He nodded, his enthusiasm growing. "Resonant amplified vibrations. That was one part. The idea that man-made seismic waves from surface impacts of a pile driver might just match in frequency the range at which the rock in the trigger area vibrates, increasing the vibrations like a struck gong. The more waves sent down, the greater the resonant vibration, until the rock loosens itself up and the trigger gets pulled on the main earthquake. And once the process starts, there's no calling it back. That's what happened when so many downtown buildings shook themselves apart in Mexico City in the great quake of 1985."

"Good grief. *Amplification?*"

"Yes! This is amazing!"

"So, where those waves come out down around twenty-one kilometers, that happens to be the weakest part of the locked subduction zone?"

Doug sighed and sat back. "That's where the guesswork comes in. Where *is* the trigger? How fragile is it? You know, does it take one more straw to break the camel's back, or a million tons? And right now, as we sit here talking theory, Walker may have unlocked that trigger and we're just waiting for a slow fuse to burn down to the dynamite."

"It's strange that a hundred nuclear bombs going off down there might not cause it to break. Yet, with this structural amplifier in the rock, it could take very little." Diane paused. "Are they still blasting around here?" she asked. "Even now?"

"No. The damage is done. If they've unlocked it, the genie is out of the bottle."

Diane stood and paced toward the balcony in thought as Doug looked more closely at the screen.

"Hold it."

"What?" she asked, turning back.

"I see the surface fault you described."

Doug reached for a stack of promotional brochures on the new facilities. He yanked open the largest of the site maps and turned it back and forth until it was aligned with the diagrams on the screen, placing the point of his pen on the collapsed convention center and marking left and right in a line that passed through both the hotel and casino.

"Dear God, he built all the main facilities right across it! A major surficial fault. How did you guys miss it?"

Diane followed his finger as it traced the shadow through the data points. "It looks fatal for this island."

"To say the least!" he replied, almost as a snort. "No one would have ever built on this place if this fault had been discovered. It means all the main buildings are unsafe, and it means that Mick Walker is going to have to evacuate the hotel, the casino, and the entire island before it literally splits apart."

"That's what I was afraid of."

"Diane, who did the basic analysis of this data?"

She hesitated, her hand waving generally in the direction of San Francisco. "We have a geologic department, you know, for soils analysis and . . . seismic . . ."

"Isn't there anyone there who's competent?"

"I thought they were. Why?"

"And you said there was a formal report, and it looked cursory?"

"Yes."

"Did the report seem too cursory for a competent geologist to have signed off on it?"

"I don't know. Now that you mention it, it did seem a little amateurish." She motioned to the screen. "You're suggesting the report I finally wheedled out of them was a sham, aren't you? The real report showed everything?"

"Maybe. If the one you were given didn't contain information about this fault, it could have been a sham to stop you from asking more questions. Maybe there was a real report that told everything and someone hid it and rewrote one just for you, or for Walker, too. Do you know for certain the report you saw . . . the one that didn't mention the fault . . . went to Walker?"

She nodded. "I'm pretty sure of it. I saw mailing receipts. You know, FedEx airbills."

"Did any of the geological staff quit about the same time?"

"I don't know."

"Maybe they never got involved to begin with."

"You know, I figured that what I was bringing you might well destroy Mick, but this will take Chadwick and Noble down, too."

"If someone purposely pulled a cover-up, you're right. It will end up being a mini-Enron. Do you have a safety copy of this somewhere else?"

She nodded. "So, what do we do now?" she asked, deftly shifting from an "I" to a "we."

"The impossible," Doug replied. "And that starts with finding Walker immediately and showing him this."

"Good. I was hoping you'd say that. In the meantime, I'd like to use your hair dryer and see if I can get some of the water out of my dress."

"Sure. There are thick robes in the closet. Help yourself."

Chapter 26

Jennifer sat bolt upright in the luxurious king-size bed, angry with herself for being too tired to sleep. She knew the routine from experience. It would take hours of tossing and turning to finally shake off the adrenalized events of the previous twenty-four hours and drop into a deep enough sleep to do any substantial recharging of her body, let alone her mind. She'd tried to short-circuit the process and force herself to sleep, but continuous tremors, the howling of the wind outside, the awful confrontation with her father, and the underlying heartache over Doug's duplicity were all marching through her mind like an army.

Doug.

Why hadn't he called her? She'd fully expected the message he'd left when she returned. He was here on the island and had no idea how angry she was. She'd phoned his room immediately, but there was no answer, and she tried his cell phone before leaving a terse message.

Jennifer tossed the feather comforter off with one flick of her hand and began pulling on clothes from her overnight bag. She grabbed her purse as an afterthought and headed for the front desk, where the desk clerk politely refused to tell her which room Doug was occupying.

There was an empty concierge desk across the lobby and she found a large envelope there, but no paper. She rummaged in her purse and pulled out a blank, folded piece of writing paper which she inserted in the envelope without marking on it.

To: Dr. Doug Lam

TIME-CRITICAL—PLEASE DELIVER TO DR. LAM'S ROOM IMMEDIATELY. LEAVE UNDER DOOR IF NO ANSWER.

She handed the envelope and a ten-dollar bill to a bellman and walked to the elevator lobby, turning instead into a small alcove where she could stay hidden and yet watch anyone going up.

Two of the elevator cars were open, and, as she expected after such a substantial tip, the bellman appeared within a minute and boarded one. She stayed out of sight until the doors were closed, watching the readout of floors until she'd confirmed where he was heading. She moved into the adjacent car then and punched five.

As she'd hoped, the bellman was still moving down the corridor of the fifth floor when she arrived and peeked around the corner. She counted the doors he was passing until he stopped less than fifty feet distant and knocked on one she could see clearly. There was a short delay before it swung open and a woman in a bathrobe stepped into view to retrieve the envelope.

The woman was young and beautiful, her auburn hair wild, as if she was freshly loved and emerging from the scene of a liaison, and for a moment Jennifer wanted to believe that the bellman had made a mistake.

But the woman turned, as if listening to someone deeper in the room who was coming to the door to take the envelope. She held it out to him as Doug Lam appeared, looking disheveled, and handed the bellman a dollar.

Jennifer caught her breath and retreated around the corner, darting into a small ice machine utility room as the bellman returned to the elevator and waited. She heard the doors open and close, but there seemed no point in coming out. There was an upturned plastic bucket in the corner and she sank onto it in stunned silence.

Who was the auburn-haired lover? Had he picked her up, or was this someone he'd arranged to be with? But why Cascadia? Because it was the last place she'd think to look? But . . . surely he would have expected someone in Walker's organization to spill the fact that he'd been there, and in the absence of earthquakes and ultimatums from her, he would be just plain cheating on her.

Like he did with his ex-wife, she thought. *I don't know this man.*

There was a choice, Jennifer told herself. Sit on the stupid bucket and cry until some shocked guest came in and tried to give her unwelcome help, or go rip his door off the hinges and demand an explanation. Be a victim or seize control. What choice was that?

She could hear voices in the corridor now and the sound of the elevator arriving and departing, and when it was quiet again, she stood and charged out of the utility room and down the corridor where she pounded on his door.

There was no answer.

She knocked again.

Still nothing, and anger began to rise within her at his audacity for trying to hide.

She pounded harder, louder, adding her voice.

"*I know you're in there, Doug! And I know she's with you. Open the damn door and come out like a man and face me!*"

Still nothing, except the sound of several other doors being opened along the corridor as other guests stuck their heads out, wondering what the commotion was all about.

The tears were flowing now, the frustration and anger boiling over as she felt the muscles in the back of her neck reaching alert proportions, tightening like steel bands, the inevitable headache already starting to rumble its way into existence. She felt her heart and pulse pounding as loudly as her hand was pounding on the door, but no matter how she willed it to open, the door remained shut, and at last she stopped and stepped back.

A portly man in a business suit was coming down the hall toward her, a deeply worried expression on his face. She could see other faces peering out of various rooms as he reached her and tried to take her by the shoulders.

"Are you all right, Miss?"

She shrugged him off and stepped back, unable to completely control the sobs that were catching in her throat.

"Y . . . yes! Tha . . . thanks."

"I think I know what's happening here . . . My wife and I wanted to know if you'd like to talk about it with someone? I'm a pastor."

She was shaking her head and backing up in confusion.

"No. Thanks."

"Well . . . okay. We'd be glad to help, though. These things are always difficult."

She turned and walked to the elevator, banging on the down button, aware the man had started walking slowly toward her again out of concern.

The stairwell was a short distance away and she darted to it, desperate to disappear from the scene of her embarrassing loss of control. The two flights to her floor went by in an instant and she paused at the landing, unsure whether to wait and collect herself or burst into her corridor and hope no one was watching as she blubbered her way to her room. Somehow she found her key card, slipped inside, and closed the door firmly behind her.

In private at last, Jennifer slid slowly down the wall to the floor where she hugged her knees to her chest and let the dam break.

CASCADIA ISLAND HOTEL

Sanjay's call came as Doug and Diane Lacombe were crossing the lobby. His voice was terse and intense, with none of the usual humor.

"Doug, we're seeing regularly spaced microquakes now in the Quiet

Zone, and they're being echoed from north Vancouver Island all the way to the southern end."

"What is it?" Diane asked as Doug came to a halt and partially bent over to hear. He held up a hand in a wait gesture.

"Are they almost rhythmic?"

"Yes, they are. But they're everywhere now north and south along the zone above twenty-five kilometers. Doug, that's along the entire eight hundred miles of the subduction front! You hear what I'm saying?"

"Stay calm. Tell me your precise interpretation, Sanjay."

"Terry and I talked. He's still monitoring his array, and he and I both think it's beyond question now that this is an overture to the big break. Nature may be giving us a final warning to get to safety, and if we're right about that, there isn't much time. You need to get the hell off that island, man."

"I'm not sure I can. The only ferry took out the dock and sank, and I can't even find Jennifer to check on the possibility of flying out."

"Doug, please call Terry as quickly as possible. You need to hear what he's seeing. And have you found the governor yet?"

"Yes, but he raced away when I told him about Olympia. He's not going to do anything, even though I told him the USGS was issuing an alert."

"You told him *what?*"

"Just so you'll know if it hits the fan."

"Have . . . have you talked to Menlo Park?"

"No."

"But you said that to the *governor?* That we'd already issued an *alert?*"

"I had to. I know we're right about this. But obviously there is no official alert yet, right?"

"Absolutely not! Our headquarters is waiting for Washington to okay it. Holy shit, Doug! I can't believe you did that."

"Well, I did, but it didn't work. What does Terry need to tell me?"

"He's seeing something strange on his seismic array."

"Strange? Good grief, Sanjay, everything about this is strange."

"He wouldn't go into it with me. Just call him."

"I'll do it now."

He rang off and quickly dialed Terry's cell phone. The seismologist had been tracking the progressive increase in the microquakes and the larger tremors in the Quilieute Quiet Zone some twenty to twenty-five kilometers beneath them, and his sensitive seismographic coastal array could "see" far more than the ones Sanjay was watching in Seattle.

"Something very odd is going on just under or on that island, Doug. I'm picking up large impacts on the surface that are not earthquakes."

"What do you mean?"

"Like . . . like pile drivers or something. Everyone I've called out there tells me there's no construction going on, but I'm seeing a regular impact signature every two to four seconds."

"Okay, but why does it matter? The zone is already unlocked, and it's unzipping itself. The genie is out of the bag."

"It hasn't hit us yet, though, Doug. Shouldn't we stop whatever they're doing?"

"You mean, in case it's making things worse?"

"Yes. Maybe if the impacts, whatever they are, were stopped, the final quake wouldn't come quite as quickly and we'd have more time to evacuate people. You, for instance."

"That's all we'd gain, Terry. The whole subduction zone is breaking. It's not just Cascadia any more. There's no way to stop it. I mean, what's been started is going to thunder on to a catastrophic conclusion now. There's just too much force behind it."

"Yeah, I understand. But Doug, can you at least take a run around that rock and see if you can tell what's going on?"

"You're suggesting a *field trip* in the middle of all this? Hell, Terry, I need to find Mick Walker and get an evacuation started, and get that buffoon of a governor to declare an emergency."

"But this could buy us time."

"What? What could? Belatedly stopping some construction activity?"

"It might. It might delay the final catastrophe."

"I doubt it. Are you seeing any harmonic responses between the surface impacts you're reading from this island and the microquakes? Anything I can hang my hat on?"

"No. Nothing I could point to and say 'see, it's responding directly.' But—"

"Then it's a waste of time."

"Doug—"

"But . . . I *will* take a look if you're really convinced I should."

"I am, man! And then you need to get off that death trap."

"Where should I look, Terry?"

"Whatever's happening is on the western side of the island. I've got it down to that area in my calculations."

"I'll call you back. Are you ready to bug out yourself?"

"Packed and ready, with the engine running."

"Good. First sign of the big one, get to high ground."

"Doug, find a helicopter, okay? This is no time for heroism."

"I'll try. I also have a lady to locate without whom I'm not leaving."

He folded the cell phone and resumed the short walk with Diane to the front drive where a doorman was talking on a handheld. He introduced himself as a friend of Mick Walker.

"We've got a dire emergency and I need to find Mr. Walker immediately. Please get him on your radio and tell him I have the critical information he needed."

The man nodded and turned away as he worked his way through his communications net, then turned back.

"Mr. Walker is at the casino, sir. We can have one of our bellmen run you folks over there."

They climbed into the back of one of the covered utility carts and headed out, but Doug leaned forward and handed the driver a twenty.

"Before we head for the casino, I need you to drive to the western side."

"Why, sir?"

"There's something important I need to check out for Mr. Walker. I know that wasn't part of your instructions, but humor me."

The bellman nodded and turned at the next intersection.

"Do you know of any construction activity still going on tonight?" Doug asked when the cart had steadied out.

"Like what?"

"Heavy stuff, like a pile driver or explosives being used for excavation."

The driver shook his head. "I haven't felt anything like that for weeks."

"Something is kind of thumping the west end of this island. Any idea what it could be?"

He shrugged. "Just the surf, I guess."

"The surf?"

"The waves usually hit us there first, especially with the new artificial barrier reef."

Diane and Doug exchanged glances

"Artificial what?"

"Well, it's kinda like a reef, but made of concrete, and shaped like some sort of curved wing. Mr. Walker built it to create spectacular waterspouts, you know, when the waves come in? The water builds to a point, like in a funnel, and then shoots straight up for sometimes as much as a hundred feet. Powered by nature. We're building a heated observation tower out there, too, but it's not ready yet."

"So, the whole thing's incomplete?"

"No. Just the observation tower. They just pulled the barriers away from the reef a few days ago for the opening. Until then, they had some huge barges out there to keep the waves off."

They rounded a series of bungalows and drove into a circular parking area on the southwesternmost point of the island, and Doug scrambled out with Diane behind him, both of them hunching down against the stiff, cold wind fresh off the water.

There was a thunderous roar accompanied by heavy vibrations beneath their feet as a column of water shot almost straight up, and Doug could see another large wave building behind the first, rising alarmingly as both sides of it were squeezed together by the massive concrete structure until the resulting monster wave crashed into the final barrier and went vertical, as before.

"Good lord," Doug said, almost under his breath, as another round of vibrations wobbled the rock beneath their feet. "This is it."

"What?" Diane asked, leaning closer to hear his reply.

"The fellow I told you about over on the coast, Terry, has been picking up large impacts on the island. He thought it might be construction, but . . . it's this thing."

"Pretty impressive, huh?" the driver asked.

Doug was nodding, his eyes following the two curved wings of the wave-shaping barrier reef to its apex, where, instead of a simple concrete chute, a large rectangular structure stood to receive the waves as well as throw them into the air.

"What's that for?" he asked the driver, pointing to the blockhouse-like feature.

"I'm not sure," the man replied. "I do know there were some pretty exotic materials shipped in here for this thing, mostly on barges. I think they preassembled some of it."

Doug looked at him. "For a concrete barrier?"

The bellman shrugged. "I don't know what all the parts were for. Just that it's very innovative. Our management, including Mr. Walker, has been fairly secretive about it, so we figure there's something else really spectacular to be announced."

Another thundering vertical cascade of water and sound and vibrations diverted their attention.

"You folks ready to go?"

Diane was hunched over and holding her coat closed against the chill, and Doug nodded as he put an arm around her to guide her to the cart. When they were on the way back, he punched up Terry's number again, thankful he answered almost immediately.

"I've found the source of those impacts, Terry, and I doubt we can do anything about them." He described the huge, complex concrete structure. "But I suspect this thing Walker's built may have induced this whole sequence. It may have pulled the trigger."

"We don't know that."

"I essentially predicted it. Well, I didn't know about this wave-shaping structure, but if you remember I said that any major series of impacts, especially regular, rhythmic impacts, could amplify and unlock the Quilieute Quiet Zone. I mean, the basic theory was that this island might be a sensitive fulcrum, but that means it's the last place you want to produce the very kind of vibrations that barrier is producing with each wave."

"You say nothing can turn it off?"

"It's literally cast in concrete, the barrier and the results, whatever they are, and whether or not they're connected."

The line fell silent for a few seconds.

"Terry? Still there?"

"Yeah. Just feeling helpless, you know? The monster is coming and I can't run."

"We still need that array of yours a while longer. You can get to high ground within five minutes if the big break hits, can't you?"

"Probably. Maybe. But neither you nor anyone on that island will have a chance."

"Yeah," Doug replied. "I'm working on that."

Chapter 27

Robert Nelms was cornered, desperate, and exhausted.

The last place he wanted to be was inside Mick Walker's office, flinching at the barely contained anger radiating from the other side of Walker's massive desk.

There was little question, Nelms thought, that he would be meeting Walker again very soon on the battlefield of a federal courtroom. In fact, the wrong words from his lips now could cost Chadwick and Noble untold tens of millions of dollars, and he was mustering extraordinary self-discipline not to just get up and race in judicious silence out the door.

Running, however, was no longer a choice. In effect, he was trapped on a tiny island with a furious client facing financial oblivion for reasons that might well involve negligent work done on Nelms's watch.

One of Walker's men had rudely snatched the chairman of Chadwick and Noble from the dinner and walked him to a waiting car to view the newly collapsed remains of the convention center. The effect had been instant nausea, and the growing certainty that somehow the world's best engineering firm had made a horrible, incalculable mistake. When the car returned him to the hotel and the executive entrance, Nelms had been ushered to the office and left to cool his heels until the quaking mad Aussie burst through the door, ranting as he entered.

"So, Mr. Chadwick and Noble, did you see the result of your handiwork?"

Nelms had sighed heavily. "Mick, I prefer to discuss this in a way that goes to the, ah, heart of any potential engineering unknowns. I have to point out, for instance, that if you're asking whether or not I've seen the wreckage of the—"

"*Don't mince words with me, Bob!*" The full-volume bellow had caused Robert Nelms to wince openly and move backward in his chair as if hit with a fifty-knot wind. The glaring heat of Walker's anger was like a furnace.

"I paid you people a fortune to make damn sure nothing like this happened, and guess what? The whole foundation was flawed!"

"I'm not mincing words, Mick. I've called out half my people down in San Francisco to try to figure out what we could possibly have missed."

"Well, guess what, mister engineering genius? I demand a refund! *And* compensation for my collapsed building, *and* for the resultant delays, loss of value, loss of time, loss of reputation—everything!"

"You know I can't make any statements about who will end up paying for what."

Mick Walker looked at the dour fat man sitting across from him and felt a compelling urge to kill. His chances of recovering from the progressive disaster were good if nothing else happened, but even if the rest of the island was invulnerable, the negative publicity could easily kill the hotel and casino before it got started.

His head reeling with figures and fading financial escape plans, Mick sat heavily in his chair. He'd spent millions more than necessary just to make sure the island was safe, enriching Chadwick and Noble *because* of their reputation as master builders. And for what? He'd been gone the week they had done the seismic testing and doubted Nelms had been there personally. But someone from his shop had, and whoever it was had obviously been incompetent.

"Goddamnit!" Mick stood with the suddenness of a rifle shot and snatched a crystal paperweight from his blotter, throwing it hard across the room. He watched it crash into one of the paneled walls and bounce back onto the carpet. The temptation to hurl the object squarely at Robert Nelms's head had been barely resistible.

As the paperweight came to rest, a bright flash of light pulsed through the window from the eastern end of the island, followed by the loud report of a large explosion.

And almost immediately the lights went out.

"*Now* what the hell?" Mick asked, standing and turning to the floor-to-ceiling windows that lined the eastern side of the office.

The distant sound of heavy engines roaring to life reached his ears, and suddenly the lights were back on.

"The emergency generators," he said absently, aware that the man who'd insisted on their installation was sitting across from him and dying with professional embarrassment.

"Was that lightning?" Nelms asked.

"I don't know. That sounded more like an explosion."

A new series of bright flashes and multiple booms coursed into the office and the lights went off again, this time remaining off.

Am I actually in hell now and nobody told me? Mick thought.

Robert Nelms pushed himself out of his chair and headed for Walker's side. "What's happening, Mick?"

Mick turned with a shocked expression, as if Nelms had materialized from thin air, but somehow the presence of the senior engineer was comforting.

"Man, I don't have a clue. It feels like I'm losing a war." He reached for the desk phone and punched up the hotline to the operations center, barely waiting for a hello.

"This is Walker. What the hell's happening?"

"Sir, we're not sure, but we lost all electrical power from the mainland, then the generators all came on line, then *they* all went away. All except our buried one here at the command post."

"Why? What caused it?"

"Ah . . . I'm getting radioed reports of explosions, as if . . . as if they were blown up simultaneously. It can't be mechanical. I think we've been attacked."

"We're out of power?"

"Yes, sir."

"You mean, the whole island is dark?"

"Yes, sir. Although . . . we still have the option of turning on the Wave-Ram."

Mick paused in deep thought for no more than five seconds. "Is it ready?"

"It's supposed to be. But we haven't tested it."

Mick chewed his lip for a few seconds. The WaveRam electrical generation system was not supposed to be unveiled until months later, but the entire Cascadia hotel complex was dark now and the most innovative source of power in a decade was a mere switch-throw away. He could formalize the unveiling later, he reasoned. Right now, getting the lights back on was the only thing that really counted.

"Turn it on. Let's pray it works."

"Yes, sir."

"How long?"

"Ten minutes to build up enough pressure in the main hydraulic cylinders to start the generator. Twenty minutes before we can get the output generation frequencies stabilized and connected."

"Then get moving."

Mick replaced the receiver and turned to Nelms, feeling the need for a confidant—even one he wanted to strangle.

"I'm going to have to use the WaveRam."

"I heard."

"Keep your fingers crossed you didn't screw this one up, too."

Nelms winced at the verbal assault, but said nothing.

Several hundred yards away, in the sophisticated interior of the Cascadia Island Operations Control Center, the director and three of his technicians hurriedly pulled up the carefully written prestart checklist for Mick Walker's patented brainchild. The metal ram which was the apex of the huge concrete structure, once freed to operate, would be shoved by each concentrated wave against a huge piston filled with hydraulic fluid. When each wave subsided, valves would close, trapping the newly pressurized hydraulic fluid in a giant accumulator while gravity coursed new fluid into the ram and expanded it back to its original extension. The next wave would repeat the process, adding more pressure to the hydraulic system, which would eventually build to high enough levels to start turning and sustaining a hydraulically operated electrical generator.

The director straightened up from peering at the computer screen and surveyed his men, pointing to one with a handlebar mustache. "All right, Bart, read the prestart items," the director ordered.

"Locking pins?"

"Pins one through four retracted and secured. Pin five still in place."

"Input and output hydraulic valves one through six?"

"Open."

"Runaround relief valve?"

"Open."

Live, low-light closed-circuit television pictures of the WaveRam from various angles were on the flat screens on the front wall and inserted on each computer screen. An electronically generated diagram of the ram's position filled a screen on the far right of the room.

When the checklist was finished, they watched the readings monitoring the incoming waves, waiting for the last one to ebb far enough to permit a slow, safe start.

"There it is. Remove pin five."

"Pin five removed."

The next wave could be seen building off shore, then flowing into the broad V-shaped concrete barrier system, concentrating itself as it accelerated in force and height toward the ram and impacted with a shudder.

But this time the ram was moving backward, inward, and a different pattern of heavy vibrations coursed through the control center. Everyone was holding his breath as the ram reached full compression and the pressure readings confirmed that the energy transfer was already greater than advertised. The valve position lights changed and the ram began extending again as the next wave rose, then rolled in, shoving more pressure into the apparatus until Bart announced that they were at minimum operating pressures.

"Okay. Here goes. Start the generator."

More commands were typed into the master keyboard and massive hydraulic valves motored open, the pressurized fluid coursing into the turbine, spinning it up faster and faster until the control boards were full of green lights and the crew began applying electrical loads, gingerly at first, then more energetically, throughout the island.

And, as promised, nineteen minutes from the time he'd ordered it, electricity was once again flowing to Mick Walker's Cascadia.

CASCADIA HOTEL ROOF

With a hand clamped firmly over Jimmy's mouth to prevent further victory whoops, Bull rolled his eyes at Lester.

"I hear a generator starting."

"Yeah," Lester replied, searching the surrounding landscape in search of lights not attached to vehicles. "But everything's still dark."

Jimmy was struggling against Bull's grip and finally snatched his hand out of the way.

"What the hell are you doing?"

"What the hell were *you* doing, Jimmy? Trying to alert everyone on this damn island where we were?"

"Man, just celebrating." He slapped Bull's hand away. "You do that again and I'll kick your ass."

"You're not big enough to kick my ass, little man," Bull shot back.

"Chill, both of you," Lester commanded, his eyes still scanning the horizon. "Over there!" he said, pointing toward the diesel noise. "Just one, but it's somewhere over there."

"We're out of C-4, Lester. Until we get to the other cache, we've got nothing left to blow it. And we need everything in that other cache to blow the casino."

"Yeah, well. An earthquake's dropped one building already and we've taken care of the lights."

"Think we should go?" Jimmy asked.

"Are we finished with the game plan, genius?" Lester shot back.

"No."

"Then we're not ready to go. You guys keep your eye on the target, okay?

We don't wanna kill anyone, but we want to destroy this jerk's whole infra-structure."

"What?" Jimmy asked.

"Infra—never mind. All the buildings on the island. We've been over this and over this. First the power, then the casino, then the sewage plant and water supplies. After they get everyone out of the hotel, we drop it, too."

"What the hell . . ." Bull was saying as he scanned the horizon.

Lights were coming on again in the hotel beneath their feet as well as the casino across a courtyard.

"Jeez, where're they getting that juice?" Lester asked, standing, his hands on his hips. Bull and Jimmy followed suit.

"You said that was everything, Lester," Bull said. "All the generators, the main connection from the mainland. I'm an electrician, man, and that's 220-base AC power if it's a watt!"

"Okay, look. I don't frigging believe this! Let's go back over it, okay?" Lester said, as a voice ten feet behind them rang out, full of nervousness and urgency.

"*Freeze!*"

Lester turned, spotting two uniformed guards, their guns drawn and pointed.

"Hey, put those down, guys," Lester said in true alarm, his hand out. We're guests."

"*Shut up! All three of you, on your knees! Put your hands on your heads. now!*"

Jimmy complied first with Bull and Lester following.

"You've got this all wrong, man," Lester said, blinking against the power-ful beam from one of the flashlights playing in his eyes.

There was a sound like a tape recorder being rewound, and suddenly Lester could hear a scratchy and distant version of his own voice being re-played.

> We've been over this and over this. First the power, then
> the casino, then the sewage plant and water supplies. After
> they get everyone out of the hotel, we drop it, too.

The recording stopped.

"You three are under arrest on so many charges I don't know where to begin."

"Hey, you can't arrest us! You're just rent-a-cops."

"Sorry kid," the other man was saying. "We're deputized by the local sheriff's department and we're duly constituted police officers protecting a special district created by the legislature. In other words, we're cops, you're terrorists, and you're busted big time!"

PRESIDENTIAL SUITE

"Where the hell is that helicopter?"

Frank O'Brien tossed away the magazine he'd been flipping through and got to his feet with a disgusted sigh. The governor of Washington had been alternately sitting and pacing for the previous two hours while his wife napped in their bedroom, waiting for word that it was time to go. The first daughter's bedroom door was still closed, and they had agreed not to wake her until the promised National Guard chopper was inbound.

The state trooper named Billy had been on the phone almost the entire two hours, working his way down from the state adjutant general to the various National Guard commanders whose units were supposed to be able to respond in timely fashion.

Billy turned to answer. "They're diverting a Chinook to pick us up, sir."

"And why the hell wasn't that done an hour ago?"

"They were calling in the pilots, but I guess the only ones on alert were working on rescues elsewhere."

"Unbelievable, isn't it? I'm effectively their commander and they can't figure out how to get out here to pick me up when I order it? Outrageous."

"Yes, sir."

"I'm having someone's head for this."

"The Chinook will be touching down at the heliport in twenty minutes, sir."

O'Brien nodded and moved quickly to the bedroom, throwing open the door.

"Janet? Time to get up and get Lindy put together. We're getting out of here."

"I'm awake," the first lady replied.

"Well, hurry."

Janet O'Brien emerged from the bedroom looking ruffled and walked the length of the huge, elegant Presidential Suite to the opposite bedroom door. She opened it and went inside, and Frank O'Brien could hear her calling for their daughter to wake up with no response. There was a rustle of bedcovers and an uncharacteristic oath before Janet appeared in the door way, her face dark with anger, holding a pillow with a blonde wig pulled around one end.

"That's it, Frank, that's just it! She's either going to a convent or I am!"

At the opposite end of the new hotel complex, Doug Lam and Diane Lacombe walked off the elevator on the floor containing Mick Walker's suite of offices just as Doug's cell phone rang with Terry Griswold on the other end.

"Doug, you're still on the island, right?"

"Yes."

"I need to tell you something. The impact waveform from that barrier thing you found on the island has changed. The impact waves are markedly different now."

"Okay. Is that a problem, Terry?"

"Yes. For the first time I'm seeing an identifiable resonant response from the zone."

"Resonant?" He stopped cold and hunched over the phone slightly. "Did you say *resonant*? Are you sure?"

"I'm sure. Whatever's changed out there is directly causing microquake responses. A shudder goes down, a microquake comes back up like an answer from the most dangerous place imaginable. It wasn't happening that way as little as a half hour ago."

Doug heard himself exhale, feeling even more desperate and equally impotent. "We had some explosions out here and the power went off twice."

"Doug, whatever's changed, if they turned on a water valve or did something, they've got to reverse it right now! I'd bet we're less than an hour away from the main break, and they're almost forcing it."

"Terry, we don't have any way of knowing or predicting that. Stop grasping at timelines!"

The voice from the peninsula was exasperated.

"Look, maybe I'm reading psychic energy or tea leaves, or maybe I've tied into the 'force,' but it's about to happen and I'm scared to death and scientific or not, I'm standing by that prediction. Can you get to Walker?"

"I'm a few yards from his office now. That's where we were headed."

"We?"

"Long story."

"Okay."

"Just . . . just stand by to head for high ground."

"I am. But again, get the hell off that island!"

Doug briefed Diane on the conversation as they resumed their course and opened the outer door. Mick Walker could be seen through a series of inner doors pacing in his office, but he disappeared just as the floor beneath their feet seemed to jerk eastward and upward as a huge seismic compression wave shuddered through the island throwing all of them to the floor.

The P wave was followed almost instantly by an accelerating washboard of staccato, shortwave vibrations that began chewing away at the interior walls and fixtures around them, grinding gypsum dust into the air from disintegrating drywall, shattering window glass and splintering wood trim as desks and chairs and rubber plants danced across the floor and turned over amid a horrid, sustained din.

Doug grabbed Diane from where she'd fallen and pulled her under a table in one corner of the reception area as a cascade of crashing, breaking objects flowed off shelves in Walker's inner office and a bookcase emptied with a series of small impacts as heavy volumes of law and history thudded to the gyrating floor.

He could hear the sickening sounds of rending metal and squealing structures from down the hall and a thunderous crash of something very large and complex in the distance. The lights went out again, but through the gaping hole where one of Walker's window walls had been, other lights could be seen burning.

Emergency battery lights snapped on inside the mauled office, stabbing beams of light through the debris-laden air as if a Hollywood crew had filled the space with artificial fog.

And just as soon as it had begun, the shaking stopped.

"My God, was that it?" Diane managed.

Doug was still prone under the table, his arm around her unconsciously as he shook his head.

"That was a major surface break. At least, it was very close to the surface."

"How can you tell?"

He was breathing hard, his hands shaking slightly. "The P wave and the S wave got here almost simultaneously. It's somewhat like counting the seconds between lightning and thunder." Doug hauled himself out and held out his hand and she took it and stood, shaking visibly.

Doug rushed into Walker's inner office, amazed at the depth of the rubble scattered over the floor, but relieved to see that both Walker and a very fat man sitting in a large corner chair appeared unhurt.

"Jesus Christ!" Walker was muttering as he peeled himself off the floor. He took note of Doug's presence as he glanced at the other man.

"You okay, Robert?"

"Shaken, but I suppose I'm okay, yes," the man answered slowly, his voice husky, his small eyes moving from Mick Walker to the woman who had just appeared in the doorway of the office. Doug could hear Robert Nelms gasp and looked around, noting that Diane Lacombe was looking equally stunned and momentarily speechless.

"You're all right, then?" Nelms probed. "We thought you'd been kidnapped."

She cleared her throat rapidly and tried to recover.

"I . . . no, I'm okay. It was all a mistake. I didn't mean to scare everyone."

Mick had been surveying the damage and looking through the shattered window to assess what had happened to the rest of his hotel, but at the sound of Diane's voice he turned around, his expression momentarily ashen as he recognized her, then recovered.

"Diane! You're okay!"

"Yes, Uncle Mick. Surprised?"

Mick's mouth was open, but before he could say anything, Doug cut in.

"*Uncle* Mick?" Doug asked, almost under his breath.

Mick recovered from his momentary paralysis and crunched through the broken remains of his office to hug her awkwardly. She turned back to Doug. "Mick has always been kind of a Dutch uncle to me."

"I've known this young lady since she was in diapers," Walker said, the remark stated almost as an afterthought, his mind elsewhere and his eyes still darting around the office. "Bad timing, sweetheart," he said.

"Isn't it always."

"I'm so glad you're all right." He rushed back to the desk and pulled a receiver to his ear, trying various lines before giving up and searching for his handheld radio, which had been off. "I've got to go find out the extent of the damage," he said.

There were excited voices in the hallway and a siren blaring somewhere in the night on the island. An assistant manager for the hotel skidded to a halt in the doorway just as the Operations Control Center answered.

"Mr. Walker! The east side of the building has collapsed, sir! You've got to come!"

"*What?* Which building?"

Robert Nelms pulled himself out of the chair and stood unsteadily, his eyes now huge as the man replied.

"Why, this one, Mr. Walker! My hotel. The whole east side . . . and it's full of guests! God, it's horrible!"

Chapter 28

Her head pounding with pain, Lindy O'Brien opened her eyes and tried to focus on the swirl of surreal sounds and feelings around her. She was aware of being very cold, aware of the wind whistling past her in the darkness, the sounds of a distant siren and frantic voices far away. There was rain and the sound of running water, as if someone had left a faucet open.

And there was a single light stabbing a small beam through a haze in the distance.

She pulled herself up, wondering why she was naked from the waist up, her feet bare and the leather miniskirt the only thing she had on. Where was she? Where had she been?

Wait. I was in bed with whatsisname . . . she thought, considering the dream that she was beginning to think might have been reality.

But this couldn't be reality, could it? There was a memory of shaking . . . an earthquake . . . and then the memories ended.

Jeff!

That was his name. She sat up straighter, straining to see something familiar in what should have been a plush hotel room, but with the only light coming through a shattered door from the hallway, she couldn't tell where the bed was, or had been.

Lindy pulled herself to her feet, taking inventory of her body, and suddenly feeling exposed. She thought of looking for her bra, but had no clue where it might be.

She stumbled toward the light from the hall, recognizing her blouse over a broken chair back, and she pulled it on as much against the cold as from any thought of decency.

The bed was over here! she thought, moving by feel in that direction. Somehow the ceiling was now partially night sky, which made no sense.

She felt the edge of the bed, her hands progressing over the top to a heavy timber of some sort. She felt around it, down to the end, and partially up the other side, ducking below the massive thing as her hand closed on Jeff's ankle.

"Jeff?" she called.

There was no response. His ankle was warm, but he was moving nothing, and she walked her hands up his body as she had from lust a half hour before, this time finding no response.

Oh, God! Her hands reached his left shoulder, but his right shoulder was inaccessible beneath the fallen timber, and as her hands felt up around his neck and the back of his head, she realized his skull had been crushed.

She pulled her hands back, feeling the gooey presence of congealing blood. He was clearly dead, and she had eight other friends in the main room next door who might have met the same fate. She could hear nothing from the next room, no voices, no screams . . . nothing.

Backing off the crushed bed was harder than she'd expected, and she noticed that something had sliced a gash in her right leg in the process—a minor matter she could ignore. She crossed carefully to the door leading to the main salon and tried to open it, but the frame had been crushed and it wouldn't budge.

Her eyes were adjusting to the dim light from outside now and the full impact of what had happened was becoming apparent. The upper floor above had given way, crashing through the ceiling over the bed, and the roof above had also been breached.

Lindy made her way to the hall and turned toward the main salon's outside double doors, which had burst open. There were sounds from within and she began calling the names of her friends as she entered, her fears rising by the moment. She had brought them here on a lark! She was responsible.

Here, too, the floor above had collapsed, but there were fixtures and large vases and tables everywhere in the salon, and they were supporting many of the fallen timbers.

"Davie? Karen?" Lindy could hear her voice being absorbed by the mess before her, but suddenly there was a response from somewhere to the right, and she picked her way through the debris toward the sound.

"Who's there? Are you okay?"

"Lindy?" a female voice asked, the strain apparent in the reedy tone.

"Yes!"

"We're . . . here . . . Jaimie and Matt. Matt's hurt."

"Where? Keep talking!"

There was just enough light to see that the ceiling timbers had been prevented from reaching the floor by a partially collapsed dining table whose legs seemed to have been pounded into the marble floor like spikes.

"Help us. Hurry!"

She shoved aside loose wallboard and broken chairs until she could peer beneath the crushed tabletop that had obviously saved them.

"Give me your hand, Jaimie. Matt? You follow."

"He's unconscious and . . . and I think he's bleeding."

She took Jaimie's outstretched hand and pulled, slowly dragging her from beneath the ledge of the table. Even in the dim light she could see her friend was covered in blood. Jaimie grabbed her in a shaking embrace and broke into sobs.

"What happened, Lindy? Oh, God, what happened?"

Lindy patted her back, thinking of the dead body in the other room and wondering how many more of her friends were hurt, or worse.

"It was an earthquake," Lindy replied, her voice otherworldly.

"Oh, God! Oh, God!" Jaimie was wailing, her body shaking.

Lindy felt something flowing through her, as if some strange elixir of liquid courage was pumping through her veins, washing away the fright and the horror and infusing a steely determination and a knowledge beyond herself.

She glanced toward the destroyed corridor, then pushed Jaimie away slightly and held her by the shoulders, searching for her eyes.

"Listen to me. Help won't be here for some time. You and me, we've got to find and help the others."

"I . . . don't know what to do!"

"Yes you do!"

"Lindy, I'm scared!"

She shook her head and took a quick breath, recognizing the pleas of her friend as a form of paralysis she had to break.

"Jaimie!"

"Wha—?"

"Get hold of yourself! The first thing we're going to do is get Matt out of there and get help."

QUAALATCH, WASHINGTON

Marta Cartwright stood at her seaside window, her heart beating dangerously as she searched the mostly darkened island across the small stretch of channel. The searchlight had stopped earlier, then restarted. Now it was dark again, and there had been no tidal wave. When the hated searchlight had gone out the first time, she had been napping in her chair, and the sudden realization that the whole island was dark, and she was still alive, had been a puzzling way to wake up.

But her heart sank when her grandson called on his cell phone to tell her why the searchlight had gone out.

She hadn't understood what Lester Brown was saying at first. He was making no sense.

"Where are you, Lester? What do you mean?"

"I mean that damned searchlight you hate so much is gonna stay dark. And their big party is gonna be ruined."

"Yes, Lester, I know. Soon."

"No, Grandmother. Now! We blew up their power station and we're gonna blow up that searchlight. I've got to go. Enjoy this moment of victory, okay?"

"Lester, wait, this isn't right."

But he was gone, and when she looked up his cell phone number and dialed it, there was no answer.

The searchlight had come back on a half hour later. Then a powerful tremor, and it was off again. She could see flashing red lights from some sort of emergency vehicles on the island, but there was no sound except the wind and the roar of the surf.

A cup of cold tea stood where she'd left it on her kitchen counter as she tortured a dish rag and waited at the window, fearing the worst for her grandson and whoever was helping him.

How did this happen? she wondered. *This is not our way!*

CASCADIA ISLAND SECURITY OFFICE

Handcuffed, shackled, and hobbled, Lester, Bull, and Jimmy had been placed in different cubicles in what was designed as a modern, if small, police station. The presence of a casino on the island had necessitated the installation, including five barred holding cells.

Lester's thoughts were on Marta and how she would react to their bravery. What little questioning they had been subjected to in the short time since the large earth tremor seemed to center around only one thing: where their other cache of explosives was hidden. He had no intention of telling them anything, other than how proud he was to be a Quaalatch brave and a defender of his nation's territory, and how easy it had been to blow up their facilities.

Bull would be equally uncooperative, Lester knew, but Jimmy was likely to squeal like a pig at the first physical prod. He'd already disgusted Lester by wetting himself in fear as the cops dragged them from the hotel.

He felt a twinge of regret that they hadn't finished the job, and fear that perhaps the threats of many years in prison would be true. He knew that would shake Bull, too. His marriage had ended, but he was still able to see his four kids, and losing that right would be a tragedy. But his new reputation as a defender of their tribe would make his kids proud. He would be a political prisoner, and he could handle that.

Once more a disgusted-looking man with a craggy face walked into the room. On his shirt was an official Cascadia nametag that said Jason Smith.

"Well, slimeball, nature is helping you. Half the hotel's collapsed so I don't have any rubber hoses to spare to beat it out of you, but you're going to answer my question."

"I have nothing to say," Lester replied, feeling powerful.

"I figured you'd say that. We called Marta Cartwright, and she almost had a heart attack at the news that you three would risk conviction and the death penalty to do something that she specifically prohibited."

"Who are you, man?" Lester asked. "How do you know our chief?"

The man leaned forward, his face in Lester's. "You don't recognize me, dude, because you're too young and obviously too stupid. My Quaalatch name is Jason Two Otters, and I was an FBI agent for twenty years before you graduated from the sixth grade. Marta is my aunt. And I'm going use some old ancient methods to skin you alive if I don't hear the location of that arms cache right here, right now."

The officer pulled a long-bladed pocket knife from his trousers and snapped it open, the gleam of a stone-sharpened blade all too obvious.

"You can't do that!"

"This is the sovereign nation of the Quaalatch, right? I'm deputized as tribal police, too. You want to regard Cascadia as still being Quaalatch? Then you'll yield to Quaalatch justice the old-fashioned way."

"What old-fashioned way?" Lester was squirming in the chair. "What are you talking about?"

"You're such a grand example of a brave, yet Marta told me you never had time to sit down and learn much of our history, or her stories. So you would never have known of the methods our ancestors used to extract information from the northern tribes when we captured one of their scouts. It wasn't pretty, it was loud and gruesome and left them crippled, but our ancestors always got the information they needed. Why do you think a poor little coastal tribe managed to survive for so many centuries?"

"You're bluffing! You can't cut me to get information! That's illegal!"

"You're not in the state of Washington. You're in a state of hurt."

He reached out and expertly sliced through Lester's shirt from neck to belly, using the tip of the blade to flick the separated cloth aside. Lester looked down, wide-eyed, aware that the blade had lightly traveled his skin without cutting him, though it was as sharp as a scalpel.

The cop was smiling an evil smile. "First," he said, "we'll change your gender. Then we'll talk."

The dream was trying to kill her again.

Once more Jennifer tightened her death grip on the controls of the big Chinook helicopter and pulled with every ounce of her strength, but as always, the controls were frozen and the ground was coming up fast.

This time she awoke to darkness and the confusing smell of dust and dampness, apparently delivered from one nightmare to another. She straightened up, remembering she'd been sitting on the floor just inside the door of her room when the whole building had begun gyrating in the latest tremor. But this one had been different, and her memory ended there.

Her head hurt, and she felt around, finding a growing, bleeding lump on the back of her skull. She inventoried her extremities and realized something was partially resting on her right leg. She moved whatever it was aside as her eyes focused on a wall of tangled beams and walls just inside what had been her room. Standing gingerly, she moved toward the interior of the room, catching enough light from somewhere outside to realize the interior—including the bed—had been crushed by a collapsing ceiling.

Somehow the door to the corridor had opened, but the confused mass of collapsed debris beyond was daunting, and she stood in what had been the only safe alcove wondering what to do. Sven's room was four doors down . . .

Dad!

A sudden cold fear gripped her as she tried to see something, anything, through the destroyed corridor. There were voices in the distance, but she could see no direct lights and the pathway, if there was one, had to be filled with sharp objects ready to make things worse for any survivor trying to flee.

Okay, she told herself. *There's no fire, I'm not trapped or drowning, and the last thing I need is a broken leg or deep cut.*

But her father was down there somewhere.

There was a flashlight in her flight kit, and she'd left it in the partially collapsed alcove to her room. A quick search found the bag wedged beneath debris. She hauled at it, finally pulling it free, fishing around in the crushed case until the flashlight's cold metal housing lay undamaged in her hand. She switched it on and its powerful beam obediently lit up the destruction all around her.

Jennifer shuddered as her eyes adjusted. She played the beam around, confirming how close she'd come to being in the wrong place at the wrong moment. The thought of Doug's betrayal now seemed a lifetime away, but she remembered sliding down the wall and sitting there in emotional agony, and apparently what had seemed an act of ultimate feminine surrender to the tyranny of her emotions had saved her life. If she'd gone to bed . . .

Using the flashlight for illumination and physical leverage, Jennifer began poking her way through the debris to get down the corridor, climbing over fallen masonry and timbers, moving around a huge block of twisted metal that looked like a destroyed air-conditioning unit, and working carefully to avoid ripping her hands and arms on the countless protruding nails and sharp edges.

The only voices she could hear were very distant and still indistinct, unresponsive to her periodic calls. There was nothing audible but the drip of liquids and the occasional groan of something big adjusting itself in the wreckage to the force of gravity.

No, she decided. *I hear the wind, too. We're open to the outside.*

She pushed another panel of broken drywall aside and stopped to figure out her position, aware that it was the mission driving her on that had instilled a calm, even in the face of her father's unknown fate. Having a mission always did that, she thought. Her training as a nurse and a pilot had molded her reactions. Handle it now, break down and cry later, if crying was required.

One more door, she concluded. The numbers on several of the rooms had been ripped away from the wall, but the one just before her father's was readable. She could see his partially collapsed door. It had buckled in half, but not fully jackknifed, and she checked to see what it was holding up before pushing it aside and moving quickly into the remains of the room.

"Dad! Dad, are you in here? It's Jennifer."

Cold fear threatened to engulf her again but she fought it down and concentrated on pushing further into the wreckage. Just as her room had been partially crushed by a collapsing ceiling and floors above, the space beyond the entry alcove was a solid mass of twisted construction materials, and she had to push and haul against them, using a broken two-by-four to force her way in.

The bathroom was empty, and she moved to the collapsed bed, her hand shaking as she felt around the top of it. If he had been on the bed, the immense weight of what had fallen from the floor above would probably not have been survivable, but she forced herself to keep hoping as she snaked her hand around heavy objects, feeling for any trace of him.

But he wasn't there, and the flashlight beam poking through the gaps in the debris showed no one on the floor beyond.

After fifteen minutes of careful, frightened exploring, she regained the destroyed corridor, relieved and scared at the same time. He wasn't here. He hadn't died here. But he was somewhere, and how much of Mick Walker's complex had collapsed she had no way of knowing.

And for some reason the thought of her father's anger at losing their investment in the Cascadia project took momentary center stage, her mind so hungry for a mundane diversion that it seemed almost comical.

There were voices now moving toward her in the debris, calling for survivors, their flashlights showing as glimmers in the distance.

"Over here!" Jennifer yelled. *"Can you hear me?"*

"Yes!" someone bellowed back. *"Are you injured?"*

"No," she yelled. *"But I can't find anyone else."*

"Hang in there! We're clearing a path."

A hundred yards away in the east parking lot of the hotel, Mick Walker stood in the wind and steady drizzle holding his walkie-talkie and watching the growing rescue effort. The fire department he'd created had brought every piece of equipment they had, including the ladder truck that had cost him over two hundred thousand dollars, but the enormous scale of the damage was going to require a fleet of bulldozers and cranes and other heavy equipment they didn't have.

The entire eastern half of the hotel had partially collapsed, the top two floors crashing into the floors below, but leaving the front part only partially compressed while the back half appeared to be flattened.

A stunned group of employees was standing at his side, paying no attention to Doug Lam and Diane Lacombe as they stood slightly apart. Doug had collared the assistant manager who brought the initial news to Walker's office pressing him for Jennifer's room number, and the man had somehow responded, easing his near panic with the news that she'd been housed in the western end of the hotel, which was still intact. He still needed to find her, but it could wait for the more urgent matter at hand.

Doug wiped the raindrops from his hair and caught Walker's attention.

"Mick, I'm terribly sorry."

Mick nodded, his stunned expression unchanged. "We're going to lose people in this."

"I know it," Doug replied.

"The Presidential Suite was on the tip of the east wing, and O'Brien and his family were there."

"The governor?"

"Yes."

"You mean, over *there?*"

"Yes. The worst hit."

"Which floor?"

"Top floor. It's gone."

Doug followed his gaze, recalling the utter refusal of the state's chief executive to even consider his pleas. If he had been in that corner suite, he was probably dead.

Doug took a deep breath and mentally squared his shoulders.

"Mick, you have to immediately evacuate this island."

Mick turned to him, the first flash of anger moving like a fast cloud across his face.

"You just can't wait, can you, Lam? If you mean evacuate the injured, that's fine. But if you think I'm abandoning this resort—"

"Mick, I mean the whole island! That last quake split you in half. You built right across a surficial fault and it's now active, for crying out loud. That's what I . . . we . . . were coming to tell you when it hit."

"I'm not abandoning this island. I'll rebuild."

"Mick, that's not the point. Your hotel's uninhabitable, there's no other place to stay, we still could have the big subduction quake any moment with a tsunami that will finish off all of us, and there's no time to lose."

Walker turned to Doug. "You know what? Fuck you, Lam. Just fuck you for enjoying this."

"*Enjoying* this? You've got to be kidding! Hey, get this straight, Walker. I'm horrified, and I also happen to be standing here in harm's way, and I've got a lover in there somewhere I'm worried about, too."

"Even if I wanted to evacuate, would you kindly tell me how we're going to do it? My ferry's out of service, the dock is toast, the wind's too high for helicopter operations, and here we are! So, genius, how do we evacuate?"

Doug exhaled sharply, knowing he'd been cornered. "I don't know. But there's always a way."

"Yeah, thank you Mary Sunshine."

Someone was tugging on Doug's sleeve and he turned to find the ashen-faced assistant manager.

"Dr. Lam, I . . . made a mistake earlier."

"Sorry?"

"Ms. Lindstrom was in 214, not 240."

"Oh. Okay."

"I thought you needed to know."

Doug stared at the man, his level of panic rising once again, Jennifer's face in his mind.

"Which wing? Still the west wing?"

"No, sir. East, I'm afraid. The east wing."

Diane Lacombe tried unsuccessfully to catch his arm as he bolted for the wreckage of the hotel, but he was too fast, and she stood in confusion for a second before turning to Mick Walker.

"Mick—"

"I'm sorry you're with Chadwick and Noble, Diane."

"Yeah, well—"

"They've done this to me. Some bastard failed to do the job and missed that fault."

She swallowed hard, all her suspicions about who had invaded her apartment and who was looking for her suddenly seeming moot.

"Is . . . is Mr. Nelms still back at your office?"

"I think so," he said, noting that she was looking around as if worried she might be overheard. "Why, Diane? Do you know something I should know?"

Her words were anything but planned.

"There are a lot of things you should have known, and a lot of great things you've missed."

"You're . . . referring to ancient history?"

"If that's what you want to call it. That's pretty insulting."

"I don't mean it to be. It's just that we agreed—"

"*You* agreed. I was forced to listen." She composed herself, throttling her emotions and returning to the mission. "I also happen to know who that bastard is you're referring to."

His eyebrows furrowed in a strange look, more worried than shocked.

"You do? Who?"

"Me."

"What?" He shook his head once as if to toss off whatever had garbled her words. "No, I mean, who did it? Who screwed up the seismic survey?"

She sighed, dropping her gaze to her shoes before looking back at him. There was anger and pain and fury there, she knew, and all of it moments away from becoming shock.

"I personally came out and led the team that did the survey. You didn't know that, did you?"

"No. You were *here?*"

"Yes. Others crunched the numbers and interpreted the data, but I got the data, and it showed the fault."

"Good God, Diane! You *knew?*" he asked incredulously, a look of betrayal already spreading across his features. "You knew and you didn't report it to me? Why would you . . ."

"How would I know? I'm not a seismologist. No, I just gathered the raw data. And until I crunched it myself much, much later, I didn't know Dr. Lam was right. By then you'd already built about half the island."

"I'm totally confused! You said you got the data and it showed the fault, and you later found out it also validated Lam's theories about this being a very seismically sensitive location?"

She was nodding.

"Go on," he said, his voice distinctly cold and precise, his attention riveted on her even as the island's remaining ambulance screamed up and stopped yards away.

She moved closer. "I had to find Dr. Lam to make sure of what I was seeing before I brought it to you. After all, I had no clue until after all your main construction was finished. He confirmed what I thought I saw—and more—and we were coming to warn you that there was this massive surficial fault splitting the island."

Mick Walker seemed staggered. "You mean . . . ten minutes before all this happened?" He gestured to the partially collapsed hotel.

"Yes. Lam confirmed it, and we headed off to find you immediately. To warn you that the reason the convention hall collapsed was that it ended up being built right across the hidden break in the island. The fault line. But, there's more."

"Go on."

"Doug Lam was going to tell you, because I can't give you all the reasons, but he thinks your wave machine is feeding these earthquakes."

Once more his expression turned dark and angry. "It's doing *what?*"

She explained the theory as best she could, her confidence sinking again as he rolled his eyes. "Diane, Doug Lam would say anything to shut me down."

"But, I heard one of his other seismologists on the phone confirming what he called resonant echoes, especially after the power generation machine was turned on."

"Bullshit."

"Mick—"

"Look! I know this guy, Honey. Okay? He's hated this project from the beginning. He says it's because of the earthquake threat, but I know the guy's a closet environmentalist who's outraged because I pushed some smelly seabirds off their filthy perch and cleaned it up."

"He confirmed the fault line and he was right."

"Perhaps. But that doesn't mean he's right about a larger earthquake, let alone our causing it. Besides, I've heard that drivel before when he opposed us in the shoreline construction permit hearings."

"You did?"

"Hell, yes! Lam was in there saying that if we used pile drivers or explosives we'd set off the subduction zone. No one agreed with him. It was junk science at best."

"So, you used pile drivers and dynamite, right?"

"Yes. Of course."

"And now the subduction zone is coming apart, right?" She let the statement sit there like a poisonous snake, watching his mouth come open and close as that part of the argument sank in. "All he's saying, Mick, is that if there's any chance his theory is correct, maybe we should stop banging away on an already fragile situation. And I . . . I happen to agree. Why take the chance?"

He stared at her before shaking his head, slowly at first, then vigorously side to side.

"No! Absolutely not! Sorry, Diane. I'm not turning off my WaveRam. I spent tens of millions on it and it's working perfectly, and thanks to someone running around blowing up our generators and main power line from the peninsula, we need the electricity. I won't turn it off. There's no way in hell it could cause a major earthquake. That's like saying a gnat could cause a stampede of elephants."

"And what if you're wrong?"

Chapter 29

The scene that spread out below the approaching Chinook was confusing. The pilot could see a mass of flashing red lights on one side of the complex and what appeared to be a darkened building, but not until he slowed overhead, trying to hold the big twin-rotor craft steady in the thirty-knot wind, could he see that part of it had collapsed.

The heliport itself should have been lighted, but only the rotating beacon heralded its location. It took the powerful landing lights to find the concrete pad where a Dauphin was tied down.

He set the big machine onto the concrete and unloaded the blades, keeping the cyclic into the wind as the crew chief scrambled out, looking in all directions for signs of a car or any other trace of the governor's party.

"I see nothing out here!" he reported into his headset intercom.

"Did they give us a phone number for their command post?" the pilot asked.

A third crewman passed up a cell phone and a notepad with the area code and number, and the pilot shoved the earpiece of the phone under his helmet after dialing.

"Is this Cascadia Control Center?"

"Yes. Who's this?"

"Guard Helicopter Bravo Sierra Two Six, here to pick up the governor's party. Do you know where he is?"

There was a hesitation on the other end.

"We've had a bad earthquake and part of the hotel collapsed."

"Yeah, we saw it a minute ago while we were landing."

"We think Governor O'Brien and his wife and daughter were in the collapsed section. We can't raise them, and we can't raise their two state troopers."

"Damn! You need us to fly over and use our light or anything?"

"Yes. Stand by while I check with our fire chief and see if I can patch you two together on some common frequency."

The man was off the line for less than thirty seconds.

"Do you have VHF aviation frequencies?"

"Yes."

"He's got a handheld. Come up on 121.5, and just hover as close as practical to the collapsed east wing and light up anything you can."

"We're on the way," the pilot said, punching the interphone to bring the crew chief aboard and brief his crew before pulling them into the air again.

CASCADIA ISLAND HOTEL

The dangling debris still threatening to fall into the crushed room was almost as much of a danger as the tangle of wreckage across the floor. Lindy, however, braved it as she moved to the edge of the ripped-open building, waving her arms and yelling until someone played a flashlight in her direction. Several men in yellow slickers moved immediately toward her, calling from several stories below to hang on and asking how many were there.

"*Five of us!*" she bellowed, knowing one of her friends was beyond help. "*Two need immediate medical help!*"

The men were in motion below and she turned back, picking her way along the same perilous pathway to where Matt was sitting, holding his head, while Jaimie sat beside Karen Sams, holding her hand and talking to her. Davie's body lay nearby. He hadn't been breathing when they pulled him out.

She knew she should feel something, looking at him lying there, his death a direct result of her party plans. But there was one more task to be accomplished, one that was roiling her stomach.

As she'd stood on the edge of the open room, she could see the east end of the building where her parents' suite had been, two stories up. The floors were now missing.

"Okay, Jaimie, they're coming. Matt? Karen? Hang on. I've got to go find my parents."

"Don't leave us!" Jaimie managed.

"I'll be right back. I promise."

Before she could hear any more protests Lindy moved quickly through the debris of the alcove to the corridor and turned toward the east side. The suite had been at the end of a similar corridor two floors up, and the remains of the floors were now compressed and jumbled in front of her. She stood for a second considering the limited options and turned back in the opposite direction, moving steadily through less and less debris until she found a usable stairway. She climbed quickly to the fifth floor and emerged into the corridor, running down it until she reached the beginning of the collapse. There was nothing but black, rainy sky straight ahead where the corridor ended in a jagged hole, and looking down she could see the remains of the fifth floor pancaked onto the fourth and third. She could see a narrow pathway along one side, the result of an uneven collapse, and without hesitating she moved out onto the ledge, ignoring the jagged metal and angular masonry waiting below to impale her if she fell.

The sound of a large helicopter grew overhead and a burst of wind from its rotor blades almost caused her to slip from the narrow walkway. A huge beam of light suddenly stabbed at the mess, probing around, finding her and remaining on her.

She was paying no attention, but was grateful for the illumination. The entrance to her parents' suite had been less than thirty feet ahead, and she could see in the helicopter's light enough of a hole to wiggle in when she got there. Unlike the floors below, there was only a roof that could have fallen in on her mother and dad, and that, she concluded, had to be survivable.

Ten feet from the entrance she had targeted, her right foot slipped on the wet ledge and Lindy felt her body sliding downward. Instinctively she jerked her legs up as she grabbed for something on the right, her hands grasping an exposed pipe which bent but held, leaving her dangling and kicking hard to get a foot back on the edge of the collapsed roof. There was a five-foot drop to a meat grinder of debris below and she could feel the pipe bending more, threatening to break. Her left foot caught the ledge and she began rotating her weight to that leg, pushing against the pipe, and finally regaining her balance.

Lindy stood there a few seconds breathing hard, refusing to let herself look down as she gathered her strength to keep going. An earsplitting PA speaker suddenly blared from the helicopter overhead.

"Stay where you are, Miss! We'll lower a basket!"

She looked up, shielding her eyes against the bright light, and shook her head no, pointing instead to the collapsed end of the building. She knew they wouldn't understand, but it would keep them from coming after her long enough to reach the hole she'd spotted, and nothing was going to keep her from getting to her parents.

The rescuers moving up the still-intact staircases on the east wing of the hotel were becoming a steady stream as Jennifer Lindstrom made her way down against the flow, unsure where to look next for her father. She paused on the second-floor landing to move out of the way while two firemen raced by carrying a Jaws of Life metal cutter. After they passed, she entered the hallway and returned to her room, recognizing the ring of her cell phone as she stepped into the alcove. Jennifer retrieved her purse and answered her phone just as the ringing stopped. She toggled up the number of the last call, her heart leaping at the sight of Sven Lindstrom's cell number. She punched the appropriate button and pressed the phone to her ear, hoping.

"*Dad?*"

"Jen, is that you?"

"Dad! Thank God, I thought you'd been in your room."

"No, I came down for a nightcap. I . . . wasn't feeling so good."

"Where are you?"

"In the entrance to your room, looking for you. You had me terrified!"

"Me too, about you, I mean. We must have passed somehow a few minutes ago. I'm almost to the lobby."

"Go back there and I'll find you," he said. "Thank God, Honey. I saw this room and I thought I'd lost you."

They disconnected and she descended the final flight and opened the door to find Doug trying to rush in, his eyes wild. He hesitated, trying to focus at close range, then shook his head to make sure what he saw wasn't an illusion.

"Jennifer!"

A small wave of guilt swept over her that she hadn't even thought about whether he was all right, or what room he was in—even though she already knew. The room with the two lovers had been in the west wing, where the building was still intact, and the thought brought back in agonizing detail the image of Doug and the young woman in bathrobes in the doorway.

Doug took her by the shoulders and she permitted it without reaction.

"Thank God you're all right, Baby! I just found out where your room was."

"Is that right?" she said as flatly as she could manage, keeping her eyes away from his.

"What's wrong?" he asked, cocking his head and trying to look her in the eye.

"We'll talk later." Jennifer removed his hands from her shoulders and took Sven's elbow, turning away. "Come on, Dad."

"Jennifer—"

She turned and leveled an index finger at him. "I said later. I meant later."

Jennifer and Sven turned together, walking swiftly away, leaving Doug standing uncharacteristically speechless in the middle of the crowded lobby.

Chapter 30

Soaking wet again and aware she was of no practical use to the rescue effort, Diane moved away from Mick Walker's impromptu emergency command post and reentered the lobby where the activity was just as frenetic. Her thoughts suddenly focused on the whereabouts of Robert Nelms. Wherever Doug Lam was, she'd already given him all her information, and unless something happened to him or the disk, the cat was effectively out of the bag. In the obvious confusion of the unfolding disaster all around her, thoughts about unknown operatives trying to chase her down now seemed trivial. Instead, she was feeling pangs of guilt about her disloyalties to Mick, and to her employer.

Especially her employer.

Somehow the sight of Robert Nelms sitting in a debris-filled corner of Mick Walker's destroyed office had tugged at her sympathies. Maybe it was her maternal instinct, or just an image inconsistent with someone who could be a threat to her, but suddenly she needed to talk to him—even if it meant throwing caution to the wind.

The lobby itself was largely undamaged except for overturned potted plants and a fine film of dust from the grinding action of the drywall. But the air of disaster was everywhere, with guests huddled under blankets, loud voices coming at her from all directions, the cold winds whipping through double doors that had been propped open, and even the sound of a heavy helicopter hovering somewhere overhead.

She'd seen the gash in the ground where it snaked right through the foundation of the hotel. The break was at the point where the east wing joined the lobby, and it was no mystery that the activated fault had pulled the building in two. The lobby and west wing had enough residual strength to survive the fault's sudden movement, but the hapless east wing—deprived of too much lateral support—couldn't keep from collapsing.

And it was her data that had been the starting point. The question that everyone would ask, however, was whether the data had been hidden to help the client, or had there been an unheard-of level of incompetence in the bowels of Chadwick and Noble?

Diane found the western stairwell and climbed back to the fifth floor, retracing the earlier path from the centrally located elevator shaft to Mick Walker's west-end office. Windows had blown out throughout the western side of the hotel, but the basic floor structure had remained intact, even though the furnishings in most of the rooms had been tossed wildly about.

Robert Nelms was roughly where they had left him, but standing now and looking out of the shattered glass wall facing south-southeast. Island fire and emergency vehicles along with a small crane could be seen around the collapsed eastern end of the hotel.

"Mr. Nelms?" Diane said, her voice tentative.

He turned his head, his eyes flaring slightly in recognition as his features softened.

"Oh. Diane." He turned back to the disastrous vista as she picked her way across the debris-laden floor to stand beside him.

"There was nothing I could do down there," she said.

The wind was blowing savagely through the shattered glass of what had been a floor-to-ceiling window, and she shivered in its grip, wondering why he seemed unaffected.

"What a tragedy," he said. "Do we have any idea how many are hurt?"

"No, sir. There are a lot of collapsed rooms, though. I . . . I think there will be at least some fatalities."

He nodded. "And we've always said that earthquakes don't kill people, Diane. Collapsing buildings kill people. That's where we were supposed to come in. Prevent it. You know?"

"I know."

He glanced at her again. "You realize this could destroy Chadwick and Noble, don't you?"

She nodded, the lump in her throat growing larger. The firm had been wonderful to her. It was a shame it had to be this way.

"I need to talk to you, sir," she said.

"Hmm," he replied absently, his eyes on the rescue efforts, his hands clasped behind his back.

Diane was shivering almost uncontrollably and he noticed and turned to put his arm around her, guiding her to the outer office, partially closing the damaged inner-office door behind them. He shoved a fallen painting off the couch and motioned to her to sit down as he sat on the far end, looking completely defeated.

"What did you want to talk about?" he said, as if they had all the time in the world to kill in idle conversation.

She took a deep breath, steeling her courage and forcing her eyes up to meet his.

"Sir, do you recall that I led the team that gathered the final seismic structural data for this island?"

He nodded. "Yes. You came in on budget and on time."

She nodded, wondering why, in the face of this disaster, that was in any way worth noting.

"Well, after I came back to the office and turned in all my data, I asked for the report, and no one wanted to let me see it."

She saw one eyebrow rise slightly as Nelms leaned forward with what appeared to be considerable effort.

"What do you mean, exactly, that they didn't want you to see it? Who is 'they'?"

"My boss, Jerrod Schultz. I kept bugging him and finally buttonholed his boss, Mr. Wong, in the hallway one day . . ."

"Yes, I know our hierarchy. Go on."

"And finally, about six months later, a copy of the report showed up on my desk."

"And, there was a problem with it?"

"It seemed cursory and incomplete." She explained in detail what she'd seen and not seen in the report. "I mentioned it to Jerry and he told me to drop it, that I was not to interfere in another department's work quality and that it wasn't my area anyway. He even sent me a memo to that effect later. I still have it."

Robert Nelms moved even closer to the edge of the couch now, listening intently as she described her forays into the brick wall of bureaucratic resistance to see her raw data again, then the off-the-books, independent effort that finally secured the raw data and her days and evenings working to decipher it.

"You took it home, so to speak?"

"Yes, sir, I admit I did. I was worried we'd put out a bad report, and no one was helping."

He took a deep breath. "And what did you conclude?"

Diane looked him in the eye and told him about the sloping strata that confirmed Doug Lam's suspicions, and the later revelation that the firm's geologists had missed the fault. It was hardly a secret now that Cascadia Island had a fatal crack running through it, and when she had finished the recitation and told him of Doug Lam's instant recognition of the surficial fault, Nelms leaned back heavily and shook his head.

"I . . . know I should have come to you . . ."

He turned his gaze back to her. "When did you know all this? When did you come to the conclusion the strata might support Lam's theory?"

"I didn't know about the amplification thing. What I saw in the strata was a direct line between the island as a hot spot down to the so-called 'Quiet Zone.' That's the part that scared me. I didn't see the amplification issue, and I had no idea about the significance of what was the surface fault."

"Diane, please. Give me a date!"

"Well . . . about a week ago. I sat there one evening and realized there was no other logical conclusion."

"All right. Only a week ago. Whom did you take this to?"

She chewed her lip for a second without responding.

"Did you approach Jerry Schultz about it?"

"Yes and no. As I said, I had asked him if I could talk to him about the raw data I had developed regarding the Cascadia project, and he had asked why, and I fibbed and told him I had found some of the readings were still on my laptop and when I'd analyzed them, it was obvious the report we'd sent did not tell the full story. He dismissed it, laughed about it, and told me to stop worrying, that the resort was about to open and there were no problems, and it was way too late anyway. He said the chances of a major quake in the next hundred years was an acceptable risk and he directed me to erase immediately all of the data from my hard drive."

"And, you didn't go higher? You didn't tell Wong?"

"No. I wasn't sure what to do. I thought I'd tell my father, but then I chickened out."

"But you decided that running to Dr. Lam was appropriate?"

"Not until someone wrecked my apartment looking for my laptop and the data."

He nodded. "And you suspected us."

She nodded.

"Which is logical," he added. "I would have suspected us, too."

"Really?"

His eyes riveted hers. "Diane, I scrambled half the company back to the office earlier this evening to answer the question of why in hell we let Mick Walker build his convention center across a major surficial weakness. Wong has called me back several times, and I've talked to Schultz. They're all say-ing that the formal report was top-quality and that the dataset that was filed with the report shows no surface faults whatsoever. They said the date of the original dataset bore your signature."

"Wait a minute! I don't know what they're looking at, but I have a verified copy of my data stored away, and the other one is in Dr. Lam's possession. He took one look at it and showed me the fault, showed how it ran right under the convention center and under the eastern side of this hotel, and in fact through the middle of the island."

"I'm sure he did. But if the dataset you're looking at and the dataset in our files are not the same, which one is correct?"

Diane felt her heart rate increasing as she felt the onus suddenly shifting to her. Maybe, he was thinking, her data had been flawed, or perhaps the disk she'd grabbed from the vault had been the wrong one or had been somehow adulterated. The questions swirled through her head for less than a second before she realized the answer was already apparent. She gestured toward the shattered end of the hotel.

"Mr. Nelms, I think Mother Nature has just demonstrated which dataset is right. The one that I gave Dr. Lam. The one that shows evidence of a major surface fault."

Robert Nelms nodded slowly. "You're absolutely right."

"What could they be looking at down there at headquarters?"

He shook his head. "I don't know. I mean, we *will* find out, but I was looking for quick answers before the lawyers and the insurance companies start swarming."

"My data wasn't wrong, Mr. Nelms, and there was only one dataset. Someone is . . . well, not correctly representing the situation."

"Lying, in other words?"

"Your word, sir, not mine. I just know what I know."

He sighed and sat back. "Well, however it came to this—whether someone in our company purposely hid or changed the data or whether it was all a monstrous mistake, Walker has apparently wasted over a hundred million dollars in reliance on our fatally flawed advice."

"Will the firm's insurance cover whatever happens?"

He shrugged. "Not if it was purposeful. And the damages will undoubtedly be more than our coverage."

"I'm so sorry," she said.

"I wish you'd come to me, but even if you had, as of a week ago, the place was already built." He got to his feet then, stopping to take a breath before gesturing to the door. "Let's get out of here, Diane."

She stood. "I'll follow in a moment. I want to check to see if Dr. Lam is still out there."

Robert Nelms walked slowly out of the office toward the stairwell as Diane opened the door to the inner office, braving the blast of chilled air to cross to the broken window. She looked closely, but couldn't make out Doug Lam's form, and was working her way across the broken bric-a-brac on the floor when the spilled contents of a file cabinet caught her eye. There was a golden-edged certificate out in the open, obviously something of value to Mick Walker, and she pulled it clear as she looked for a plastic sleeve or something to protect it with.

The seismic report folder was next to it, exactly as it should be with the familiar red cover, and her eye ran over the printed title in passing: "Seismic Safety Report, Cascadia Project."

She moved into the outer office and searched his secretary's desk for a plastic sleeve, finally finding one and carefully inserting the certificate. She returned to the spilled file cabinet and reinserted the certificate where she'd found it, flipping open the seismic report folder before standing.

The cover of the report was identical to the one that had appeared on her desk in San Francisco. Beautifully printed on heavy, slick, red card stock, it was emblazoned with the gold Chadwick and Noble logo.

But this one contained her full dataset from Cascadia. She flipped quickly through the hundred or so pages of printed-out charts, graphs, and tables, verifying it was the full, damning presentation of the seismic story. It looked as untouched as the day it had been slipped into the filing cabinet.

Footsteps were echoing in the corridor, and she did not want to be caught snooping in Walker's private files, overturned or not. Diane closed the report and slid it back in the folder, standing quickly as she caught a glimpse of another file with the same familiar red spine. There was no time to look more closely and she mentally filed the small detail away for later perusal and moved to the outer office, trying to look as casual as one could in the middle of an emergency as she rounded the corner to the corridor.

There was no one there.

Robert Nelms could be seen a hundred feet away opening the door to the stairwell. But there was no one else within view, despite the footsteps she'd heard. A creepy feeling began pushing her to hurry after Nelms.

———

To the National Guard crew aboard the Chinook helicopter hovering over the collapsed eastern wing, the sudden reappearance of a young woman in a flimsy blouse and a miniskirt was impossible to miss. The pilot and two crewmembers had watched earlier as she ducked into a hole leading to the ruined interior of the building just as they were preparing to pluck her off, but she was obviously searching for someone, and they were relieved when she reappeared to stand on a ruined section of roof and wave at them, pointing downward, holding two fingers aloft, and then giving a hurry sign.

Lindy O'Brien had grabbed up a heavy emergency battery lantern that had fallen from its perch along one of the corridors and hauled it with her into the collapsed remains of the Presidential Suite. Without that light, the search would have been hopeless, since the noise of the helicopter drowned out any hope of hearing a reply to her repeated calls for her parents.

The helicopter's noise had faded slightly, but she still couldn't hear a thing.

It seemed to take forever before she found her father, alive but unconscious in the middle of the room. She figured she had crawled right past him twice. Her mother was fifteen feet away and in severe pain, her leg badly broken and trapped beneath a desk by the eastern window. She was conscious but woozy, and Lindy left her to go back to her father. She checked his breathing. It was steady, but shallow, and she went to work to try to free him, finally succeeding.

"Dad? Can you hear me? Please be all right!"

She searched for a blanket and found a fallen tapestry. She pulled it over her father before she crawled back to try to help her mother.

"Mom, I'm going to get help up here. Hang on!"

"I'm really hurting, Honey! Is your father okay?"

"He's unconscious, but breathing steadily, Mom. I think he's okay."

She could see her mother wincing against the pain as she lay on her stomach and tried to look at her daughter.

"Thank goodness you're all right," she said. "I'd just discovered your little ruse when the earthquake hit."

"Sorry, Mom."

"We'll . . . talk about it later."

"Yeah."

Lindy patted her mother's arm and slid backward until she could turn around again and regain the exit.

She climbed back onto the partially collapsed roof and began waving the helicopter in, watching as best she could against the glaring searchlight as the crew chief swung free of the Chinook and let his partner winch him down. He had barely reached the roof and disconnected when

Lindy plastered her mouth to an earhole in his helmet and cupped her hands.

"Can you understand me?"

He nodded.

"I'm Lindy O'Brien. My mother is hurt and trapped. I can't lift the stuff holding her. My dad—the governor—is unconscious. I pulled him free but he's obviously hurt." The tears were streaming down her face now. "I can't do any more by myself!"

"We'll take it from here."

———

After the uncomfortable encounter with Doug, Jennifer had left the hotel lobby with Sven trotting to catch up. They had marched outside into the cold rain and wind before she turned to her father and confessed that she had no clue where she was going.

"I was wondering," he said, still eyeing the area behind them in case Doug Lam came storming after them. "It was a good exit, though."

She tried to laugh, the tears in her eyes blending with the rain trickling down her face and invalidating the attempt at nonchalance.

"Honey, I don't know how many people are hurt in there, but we'd better call dispatch and scramble as many birds as we can get in the air. This is very serious, Jen. From what I saw back there, we're going to have some terrible injuries."

"But the winds—" she began.

"Are a bitch, I agree. But if they're anywhere close to the limit, we'll have to handle it, and if you've noticed, that Chinook is holding his own."

She glanced involuntarily at the rescue operation in progress over the shattered east wing and nodded, her cell phone already open as she followed him back into an empty meeting room unlikely to be visited by Doug or anyone else she didn't want to see.

Norm Bryarly was still manning the desk in Seattle and already ahead of her.

"I figured you'd be calling, Jennifer. The island's command post just called begging for immediate help and we're launching. With all the military helicopters going down to the Long Beach Peninsula, we're the only other source of medevac help."

"It's still blowing hard out here, Norm. I'm not sure it's not out of limits."

"They say it's just *at* the limit, Jennifer."

"Who can we launch?"

He went down the list of available pilots and helicopters.

"We can send the Dauphin back, dispatch both of our BK-117s, and the EC-135, and then there's the 412 you're flying."

"We may have to evacuate up to three hundred people, Norm."

"*What?*"

She explained the loss of the ferry and the splitting island. "As soon as we get the stretcher cases out of here, we'd better be ready to start shuttling them to the mainland."

"Well . . . I estimate . . . given our fleet . . . ah . . . about thirty-two to thirty-four people with each run of the fleet, with all the choppers at max capacity."

"I was thinking we could shuttle them to the ferry parking area on the peninsula fairly rapidly. It's less than two miles."

"If so, and if the winds don't go out or stay out of limits, we can probably airlift three hundred people out of there in five hours. But we'll need jet fuel from somewhere to keep going at that rate."

"They've got fuel here. I just don't know if they've got the power to pump it."

"I'll get a fuel truck started in that direction. But it'll take four hours to get him there, and that's if the roads aren't cut. Jennifer, may I ask a personal question?"

"Sure."

"Are *you* okay? You sound really stressed."

She chuckled as convincingly as she could, wondering if being so empathetically joined with your employees was always a good thing, especially when you were trying to hide personal upsets.

"Yeah. Just a bit tired and . . . you might say I've been a little distracted. Do we have enough crew?"

Norm hesitated, deciding whether to press further. He'd known her long enough to spot a lie.

"Yes and no, Jennifer. We'll man them, just don't ask about crew duty time."

"I know nothing. A flight nurse with each?"

"Three crewmembers per bird."

"As soon as you can get them airborne, Norm. We'll sort out the financial later."

There was a hesitation on the other end. "A lot of money is involved here, Jennifer, and normally we've got a billable client."

"Don't worry about it. Let's just get rolling. According to Doug . . ." she hesitated, something catching in her throat.

"Sorry?"

She cleared her throat, but not before Norm Bryarly understood what was troubling her. They'd permitted Doug Lam to hitch a ride to Cascadia Island, and whatever had happened since had shaken his boss.

"Just got a tickle in my throat. I was saying, Norm, that according to Doug Lam, we're all standing in the shadow of a huge tsunami, so every second counts."

Chapter 31

"What?"

The sharp, angry answer was anything but characteristic of Doug Lam's normal telephone manners, and for a moment Terry Griswold thought he'd reached the wrong number.

"Doug?"

"Yes—who's this?"

"Terry. Are you okay?"

"Yes. It's just a hell of a mess here. What do you have?"

"Doug, at the risk of sounding like Chicken Little, the ground is, in fact, falling. Cascadia has now dropped 1.8 feet, most of it with that large shaker less than an hour ago. And if you can't get those impacts stopped, it's going to be all over in a matter of hours. Every hour the resonant answers from the Quiet Zone become more directly linked to those impacts. Have you talked to Walker?"

"We were on the way when it hit." He quickly described the collapse of the hotel's eastern wing, and the fact that the governor was missing in the wreckage.

"I hate to sound unsympathetic, but if O'Brien's dead, the lieutenant governor has the power to make the evacuation decision, so we should talk to him. I agree with your earlier analysis. It's too late to stop this disaster, but we might delay it."

"Okay, I'll look for Walker again."

"Doug, I'm begging you, man, don't take no for an answer. Get it stopped any way you can."

"I never accept 'no' for an answer, but unfortunately I can't make the damn world do my bidding every time."

"Doug? I've been in touch with Menlo Park and they agree. They've issued the warning, so you're okay there, but they've also seen my data and they agree those impacts have got to be stopped, whatever it takes."

"It may be impossible, Terry. That barrier is a giant concrete dam, and even if he stops his electrical generator, it may not be enough."

"Do what you can."

"This can't get more bizarre."

"I'm going to call our senior senator," Terry continued.

"You *know* her?"

"Yes, I know her well. Another story for another time. I'll call you back."

Terry disconnected and Doug folded his cell phone and headed for the parking lot where he'd last seen Mick Walker. Having a mission again was a relief. He could see the huge Chinook hovering over the eastern end of the building and recognized it as National Guard, and at first the thought that a hundred Army helicopters could rapidly pick the island clean of potential victims seemed a deliverance. But he found the idea was already being discussed, and dismissed, when he came up next to Walker, who was being briefed by a man Doug hadn't seen before.

"At best they can spare one more helicopter, but not for an hour. All the rest of them are down in the Long Beach area. Half the peninsula's cut off by water and there are a huge number of collapsed buildings between here and there. They say we're far down the list."

Mick Walker was incredulous. "How about medevac?" We've got injured people all over the place!"

"They said we'd have to wait."

"Okay, where's Sven Lindstrom and his daughter? Find them, and get one of them over here."

The man nodded and rushed off as Walker turned to Doug.

"You again?" he asked.

Doug sighed. "I'm too tired to spar with you, Mick. But I wanted to tell you two things. One, my people in Menlo Park have formally posted the earthquake warning, as I told the governor a while ago. And two, your WaveRam has got to be turned off now, or it's highly likely the federal government will get involved."

"And what is that supposed to mean?"

"If they have to they'll issue a court order. Maybe they'll send the Navy in to blow it up. You've created a major public threat."

"So what do we do for power?"

"We'll do a lot better in the dark than washed away by a fifty-foot wall of water."

"Now it's a fifty feet?" Mick snorted. "Before, you predicted thirty."

"Oh, Christ, Walker, who cares? We're dead if it hits, okay? How many angels can dance on the head of a pin, anyway?"

"I can't black out the island in the middle of a rescue."

"Don't you have portable generators?"

"One, yes. Only one."

"Isn't that enough?"

"Damnit, Lam, why should I believe you? And don't start with the convoluted scientific explanations."

Doug sighed and met his eyes. "Okay, this is as simple as I can make it. There's a trigger down there and your machine is pulling at it with every impact. How do we know? Because every impact that thing makes sends seismic waves down that are being amplified and echoed right back up. We can literally *see* the effect on our seismographs. That thing is progressively pulling the pin on the big one."

"Not creating it?"

"No, the trigger was already there."

"So, we're just making it happen faster, which isn't going to help with an island full of people I need to get to safety. The question is, how much faster?"

"We've seen unprecedented changes in the patterns in just the last hour. That probably means the big break will come before daybreak if we don't stop pounding on the trigger, and maybe next week if we turn it off."

"So, what happens if I turn it off and nothing changes?"

"Then your wave dam out there has to go. I heard you had barges blocking it before Thursday. Are they still available? Could you pull them back in place?"

Walker shook his head. "The tugs have gone. It would take six hours to get them back, maybe more."

They stared at each other in silence for a few seconds as another small tremor shuddered beneath their feet, then stopped.

"It's talking to you, Mick. It's answering your call."

"I detest anthropomorphic analogies, doctor, but I'll . . . turn it off, if your man on the coast will watch his equipment and report whether it does any good."

"Fair enough."

Mick raised a radio to his lips and pressed the button, issuing orders to the command post to get the remaining generator to the hotel immediately, then turn off the WaveRam.

"But, it's working better than we'd hoped, Mr. Walker," the coordinator's voice whined from the unseen command post.

"Do it anyway. We've proven our point. And save the records." He lowered the radio. "Okay, Lam, I need a serious answer to this. You and Diane say the casino also straddles the fault line, but so far the building is still intact. I'm worried about the rest of the hotel staying up. Should I move everyone into the casino? Can I trust it structurally?"

"Do you have a big tent? Anything that can't collapse?"

"A *tent?*"

"Like a small circus tent for outdoor functions."

"Not with sides, and not in this wind." Mick had his hand up to stop the questions. "Wait! My first question should be, Are the hotel lobby and west wing safe?"

"Lord, Mick, I can't tell you about the hotel. I'm not a structural engineer. But I can tell you the fault is going to split more, and the casino is right on top of it. I can't imagine it *not* being torn apart or coming down."

"Okay, answer this: are we likely to have more big surface quakes, as I think you called them?"

"Yes. Absolutely. At any moment."

"Then the hotel isn't safe?"

"Maybe Diane Lacombe can answer that."

"Let me personalize this for you, Doctor. Would you want the love of your life to be standing in the lobby right now?"

Doug stopped cold, Jennifer's image playing in his mind.

"Ah . . . the answer is, 'Hell, no,' and I'm afraid, now that I think about it, that that's exactly where she is."

Mick cocked his head slightly. "You mean, Diane?"

"No. No, someone else."

Walker sighed. "All right, if you're sure more shakers are coming, there is no choice but to evacuate."

"How about the buses? They've got their own power and heat."

Mick nodded. "Maybe. I've got three of them at forty-five passengers each. That's a start." He raised the radio again and gave the requisite orders for all the passenger vehicles they owned to assemble in front of the hotel.

"Mick, where do you keep them?"

"What, the buses?"

"Yes. That fault line is likely to split open wide enough to prevent driving over it. Once you get them loaded, you need to get them to the heliport, which is clearly on the southwest side of the fault."

"Split open? You mean, like a chasm?"

"Yes. The island is sinking, Mick. It's likely to split drastically and literally pull apart as well. I don't mean by a hundred feet, but enough to be impassable."

"You're just a barrel of fun tonight, aren't you Doctor?"

"I'm sorry. I wish they'd told you about that fault line long before you turned a shovel of dirt here. I wish I'd seen the data. But I've been trying for a long time to warn you and everyone how dangerous this place is. I just didn't know about the fault."

"Do you have your man standing by?" Mick said, brushing past his comments.

"Not yet. Hang on."

Terry answered on the first ring and toggled up the appropriate screen as he sat at the temporary monitors across the channel, his truck still idling a few feet outside the cabin door.

"I'm ready, Doug. Relay to me exactly when that generator goes off line, and keep your fingers crossed."

————

Diane Lacombe had followed Robert Nelms down to the lobby before the image of what she'd seen in Mick Walker's files fully coalesced. A second copy of the same report in a different file folder seemed strange.

Why would there be a second copy in the files? Was that an earlier version? And if so, did it point out the surficial fault? The question of what the other copy said was already burning in her mind, and she decided there was still enough confusion going on to permit a stealthy attempt to answer it.

With Robert Nelms resting his bulk on the edge of the grand fireplace hearth in the lobby, she slipped away and returned to the fifth floor and the corner office. The spilled files were where she'd left them, and she bent down to extract the folder once again.

It wasn't there.

She got on her knees to look more closely.

It was right here, wasn't it? she thought. Everything looked as it had when she'd left it less than ten minutes ago, but the folder with the report analyzing her dataset was suddenly eluding her.

Diane sat back on her heels for a second in confusion.

Okay, what in the devil is going on? I was just here, and I remember clearly what I saw and where, and nothing has been disturbed. So where is it?

The other folder she had glimpsed with the signature red cover was still there, and she opened it quickly, flipping to the title page and recognizing it as a preliminary version that never mentioned fault lines or any other problem with the substrata. Now it was the only one left, and, as such, the only evidence of what Walker had seen and acted on.

She got to her feet, the report and its folder in her hand, and stepped back, surveying the office again as if she might have headed for the wrong stack of spilled files, but there was only one.

Did I move it somewhere else? No! I distinctly remember putting it back.

She retraced her steps to the outer office, scanning for anything resembling a loose file folder, but nothing caught her eye, and she sat on the same couch as before in deep thought.

Everything's the same in here, too, she thought, her eyes coming back to the potted rubber plant by the door. It had survived the earthquake's effects and looked just as fresh as it must have when they bought it.

Diane jumped to her feet suddenly and crossed to the plant, kneeling down to run her fingers through the trace of dirt on the rug, potting dirt that had fallen from the ceramic base when the quake turned the plant on its side. She had been forced to step over the overturned plant ten minutes ago when she left to catch Robert Nelms. The dirt was still there on the rug as she remembered it, but now the plant and its base were upright.

For the second time in the past half hour she felt a shiver slither up her back, as if she were being watched. Diane whirled around, visually examining every possible hiding place in the outer office before returning to the inner office and staring at the spilled files for the last time.

The conclusion was inescapable. Someone had been waiting and watching her earlier, and that someone had taken the file and the report. She remembered the phantom footsteps and the empty hallway and shivered again to think someone could have been lurking nearby.

On a whim she opened Mick Walker's desk drawers, scanning for the folder, but found nothing. She looked carefully at the wall of bookcases along the side opposite the now-shattered floor-to-ceiling windows, but if the file had been hastily stuck there, she couldn't locate it.

The noise of an elevator door opening reached her from the hallway and she moved swiftly to the outer-office door to peer around the corner. Once more the corridor was empty, and with the hair standing up on the back of her neck, she hurried to the nearest stairwell and slipped inside, carrying the purloined file and descending to the lobby as rapidly as possible—fully expecting to hear footsteps behind her.

Chapter 32

Several hundred yards away, Sven Lindstrom burst through the door to the vacant hotel meeting room they'd commandeered and flashed a thumbs-up to Jennifer, who was holding two cell phones, one to each ear.

"Hold . . . hold on . . ." she said, pulling both away with a questioning look.

"I found Mick Walker, and he agreed to the evacuation and whatever it costs. We should launch everything we've got."

She nodded, relaying the message to Norm Bryarly as she waited for the FAA Flight Service Station briefer to come back on the line with the latest weather. She signed off with Norm and folded one of the phones.

"The 412 and the first BK-117 are lifting off as we speak. The other BK-117 is headed to Tacoma to pick up two more of our pilots. First arrival will be just under an hour."

"They're loading up the buses right now, and we should probably get the hell out of this death trap of a hotel. The tremors are coming every few minutes now."

She raised a finger and pressed the remaining phone to her ear.

"Yeah, I'm here. The lights are still on in this section—they've got a generator going—but there's background music playing too loudly in this room. Speak a little louder and go ahead, please."

Sven began searching the walls for a volume control as Jennifer rapidly transcribed the information and thanked the briefer.

"I can't find a volume knob," he said in frustration.

She waved it away. "It doesn't matter."

He shrugged.

"Okay, Dad. This is going to be a real challenge. They'll be on instruments all the way to Port Angeles and then they're going to have to follow the coastline. No other way to do it."

"And the winds?"

"Here, thirty-five, but steady. We're going to have to turbine-wash every one of our birds, though, when this is over. I don't want to think about how much salt spray they're going to be ingesting."

"I know. The Dauphin was already soaked."

She was rubbing her eyes. "Let me sit here a few minutes. This whole evening has been a nightmare."

He nodded silently as he leaned on the edge of a table, then sighed.

"Honey, what happened between you and Lam this evening? I mean, if you don't want to tell me . . ."

She shook her head, tears suddenly glistening in her eyes again as she grimaced and turned away to hide them.

"It's not that, Dad . . . I just . . . I guess it was time."

"For what?"

"To give up on him. I wasn't expecting a proposal, just some form of commitment. And I guess he's incapable of it. Too many years with his ex to reform."

"But, it sounded like you'd caught him with a woman."

She nodded, eyes squinted against the tears she couldn't stop, her mouth tight with determination to get past it. She sighed and cleared her throat, getting hold of herself.

"Yes, I did." She related a capsule version of the story.

"The bastard."

"Yes." She looked up and smiled at him. "But, it was about time I found out."

Sven was chewing his lip again as a modern symphonic piece filled the room. "You know, Lam has never impressed me as being bold enough to juggle women."

Jennifer cocked her head, wondering if he had just jumped to Doug's defense, or was on the track of something profound. She wasn't sure she wanted to go there in any event, but it was obvious he wasn't through.

Jennifer stared at her father, defensiveness and anger rising within, but something about his demeanor and his tone of voice was different. She remembered her heart almost breaking at the image of him in the rain a few hours before, looking broken and old. But this version of Sven Lindstrom wasn't the sneering know-it-all father. His tone was soft and respectful, and for the first time she could remember, he was actually *asking* her if she'd considered his viewpoint.

The realization was startling, and her expression softened.

"Jen, despite some of the flippant things I've said to you about Doug Lam, my real perception is that he's a very good man, and could be exactly what you're looking for."

"I thought you considered him a weakling."

"Yeah, well . . . I've been doing an awful lot of thinking in the past few hours about everything you said, and . . . maybe you'd better stop listening to my overblown point of view."

"About Doug?"

"About a lot of things. An ex-friend of mine once told me I had a tendency to draw, shoot, and then aim with my mouth. I've always known that was true, it's just painful to admit."

The need to comfort him welled up again. "Your advice is usually sound, Dad."

"Yeah, when I'm not trying to impress you with how much I know. It becomes a habit over time."

Changing the subject was becoming an urgent need for her. "Well, it's over anyway with Doug."

"All I'm saying, Jen, is be absolutely certain he's a rat before you throw him away. Some men actually do tell the truth."

"Maybe, Dad, but being in a relationship where you've got no control regardless of what you do is not satisfying."

They fell silent, each looking away from the other as background music filled the void. It was an introspective, haunting choral and orchestral piece heavy with violins and Celtic flutes, evoking images of grand ivy-covered collegiate halls steeped in generational tradition—music capable of broadening perspectives in the passage of a stanza. Jennifer felt her mind resonate to the piece, flashing through a mix of sweeping landscapes and noble causes and stirring moments from countless movies experienced over her lifetime, all of it leading somehow to the exasperated voice of her closest female friend a month before: "You're going to control yourself into spinsterhood!" Rachael had snapped after another rant from Jennifer about Doug. "He's the best thing that ever happened to you, girl. For once in your life, let go, follow his lead, and learn to enjoy the journey moment by moment."

The door to the meeting room opened suddenly and a harried-looking hotel employee stuck his head in, startled to see people inside.

"Ah, we're evacuating the hotel, folks. I need you to leave now. Please."

Sven pushed himself away from the edge of the table.

"We'll be right there."

"Okay," he said, hesitating, then deciding to leave it alone.

Jennifer got up as her father put his hands on her shoulders, surprising her.

"Jennifer, two things. One, whether you believe it or not, I've always been proud of my daughter, *as* a daughter, and proud of your strength as a woman. Obviously, I've been a bastard about showing it. Two, it's okay to be a girl every now and then. Slowly, even I'm learning that I can't control everything. You, for starters."

She struggled to keep composed, merely nodding as she turned away to move toward the door, avoiding his eyes.

"Let's go, Dad."

Chapter 33

Doug stood just outside the hotel pressing a cell phone to his ear as the last bus full of evacuating guests rolled out from beneath the covered drive.

Terry Griswold was returning to the line and the low-battery warning on the phone was beeping.

"Okay, Doug. I've got triple confirmation. The pattern did change back when they turned the wave generator off, but the remaining wave impacts are still being echoed one-for-one from the Quilieute Quiet Zone, and the echoes are growing stronger."

"Damnit."

"What do we do? You say that thing is made of tons of reinforced concrete?"

Doug rubbed his eyes, trying to think. He'd mentioned Navy vessels and thought about every other possible way of destroying the strangely curved structure, but the mere bulk of it was formidable.

"Terry, I think we're too late. They had barges in front of it, blocking it, until Thursday, but they're gone now. Walker says it would take six hours or more to get them back. We may not have six hours."

Terry's voice was clearly stressed, his tone higher than normal, his desire to fold his tent and run palpable.

"They pulled them on Thursday? Do you know what time?"

"I think he said late afternoon."

"And . . . Doug . . . the first tremors from the Quilieute Quiet Zone were a few hours later. You realize that?"

The realization was a small roar in Doug's mind, and several seconds went by before he answered.

"Good Lord. No, I hadn't quite put that together, Terry. The confusion factor out here is unbelievable."

"Okay, so God only knows if we have six hours or six minutes, Doug. I think it's likely to hit us at any moment, but you know better than I do. It could be a few days."

"Terry, hold on. Let me think." We've got a huge concrete barrier in salt water made of reinforced concrete laced with steel designed to curve the waves in just so.

Doug raised his head suddenly, examining his last thought. The barrier wasn't just a barrier, he realized, it was a specific, hydrodynamic shape. Hydrodynamic shapes, like aeronautically engineered shapes for airplane wings, were designed with complex formulas to do very specific things. The image of the Concorde's wing and its constantly changing compound curves came to mind. Change one angle or curve and the wing would be drastically less effective.

So what section of the WaveRam was critical to the function of concentrating the waves?

"Terry, I may have an idea. Hang on. I'll call you back."

Mick Walker was still in the lobby, monitoring the rescue efforts under way in the east wing. More bodies had been found in the wreckage of the east wing's top three floors, but more than two dozen survivors had been rescued as well. Many guests trapped underneath debris that had fallen on them were being liberated as rescuers continued searching through the tangle of broken and shattered metal, wood, tile, and glass.

Doug hurried across the drive and directly to Walker's side.

"Mick, sorry to interrupt."

Mick's resistance was all but gone, his eyes now flat and lifeless as he looked at the seismologist.

"Yes?"

"First, the waveform *did* change for the better when you turned off the WaveRam generator. But the original seismic impacts produced by the barrier itself are still a major danger. We've got to stop the wave impacts."

Mick sighed. "I can't turn off the barrier, Lam."

"No, but you can tell me who designed its shape, and whether that person is on the island."

Mick Walker cocked his head in thought, not bothering to ask the reason for the question.

"The designer is a hydrodynamics professor at the University of Washington. As I recall, I invited him here tonight but he couldn't come."

"Lucky guy."

Mick ignored the editorial comment. "I take it you need to talk with him?"

"Immediately."

"All right. His name is Dr. Fred Kopp." Mick quickly called Sherry Thomas to get Dr. Kopp's phone number, which he relayed to Doug.

"Thanks," Doug said, moving away and snapping the last spare cell phone battery into place before dialing Dr. Kopp's number. After two rings, a woman answered and reluctantly handed the phone to Fred Kopp, who sounded cautious. His accent was vaguely British, his tone imperious.

"Dr. Kopp," Doug said, "this is an emergency and you're speaking with Dr. Lam of the geophysics department, a fellow professor."

"What's going on, Dr. Cam?"

"Lam."

"Lam. Very well."

"Doctor, we're on the brink of a catastrophic subduction zone earthquake that will level your house when it happens, and the wave barrier you designed for Mick Walker's Cascadia project is triggering it."

"What? *What?*"

"Are you listening carefully?"

"What the devil do you mean, my barrier design is causing it?"

Doug explained the details in brief, including the fact that the island was in the process of splitting apart.

"Good heavens!"

"What I need to know is this, and it is a very critical question. In order to silence the seismic impacts produced by each wave—and those impacts are thanks to the great effectiveness of your design, by the way—in order to stop it, turn it off, do we have to remove the whole thing, or is there a strategic section of it that, if removed, will significantly change the pounding effect and the seismic waveform?"

"That's a very good question, Doctor. The answer is yes. It's the outer forty feet of each wing that begins the reinforcement process with each inbound wave. Without those curved elements in a compound sine-wave effect, the concentrated power of each impact would be reduced by one order of magnitude, roughly . . . ah . . . down to 10 percent of what's happening now."

"Is there . . . *are* there break points, or points of weakness, at those very junctures in the structure? Like a production splice in the fuselage of an airliner?"

"That's how they assemble the airplane fuselage? In sections, like sections of pipe, yes?"

"Right. Is that how the WaveRam barrier is put together?"

"Well, yes, actually. We formed the critically shaped elements—the prestressed concrete curved portion—in a dry dock in Tacoma and shipped it out on barges. The rest of the concrete wasn't critical in shape, so they poured it in place. But you're correct that the shape of the outer wings is a complex, running compound design in which the focal point is ever changing. Where they're joined to the straight section, there is a splice on each end. But, you can't just unbolt the bloody thing."

"Could we yank it off the bottom with a large tug? How well anchored is it?"

"The main section is impermeable. It'll be there two hundred years from now. The wings . . . well, if you could break them free of the attach points, they could be dragged seaward, but you'd need an oceangoing tug. You'd have to drag them out, though, because they're backed by solid concrete footings. So just detaching them wouldn't be enough."

"Thank you, Professor. I warn you, I might need to call back."

"That's . . . all right. I'm wide awake and considerably worried."

Doug rang off, letting the information ricochet around his head. He was tempted to dial the man back and ask the weight of the so-called wings, but what was the difference if they couldn't even detach them, let alone pull them out of position?

He called Terry back and ran through the conversation.

"Damnit! Can't we try something?"

"You have any bright ideas?"

"Yeah, head for the hills. But if there's a way to solve this and slow that mother down, we've got to try it."

"Even if Mick Walker agrees to destroy his creation, how do we do it?" Doug wondered.

"You did consider the Navy, right?"

"There's no way the Navy's going to send something out here big enough to shell a shore installation with people on the island. Besides, I think that takes a battleship, and they don't have any left."

"Well, you mentioned an oceangoing tug. What if there's one close by?"

"I was thinking that. We could try calling through the Coast Guard. Undoubtedly they know who to call."

"Or, there's always dynamite."

"But where would we get that much in time? And besides, Terry . . . oh, brother . . ."

The floor had begun vibrating again.

"What?"

"Another tremor."

"Uh, oh. Yeah, I feel it here. Hang on!"

The shaking lasted no more than ten seconds, then subsided.

Doug continued, his vocal register a little higher and more strained than before. "What I was saying is that we have no real reason to believe that we can actually slow it down now. The pin has obviously been pulled from the grenade."

Terry's voice conveyed a weary tone of defeat. "I guess I knew that. I know it's just a matter of hours."

Doug sighed. "You go ahead and get out of there, Terry. I'll check with the Coast Guard and leave by helicopter as soon as possible."

There was a long sigh. "God, I wish we could have done something, Doug."

"I know. Take care, my friend. I'll see you back in Seattle."

"Right," Terry replied, his tone carrying an undercurrent of doubt that Doug would ever make it off the island.

CASCADIA ISLAND HELIPORT

The big National Guard Chinook lifted off from the hotel parking lot with fifteen injured people aboard, including the governor, his wife, and daughter. They were headed directly for Madigan Army Hospital at Fort Lewis, south of Tacoma. But there were still eleven other injured guests to evacuate, and Jennifer was moving now between two ambulances to determine who had to go first. The rest of the Nightingale fleet was inbound, and the decision on whether to risk the Dauphin or wait for the heavier helicopters was weighing heavily on her when a hand landed gently on her shoulder, accompanied by a deep male voice she really did not want to hear.

"Jennifer? I need your help."

The icy expression she turned on Doug was as much a defensive reaction as an expression of anger, but within ten minutes they were walking together toward the Dauphin as a startled Sven turned to appraise the situation. She inclined her head toward Doug.

"I need to fly him briefly over that artificial reef."

"What?"

She had her hand up. "Don't ask, Dad. Just take off the tiedowns."

Doug climbed into the left seat of the Dauphin and shut the door, fumbling for his seat belt as Jennifer pulled on her headset and began the start sequence.

"Hang on," she said. "We're in for a very rough ride."

The Dauphin was rocking in the thirty-knot winds even with the rotor up to speed.

She pulled on the collective and the Dauphin leapt from the pad, tilting dangerously to the left. A quick pulse of the cyclic to the right dampened the roll and within a few seconds they were moving forward and climbing through twenty feet, safely away.

The turbulence was nothing short of frightening, and Jennifer could see Doug was literally hanging on to the edge of the copilot's seat, his knuckles white. She settled into the task of riding out each gust, but the controls were in constant motion.

"Okay, where do you want to go?" she said over the intercom, her voice all business.

He pointed straight ahead.

"See the concrete barrier out there?"

"The wave thing? The one that causes the waterspouts?"

He nodded energetically. "Yes. The waterspout thing occurs at the center of it. It's kind of like a long, swept-back, curved wing. I need to look at the outer forty feet or so of each side."

"How close?"

"As close as you can safely get."

As if on cue, a towering explosion of water shot skyward less than a quarter mile away, and she altered course to the south side of the structure, avoiding the corrosive mist that remained in the air after the tons of salt water had crashed back down.

Rain had begun again, although it was light and sporadic, splattering the canopy of the Dauphin while the rotorwash tried to blow it off.

"Okay, right around that end," he said. "Can you put the spotlight on it?"

The wind was blowing from the same direction they were flying, their speed through the air a comfortable seventy knots, but the Dauphin was actually moving over the surface of the water at forty knots. She slowed until they were barely moving over the surface, aiming for the right side of the concrete reef. Doug pressed his nose to the forward left side of the canopy, straining to see. She snapped on the Night Sun searchlight and toggled its small joystick on the top of the cyclic with the thumb of her right hand.

"You may want to open the door," she said. "For a better look."

Doug shot her a worried glance and she chuckled in spite of herself.

"Don't worry. I won't boot you out."

"Thanks!"

"Not that it isn't a tempting idea."

Doug reached down and cinched up his seat belt even tighter before working the handle and cracking open the door against the hurricane of cold wind. The thermal onslaught instantly sucked at his body heat, dragging it through his pores and his coat, the wind blasting his eyes and face as he struggled to make out what he was looking at below.

"Can you get any lower?" he asked.

"Yes, but not without getting more salt spray in the engines. How low do you need?"

"As close as you dare, Jen. I see the end splices . . . at least I think I do."

"And why are they important, again?"

"You see that break . . . that line in the structure? Just below us?"

She used the rudder pedals to yaw the Dauphin to the left slightly, following his gesture.

"I think so."

"If there's a way to detach the outer portion at that joint on both sides, I'm thinking we could get a big tug to yank them out to sea, or at least get them pulled far enough . . ." His voice trailed off.

"What?"

There was a sigh transmitted over the intercom and she thought she saw his shoulders droop. "No. This is impossible," he said.

"Is it? Why?"

"Look at the way the pieces interlock, and how massive that thing is. I don't know how they barged it in to begin with."

Jennifer slowed the Dauphin, matching her forward airspeed against the windspeed and achieving a surprisingly steady hover. She studied the structure in the Dauphin's searchlight, moving the focal point of the light back and forth along the dark crevice of the splice.

"Has Mick Walker agreed to disassemble it?"

"The whole island is toast, Jennifer. He's acquiesced."

"Really? Are you sure of that? Somehow I can't picture Walker agreeing with your theory even now."

"Point is," Doug continued, "what's the difference if it goes or stays? The island is now useless for a resort, the entire project is a disaster, and if there's one iota of a chance that breaking up this wave barrier will delay a gigantic earthquake, he won't stand in the way."

They studied the barrier in silence for nearly a minute as she kept them fifty feet above it.

"You really think this would make a difference? To get rid of it, I mean?"

He nodded, his lips tight in concentration.

"Well, how about dynamite? Is there any on the island?"

Doug was shaking his head and searching for the interphone button.

"I asked. They don't have any they'll admit to. Anyway, it would take a huge amount and looking at it in person, I don't know how the hell you'd attach it, or detonate it, you know?"

"It could be done."

He turned to her, his expression startled. "How?"

"Either radio control or a long detonator line . . . pack the charge in two separate bags connected by a heavy rope, drop one in front, the other behind, with the rope over the top, then move away and trigger it."

"You make it sound easy," Doug said.

"No. Not easy. Just possible. But you'd need enough explosive power to do the job. Just chipping the concrete a little wouldn't be enough. You said forty feet either side?"

He nodded, then brightened. "Wait. What we need is to ruin the compound curves of the thing so the waves won't reinforce themselves. Any large hole in it might work."

She turned right and flew to the northwest end of the structure and dropped the Dauphin down to less than ten feet above it, pointing to the spliced area.

"Doug, you said they brought those end pieces in on a barge. I don't see how they could have floated them in if they're solid. I think they're hollow, like those on the Seattle floating-bridge sections."

"And if they are?"

"Well, you blow a hole in the front part of a hollow structure, it's going to fill with water. Won't that do the trick?"

Doug shrugged. "I don't know."

"You said any disruption to the waveform, right?"

"Yes."

"Then I'd say it's worth a try. If each wave is a carefully formed critical thing, then hitting a huge hole will screw it up."

"Maybe. But where we could get explosives at the last minute I have no idea."

"Doug, are those steel hooks on top?"

"Where?"

"There. Along the entire length of those end pieces."

His head was against the Plexiglas trying to see the barrier.

"I think so. You're thinking of lifting them with a helicopter?"

Jennifer laughed. "Not even a Skycrane could lift those. But you mentioned tugs, and at least they'd have something to latch on to."

"I'm ready," he said.

"For what?"

"To go back."

She nodded and turned the Dauphin away from the wind for a rapid flight back to the helipad. The mission accomplished, they fell silent for a few moments, the noise of the helicopter's engine and rotor partially muffled by the noise-cancelling headsets into a dull roar.

"Jennifer?"

She turned slightly.

"Yes?"

"Are you ready to tell me what you are so angry about?"

"You haven't figured it out?"

"No."

"After hiding in your hotel room with a bathrobed bimbo while I made a fool of myself banging on the door, you still don't know?"

He was silent for a few seconds while the images coalesced.

"Oh, jeez, Jennifer! You're the one who sent that blank piece of paper and saw us at the door and thought the worst, didn't you?"

"I think the colloquial term is *busted*."

"No, you're grossly misinterpreting the whole thing. She's an engineer named Diane Lacombe."

"How nice for you. All I had was an MBA, and we know how limiting that can be in bed."

"Jen, she's the one who sent me the e-mail and brought the seismic data. We got caught in a downpour on the way back from the casino where she found me and she was just drying out. Nothing sexual was happening. This was purely technical."

She chuckled ruefully. "So, you two were just screwing for scientific reasons? Maybe discussing the engineering theory of human coitus, and it wasn't like an enjoyable boy-girl thing, right?"

"We were not, as you put it, 'screwing'!"

"Okay, I see . . . the bellman interrupted your foreplay! How anticlimactic of him, to coin a phrase."

"Jen, be serious! I never even met the woman before tonight."

"Oh, *that* makes me feel so much better."

"You know what I mean."

"Doug, you're shocked I don't believe you as easily as I believed that your phone calls from Menlo Park last spring were really from Menlo Park. Maybe I'm wising up."

"Menlo Park? I was in Menlo Park when I said I was."

"Except when you took your estranged wife on a cruise, had your picture taken in Alaska, and decided to lie to me about it."

"*What?*"

"I saw the picture."

They fell silent for nearly a minute.

"Jennifer, I love you, but you are an exasperating woman. All action, control, and snap decisions, and no trust. You're wrong about Diane Lacombe, and you're wrong about Alaska."

"We'll talk later, as I said."

Jennifer was silent as she overflew the helipad and swung the Dauphin back into the wind for the approach and landing.

"In other words," he continued, "I love you, I have not betrayed or cheated on you, and as far as I'm concerned, we're not through."

"Wish that was true," she said, half mumbling.

She sat the helicopter down harder than normal, quickly unloading the blades as Sven and two other men she had not seen before rushed up to tie it down.

"Okay, you've had your free flight," she said as she ran through the shutdown checklist. "Now we've got to evacuate this island."

"I may need you again."

Her right hand flailed at the air in front of her. "What does that mean? Personally or professionally, you may need me?"

"The helicopter. If there's any hope of blowing that thing up."

"Oh."

"Can you stand by for a few minutes while I call the guy that designed it?"

"Go ahead."

"And, yes, I was worried about your seeing Alex Jamison again. You still melt when his name is mentioned."

"I do not," she said, her face visibly reddening even in the subdued light. Jamison was an obscenely wealthy cofounder of the world's largest software company who'd wined, dined, and romanced her for a year before deciding that any female over twenty-five was too old for him. She had almost fallen in love with him, and the rejection had been confusing and impossible to understand, since there was nothing she could do about changing her age to fit his new criteria. Alex had been scheduled to be at the gala opening, but she hadn't seen him. Yet the fact that his presence had worried Doug was somehow confusing her feelings about his conduct with ex-wives and female engineers.

Jennifer stole a glance at him, eager not to appear swayed, but he was hunched over the copilot's cyclic pressing his cell phone to his ear, apologizing to someone for calling so late again. She interpreted the other side of the conversation from his reactions and words as Sven flashed her a questioning glance from outside. Jennifer held up an index finger to wait, wondering why she was indulging him. The unsettling possibility that she could have misinterpreted everything was eroding her defenses, like an acid of self-doubt eating away at her decision to end the relationship.

"Okay, Professor," he was saying. "So they *are* hollow, and any large hole *would* exponentially reduce the wave-formation effectiveness, right? Okay, wave *concentration* effectiveness." He listened and nodded a few more times before speaking again. "Okay, you mean anything placed in front of it would do the job?"

He snapped the phone closed before turning to her.

"Jen, if you're flying evacuation missions, does that mean all the way back to Seattle, or just across the channel?"

"Across the channel. We have the bigger birds inbound to do the medical evacs."

"I've got to find explosives. If I can, I'll need you to fly me back out there."

She nodded, suppressing the need to ask him just how in hell he thought he could place them by himself.

Chapter 34

Diane Lacombe stood in the shadows under an emergency exit stairway too stunned to move. She'd put the file she'd taken from Walker's office in her bag, which she'd retrieved from her room and left in the lobby earlier. Her deepening concern over who had watched her in the office had caused her to double back to the lobby-level stairwell during another small tremor. It might already be too late, she reasoned, but there was a chance whoever it was might not have had time to leave the upper floors and get lost in the crowd of evacuees. If so, maybe she could spot him.

Ten minutes and two more small tremors had passed before she heard a stairwell door on an upper floor open and close quietly. Footsteps moved progressively downward, their owner stopping at intervals, apparently listening for any indication that someone might be waiting or watching. She adjusted herself in the shadows to be all but invisible and still have a clear view of anyone coming off the stairs. Whoever was coming, she would have to memorize the face in order to pick it out later in the crowd of refugees.

The approaching footsteps reached the bottom, and her boss, Jerry Schultz, pushed through the exit door to the lobby, carrying a red folder in his hand.

Sure that he hadn't seen her, Diane forced herself back into motion, cracking open the same door as he moved away across the still-crowded lobby.

She leaned against the wall for a second in shock.

My God!

She peeked out again. The item he was carrying had to be the other report from the file cabinet in Walker's office.

Diane moved through the door and remained in the background until she saw him board one of the buses. When it pulled away, she took her bag and boarded the next bus, retreating to a seat toward the back, her mind whirling through the possibilities.

What on earth is he doing here skulking around?

Schultz was a coward, afraid of everything, a tail-kissing company man for whom the word *obsequious* was a personal pronoun. Diane had never considered the possibility that he could have been found voluntarily outside the defensive confines of his office. Somehow one of the panicked calls from Robert Nelms had brought him jetting to Seattle and somehow to Cascadia, and that by itself was amazing. He had to be terrified that he'd be blamed for what was happening. Since he was her boss and he was ultimately responsible for the correct presentation of her seismic data—and since the island was coming apart at the geological seams—and since she, Diane, had gone missing, he must have panicked.

But that's important evidence he snatched!

But why would Schultz, of all people, be creeping around the shattered hotel waiting to pull that specific report out of Walker's files? Or had he been merely watching her?

She'd come on the island under an assumed name. How on earth could he have anticipated her sneaking in? What did he suspect about her activities that could have led to such a precautionary move?

Her head was all but spinning with possibilities. Only Doug Lam was above suspicion, and suddenly she wasn't even sure of that. There were shadows of possible alliances everywhere, webs of questions of who had known what, and at the heart of it all was a naïve little female engineer who had pranced right in, threatening to expose a monumental deception.

The now-familiar chill of apprehension shuddered up her spine again and she hunkered down further in the seat, keeping her face away from the window and trying to force the butterflies in her stomach to land.

CASCADIA ISLAND HELIPORT

Doug had climbed out of the Dauphin as his cell phone rang with Sanjay on the other end.

"Is there any way you could get to a computer and the Internet?" Sanjay asked.

"I don't know. Maybe. Why?"

"You need to see the latest response patterns, and they're far too complex to describe."

"You mean, responses from the wave impacts out here?"

"Yes. The whole zone is quivering with each one."

"That's a pretty apt description by itself."

"Please try to find one quickly and call me back. I'm sending the package to your e-mail address with this as an attached file."

Doug made a beeline for one of the Cascadia employees standing by. He asked to be taken as quickly as possible to the command center. The woman motioned him into a golf cart and drove the short distance to the embedded, partially buried center.

Finding a computer and Internet connection took only a few moments, and a minute more to download the seismographs Sanjay had found so compelling. Doug knew him well enough to know that urgent requests were to be taken seriously. Three members of the command center staff were looking over his shoulder, none of them having any idea what they were seeing, as Doug examined the pulse of the Cascadia Subduction Zone's most dangerous area.

He sat back at last, nodding to himself, before turning to catch the eye of the supervisor.

"Do you have a stock of explosives on this island?"

"Excuse me?"

"Dynamite, plastique explosives, detonators, that sort of thing?"

The man shrugged, but he was seriously engaging the question. "I don't know, other than what they might have found on those bastards who blew up our power lines."

"Sorry?"

The supervisor gave a capsule version of the arrest of three Quaalatch tribe members.

"*They* were responsible for the power loss?"

"Apparently. Our security director is still questioning them."

"And you say they had some explosives with them?"

"I don't know. He's right here in this building if you'd like to talk to him."

Doug snapped to his feet. "It is vitally important that I get a reasonably large quantity of explosives as quickly as possible. So please. Yes."

A short walk down the corridor and an introduction to Jason Smith led Doug to give a capsule version of why the WaveRam had to be destroyed. Smith seemed stunned.

"I'm supposed to help you destroy something that Mr. Walker spent tens of millions building? On whose authority?"

"Get Mick Walker in here and he'll give it to you. The question is, can we find the explosives? Did the guys you arrested have more?"

Smith nodded, a rueful smile crossing his face. "They have a large cache they didn't want to tell us about, but we just secured the information. Two of my guys are on the way to check it right now."

"I need to know if there are detonators, and whether anyone on the island knows how to use them."

"Well, at least one of those jerks does," he said, gesturing toward an unseen holding area. "But they're under arrest and anything but trustworthy."

Doug reached out and carefully placed a hand on the man's upper arm, looking him dead in the eyes. It was very obvious that the ex-FBI agent did not like unauthorized touching, but he was making a tenuous exception in this case.

"Listen to me carefully, please," Doug said. "I am a scientist, a professor, and a member of the U.S. Geological Survey. We're about to have an earthquake larger than anything in the United States since at least 1964, and perhaps in three hundred years. When it comes, it will drop this island below sea level and wash it clean with a thirty-foot-high tsunami before we can evacuate it. It will kill all of us, collapse buildings from Vancouver to Portland and all the way down to Northern California, destroy the ports of Vancouver, Seattle, Tacoma, Portland, block the Columbia River for six months minimum, and essentially destroy the economy of the Pacific Northwest while killing at least a few thousand people and causing losses greater than a hundred billion dollars."

"Jesus Christ!"

Smith relaxed as Doug dropped his hand and nodded solemnly, adding "There is one chance, and one chance alone to stop it."

"You can stop an earthquake?"

"It's never been done, but there's a chance, and I didn't know it until a few minutes ago. It will require explosives to partially destroy the WaveRam, which unfortunately is the very thing that's unlocking three hundred years of pent-up seismic energy. If we hesitate more than a few minutes, it will be too late. I can show you why on the computer back there."

"I wouldn't understand any of it, Doc, but I see the look in your eyes and I'll have to trust you're right. This resort is doomed anyway."

"Where is Mick Walker?"

Smith yanked out a radio.

"As good as here."

Chapter 35

Two of Nightingale's helicopters had flown in close formation along the coastline for the previous twenty minutes, dodging low clouds and staying slightly out to sea to avoid blundering into the low hills and sudden cliffs around Neah Bay and to the south. Whipped by rain and disoriented by darkness, the two pilots were relieved to see the sparse lights left on at Cascadia Island, even though they were not visible until the last two miles.

One after the other, the BK-117 and the EC-135 slowed and touched down, their rear doors opening immediately to load the waiting injured. Jennifer was waiting as well to talk with the pilots, arranging their quick return and the beginning of the evacuation of the island.

When the two machines were airborne again and turning around to retrace their flight path to Seattle, she strapped in and motioned Sven to load the first four people for transit to the ferry landing parking lot on the mainland where a small collection of State Patrol cars and a bus were waiting.

This time, with the added weight, the Dauphin was noticeably more stable as she lifted off. Jennifer climbed to several hundred feet, skirting the bottom of the clouds, and headed for the lights across the channel. The approach and touchdown were fairly calm, and when the four passengers had been helped out of the helicopter, she ran through her checklist again prior to securing the door.

But the door was opening again, and a small, silver-haired woman who had to be in her seventies was adroitly swinging herself into the copilot's seat.

"Ah, excuse me! What are you doing?"

The woman picked up the spare headset and put it on awkwardly before replying. The "hot mike" position was still on, so her voice came through instantly.

"I am Marta Cartwright of the Quaalatch. I need to go see Walker."

Jennifer shook her head. "Ma'am, I'm trying to evacuate the island, not bring more people onto it! Do you have any idea how dangerous that place is right now?"

Marta looked at her with a gentle smile, as if addressing someone who had never had the chance to acquire the understanding she needed.

"I am going to die in a few hours anyway with the island. The only danger I'm in is not being able to save my grandson."

"I don't understand,"

"You do not need to understand. Fly me there, please. I am the leader of the Quaalatch Nation."

Jennifer felt off balance. Self-confidence was one thing, but in the midst of rain and mist and impending disaster, and with the ear-shattering noises of a turbine helicopter all around her, Marta Cartwright seemed as at peace as if she were sitting in a favorite meadow on a mild, spring afternoon.

How does someone achieve such calm? Jennifer wondered, the question fleeting but profound. There was a form of control there she needed to understand.

"You know Mick Walker?"

"Oh, yes. He's expecting me."

Jennifer nodded. "Very well. But you assume all risk yourself, okay?"

"I always have," was the reply.

CASCADIA ISLAND HELIPORT

It was confusing to see Doug Lam walking by the bus. Diane Lacombe hunkered down in her rear seat, trying to stay invisible before reminding herself that he was the one person on the island she could probably trust.

Probably.

The urge to run to him and report all that had happened was strong, but she stayed rooted to the seat. What was the point of telling him everything? He had no power to change anything, nor do anything about the apparent collusion between Mick and her own boss. It would appear to anyone that they had hidden the very surficial weakness that was splitting the island, and that made her a whistle-blower. While whistle-blowers usually ended up with a clear conscience, they also ended up with a registration number at the nearest unemployment office.

Or worse.

Diane let the chance to bolt from the bus and catch Doug pass, since that would have been noticed by virtually everyone. With Jerry Schultz himself sitting in the bus parked just ahead of hers, she didn't dare take the chance. She watched as Lam slid into a Cascadia golf cart and motored out of sight.

The urgency to do something returned, and she spotted a small emergency exit door several rows ahead of her. There had been at some point a small galley below, and the steps led down to it, and then outside.

Diane got out of her seat, being careful to attract as little attention as possible. The lights in the bus were on, and while most of the refugees were quiet, they were wide-eyed and frightened, and watching everything and everyone.

She knew a dashboard warning light would illuminate as soon as she opened the emergency hatch. Even if it went off again just as fast when she closed the hatch from the outside, the driver was likely to come out of the front entrance to see what was happening. At the very least he'd check his rearview mirror.

She waited until the right side of the bus was deserted before working the latch and stepping quickly out, reclosing the door behind her, moving with lightning speed around the rear of the bus and walking quickly away.

The same resort employee she had seen driving Doug Lam was back, and Diane approached her.

"Dr. Lam was expecting me and we got separated. Could you take me to him?"

The woman agreed and repeated the same short drive, escorting Diane into the command center and to the main control room where Doug was standing with another man, his eyes on an overhead screen.

Diane approached him silently and touched his shoulder. He turned and saw her and jumped slightly, backing up a half step.

"Hi," she managed, confused by his obvious recoil.

"Diane! Ah, hello."

"Is . . . something wrong?"

He shook his head too aggressively. "No, no, no!" Just . . . surprised to see you here."

"Well," she began, her instincts demanding an explanation that didn't seem to be forthcoming, "I have some interesting things to tell you."

He brightened noticeably, deepening the small mystery.

"Good. What?"

She related the story of the disappearing file folder and Jerry Schultz's involvement.

"He was carrying the copy you found in Walker's office?"

"Yes. All the way across the lobby. He's sitting on one of the buses now with it."

"Does Mick Walker know this?"

She shook her head. "I mean, he obviously had the report and knows what it said, but he doesn't know that Jerry Schultz spirited it out of there. Jerry hasn't had time to tell him."

"So you're saying Mick Walker *did* know about the surficial fault?"

"Yes, he had to. *When* is still a question. And it was probably someone he hired who ripped through my apartment."

"Then he's a great actor."

"What?"

"Walker. Your Uncle Mick. I've watched his reactions carefully, and I didn't see a flicker of an indication that he was aware."

"He probably never expected an earthquake to hit."

"Maybe," Doug replied, unconvinced. "But let me ask you this. If you didn't have a chance to read the whole report, how can you be sure it told the whole story? How can you be certain Walker knew about the fault?"

"Because I could see at a glance the report was done in the proper, usual format. It wasn't the one I was provided. That one was definitely a sham. This one referenced my data on the flyleaf, which meant they analyzed it, and I flipped through the entire dataset in the back. It was all there, and you said yourself it took only a glance from a trained individual to see the fault."

"Yes, but Walker isn't trained in such things."

"Whoever prepared it in our analysis department would have known, and they would have had to state it in plain English before shipping it to Jerry, who then had to approve it and send it on."

"Could this Schultz guy, your boss, have altered it?"

She shook her head. "No. It would have taken too many steps, and he's not capable of a good alteration, nor could he do it without the data analysis department knowing."

"How on earth could a responsible man go ahead and build after finding out something that staggering?"

"Because he had already signed the contracts and committed his money. No, trust me on this. Mick Walker doesn't like to lose, and he knows how to gamble. He probably figured there would be no quake in his lifetime, so as long as he could pay the right people in San Francisco to suppress the truth, all would be well. Don't forget how much money was involved. After all, someone broke into my apartment, and I'm sure Jerry wrote that pitiful version of the report left on my desk just to shut me up."

A deep roar and shudder rippled through the building and Doug instinctively grabbed for the edge of a desk with one hand while reaching for Diane's arm with the other.

"That's another P wave, and a large one." He turned to the shift supervisor. "Everyone, hang on!"

In seconds the building began to vibrate laterally as a large tremor shook the blockhouse-style structure, throwing a few small items to the floor as it continued for nearly fifteen seconds.

When the shaking stopped, Doug realized he had a death grip on Diane's arm and let her go.

"Thanks," she said.

"No problem."

"How big was that?"

"Too big. The full release can't be very many hours away, which is what I'm trying to stop."

She moved a half step closer. "Excuse me?"

"The big one. The subduction zone quake we've been fearing. I think I may be able to stop it."

"Stop it? You're joking. No one can stop an earthquake!"

"If you can artificially trigger one, you should be able to artificially stop it."

"You . . . thought earlier you might be able to delay it, but you said it was unstoppable!"

"I hope I was wrong, Diane." He outlined the growing urgency of his plan, as Jason Smith came back in the room.

"Dr. Lam? Mr. Walker says you can do whatever you think best if you're sure it will benefit public safety."

"Okay. Thanks."

"And I've got the ringleader of those jerks ready to question on how to fuse the explosives. We've picked up their cache now, and it's enough to blow up a full-sized building. He's ex-military and apparently learned demolitions in the Navy."

Doug and Diane followed Smith back to the holding cells where a sullen man in jeans and a pullover sat on the edge of a bunk, handcuffed and shackled. He didn't look up when they entered.

"Lester? This is Dr. Lam of the U.S. Geological Survey, and—" He turned to Diane, and she gave her name as a Chadwick and Noble engineer.

"Okay, son. You're going to give Dr. Lam here a quick course in fusing and detonating plastique."

"It's C-4," the prisoner mumbled.

"Whatever it is. You gonna cooperate?"

Lester looked up. "You gonna let me go?"

"Lester, you could be facing a lot of years in prison."

"Bullshit. I hurt no one. I blew up property, that's all."

Smith shook his head and turned to Doug.

"I gave him a quick briefing on what you're trying to do, and how urgent it is."

"Lester," Doug began, "I'm trying to save thousands of lives."

"How?"

"Let me talk to you for a moment and I'll tell you. But we don't have a lot of time, and I need to know how to work with your explosives."

"What are you, suicidal? You can't learn demolitions in a few hours."

"Well, is there anyone on the island not in handcuffs who knows how to handle them?"

Lester shrugged. "Beats the hell out of me."

"Then you'll have to do." Doug sat on a steel chair as Diane left the room with Jason Smith, who turned to her as soon as he had secured the door. She introduced herself and quickly explained her suspicion that her boss—now sitting on a bus a quarter of a mile away—had stolen a valuable report from Mick Walker's files. Smith was openly skeptical, but she worked hard to win him over to the idea of a quick interrogation.

Smith scratched his chin and ignored the now-familiar side-to-side shaking as another tremor began. "All right, I'll have one of my guys go to the bus and ask him to produce it. If he has it, I'll show it to you and then give it to Mr. Walker."

"Fair enough," she said, reaching out to hold on to the doorknob. "Should I wait here?"

He nodded as he pulled out his handheld to issue the orders. The shaking was getting worse, the roar and rattling of items through the command center making almost too much of a racket to hear the radio.

The seismic waves ended as before, and whichever security guard was on the other end acknowledged his call. Smith was reholstering his radio when an excited voice broke through the squelch.

"Control center, Twenty-Six! The rest of the hotel has just collapsed! Repeat, the western end and the lobby just collapsed!"

Chapter 36

The Nightingale air force was converging on Cascadia Island, and Sven Lindstrom had assumed the role of air traffic controller.

From inside a utility van parked at the edge of the helipad, he'd found a grease pencil and was using the inside of the windshield as a tracking board.

The remaining injured had been lifted out in the big Bell 412 minutes before, and two more BK-117s along with all of the Eurocopters and a Jet Ranger were approaching, several of them flying formation along the coastline as their brethren had done a half hour before.

Fuel trucks were due at the mainland ferry slip inside of an hour, and as soon as the first BK-117 touched down, battling the fierce winds, six passengers were ushered into the aft compartment. The chopper was off again almost as soon as the pilot had alighted, since he'd already been briefed on the pathway across the channel.

Sven made a notation of the outbound passengers and the pilot's name on the inside of the van's window, and made a check mark by the next incoming ship as he raised a borrowed walkie-talkie to his mouth.

"Okay, bring on four more passengers for an inbound Dauphin. Three in the back, one in the front left. The next flight will be on the ground inside one minute."

The ground crew had been cobbled from the small force of Mick Walker's staff who had left the hotel to keep attending their refugeed guests. With news that the rest of the hotel had come down, there was a somber mood among the occupants of the buses as they all thought about where they had been standing an hour before.

Jennifer had been cleared in by Sven on the radio after the BK-117 departed, touching down in the Dauphin and having as much trouble stabilizing the landing as before. The winds were holding steady at thirty-one knots, but the effect of the various burbles and eddies in the wind currents flowing over the helipad was nothing short of frightening to any passenger, with the exception of the elderly woman who emerged from the helicopter to the complete surprise of those pressing to get aboard.

Marta Cartwright smiled thinly at the crowd, her heart pounding now from the reality she was glimpsing. She had asked for this kind of ruination of Cascadia Island, but she had not imagined the traumatized faces of the ordinary, innocent people who would become victims.

"Thank you," she said to Jennifer, smiling as broadly as she could with her heart heavy as she climbed out.

"Be careful, Marta. And be quick! Our last flight off this rock will probably be in three to four hours. Please don't miss it!"

Marta smiled and nodded, hiding the shame she was feeling. Her destructive wishes had been as real as these refugees, and if she had made this a reality through her dreams and thoughts and her hatred, then she had surely fallen into evil.

Marta suppressed the powerful urge to apologize and take responsibility. No one would understand a batty old woman running around apologizing for something no one would believe she could cause.

But *she* knew. In the guiding philosophy of her people, for thousands of years shamans always had an extraordinary responsibility to be very careful of their wishful thoughts. To wish something evil was to commit it.

CASCADIA CONTROL CENTER

Lester Brown sighed and shook his head. "Man, if you get the sequence screwed up like what you just said, you're dead."

"What? Which step was out of sequence?" Doug asked, alarm showing on his face as he thought about the lethal consequences of an accidental detonation. He'd written down each step in priming and fusing the plastic explosive. What could be wrong?

Lester looked up at him.

"You know what, man? Just go away. I'm not going to help you kill yourself. I'm in enough trouble already."

A woman's voice, reedy and redolent with the tones of advanced age, found his ears. "You certainly are."

"Grandmother?"

Lester Brown looked around, his eyes wide, finding no one but Doug and a deputy in the room.

"What?" Doug asked.

"I . . . just thought . . ." he stammered.

The door was opened by Jason Smith, who stepped aside to admit Marta Cartwright. She snapped a finger at Lester to quiet him and turned to Doug.

"Would you excuse us for a moment. My grandson and I must talk."

Doug glanced at Jason Smith, who nodded.

"Lester, I've got to try this whether you help me or not. I have no choice and less time. So, if it means anything to you to not let me kill myself in the process, I need to know what you know."

"There's no way—" Lester began, but once again Marta snapped her finger and he shut up in midsentence.

She turned back to Doug.

"Please allow me a couple of minutes and he will be ready to help."

Doug followed Smith into the hallway and waited until the soundproof door was closed behind them.

"That's his grandmother?" Doug asked.

"Marta Cartwright is . . . was . . . the spiritual leader of our tribe."

"Our?"

"I'm Quaalatch."

"I didn't know that."

"That turkey really is her grandson, and she is *not* happy."

"He called her, I take it?"

"No."

"Then . . . *you* called her?"

"No. She's a shaman. She doesn't need a call."

The explanation was obviously meant to be complete, and Doug let it pass.

"Were there . . . any new casualties at the hotel?"

Smith shook his head. "No. Fortunately we had it completely evacuated. The state is now ordering everyone off the island and away from the coast. It's the largest evacuation since World War II, from what the State Patrol is saying. But I still can't believe two of our three main buildings have collapsed." He laughed in a staccato explosion of pain. "This is going to turn out to be the shortest job I've ever held."

"Where is Mick Walker?"

"At the helipad, supervising the evacuation, I think."

Diane had returned from a trip to the ladies' room and was giving Doug a questioning look when the door to the interrogation room came open and Marta Cartwright appeared.

"Who is Dr. Lam?"

"I am, Ma'am."

"I apologize for the criminal behavior of my grandson. He is ready to help you now."

"Good! I've got to learn how to prepare the explosives."

"No, he will do that himself for you."

"I'm sorry?"

She turned to Jason Smith. "Jason, I need you to release Lester to Dr.

Lam's custody. He will prepare whatever needs to be prepared and turn his evil to some good."

Much to Doug's surprise, Smith nodded.

"If that's what you'd like, Marta."

"That's what is needed," she replied, turning her gaze on Doug. "Doctor Lam? Lester will prepare this explosive you need and place it himself for you. It's the least he can do."

She turned without waiting for a response and started down the hall.

"Marta?" Jason called after her. "We need to get you back off the island to safety."

She stopped and turned, smiling. "I'm safe wherever I am, Jason Two Otters."

"Well . . . where do you want to go?"

"Wherever I'm bound. This island's fate and mine are the same."

He sighed. "Why don't you rest here for awhile, then."

"If you say so."

"Just have a seat in my office there on the right and I'll be there in a few minutes."

The walkie-talkie on his belt beeped and Jason acknowledged the call.

"Jason, we've completed searching through all the buses and the lists of those waiting for evacuation."

The transmission ended.

"Yes? And?" Jason prompted.

"Sorry . . . someone was asking a question. Yeah, the thing is, we've checked and there is no Jerry Schultz out here anywhere. Robert Nelms is here, but no Jerry Schultz."

"Which means," Diane said, "that Jerry's run to his confederate."

"And that would be?" Jason asked.

"Not important," she said with a sigh. "But thanks for the help."

MADIGAN ARMY HOSPITAL, FORT LEWIS, WASHINGTON

The fact that the governor of Washington and his family were injured and inbound had caused the state's adjutant general to order his pilots to go directly to the preeminent center of military medicine in the Pacific Northwest. A quick call to his active-duty Army counterparts sealed the arrangement, and a formation of physicians and nurses were waiting as the Chinook settled onto the Madigan helipad.

With Frank and Janet O'Brien whisked away, followed by the three injured teens who'd survived Lindy O'Brien's party, Lindy was escorted to another section of the emergency department to attend to the cuts on her forearms. Bandaged and impatient, she'd enlisted one of the younger doctors to take her to her friends.

Matt had a concussion and broken ribs, but nothing life-threatening. Karen, however, had collapsed during the evacuation flight and had been rushed to the OR with severe internal bleeding. While Jaimie would be ready for immediate release, Karen's life hung in the balance.

And the bodies of Jeff and Davie had yet to be recovered, or their parents notified.

Lindy felt somewhere beyond numb. She stood like a zombie trying to process it all before the doctor placed a hand on her shoulder.

"You want to check on your mom and dad now?"

She looked at him as if she'd been in the process of drowning and he'd interrupted from somewhere above water. Her parents. For a second she'd forgotten.

"Yes," Lindy managed, and he pointed the way down yet another hallway.

The governor's injuries were confined to broken bones and a mild concussion, but her mother was in another operating room, and when she pressed a circulating nurse for the reason, all she could get was a sympathetic word of useless encouragement.

"I . . . I asked you what they're doing in there?" Lindy said again, having caught the nurse, an Army captain, by the sleeve.

"Miss O'Brien, I told you, they're working to stabilize her."

"Do you know what her injuries are?" Lindy asked, her voice shaking but rising in volume.

"I can't discuss that with you right now," the captain replied.

"The hell you can't! That's the first lady of Washington in there and I'm her daughter! Tell me the truth, damnit!"

"Look—"

"*That's an order!*" Lindy bellowed, tears streaming from her eyes.

The nurse looked closely at her for a few seconds. The young girl with the shaking shoulders would have bordered on the ludicrous trying to pull rank if her mother's life wasn't in question. The captain moved toward her and gathered her in a hug.

All the fight went out of Lindy, and she let herself be enfolded as she sobbed openly.

The nurse waited for more than a minute before speaking.

"What's your first name, Miss O'Brien?"

"Lindy."

"Well, your mom is fighting for her life, Lindy."

Lindy looked up, feeling like a five-year-old but unable to help herself.

"Really?"

"Yes. Are you strong enough to hear the details?"

Lindy nodded.

"Very well. There are broken ribs, a collapsed lung, internal bleeding, a crushed left leg which will take massive effort to save, and when we got her on the table, she went into cardiac arrest. We got her heart restarted within a minute, but she's in very critical condition, in surgery, and you need to be prepared. We may lose her."

Chapter 37

A sudden burst of rain had wiped out visibility around the island for just long enough to force the Dauphin and one of the Eurocopters back to the peninsula, wasting precious time. When Sven called to report the squall had cleared, Jennifer let Gail Grisham take the Eurocopter in first. She held the Dauphin in a hover for the two minutes it took for Gail to load the next group of escaping passengers. Five Nightingale choppers were now churning back and forth between the island's helipad and the mainland ferry parking lot, and the three that had been used for emergency evacuation earlier were now on their way back from Seattle to join the effort.

Sven cleared the Dauphin in as soon as Gail had lifted off, and once more Jennifer battled the controls to stay on top of the fierce wind and occasionally surprising side gusts.

She had expected someone to open the copilot's door, but the face of the auburn-haired young woman in the doorway was unfamiliar at first. Jennifer pulled part of her headset away from her left ear and leaned in the woman's direction.

"Are you getting in?" Jennifer yelled over the noise of engine, rotor, and wind.

"No. They need you for a special mission, but I need to talk to you first."

"What?" The woman's voice was getting swallowed, and Jennifer offered the spare headset to her as she balanced on a footstep mounted on the left side. The woman put on the headset after fumbling to determine which side was which.

"I said I needed to talk to you."

"About what?"

"About your fiancé, Dr. Lam."

Jennifer froze for a few seconds, her mind flashing to a picture of the bathrobe-clad female next to Doug Lam in the hotel. Diane Lacombe!

What is she doing here?

"He's not my fiancé," Jennifer said, her tone instantly hardened.

"Whatever. He told me you'd seen the two of us together earlier, and that you got the wrong idea. I wanted to tell you, woman to woman, that absolutely nothing sexual or even suggestive was going on! I took a terrible chance coming to this island, but I needed his help as a scientist. He stood out in the rain and listened to me. I was trying to avoid pneumonia and get dry. I was in a bathrobe just to avoid pneumonia!"

"Nice speech," Jennifer shot back, watching Diane's eyes, which narrowed in frustration.

"Speech?"

"Yes. You delivered it well."

"It wasn't a speech. It's the truth."

"Thanks. Anything else?"

"You don't believe me?"

"Why should I?"

"Because there was no time for it to be anything but the truth. Let me ask you this. You know the man, and I don't. Is Dr. Lam an impulsive type who would jump in bed with the first girl he found, especially when his fian—his steady, is on the same island?"

Jennifer hesitated just long enough to validate Diane's point.

"See? You know he isn't, and yet for us to be fooling around, that's what would have to have occurred."

"All right. Thanks."

"Look, you've taken a position that he's guilty, but you need to change it. I've worked for men like you, and when they refuse to reexamine something, they make terrible mistakes."

Anger was bubbling around the confusion Jennifer was feeling at being confronted by the very woman she assumed Doug had strayed with. But in the end, the whole exchange was little more than a personal distraction which was interfering with the mission and her duties, and that was unacceptable.

"I'll take the headset now," she said with as much finality as she could manage.

But Diane Lacombe hadn't budged, her eyes boring holes in Jennifer's face until she turned and snapped at her one more time.

"What?"

"He's innocent, okay?"

"No male is ever innocent, Honey," Jennifer responded, reaching over and pulling the headset off the woman's head to end the exchange. She turned her eyes away to avoid Diane Lacombe's reaction.

The left rear door of the Dauphin opened at the same moment and a large-chested male climbed in carrying a coil of rope and wearing a safety harness. He placed a jump bag on the seat beside him and nodded unsmilingly to her. Lacombe disappeared and Doug now came running toward the Dauphin and clambered into the copilot's seat, sweeping on the headset.

"Hi."

"Hello," she replied, her voice sounding all but computer-generated. "What now?"

"The fellow in the back seat is Lester Brown of the Quaalatch tribe. He has enough C-4 plastic explosives in that bag to hopefully cripple the Wave-Ram's outer wings, and he has the detonators. We need to get him low enough to go down by rope and place charges on either end. We can detonate them by radio from the air."

Jennifer's jaw must have dropped involuntarily. "Are you out of your mind? You brought a bag full of C-4 on my helicopter? Without asking?"

"Okay. Can we please get this done and perhaps save a few thousand people from being killed?"

"I can't fly explosives! Do I look like an Air Force Special Operations pilot?"

"Jennifer, I can't fly, and the only way to do this is with masterful piloting."

"Flattery will get you nowhere." It was a phrase she'd always liked, but she couldn't even muster a smile to accompany it. The knowledge of what was a mere two feet behind her in the passenger seat was distracting.

"Come on, Jen. Why do you think I had you fly me over that big barrier a little while ago?"

"I . . . I don't know. You seemed to think it was important. I surely didn't think you'd try to involve me in something like this."

"How could I not involve you?" he said, closing the door and fishing for his seat belt. "I wouldn't trust any other pilot, and . . . *and,*" he said, holding out his hand to stop her impending response, "that's not flattery. That's fact."

She was breathing hard now, the C-4 truly frightening her where high winds and rain and impending seismic disaster had failed. If it went off, of course, she would at best have a microsecond of consciousness to be pissed off at him before being blown into oblivion. There would be no time for pain.

And then there was the matter of Doug's presence. Doug would die with her. Why, she thought, did that make it seem all right? The reality was almost comforting, and that fact by itself was truly disturbing.

Clearly there was no time for deeper examination of her feelings, or his. They were already aboard, the island was clearly splitting apart, and the surreal nighttime evacuation had already taken on the appearance of a Buck Rogers movie. The planetary panic in black and white she'd laughed at as a girl.

She shook herself mentally back to the present. "All right. Lay out your plan."

He took her through the steps in a quick but comprehensive briefing. She could hear the man in back working with whatever he'd brought aboard, and hear as well the click of his seat belt. Sven, she figured, couldn't possibly know the details of this mission or he wouldn't be standing calmly outside watching his daughter prepare to lift off with enough firepower aboard to vaporize her body, and his newest helicopter.

"Does he have the proper clips and rope for using the winch?"

"He says he does. He's mountain-climbed."

"Which end of the WaveRam first?"

"Ah . . . let's do the southernmost wing."

She finished the checklist and lifted off into the wind, this time more smoothly than before, anticipating the vicious wind burbles cascading around the forward corner of the helipad. She brought the Dauphin into position again over the massive concrete breakwater just as she had before, noting that the waves were even higher now, which made the chances of losing anyone dangling from the end of a rope even more likely.

In the back seat Lester Brown had finished laying out the materials before liftoff, dividing the eight remaining blocks of C-4 among four small knapsacks. In each block of the explosive he carefully inserted a blasting cap, feeling the same jitters as before when he connected the wires to the waiting leads from the encrypted radio detonator. They had used timers on the central power station and modified cellular phones for the emergency generators. There were now just two of the phone detonators left, one for each side, and he had just enough wire to connect the two knapsacks together across a twenty-five-foot length of rope. One knapsack would be laid on the front face of the WaveRam, the other in the back, with the combined explosive power acting somewhat like a shaped charge and blowing a hole all the way through.

That, at least, was the theory.

They were almost over the target when he finished, his hands shaking slightly as he rechecked the inbound phone numbers and the special six-digit code which would actually trigger the blast.

Doug was looking back over his shoulder and Lester gave him a thumbs-up. He connected a ring from the end of the winch cable to the central ring on his harness after opening the right-hand door, and on word from Jennifer relayed by Doug, he swung himself out, supporting his weight entirely on the winch as Doug took the remote control and began lowering him.

Hanging thirty feet below the Dauphin, the surreal oceanscape of the WaveRam barrier illuminated by the downward spotlight, Lester held on to the two bags and used hand signals to motion Jennifer lower.

Ever so slightly, she lowered the collective, causing the Dauphin to settle until Lester's feet were at the top of the barrier. He kicked around for a few seconds before another lowering gesture brought him down right on top of it, and he could stand on his own. He started to remove the hook attached to his harness but thought better of it, and knelt down to begin the job of laying the connecting line between the two knapsacks over the top of the barrier. He flopped one deadly sack over the front face, the other over the back, horizontally aligned.

Jennifer had been fighting the winds and the visual illusions much too consciously, her control inputs falling behind the responses of the Dauphin. Each successive movement of her hand slightly reinforced the deviation, rather than damping it. It was as if her car had started drifting to the right and she'd mistakenly corrected to the right, worsening the situation.

At first the gyrations were little more than a slight annoyance, but fatigue and distraction were taking their toll, and within a few seconds the malady had become significant. The Dauphin began popping up and down with uncharacteristic suddenness.

She forced herself to reacquire her alpha state, the calm control that had always characterized her flying at critical moments. *Breathe! You can do this!* But it wasn't working.

Still attached to the lifeline and winch, Lester was too busy to notice the gyrations of the helicopter until he reached over the front of the WaveRam at a critical moment, and the rope tightened enough to yank him off balance. It slackened almost as fast, leaving him toppling headfirst toward the waves and flailing the air to no avail, unable to stop his tumble, his back hurting from the sudden snap upward. He hit the water just ahead of a huge wave, but was yanked back in the air by the line to the helicopter before the wave could completely engulf him.

Lester looked back around, relieved to see the knapsacks of C-4 right where he'd left them. There was no need for realigning them, and he frantically gestured to be pulled up. Jennifer yanked him up energetically enough to cause him to bounce and twist at the end of the rope before the winch could begin pulling him in.

She gained a hundred feet in altitude, calming herself and looking for her "hover button," the almost mystical melding of pilot and machine which had shocked her so long ago as a student helicopter pilot. One moment she'd been all over the sky, the next hovering rock-steady with the ease of a hummingbird. Calm again and fully in control, she flew over the northern wing of the giant concrete structure. Doug confirmed Lester was back aboard and was ready to use his cell phone, and gave him the go-ahead signal. Lester dialed the requisite number and heard it answered automatically by the cell phone in the package of C-4. Carefully he punched in the destruct sequence he'd programmed, and with the last digit the night sky lit up in a double report of light, concussion, and sea spray.

"God! That was impressive!" Jennifer said.

"Certainly was," Doug responded. "Maybe we should go back and assess the damage first."

"You said we had little time, right?" she asked.

He thought for a few seconds. "No, you're right. We'll blow the other side first." Doug leaned over the seat back to confirm that Lester was once again ready to go down. He could tell the man was freezing cold, his clothes soaking wet from the first encounter, but Lester didn't complain as he once again checked the security of his tether and opened the door, carrying the knapsacks with the second round of explosives.

From Lester Brown's perspective, the disapproval of Marta Cartwright had been a far more crushing disappointment than the possibility of prison. He'd organized the strike against the hated Cascadia development to honor her, only to discover that far from being pleased, he had shamed her. Their brief conversation in the island's command center removed any doubt that he owed an act of redemption, and one normally achieved only by sacrifice and bravery. It had amazed him that the pathway was right in front of him. From that moment, helping Dr. Lam blow up part of the wave barrier had become a grateful duty.

His thorough military training had rendered the handling of explosives a comfortable and familiar process, but the equipment he'd been using to damage the Cascadia facilities was far from military standard, and that had already created a few moments of panic.

Suspended now from the helicopter, he struggled to hold on to the second two knapsacks containing plastic explosives and trigger devices, all of which were moving around loose inside. They were trying to turn upside down in his hand, and he was losing control of them. With the main flap not completely secured, the prospect of dumping the trigger devices in the water was very real.

Once more he strained to reach around beneath the principal sack and stop the tilt, but the motion caused him to start spinning slowly on the end of the tether, making the problem even worse.

There were only a few feet left to go before his feet could get a grip on the top of the jetty, but the gyrations were getting wilder and he found himself almost upside down, holding on to the flap of the knapsack with every ounce of control he could maintain. In such an undignified, unplanned position, there was no way his feet were going to land first.

Overhead, Jennifer was relying on Doug's verbal instructions through the interphone to know how to position Lester over the concrete barrier. Now he was reporting the man had begun spinning and was going to land on his side.

Jennifer pulled up slightly, the Dauphin fighting the winds as she pulsed the controls.

"Where is he?"

"In the right place, but he's on his side and spinning around. Not like before."

"Is he giving you any signals?"

"No. I think he's having too much trouble holding on to the sacks. Take him down more. Let him touch down sideways. That'll stop the rotation."

"You're sure that won't hurt him?"

"I don't think so."

A vicious side gust hit the Dauphin at the same moment and Jennifer worked to get them back under control, but the movement was enough to start Lester swinging, a motion which further confused the inputs to the chopper's controls.

"I'm going to bring us up. You need to winch him in."

"No, he's motioning for you to come down, Jennifer."

"*Down?*"

"Yes."

"But . . . is he swinging? It feels like he is."

"A little, but he wants down, and I think he can land on top."

She lowered the collective too fast and too much, her correction coming too late.

Twenty feet below, Lester Brown had almost righted himself when the line dropped a few feet at the apex of a lateral swing. He was on his side, struggling to come back to the vertical, his body beginning a downward arc toward the wave-pounded concrete abutment. He could see what was coming, but there was no way to avoid the impact between chest and concrete, and even over the noise and the wind he could hear his ribs snap and feel the breath knocked out of him.

Somehow the impact dislodged the lifeline, unclipping it from the chest ring and whipping it away in the wind. He could imagine the startled response overhead in the helicopter.

Lester felt himself slipping over the side of the slime-slicked wall and scrambled hard to gain a handhold and boost himself up. With his feet churning against the front of the barrier and slipping with each cycle, his hands closed around an exposed piece of rebar and with a focused, mighty effort he yanked his weight up and got a foot over the ledge, working the other leg up until he was sprawled on top, all too aware that there was no longer a lifeline to cling to.

His chest was on fire with pain, his breathing shallow and his body rebelling, hurting with every breath and protesting against the amazing cold and windchill. Somehow the knapsacks were still with him, and he checked to see if the contents were safe before slowly inching one over the back side, then reaching in the other one to check its contents.

He dug around inside, his fingers finding the awful state of the phone before he could see it. The impact had broken the case open, strewing the electronic contents uselessly inside. There was no way it was going to work.

He stole a glance upward at the Dauphin and saw the worried face of Doug Lam leaning out. He tried to give him a thumbs-up, but it hurt too much, and he concentrated his efforts on trying to figure out how to detonate the remaining charge.

There was no fuse to light, even if he had a lighter that could brave the water all around him. Either the C-4 would be exploded with a blasting cap initiated by an electrical pulse, or there would be no explosion. With the shattered phone there was no longer any way to trigger it remotely.

But, he reminded himself, he did have an extra coil of insulated wire in one of the sacks. At least a hundred feet of it. If he could manage to rig up a temporary connection with the blasting cap on one end, and the battery from the smashed cell phone on the other, he might be able to get winched back up and detonate it safely from forty feet in the air. The explosion would be terribly loud, but it shouldn't hurt the helicopter or its occupants.

Aware that the line was being dropped once again, Lester carefully reached inside the sack and began assembling what he needed, working hard against the pain to keep his focus and avoid what would be an instant, fatal mistake.

The hook on the end of the line suddenly hit him in the buttocks and spun away, but he paid no attention, knowing they wanted him to grab it and hook it up again. The thought of putting pressure on the harness and on his damaged ribs took his remaining breath away, and he tried to wave "No" with his left hand, a gesture they were apparently not getting.

There it is, he thought, his left fingers closing around the end of the extra wire, which he had already stripped and prepared. The two screw-down terminal poles he'd mounted to the case of the specifically configured cell phone were still in place and hardwired to the battery's terminals, and he removed the existing wires and attached the new leads before realizing he wasn't thinking clearly.

No, no, no! Jeez! I need the new long wire to go to the old ends which go to the blasting cap. The new end I carry up to the chopper and just touch the actual battery poles to them. Not before!

He knew there was a chance that some sort of unplanned pathway might now exist in the shattered phone case, porting electricity to some unsuspected spot. If he accidentally touched a lead wire to such a spot while the other lead was grounded, this life would be ended instantly and painlessly. Just as he'd warned Doug Lam when he thought the scientist was going to try it himself, one mistake would be fatal.

Move by move, he got the shunt and bypass attached and quickly worked the battery out of its housing in the shattered phone. He held it tight as he automatically slipped it into his right pants pocket, then removed the new end of the connection and painfully strained to raise his head and look up.

He was shocked to find a pair of feet practically landing on his back.

———

When Doug had seen the brutal impact between Lester Brown and the concrete jetty, he knew instantly the man was in serious trouble. Although he was gesturing that all was okay, it clearly wasn't. Doug couldn't get him to look skyward again, and then he realized that Lester was fumbling around in one of the knapsacks and might accidentally blow himself up. Apparently, Doug concluded, the man was delirious with pain, and therefore there was no choice but to go down and get him.

"No, Doug!" Jennifer had responded. "You don't have any training as a parajumper! How are you going to get yourself back up, let alone pull him up if he's injured?"

"We can't leave him down there! Do you have a remote control for the winch at your console?"

"Yes, but—"

"Then you'll have to use it. One of those waves is likely to wash him off if I don't get to him."

"I can take the chopper down and put the wheels right on the concrete, and you can haul him in from there. You don't need to ride the winch down."

"Jen, the waves will wash *you* out of the sky! You can get me a lot lower, but you can't land on that thing."

There had been a telling silence from the right seat.

"Okay," she'd said at last, "but take that second harness and put it on, and when you reach him, click his ring into the same clip as yours. As long as his spine isn't injured, he'll survive it."

What had seemed straightforward suddenly became terrifying as he zipped his jacket up and tested his weight, then swung out suspended only by the harness running between his legs and cutting painfully into his crotch.

Jennifer began winching him down as she struggled to see his position. The thought of jettisoning her right side door and peering out like a long line pilot was becoming more attractive by the second, but there was no way to ensure it wouldn't hit the tail rotor. Instead, she pressed her face to the side window, struggling to see. When she had him down to approximately ten feet, she stopped the winch and began maneuvering him back toward Lester's position, working hard to maintain her visual orientation in the dark, the Night Sun providing the only horizon references by reflection.

Slowly, she walked the helicopter forward, watching Doug as best she could until he was right over the wall and just next to the stricken man. She gently lowered the collective until she glimpsed Doug steadying himself on his feet and gesturing a thumbs-up, then she dropped another couple of feet to give him slack and backed the Dauphin a few feet to one side, holding the machine into the wind as she watched him examining Brown and then trying to hook the man to the line. She could see him working at it diligently, but to no avail, and she realized with a sinking heart that the hook device on the end of the line was too small to take two rings at once.

At last Doug reached the same conclusion, and, much to Jennifer's relief, gestured to be lifted up.

She pulled him carefully off the concrete and then triggered the winch until he was aboard and on headset once more.

"I couldn't get it hooked to both of us!"

"I was afraid of that. How badly hurt is he?"

"Cracked ribs I think. He was working on rigging a longer fuse."

Jennifer looked back, startled. "Fuse? I thought it was radio-controlled like the other side."

"He broke the receiver when he hit."

"Oh, no."

"Stay in position and get as low as you did with me, Jen. I'm sending the hook back down to him."

She edged the Dauphin a bit more to the right and adjusted her hands on the controls again, fighting the wind which was gusting now even more, taking a deep breath as she brought them down to ten feet over the jetty while Doug winched the line down one more time, manually swinging it as close as he could until it literally brushed Lester Brown's back. The sea spray was almost constant, splashing onto the canopy and temporarily fuzzing up her vision.

In the helicopter's searchlights, she saw Brown reach around and grab the line, pulling it toward his stomach and hooking it on before pushing the second knapsack over the front side of the wall, and rolling over with a coil of wire in his hand. His eyes were closed tight as he gestured to be raised up, and Jennifer began pulling the Dauphin back to a higher altitude as Doug started the winch once more.

Lester Brown was grimacing from pain as he played out the coil of wire. Foot by foot the winch pulled him closer as Jennifer held them at twenty feet above, but Brown was gesturing for more altitude, and Doug could see the coil of wire was still less than half played out.

"Jen, he wants more altitude, and I think he has enough wire."

"Okay, I'm coming up slowly. Is he almost in?"

"Still five feet down. How high are we?"

"Twenty five."

"Give me fifty feet and I'll watch how much wire he has left."

"What the hell is he planning, to detonate it from fifty feet up?"

"I don't know. I'm afraid so."

"We can't do that! Did you see the strength of that explosion?"

"Just . . . keep coming up."

"Bring him aboard as quickly as possible."

Doug leaned over to the winch control and continued motoring it in as slowly as possible. He could see the wire uncoiling foot by foot and see Lester Brown looking down and trying to gauge how much was left.

At last the injured man was at door level, swinging painfully by the harness as Doug reached for his hand to pull him in.

"Up! Go up!" Lester yelled.

Doug cupped his ears and leaned as close as he dared out of the door. "What?"

"I said, go up! I have at least a hundred feet of wire."

Doug relayed the word to Jennifer, who climbed slowly to ninety feet.

Lester was at the top of the winch now, his feet just shy of floor level. He shifted the remaining unwound coil of wire to his right hand as he reached with his left to catch Doug's hand. They connected and Doug struggled to pull him in, both of them realizing the line to the winch was holding him tight.

Doug reversed the winch and tried to motor some slack to the line, but it had jammed in the up position and refused to move.

Lester saw the problem as well and placed his hand on the release for the hook holding his harness to the winch line. With one hand on the release and the other gesturing for Doug, he prepared to get a foot on the doorsill and use Doug's help to pull himself in as he released the safety line.

But the wire was getting in the way, and he stuffed it in his pocket quickly, caught the outstretched hand, and pulled the release just as a gigantic flash of light and a thunderous roar of impacting shock wave announced the fact that the wires and the battery terminals had met in the depths of his pocket.

Doug was blown backward onto the rear seat of the Dauphin, his hand yanked away from Lester's by the shock wave. He scrambled back to his feet instantly, but the doorway was empty.

"Oh, God!"

"What happened?" Jennifer yelled in his headset, her voice tense and shrill as she struggled to adjust her headset back on her head.

"He . . . he accidentally triggered it, Jen, just as he was getting in, and—"

"Is he okay? Is he in?"

"No."

"What? What does that mean?"

"He's gone, Jen! He fell. He had pulled the release . . . and he's gone."

"The harness release?"

"Yes! It was stuck. He had to, to get back in."

He felt the Dauphin turn suddenly and drop in altitude as she adjusted the Night Sun and backed away downwind to turn and come back over the jetty in the slim hope Brown had survived the fall.

"I can't believe we've lost him," she said, true alarm in her voice. "He's got to be down there somewhere visible."

"Jen, he may not have survived the fall."

"A hundred feet into water can hurt, but it doesn't have to be fatal."

Lester was nowhere to be seen, and after a few minutes of searching, she focused the light along the front of the concrete structure where they had intended to blow a huge hole. Between the impacts of the waves, they could see the huge gouge the explosion had made, but there was no hole, and no breach in the ability of the WaveRam's northernmost wing to properly form each wave in accordance with Dr. Kopp's ingenious design.

"I just don't believe this! I'm going to check the other side," Jennifer said, flying them quickly across the expanse of angry, churning water and bringing the powerful spotlight to bear on the opposite explosion site. "We've got to find him!"

She played the searchlight back and forth across the surface of the water behind the WaveRam, then played it momentarily on the back of the barrier itself. There was a slightly greater gouge on the south wing, but again no hole in either front or back.

"What do you think?" she asked.

"What do I think?" Doug repeated quietly, "I think Lester's gone and we can't disable that thing."

Her eyes were wide, her voice bordering on the frantic. "We can't just leave him out here!"

"What else can we do, except notify the Coast Guard?"

She was silent for nearly a minute as she urged the Dauphin back to the front side of the structure, raking the water with the Night Sun until her shoulders fell.

"Oh my God. We've really lost the man."

"I think you're right."

"And you've lost the battle with the explosives, too. Right? Are there more explosives? I don't believe I'm asking that, but . . . this can't be it."

Doug was shaking his head. "No. We've got nothing else. There's no time."

Jennifer keyed her radio and relayed the sad news about Lester Brown along with his last known location to Cascadia Operations.

"Please get that to the Coast Guard immediately."

"Roger."

"There aren't any rescue boats on the island, are there?"

"Not anymore," was the singular response.

A lengthy silence fell between Jennifer and Doug before she broke it. "If there's nothing more to be done here, we'd better get back. Now more than ever we need to rush the evacuation."

He climbed back over the partition to the copilot's seat and nodded. He snapped his seat belt on, his eyes falling idly on a ship passing a mile or so seaward. The forward section was brightly lit, and he wondered if any of the crew knew of the immense drama playing out so many kilometers beneath their feet. It could be a cruise ship, he thought, the idle curiosity a grab for anything to concentrate on other than the lost quest and the man they'd just left for dead.

There were more of the ship's lights showing at what had to be the stern, but as he watched, even more lights appeared to the south, which didn't make any sense.

"What kind of ship do you suppose that is?" he asked Jennifer.

"Where?"

"At your three o'clock. It looks incredibly long."

She looked as she turned them slowly back to the east.

"Oh, that would be an oceangoing tug and a barge . . . or two barges, I guess."

"Barges?"

"Yes. Dangerous work, but those tugs are huge and powerful."

The Dauphin took up a northeast heading as Doug came forward in the left seat.

"You suppose they could come over and look for him?"

She was shaking her head. "No way. Not with barges in tow."

"Wait! Could you fly me out there?"

Jennifer looked at him like he'd lost his mind.

"What? Even if you beg them in person they can't do it without cutting their load loose, and I promise you that's not going to happen."

"No, no. That's not the reason," he said, excitement creeping into his voice. "That tug and the barges. I need to see how big they are."

"Why, for God's sake? We've got to evacuate an island."

"Jen . . . it's a long shot, but . . . several days ago they activated this wave shaper by pulling the barges they had blocking it out of the way. That more or less turned it on."

"What are you thinking? Go hijack that crew's barges?"

"Hell, I don't know. Can you get close?"

"Of course. I'm a helicopter. If you think it's really necessary."

"I do, Honey."

She let the term of endearment hang in the air for a few seconds as she turned the Dauphin back to the west.

"All right, Doug. I have to ask you. Did you tell Diane what to say to me?"

"Diane Lacombe? What do you mean? Did she say something to you?"

"You tell me."

"I didn't ask her to say anything. Why?"

"I'd like to believe her. I'd like to believe *you*. Is she really in trouble with her job?"

"Yes. Big time." Jennifer heard him take a deep breath. "Look, I don't know what she said, but what I told you about her earlier was the gospel truth, and I assume she confirmed it. We weren't fooling around."

"We need to talk about this on the ground."

"I agree. I love you, Jen."

There was no answer, but he could see her wince, and that, he figured, was progress.

"Fly over the first barge there, okay?"

"That's not a barge."

"What is it then?"

"It looks like . . . like one of the old floating bridge sections they just removed from Lake Washington. Same for the one behind."

She dropped them down to a hundred feet with the Night Sun on while they banked over the floating roadway, confirming its length to be at least two hundred feet, the old center line highway markings still visible.

"I've driven over that very roadway. So have you."

"Now the one to the rear."

It, too, was two hundred feet long.

"What now?"

Doug was deep in thought as she headed toward the tug from astern.

"We've undoubtedly attracted their attention by now. They probably think we're the Coast Guard getting ready to warn them something's wrong with their tow."

"You see anyone on deck?"

"Not yet."

"Jen, can we call them on some radio?"

She shook her head. "They monitor marine frequencies, and we're too low to talk to Seattle Center and get their help in relaying. But I could try."

There was more silence between them as she flipped on the Night Sun again and caught several crewmembers on the aft railing of the massive tug, blinking against the bright lights. They had been watching and wondering what was going on.

"Jen, can you lower me onto that tug?"

"*What?* Good God, no! It's far too dangerous! What we were doing back there was bad enough. I never authorized you to go down after him."

"Jennifer . . ."

"I could have lost you back there!"

"I didn't have a choice, and I don't now, either. I'll admit I'm grasping at straws, but how can we not try? *Can* you do it, without endangering yourself?"

There was a telling pause. "Maybe. Probably. But, Doug, what are you thinking? That they'll let you seize those bridge sections? They'd be risking their jobs."

"Then get me down there and go back and get some authority."

"Authority? What authority?"

"Jason Smith, the island security director, is a sheriff's deputy, too. He can commandeer anything under the state's police power."

"This tug may be outside the international limit."

"Jennifer, please! We're desperate, remember? It's the only chance we've got as far as I can see."

She passed over the tug and turned to the left slowly, the Night Sun still raking the waves ahead of them.

"Oh, Lord," she sighed, shaking her head in frustration, knowing he was right, but realizing at the same time he'd been lucky on the first trip down the winch. "Let me match speeds here and check the wind before I agree to this suicidal idea."

"How long?"

"Two minutes, maybe three."

"Okay. Then while you're flying, I need to tell you something."

"What is this, another defense? Can't this wait, Doug?" she asked, shaking her head as she kept her eyes on the tug below and worked to match airspeed. "Let's just shelve it for now."

"I was going to get into this at the Space Needle last night, but I shouldn't have let it wait this long."

"All right. What? Quickly."

"Jen, Deborah is dying, and I can't divorce her while she's alive."

Jennifer looked at him in stunned silence, her attention suddenly ripped away from the tug several hundred feet below and the three crewmembers standing on the forward deck wondering why a helicopter was keeping pace.

"Dying?"

He nodded. "After we separated—three months, to be exact—she flew to the Mayo Clinic in Minnesota out of frustration at some weakness in her right arm. It took them nearly a month, but they diagnosed ALS, amyotrophic lateral sclerosis, otherwise known as—"

"Lou Gehrig's disease. Oh, God, Doug! How long does she—I'm sorry! Don't answer that."

"No, Jen. You have a right to know. They've tried all the new therapies and slowed it a bit, but she's now in a wheelchair and they're saying no more than eighteen months."

"Why didn't you tell me?" she asked, her voice low and nonaccusatory. "I would have understood."

"Deborah has always been a strong, controlling woman. Too controlling, which is where we clashed so often. But she was horribly embarrassed by a disease that would end up leaving her on a ventilator, unable to communicate or do anything for herself. The prospect of being imprisoned in a sharp mind with nothing to do but watch her body die was too much. She begged me not to tell anyone, and I felt I needed to honor her promise, even with you."

Jennifer turned her attention momentarily back to the tug, sliding the Dauphin a bit more to the left.

"The winds are not that bad out here. I think we can do it," she said.

"Jen, if I divorce her now, we lose the health insurance, among other problems."

She was shaking her head. "Don't say anymore. If you divorced her now, you wouldn't be a man I'd want to be with. Now or ever. I'm so sorry I pushed you."

"About the Alaska thing . . ."

"It doesn't matter, Doug. Say no more."

"No, I want you to know that I didn't lie to you. I sent her on the cruise with two friends, but I had to fly to Seward from Menlo Park for a day and I came aboard to see the ship and talk to her. That's it."

She looked over and smiled. "Let's get this done, okay?"

"Yeah."

"Provided you still want to get down there."

"I do. I'll have to get the winch unstuck first."

"Okay, climb to the back and get into the harness, and put on that life vest. You're going to have to hit the winch pulley to unjam it. Use the crash axe—the blunt end."

"Okay."

"I'll put you on their forward deck. Raise your feet and ground the hook before you touch their deck, like I told you before with the water."

"All right."

"I'll go get Smith, if he'll come."

"Wish me luck."

"I do, but you know I think this is too dangerous."

He was already climbing over the center console between the cockpit and the cabin and grabbing the harness, fitting it over the life preserver she'd indicated and checking the crotch straps for a better fit.

Jennifer noticed. "Tighten them to where you can barely stand. The straps need to clear your scrotum on each side so you can literally hang from those straps."

"Got it."

"And if it looks too dangerous, I'm going to winch you in and I don't want any arguments, okay?"

"Okay."

"Doug, this is very, very dangerous."

"Stop worrying and let's do it."

"All right. Go ahead and swing out on the winch. Godspeed."

"Thanks."

He pushed himself over the side again, feeling the same desperate need to claw himself back into the cabin, realizing at the same time that he still had his headset on. Jennifer's eyes were on the tug below as she fought to maneuver into position, but she was having trouble with the lump in her throat and the inconvenient mix of guilt and relief that were forcing tears into her eyes at the worst possible moment. She blinked them back as she spoke for herself alone.

"Please come back to me, Doug. I do love you."

Chapter 38

"Are you Miss Lacombe? Diane Lacombe?"

The driver of the bus watched the young woman climb aboard. Her eyes were systematically searching his passengers, and she fit the description he'd been given.

Diane looked at him, trying to be appear startled, yet somehow glad she wasn't yet completely numb from the events of the last few hours.

"Yes."

"Okay. I have a message for you."

"From Robert Nelms? That's who I was looking for."

"I don't know. One of our staff handed it to me a while ago."

"Was there a large, heavyset man aboard a while ago?"

"I think so. But he got off. Mr. Walker apparently knows him."

"Okay. That's the one."

She took the note and opened it.

> Diane,
>
> I'm assuming you'll be looking for me. I need to talk with you immediately. One of Walker's staff has provided a bit of shelter with telephones in the small utility building just across the street from where the bus is waiting. Please join me there.
>
> Bob Nelms

"Thanks," she said, refolding the note and stepping out. The only structure close by was a small, windowless building some thirty yards away, and she hurried in that direction. There was a single door on the side and she tried it, unsurprised when it opened. She stepped inside and moved, through a small entryway, then through another door into a small room with a line of desks facing a wall of dark screens which looked like some sort of emergency command post. There were a few low lights around the perimeter of the room, but in the subdued light she couldn't make out where he might be.

"Mr. Nelms?" she called. "Are you here?"

A bright overhead light snapped on suddenly and she blinked at the painful intensity as she tried to shield her eyes. Someone had moved into the room from the far end. No, there were two people there.

"Diane, sit down, please."

"Excuse me? Who's that?"

"Bob Nelms. And Jerry Schultz is here as well."

"Jerry? Why? What's going on here?"

"Sit, please," he repeated.

Diane pulled a swivel chair toward her and sank into it, a guarded expression on her face. The threatening nature of the ambush was overwhelmingly obvious, and she quietly refreshed her memory of where the exit was in case she needed to bolt.

Robert Nelms was standing a few feet away, his face stern and ashen, his demeanor one of tired outrage.

"Diane, I've got some serious conflicts in the stories I'm being told."

"Such as?"

"Well, Jerry here says he never sent you a memo telling you to stop asking for the raw data or interfering in another department's work."

"You deny sending me that?" she asked Jerry Schultz, who was looking alarmingly ill.

"Diane, I never sent you any such memo."

"I have a copy, and it bears the filename of where the thing is on your computer."

"That's not possible . . ."

"It is what it is," she said. "Did I see you type it and print it and hand it to me? No. But I did ask you several times about getting the raw data and you told me no."

Schultz was moving toward her now, his hands shaking slightly.

"Diane, you asked me to take you off another project to let you go reexamine that data, for which you're not even qualified. You kept bugging me about it without an explanation."

"And you remember very well I said I was less than pleased with the copy of the report I'd received regarding my data. Remember? We were at Jane's farewell party, and you'd—"

"He'd what, Diane?"

She looked down, embarrassed. "I'm sorry, Jerry. I shouldn't have brought it up."

"What?" Nelms asked more sharply, noting Jerry Schultz's reddening face.

"He'd had a lot to drink, Mr. Nelms," she explained.

"It was a party, for God's sake!" Schultz exploded

"He was drunk?" Nelms asked her directly, ignoring Jerry Schultz.

She nodded. "Enough so that I discounted two dirty jokes and a pass at me, but when he started fussing at me about my requests for the data, I explained about the report, and he got really angry." She turned to Schultz. "Jerry, I know you remember that!"

"Maybe a little," he sighed. "I just don't remember your telling me the report was bad."

"I didn't. That would have been presumptuous of me. I was worried about it."

"Okay, that one's resolved," Nelms was saying. "What is not resolved is this." He reached around the edge of the counter and plopped the copy of the report Jerry Schultz had taken from Mick Walker's files. "Jerry says he saw you looking at this."

"He was *watching* me? From where? And why?" she replied, her eyebrows shooting up, studying their reactions to spot who was responsible.

"I was worried that—" Schultz began.

Robert Nelms raised his arm sharply to stop the rest of the response and Schultz shut up in midsentence.

"He was where he was supposed to be, Diane. But that's not the point. Did you know what was in that report?"

"It appeared to be the same report I saw and was worried about. It was too cursory, and now we know for certain that it was obviously very flawed since it didn't say anything about the fault line that's tearing this place apart."

Nelms was shaking his head.

"That's not what this report contains."

"No? Well, I didn't get a look at anything but the cover and title page. What does it contain?"

"The complete story, Diane. All your data, just as you presented it to me verbally a while ago, and a very comprehensive warning that a surficial fault exists that could split the island in half."

"God! Really?"

He was nodding as she looked between Schultz and Nelms.

"Well . . . then the firm is off the hook, right?"

"Jerry says that's not the report he approved."

Jerry Schultz had apparently experienced a jolt of courage and moved a step closer, his hands flailing the air for emphasis.

"I never saw that version! I never knew anything about a hidden fault, or any of this Douglas Lam theory stuff!"

"I'm confused!" Diane said.

"So am I," Robert Nelms added, glancing at Jerry Schultz again. "If that's not the formal report we approved and sent, who wrote it and what the hell is it doing in Mick Walker's files?"

"I don't know," Diane said. "But if he had it and read it and built this complex anyway, then clearly he's the bad guy," she added. "Wouldn't that be your read?"

"Diane, why in hell would anyone as sophisticated as Walker ignore information like that and build a time bomb?"

"As I said, I know him through my family, and I can tell you that Mick Walker is a gambler who doesn't like to lose."

"Fine," Nelms sputtered, "but why in God's name would he be dissatisfied with a seismic report that wrongly gave him a clean bill of health and go out and fabricate a second version that would squarely implicate him in any seismic disaster? That doesn't make a lick of sense. I mean, I assume the man doesn't have a financial death wish."

"Of course not," she replied.

"Then, there's the question Jerry came up with before we asked you to come in here. If not Walker, then why would anyone at Chadwick and Noble fabricate this bogus version of the report—even though it's a version which ironically happens to be correct? And why would anyone in our shop plant it in Walker's files?"

Diane looked at Robert Nelms before glancing at Jerry Schultz, on whom the import of the question had just dawned. What little blood remained in his face was draining rapidly, and his mouth was flapping up and down without noise.

Diane took a deep breath and returned her gaze to the chairman.

"I think," she began, "that you just asked and answered your own question."

"What do you mean?"

"If someone at the firm didn't do it to get the firm off the hook, then he did it to get himself off the hook, especially if the first version that found no faults on the island had been signed off on his watch."

She could see the light go on in Robert Nelms's mind as he snapped his gaze to Jerry.

"You signed off on the original report, didn't you?"

"Well, yes, but the data—"

"The data was what Diane found in the vaults! Who else, Jerry, do I then look to as a possible cover-up artist here?"

"Cover-up? No! No, you have it all wrong! She's behind this somehow, and I—"

"Shut up, Jerry! That's pathetic. You're the manager. You're the one I charge with the responsibility for keeping our work products unassailable. So what did you do, make a mistake and ship the wrong dataset to geologic engineering, and then try to hide it later?"

"No!"

Nelms was moving closer to Schultz, his face dark with rage.

"And the most suspicious thing of all, Jerry, is the question of what the hell you're doing up here? I called you in San Francisco not eight hours ago and suddenly you appear here. Why?"

"I told you, sir, I got a call from your secretary saying I was to get a cab to the airport and get on the company jet immediately and then charter a helicopter."

"Guess what, Jerry? I called and checked. She made no such call. In fact, I'll bet you're the one who scrambled the jet and the crew without authorization. You came up here to protect yourself from someone finding the wrong report in his files, didn't you? You chickened out on your own plan. So when did you plant it in his files?"

"I didn't!"

"Was it supposed to be an insurance policy for you? Or were you planning on blackmailing him somehow?"

"May I go now?" Diane asked quietly.

Robert Nelms whipped his attention around to her, his face softening.

"Yes, of course, Diane. I'm sorry I thought for even a moment that you might be the culprit here."

"Goddamnit, sir, she *is* the culprit! I don't know how, but—"

Nelms whirled on him. "Shut up, Jerry! If I hear that once more I swear I'm going to slug you. I've got to figure out what to do now. I don't want another word. And Diane? Please, say nothing to anyone, especially not Walker, until . . . until I can figure out how to handle this."

"Yes, sir. I should warn you, that Mick Walker is well known for keeping duplicate files in different offices and backing up everything. Whatever he really had in his files he'll have copies of elsewhere."

"And that means?"

"Whatever we *really* gave him as the seismic report he relied on will be very much in evidence."

"Thank you."

Diane left quickly, closing the door behind her and spotting her bus still sitting in the number-three position as another round of people were offloaded to board the helicopters. She took a deep breath, letting her mind record what had just transpired in exquisite detail.

Behind her, Jerry Schultz was on the verge of tears.

Chapter 39

The skipper of the tug *Vivian O. Speetjens* took one look at the man dangling over his bow from a helicopter and broke out his sidearm. Never in his thirty-two years at sea had such a thing happened on a boat he was crewing or commanding, and thoughts ranging from terrorists to pirates were pinging in his mind as he considered and rejected the idea of ringing for the engines to come to idle.

There were two heavy floating-bridge sections trailing behind them, and idling the tug in rough seas could cause their loss.

"Go out there and retrieve that idiot!" he snarled at his first mate, who had already pulled on his coat.

The man had been swinging in a narrow arc but now thumped to the deck and fell over. He could see a small blue spark and understood whoever he was had just grounded himself successfully. He watched the man unhook the line and motion to the pilot, who immediately pulled up and away, the flashing red beacon on the belly disappearing rapidly in the murk.

Within a minute, the first mate brought their new arrival to the bridge.

"What the hell are these dramatics about?" the skipper roared. "Flashing lights over my boat and buzzing us?"

"Request permission to come aboard, Captain," Doug managed, trying to brush some of the water off his face.

"And if I say denied, are you going to jump overboard?"

"That was meant to be a courtesy. I'm not planning on jumping overboard."

"And I wasn't planning on having my crew scared out of a month's productivity. What kind of maniac was flying that thing?"

Doug fixed the captain with a steady gaze and smiled to think of Jennifer's reaction if she heard what he was about to say.

"My fiancée was the maniac flying that thing."

"What?"

"She owns the helicopter company. Could I formally say hello to you now and exchange names? There's a major emergency in progress that brings me here."

The captain hesitated, then took his outstretched hand and shook it roughly, releasing it as if he'd been forced to pick up a rotting fish.

"I'm Noel Speetjens, captain of this boat."

"Dr. Doug Lam. I'm an affiliate professor of geophysics at the University of Washington and a scientist for the U.S. Geological Survey."

Doug could see Speetjens relax just slightly.

"Doctor, what the hell were you doing coming aboard a working tug in rough waters in a damned helicopter?"

"Trying to stop a major earthquake."

Noel Speetjens was in the process of shaking his head and asking him to repeat the answer when an elderly woman in a deep-blue velour bathrobe climbed past the top rung of the internal stairway to the bridge, eyeing Doug with an unyielding expression. She stood no more than five feet tall with a head of pure white hair, and a demeanor of unquestioned authority.

The captain caught the movement out of the corner of his eye and turned around to confirm who it was, then turned back to Doug.

"Doctor Lam, you've dropped aboard the motor vessel Vivian O. Speetjens, and this lady is the original Vivian O. Speetjens, and the owner of our company."

She said a few words in a foreign language to her son, who nodded.

"My mother's Dutch," he explained.

"But she understands English perfectly," Vivian Speetjens continued, moving forward with a firm handshake. "You were saying something about earthquakes, Doctor?"

"Yes . . . as bizarre as it sounds."

Doug ran through as succinct and rapid a narrative as possible of his theory, the validation, the massive consequences of a major subduction zone earthquake, and the fact that they were running out of time to shut down the effects of the WaveRam.

"This is a utilitarian visit with a gun to my head. We may already be too late."

"Can you really stop an earthquake?" Noel asked.

"I don't know the answer. It could be that even blocking the WaveRam won't stuff the genie back in the bottle, but I have a sixth sense that the only thing unlatching the Quilieute Quiet Zone is those amplified impacts. The bottom line is, we have to try."

"Those bridge sections belong to someone else," the captain said. "We're completely liable for a huge amount of money if we lose them."

"What if you were commandeered?"

Noel Speetjens straightened up, a defensive tone in his voice.

"By whom and how?"

Doug already had his hand up to defuse the impression. "I don't mean by force, Captain. I mean by law. The same as a police officer can jump in and commandeer a car under the state's police powers in a valid emergency."

"What do you have in mind?"

Doug quickly sketched out the WaveRam and where the two barges would have to be tied up to cancel the hydrodynamic effects of the structure.

"Are there secure tie downs, or attach points, on that thing?"

"Yes. I've seen them."

Noel and Vivian exchanged a few words in Dutch before she looked at Doug.

"Lam, if you can get this police chief on the radio or on a phone and have him order me to divert, we'll consider it. I need a name and a voice."

Doug whipped out his cell phone, punching in the number of the Cascadia Command Center which was still on his screen from the previous call. After reaching Jason Smith and explaining what he needed and why, Smith agreed.

"Put the captain on and I'll do my best."

Noel Speetjens took the cell phone and leaned over the chart table, writing several detailed notes in a highly readable cursive before thanking the security director and handing the phone back.

Noel picked up a pair of dividers and placed the respective points on the chart, one on Cascadia Island, the other somewhere to the west in the water, comparing the resulting gap.

"Well! Bless me." He looked up at Doug and smiled. "Seems we blundered into the territorial waters of the Quaalatch Nation, and I guess we've been duly commandeered."

"Terrible blunder, that," Vivian said, swatting her six foot two son on his arm. "Better navigating in the future, Mister!"

"Aye, aye, Ma'am."

She turned back to Doug. "Now, the serious part, Doctor. First, I want to see every scrap of identification you have in your wallet, I want to talk to someone at the University who can vouch for you, I want to talk to the emergency services director of the state or some higher authority, and I need to talk to the Coast Guard. In the meantime, we've got to change our course, figure the currents, get the crew briefed, and decide how to do this without sinking the bridge sections, or us."

"It's that complex and difficult?"

"You have no idea the magnitude of what you've asked us to do. But I built this company doing the impossible while a galaxy of sexists snickered up their sleeves. I'm not about to run from a challenge now. So, let's just hope you're right."

DAUPHIN, AIRBORNE

Jennifer had been halfway back to the Cascadia helipad when she suddenly turned around, unable to accept defeat in the matter of her missing passenger. She banked the helicopter to the south and headed for the northern wing of the WaveRam, where she'd been hovering when Lester was blown overboard. The chances an already-injured man could have survived a ninety-foot drop to the water were minimal, but she couldn't discount the possibility.

With the Night Sun turned on again, she descended and stabilized the Dauphin at thirty feet above the waves, raking the outer wing with light several times before deciding it was, indeed, hopeless.

Wait a minute. This thing focuses the waves inward, I haven't checked the rest of it.

She turned south and began walking the light beyond the curved concrete to the long, straight portion of the wave-shaping structure, spotting something a hundred yards ahead, a dark mass that was almost certainly seaweed.

But as she brought the Dauphin within fifty feet of the seaweed, she could see it was something else. A body, with arms and legs, lying facedown on the top of the concrete wall where it broadened into a wave-swept, three-foot-wide flat walkway.

She gauged the height and timing of the inbound waves and moved the Dauphin closer, the retractable landing gear almost on the edge of the concrete. If that was Lester Brown, she decided, he was either dead or unconscious. There was no movement, other than his clothes rippling in the gale-force rotorwash.

Now what? she thought. *If I go for help, he'll wash off of there by the time I get back.*

The enormity of the problem was the immense frustration. Lifesaving was her business, and here was a life to save and she was the only living soul aboard the helicopter.

I've gotta get help.

Jennifer keyed the radio, waiting for Sven to come back on frequency, which he did quickly.

"Dad, can you send someone out here with a crew that can pull this guy off the ledge?"

"In ten minutes or so, yes," he said. "The 412 is just landing on the peninsula."

"I don't know if we have that long."

"Hang in there, Jennifer, and stay on frequency. I'm calling them now by cell phone."

She could see another large, shaped wave bearing down on her and popped the Dauphin back twenty feet higher, watching with her heart in her throat as the unconscious human form was shoved several feet along the top of the wall, both arms now dangling over the far side. One more wave like that, she thought, and he's gone.

There was no conscious decision behind the quick descent back to the wall, but the idea seemed feasible enough to try, with the unspoken understanding in her head that the slightest problem and she'd be out of there.

Quickly she positioned the Dauphin's main wheels over the top of the wall, keeping the helicopter into the wind and locking the brakes. Lester Brown's unconscious form was just to the right. She unloaded the collective fully, putting the weight of the machine on the landing gear, and sat for a second, communing with the machine to check its balance and whether the wind might topple her backward.

It felt stable enough to try.

She unsnapped her seat belt as she popped open her door and swung her feet onto the step and then to the concrete, moving as quickly as she could to the man.

"Lester! Can you hear me?"

Nothing.

She tried to get her arms under him just as a large gust of wind caught the Dauphin. She could see it teeter backward slightly, the rotor blades still churning the air at full rpm for a quick getaway.

Once more she attempted it, but the man had to weigh over two hundred pounds and as dead weight on a slimy, slippery concrete surface, it wasn't going to work.

Jennifer looked to the northwest. The shadow of another huge wave was forming. There was no time.

She leapt for the back door and the winch, trying to motor it downward, but it was jammed again. There was a flashlight in the pocket of the copilot's seatback and she grabbed it and took a large swing at the pulley, hearing an assaulted "thwang" in response.

And suddenly the winch was free. She grabbed the hook and backed away with the line until it reached Lester Brown, then she rolled him over and snapped the hook back into the ring of his harness.

The wave was bearing down on them now, less than a hundred yards out. She launched herself back at the pilot's seat, struggling against heavy gusts of wind that rocked the Dauphin back, feeling the wheels themselves skidding slightly over the slimy green covering of the top of the wall. She slammed her left thigh into the edge of the floor before hauling herself in, being careful not to touch the controls until ready. There was no time for seat belts, but she flailed for and finally caught the door and slammed it shut as her left hand closed around the collective and rotated the throttle, her right shoving the cyclic forward just as the Dauphin's rear landing wheels slid far enough backward to tumble off the wall.

She caught the motion and checked it as she brought in the collective, the dark shape of the approaching wave on her right filling her peripheral vision, the entire sequence unfolding in slow motion as time dilated. She felt the Dauphin stabilize on the edge of the wall, felt the blades bite into the turbulent air for lift, and felt the machine become airborne only to be yanked into a right bank with the weight of Lester Brown hanging from the winch on the right side.

The wave was almost on her as she fought the helicoptor's roll to the right, demanding every ounce of lift it could provide. She was trading rotor rpm for altitude, feeling the man hanging from the line on her right pulled by the massive wave as it brushed him in the process of breaking over the wall in a cascade of hydrodynamic energy.

She let herself take a deep breath and pulled them up to sixty feet of altitude, heading directly for the heliport. She called her father to have someone prepared to catch Lester Brown before she lowered him to the concrete of the helipad.

"CPR may be needed. I couldn't triage him. There was no time."

There was a momentary silence on the other end before Sven replied.

"Jennifer, how the hell did you get him aboard?"

"Not now, Dad. We can talk about it later."

Chapter 40

"Dr. Lam, it's not possible for this boat alone to do what you ask, so I'm calling in another of our tugs. She passed us seaward fifteen minutes ago."

Vivian Speetjens lowered her cell phone after an intense series of calls. The wave state outside was approaching thirty-foot swells, and the wallowing of the big oceangoing tug was making Doug queasy. Salt spray was hitting the windows of the boat at intervals.

"How long will that take?"

"Thirty minutes. She's the *Linda S,* and we'll have her take the aft bridge section and hold it a mile off while we position the first one against your wave barrier. I'll need two of my crew on the first bridge section to tie her down, and that will be the most dangerous part. Can you get that helicopter back, or a bigger one that can lift more weight?"

He nodded. "I think so."

"Please do so. As quickly as you can."

With Lester Brown safely removed from the Dauphin's winch line, Jennifer settled the helicopter back on the concrete and sat in semi-exhaustion for a minute as the rotor blades slowly wound down. She could see Brown beginning to respond to the CPR one of the emergency medtechs was administering, and she resisted the impulse to go join the effort. She saw Lester lift a hand and felt a wave of relief.

Sven Lindstrom opened the pilot-side door and stood assessing his daughter's condition, fighting his own internal battle with the lifelong tendency to instantly issue commands to subordinates and orders to children.

"Honey, you look wrung-out," he said, avoiding the obvious question of how a single pilot could have gotten an unconscious man hooked to the end of a winch line. There was only one answer, but they could discuss it some other time, if ever. He could see she'd begun to tense for that very discussion, but when it didn't come, she sighed and smiled.

"I'm okay, Dad. What are we now, about 50 percent complete on the evacuation?"

"Little over that, Jen. But it's working."

"I'll be ready in a minute."

"Okay. Obviously, it's your choice whether to keep flying, but may your old man make a suggestion?"

"If you put it that way, of course."

"Since the Dauphin is obviously our best rescue ship, and since the rest of the group is doing fine on the turnarounds, maybe you should stay on the pad awhile."

"You've got a point."

Without a word she unbuckled her seat belt and swiveled her aching body around, accepting his hand as she stepped down from the Dauphin and hugged him.

"Thank you, Dad."

"Why?"

She pulled back looking at him. "For asking. For not ordering."

"Old dogs and new tricks, Honey."

"I know, but I appreciate it. And normally I'd tough it out, but I think maybe all of you have it under control without me."

"How about under control because of you?"

She laughed, the sound getting lost in the wind. "The operable word is *control,* and I'm thinking it's time to stop chasing after it so hard."

"There's a mobile lounge over there Walker ordered in and it has several unoccupied sofas you can use. I'll come get you when we're down to the last of us."

She nodded, waving as she walked toward the indicated lounge, which was a very long, very modern motor home.

There were several people sitting in the front room of the coach, and they nodded to her before resuming their own conversation. She moved to the aft sitting room and sat down on one of the facing couches, letting her body rotate slowly to the horizontal as she permitted fatigue to wash over her.

She sat bolt upright just as quickly, remembering her forgotten mission: *Oh my God! I was supposed to find Jason Smith and fly him back to that tug!*

Jennifer jumped to her feet and raced out of the coach, standing in momentary confusion in the cold wind as she tried to recall where the command center was. Instead, she headed directly for the first Cascadia employee she saw carrying a walkie-talkie, enlisting his help in locating his security chief.

The man hunched over the radio for a few exchanges before straightening up.

"He's on his way over here already, Ma'am," the man said.

"Okay. How long?"

"It's a small island, and getting smaller. Two minutes."

"Will you please point him out?"

"Well, he's right there," the man said, gesturing to an approaching electric cart. She waved at Smith and he slowed and got out, listening to her self-introduction as she relayed the need for his immediate presence on the tug.

"Already taken care of, Miss Lindstrom. The tug captain called me a short while ago and I formally commandeered him, and he agreed."

"Really? That's a relief."

"As I understand it, they're going to be placing some sort of floating-highway sections back against the WaveRam, similar to what we had blocking the thing up until several days ago."

"Good. Any word on Mr. Brown?"

"Bruised and a bit hypothermic, but I think he'll be okay. I heard the details of the rescue. That was amazing."

"That's what we do," she answered, feeling uncomfortable. She thanked him and excused herself, returning at a more sedate pace to the coach and the aft sitting room and readjusting to lie down again on the couch.

Jennifer felt her eyes closing and the fuzz of fatigue competing with her mind, which was all but racing around wildly questioning everything.

Can they handle the rotation of the helicopter fleet without me?

Yes. Dad's been doing that.

But did the fuel truck arrive on the other side?

You think our pilots don't know how to monitor their fuel? Besides, it's either there or it's too late.

But how about Doug's progress? Who's going to monitor that?

You mean, who's going to actively worry about that! Damnit, you need sleep. Stop trying to control everything.

Once again she began to drift into the higher realms of sleep only to be jolted out by another disturbing thought.

We're going to have that damned dream again, aren't we? We're going to lose control and crash again because at the critical moment, we let go. What does that tell us?

Her eyes fluttered open and remained open, and the more she tried to force them closed, the more she thought of reasons not to, the small cerebral war escalating to a mental shouting match until she sat bolt upright again, rubbing her eyes and inadvertently voicing her thoughts out loud.

"Damnit! I can't get control of *anything!*"

A man and woman had been standing in the middle part of the coach in conversation. They stopped now and looked in her direction, wondering whether to say anything to the young woman looking so frazzled and frustrated on the rear seat. Jennifer noticed them at the same time and attempted a smile.

"Sorry! It's been a long day."

"Sure, no problem!" the man said, turning back to the woman.

Jennifer, they're doing all right out there without you, okay? Give it up. Relax. Let the world take over.

Once more she lay down, strangely relieved, her immediate burdens formally laid aside, and her eyes closing before her head hit the tiny pillow.

ABOARD THE MV *VIVIAN O. SPEETJENS*

When the first floating-bridge section had been placed against the Wave-Ram, Doug hurriedly punched in the direct number to the seismology lab to find out if the resonant reactions from deep within the Quilieute Quiet Zone had diminished.

"It's hard to say, Doug," Sanjay said. "We just had another 5.3 under Seattle. We're checking right now. Hang on."

A helicopter and crew were working on securing a third line before moving over to the second bridge section, which was already being towed inbound by the *Linda S.*

Sanjay came back on the line, sounding excited. "Doug, this is very preliminary, but the seismic impacts have diminished!"

"By how much?"

"At least a factor of 50 percent, maybe more. The echoes are way down."

"And from the Quiet Zone?"

"Well . . . it's still sending its resonant waves back up, one for one, and the zone is active now from Mendocino County, California, all the way to northern Vancouver Island. The whole thing is alive with activity. But there are changes in progress, so we can hope."

"Keep me posted. The second section is being moved in right now."

Chapter 41

Several dark suspicions had flickered around the edges of Mick Walker's mind during the previous hours of chaos and destruction, but before the unexpected note from Diane Lacombe, he'd rejected them all. The note had been written on a computer and formatted like an e-mail and handed to one of his employees.

> Mick—I'm in your command post and I just found out some amazing and damaging information about Jerry Schultz's involvement in the seismic data deficiency. I've also discovered, much to my shock, that he's here on the island. As you recall, he's my boss at Chadwick and Noble and the man ultimately responsible for the report you received, and its lack of information on the fault. I caught him taking a version of the seismic report from your office after the quake that collapsed part of the hotel! I don't want to be overheard or seen. Could you possibly break away for a few minutes and meet me at the WaveRam overlook?
>
> Diane

Mick took one of the Lincoln Town Cars and drove the short distance to the overlook, crossing the widening break in the roadway caused by the fault. He stopped the car and put it in park, leaving the engine running and the lights on, searching in the perimeter of the darkness for some sign of her, aware that fatigue was playing tricks on his mind. He was mentally exhausted, and among other wild mood swings, it was making him a bit paranoid.

At least he hoped that was the cause of his growing suspicions.

Mick pulled his trench coat around him and buttoned it up against the stiff, cold wind as he got out of the car and walked toward the railing. If Diane was out here somewhere, she had to be freezing, he thought. He stood at the railing, watching the lights of what appeared to be two tugs and a helicopter in the distance as they worked to dismantle his proudest creation. It was a surprise when her voice reached him from less than two feet away.

"Thanks for coming, Mick."

"Diane!" he said, turning and placing his hands on her shoulders. "You must be cold."

She shook him off.

"You have no idea," she said, walking slowly around him like a cat circling its prey, watching his baffled expression.

"What's all this about your boss Schultz and something taken from my office?"

She continued circling, staring at him with an unnerving look that seemed to confirm his worst fears as he kept turning to face her.

"Diane? What's the matter? Talk to me."

She chuckled, looked at the ground, then back at him, having completed a full circle.

"Open your coat, please."

"Excuse me?"

"Open your coat."

He shrugged and unbuttoned his trench coat and she came forward and reached into his inside coat pocket for the small digital recorder he always carried. There was no tiny red light indicating it was on, but she threw it over the railing anyway, a small splash marking its entrance into the water below.

"What was that about?"

He hadn't noticed the tears in her eyes before, but now they were there, streaming down her face.

"I loved you," she said, her voice very controlled.

"Diane, for God's sake. Is that what you wanted to see me about?"

"I loved you, Mick Walker. Since I was, as you have always put it so indelicately and embarrassingly, 'in diapers,' I loved you and wanted you to love me."

"Diane, look—"

"*No!* You look. You listen. This is *my* scene. *My* finale."

"Finale? What are you talking about?"

"I loved you as a little girl, Mick. You had to know it. I collected pictures of you. I hung on your every word when you were at my house. I always hugged you and you hugged me back. When I found out what sex was, I went to sleep each night dreaming of making love to you, giving my sex to you, molding myself to you every night, being your lover, your mistress, anything. And one night on your boat—a magical night when I was just starting college—you took me to your bed and had sex with me."

"Yes, and it was beautiful, Diane. In every way. But it was wrong to make love to you. You were my best friend's daughter. I had no business making love to you."

"You didn't make *love* to me, Mick! Oh, that's what I wanted, all right. I made love to *you,* but love had nothing to do with your motivation, although I didn't know it at the time. No, you just *screwed* me. That's all. You were just using me. There I was, surrendering mind and body to you, deliriously in love with you and all you wanted was to screw me and send me away, like some two-bit whore."

Diane, that is absolutely untrue! That night . . . you were incredible in that red dress, your hair, your face . . . You'd grown up to become a sexy angel and . . . you came on to me. Surely you remember? You were insatiable with your kisses and your hands and . . . and I simply couldn't resist you. I felt terrible about it afterwards. We talked about it, too. I thought we understood each other."

"So why didn't you want more sex? Was I a bad lay?"

"Good Lord, don't be crass. You were a wonderful lover. Amazingly good for your age, but it was wrong."

"No, it was my dream, Mick. You screwed my dream and me, and then walked away without a thought." Her voice became a mocking caricature. "Ya nailed little Diane! Got that little piece of ass and put another notch on your bedstead, didn't you?"

"That is so wrong, Diane. I never thought that way for a moment."

"But you also never held me again, never kissed me, wouldn't take me anywhere. It was back to patting the silly little girl on the head."

"Diane, I am so very sorry that . . . that the way we interacted has hurt you. I never knew you had a crush on me."

"A crush? Is that what you think? A *crush*? I was head over heels in love with you!" Her voice had become a pained cry now, and the tears were flowing again as she spoke through gritted teeth. "I gave myself to you! You were the first."

"Now, Diane, that's just not true."

"Oh, yes it is! I would know."

"Well, so would a guy. I mean, I was not the first."

"You were the first. You were! I handed you my heart and you crushed it, and now . . . now I'm returning the favor."

"I'm sorry, what?"

She was circling again, her face hardening to anger.

"You're ruined, Mick Walker."

"Well, you may be right, but—"

"You're ruined, just like you ruined my life. You've heard the old statement that hell hath no fury like a woman scorned? Well, welcome to hell, bastard!"

"What do mean, exactly, you're returning the favor?"

"You want the details? Start with this. You can't blame Chadwick and Noble for failing to tell you about the fault line, because they did."

"What? You know that's not true!"

"Oh, *you* may believe that's not true, but the evidence will prove otherwise. Your records . . . which are being seized by the FBI in San Francisco as we stand here . . . clearly show that you were given the real report, and you had a bogus version with no fault-line warnings prepared by a confederate and you tried to stick it in our files."

"Diane, that's bullshit and you know it! And I don't care who seizes my records, by the way. I know what's there."

"Do you?"

"What do you mean?"

"I discovered the fault when I crunched my own data before leaving this island. I was shocked, and at first I was going to tell you. Protect you. And I decided to call and see if you'd call me back. You remember that?"

"When?"

"Right before the construction permits were granted? Remember the calls you got from poor naïve little Diane that you just couldn't return yourself?"

"Vaguely."

"Remember my note? I asked you to meet me in Carmel. I said I loved you and that I had something you needed to hear. You ignored me."

"I don't recall any note."

"You didn't want me anymore, and that was your test and you failed it. If you'd just taken me to dinner, kissed me once more, been nice to me, I would have told you what the data really showed before you were committed to lose a hundred million dollars. You didn't care, so guess what? Neither did I."

"I told you I didn't receive any note from you. And regarding the report, the seismic data itself showed nothing about a fault. How do you explain that?"

"Because I doctored the data! Yeah, that's right. You *should* look incredulous. That's the price you pay for using and abusing a young girl's heart. Chadwick and Noble's geological survey department got the doctored data and produced the report you'll be trying to tell everyone you saw. But there's no record of that doctored data anymore, Mick. It's a figment of your imagination. Yet there are plenty of copies of the real data, and of the real report that was prepared and, as all the evidence will clearly show, sent to you personally a long time before construction began."

Mick Walker's face had turned dark with anger. "You'll not get away with this. I have extra copies of the original report that showed no problems, and they were filed with God knows how many different loan applications and other official papers."

"Right. All of them fraudulent. And that was the version Jerry Schultz prepared for you, or so everyone will think. Maybe you shouldn't have secretly put Jerry Schultz on your payroll to make sure you got only the good stuff."

"I never paid Jerry Schultz a cent! I don't even know the man."

"That's not what the records show. And I'm very, very good at making the records airtight."

Mick was shaking his head. "You think I'm not going straight to the authorities with everything you've told me?"

"Oh, I was counting on you to make that threat. Of course, we're out here with the roar of the surf and the wind and no light on my lips. Not even the best surveillance equipment would have a chance of hearing or interpreting what I'm saying to you. Your little recorder's gone, there are no witnesses, and this meeting never happened."

"I have your note."

"So what. Did I sign it? Or did you fabricate it on your computer?"

"Obviously, you're here."

"No, Mick, there is no way to prove that note came from me, or even that I'm here. In fact, I can prove I'm somewhere else on the island right now. But I'll tell you what *can* be proved: a trail of evidence that will show the world Mick Walker doesn't give a damn about safety, or about hearts."

"How can you be this . . . this sinister to me? This hateful?"

"You crushed my heart. You led me on for all those years as a little girl."

"I led you . . . *what?*"

" 'Diane,' you'd say, 'you're so cute! You keep growing and one of these days I'll marry you!' Remember that?"

"Good Lord, Diane, those are just things a man says to flatter and encourage a little girl. No one takes them seriously!"

"I did! And I grew! And I waited for you, and you took me and threw me away, you bastard!"

Mick was all but frantic, his voice barely controlled as the enormity of her preparations unfolded.

"Diane, my God, even if you misunderstood, how could you try to ruin me like this? Have you no heart?"

"I did. And it was yours. And you destroyed it like I'm going to destroy you."

"You need serious professional help, Diane. I mean it! I know you think you've got all your bases covered here, but you don't. This attempt will fail, you'll lose your job, and you may even go to prison. But if you drop this nonsense right now, tell me what you've done to the files so I can repair it, I'll make sure nothing happens to you, provided you agree to some deep psychiatric work."

"Oh, nothing's going to happen to me, Mick. Know why? Because if I have any legal troubles, you're the one going to prison."

"For what? I didn't write any reports, and my attorneys did all the filing in good faith."

"My diary contains the details of that heavenly night in your arms. That and my driver's license will put you away."

"What on earth are you talking about?"

"You forgot my birthday, Mick."

"Your birthday? What does that have to do with anything?"

"I hadn't had it yet. I was still seventeen. I was incapable of giving sexual consent in the state of California."

"No!"

"You raped me, and I can prove it."

For a few moments he couldn't respond. The enormity of the mistake he'd made in having sex with her to begin with was bad enough, but now to be told that she was underage, even if it didn't lead to an indictment, would be unforgivable in Ralph Lacombe's eyes.

He sighed deeply, rubbing his eyes before looking back at her. "All right, Diane. This is the worst night of my life. I surrender. What do you want?"

"What I'm getting. You, ruined."

"What does that accomplish? You said you loved me. Is there no chance of . . . of reinvigorating that?"

She laughed. "Ever the negotiator and the deal maker, aren't you, Mick? But this time you can't wheedle your way out. No, Mick. I don't love you anymore. I just wanted you to know why all this is happening to you. You tromped on the wrong little girl."

She turned and began walking away and Mick rushed after her, roughly grabbing her elbow and turning her around, unnerved by the smug expression on her face.

"Yes, Mick? What are you planning? Want to beat me up? Strangle me? Rape me again?"

"Do you think for a second your father would be anything but mortified at your behavior?"

"Not if he understood what you did." He knew she was right.

She pulled away and resumed walking back toward the helipad, leaving Mick in the middle of the road thoroughly stunned and profoundly frightened at the very intensity of her hatred.

What was worse, he thought, she was just clever enough to pull it off.

Chapter 42

Doug's cell phone rang with Sanjay on the other end just as the last section was tied in place.

"We've had a 6.2 tremor in the Eureka, California, area, Doug, at the southern end of the zone. No major damage as far as we know."

"Sanjay, we're complete out here. The barriers are in place. Please tell me the resonant tremors are decreasing."

"I wish I could. What I can confirm is that all the descending seismic impacts have stopped. But nothing has changed below in the Quiet Zone. It's still roiling."

"I thought what it was sending back up were almost echoes of the pounding this island was taking. You know, for each impulse that goes down, one comes back."

"Maybe we were, but now it's generating its own activity without that stimulus. The hypocenters are in the same place in the middle of the Quiet Zone and the microquakes are all but constant."

"Not just here?"

"All up and down the axis of the zone."

"Oh, shit."

"I'm sorry, Doug."

"So am I."

"We were too late. But it doesn't mean your theory is wrong."

"To hell with my theory!" Doug said, wishing his response hadn't been as sharp. Vivian Speetjens was watching him carefully, obviously aware of the overall nature of the report. The implications were clear: all their efforts had been in vain, and the monstrous subduction zone quake with all its costs now seemed inevitable.

"Doug, I just meant . . ."

"I'm sorry, Sanjay. I didn't mean to take it out on you. It's just that I don't care whether I'm right or wrong about the trigger thing, I just thought we had a real chance of stopping this nightmare."

"Yeah. So did I."

Noel Speetjens was backing the tug away from the secured bridge span with all the crewmembers back aboard as he briefed them on the disturbing results.

"So what do you do now, Doctor?" Vivian asked.

"I guess I hitch a ride with you back to Seattle and get ready for the worst."

"How soon will it hit?"

"I don't know. This is all uncharted territory. Ten seconds. Ten minutes. Ten days. But it's coming."

CASCADIA ISLAND HELIPORT

At last the number of empty seats in the two waiting helicopters equaled the number of humans left on the island, but one was refusing to board.

Sherry Thomas had spent a working lifetime quietly guiding Mick Walker's daily professional life, but all attempts to change his mind now were hitting a brick wall.

"What?" she asked at last, as much out of fatigue as resignation. "You want to go down with the ship, so to speak?"

He pointed to the first helicopter. "Sherry, get aboard. I'll follow later. I have a few things to recover from the office."

Her hands migrated to her hips, her wild, windblown hair too disastrous now to worry about. She figured she looked like a medusa in the stiff, cold wind that had once again accelerated to thirty-knot gusts.

"Mick, stop being stubborn!"

"I can't," he replied, trying and failing to smile. "That's who I am."

"Then I'm staying with you, because that's who I am. Okay?"

"Sherry, I'll be fine."

"We could get washed away any minute, Mick. It's time to go. There's nothing in your office we don't have copies of in San Francisco. We've got all the staff evacuated and it's down to us, and this is stupid."

"There's no time to explain." He was just standing there, hands shoved deep in his pockets, his broad shoulders hunched over against the wind, looking at her with what she once described as Lyndon Johnson eyes.

"Explain what?"

He shook his head, looking down.

"Nothing."

"Then let's go, Mick."

"Just a moment." He pulled out a small notepad and wrote something, pocketed the note, and wrote a longer memo before putting the pad away.

"Okay."

She guided him by the hand toward the open door of the helicopter and he helped her up before following, snapping her seat belt in place and handing the pilot one of the notes when she wasn't looking.

"You're sure, Mr. Walker?" the pilot asked, half turned in his seat.

"I'm sure," he replied, waving away the concerned expression from Sherry as he tore several pages from the small notebook, then folded and handed them to her.

"Read this once you're airborne," he said, backing out of the helicopter and closing the sliding door.

Sherry's hand triggered the seat-belt release and she jumped up intent on reopening the door, but the pilot was already lifting off.

"No!" she yelled forward. "Land! We can't leave him behind!"

"That's what he wants, ma'am," the pilot replied, his eyes still locked out front as he accelerated and climbed away into the stiff, gusty wind.

"No, I said *land!*" she yelled, startled when he took his left hand off the collective long enough to hand her the slightly crumpled note.

> Captain, I'm staying here and will use a lifeboat to get to shore. Do not come back for me, and do not follow Miss Thomas's orders to land again.
>
> Mick Walker

Sherry moved to the cabin window, pressing her face against the Plexiglas to catch a glimpse of Mick still standing alongside the helipad, his right hand raised in a good-bye wave. She saw his hand drop and watched him turn and walk away as the clouds enveloped the helicopter, drawing a misty curtain over the scene.

She sat back in the seat, thoroughly stunned, almost forgetting to open the folded note he'd handed her.

> Sherry,
>
> I know you'd walk with me through hell, and I love you for such blind loyalty, and more. But the hell I've got to traverse now must be traveled alone. Go home, keep the office running, and pray I can untie the noose Diane Lacombe has around my neck. No time for the details, but know that she's insane and determined to ruin me.
>
> Mick

NEAH BAY, WASHINGTON

Noel Speetjens had executed a flawless touch-and-go maneuver at the Neah Bay dock, letting Lam step off the powerful tug to hire a ramshackle local taxi for the almost four-hour drive back to Seattle.

With his cell phone car charger hooked into the aging beater's grimy cigarette lighter he was rapidly back in communication, relieved to find that everyone had been successfully airlifted from Cascadia Island, and equally disheartened to hear from Sanjay that nothing in the Quiet Zone had quieted. By the time the smoky, drafty old cab had rumbled past the town of Sequim on the northeast side of the Olympic Peninsula, he'd given up worrying about carbon monoxide asphyxiation and fallen asleep in the backseat.

Doug awoke on the outskirts of Seattle with the sun slowly poking through the low-hanging clouds to the east. They rolled past downtown Seattle and made the turnoff to the university district, and within minutes he was walking back into the familiar confines of the seismology lab, feeling defeated on too many fronts to count.

Sanjay greeted him at the door with the look of an exhausted mad scientist, his hair uncombed and wild as he hugged his boss and accepted the order to go home and get some sleep.

When he was alone, Doug tried to locate Jennifer, leaving messages everywhere in vain. He settled into a chair in front of the array of seismic drums, a pencil gyrating between his fingers as he watched the needles faithfully recording the continuous microtremors with old-fashioned ink lines across the curved paper surface. The adjacent computer screens showed even more detail, as the Cascadia Subduction Zone continued to shake off its restraints, moving inexorably toward what had to be the ultimate eruption.

It was, he thought, a death watch.

CASCADIA ISLAND

The remains of his office had pancaked into the floors below, but it was still reachable, and Mick was gambling it would be worth the climb.

He was all alone now, the cold wind howling in his ears as he climbed around the jagged, broken rebar with a large flashlight and carefully scaled the disastrous pile of rubble that twenty-four hours before had been one of the world's most beautiful new hotels. Nothing looked familiar when he reached the top, but there were still enough sections of the floor intact so he could make his way to what had been the entrance to his office suite.

Mick stopped for a few seconds and sat on a cold, wet piece of concrete slab, planning his next moves. One slip and he could break a leg or worse, with no one left on the island to rescue him. But he had no choice. The office procedure he'd instituted many years ago of making a sequential copy of virtually every piece of paper that crossed his desk had long since been reduced to the ones and zeros of digital scanning, the voluminous resulting files stored on removable hard drives with incredible capacity. It was a habit only he and Sherry and one secretary in each office knew about, and the resulting pristine record had already helped him win two lawsuits.

The built-in safe had been behind a panel in the wall, hidden behind the bookcase across from his desk, but there was little to mark where things had been. The roof had cascaded onto the furniture below, crushing everything, and he played the powerful beam of light around carefully, looking for something to triangulate on. His steps had been carefully placed, but one teetering piece of broken ceiling too many shifted beneath his foot and for a moment he was grabbing air, twisting and frantically trying to avoid a headlong plunge to a black abyss of tangled steel and concrete below.

The palm of his hand found something to grab just in time, and he rebalanced himself with a death grip on the piece of protruding metal, realizing with a start that the lifesaving shard had hours before been part of the wall behind his desk.

Okay, then the bookcase is over there!

Was over there, he corrected himself.

Carefully Mick made his way across the angry tangle of debris, kicking aside the remains of a prized bronze sculpture of a wild mustang, the twenty-thousand-dollar purchase now jagged junk waiting to impale the unwary.

There was a slab of splintered, finished wood ahead and a jumble of books below, and he walked the flashlight to one side, seeing a glint of steel beneath a piece of concrete from the roof.

Getting to his knees to see beneath the concrete was a delicate and painful maneuver, but the reward was immediate: the undamaged inner shell of the steel safe was there, its door facedown in the rubble.

Mick pushed at the concrete, realizing with a sinking feeling that it probably weighed several hundred pounds. He tried bracing his back against another large, angled slab and pushing with his leg muscles, but the massive chunk barely moved. In a sustained battle between muscle and the inertia of concrete and steel, the latter would win.

He began looking for something stout to use as a lever, trying and breaking the shaft of a brass hat rack before finding a steel tube that might be stout enough. He carefully wedged the end of it beneath the concrete, calculating which way he needed to push it before checking his own footing and starting the process of transferring every ounce of energy he had into sending the chunk of concrete over the edge.

There was an eternity of pulling, with pain rippling through his arms and sweat pouring into his eyes, despite the freezing windchill. He was coming to the end of his endurance. But suddenly, there was a small movement, then more, and he pulled harder, fearing the consequences if the metal rod broke and snapped back in his face.

It held, and the slab slid over the edge, dragging the steel bar along with it, thundering into the debris below and dislodging a small cascade of unseen items in the dark.

When everything had quieted, Mick picked up the flashlight again, his hands shaking with the effects of his exertion, the beam revealing the welcome sight of his safe, now free of its restraints.

He crawled down to it, turned it upright, and dialed in the combination, feeling as much as hearing the precision-made tumblers clicking into place. The door swung open easily, revealing a small counter with a number that confirmed he had been the last person to open the safe.

And inside was exactly what he needed to find. There was no way Diane Lacombe could have known.

UNIVERSITY OF WASHINGTON SEISMOLOGY LAB

The jumbled, troubled dream Doug had been battling ended and he awoke abruptly. The seismograph drums were still right in front of him, but something had changed. His eyes focused and he froze, almost afraid to breathe lest any movement alter the flat line he was seeing at the end of the needles.

Apparently, the microquakes had stopped cold.

No squiggles.

Nothing!

He glanced at the adjacent drums and saw the same flat-line reading.

Gingerly, he reached for the laptop keyboard and triggered a circuit check. The quick-acting program flashed around the seismic array of western Washington and reported everything normal.

Doug felt his heart accelerating. In several great quakes around the planet in previous years, the onset of the main quake had been preceded by an eerie seismic quiet, sometimes lasting hours. The hairs stood up on the back of his neck as if an electrical current was pulsing through his brain, trying to deny that he might be seeing the curtain coming up—or down—on the big one.

But after nearly a minute, he dared to take a breath, looking around in vain for someone to corroborate what he was seeing.

The drums recording the deeper areas of the subduction zone beneath Seattle were located off to one side in the lab, and their needles were still moving back and forth as normal, telling of background seismic activity forty to fifty miles down.

But what he had named the Quilieute Quiet Zone—the trigger point—was once more living up to its name.

Doug sat back, mind racing, eyes glued to the needles, a pencil once again gyrating at a frantic pace in his right hand as he forced himself to keep breathing normally. He reached for the intercom to call the team back in from an adjoining room where they were trying to grab some rest.

"Either it's about to happen," he told a sleepy Sanjay, "or we stopped it. Not that I can dare to really believe it worked."

"It's possible. And it could also be the calm before the break. I'll be right there."

Two hours passed, then four. The rhythmic tremors beneath Mt. Rainier became anemic and began to decline in strength.

The media caught wind of the sudden change. No one had yet relayed the story of how a decommissioned floating bridge had come to be jammed against a breakwater on Cascadia Island, or how that might relate to the sudden reversal of the USGS earthquake warning, but the fact that something had changed was altering the national story of the Pacific Northwest's coastal evacuation.

By late afternoon, the TV microwave trucks that had been chronicling the exodus from coastal communities were once again lining the street outside the lab, their cameramen poking their lenses over the shoulders of the scientists to record the continuous seismographic signature of a subduction zone going back to sleep. In interview after interview Doug stressed all the right caveats and warnings, but as the hours passed, he slowly began to hope.

Chapter 43

The panel of impeccably dressed senior lawyers representing the Chapter 11 filing of Cascadia Island Resorts, Incorporated, had spent the previous ten minutes arranging a stack of neatly prepared notebooks on the counsel table. The chairman of the corporation, Mick Walker, had been in the hallway the entire time talking to reporters, but now he, too, entered the ornate courtroom and walked to the counsel table exuding confidence and control.

"Everything go okay out there, Mick?" Dane Henry, his lead attorney asked.

Mick nodded and smiled. "They just can't get their arms around someone being honest, I guess."

"You've made all the tabloids, you know."

"I know."

"Most of it is leering, but essentially favorable."

"How can it be favorable, Dane? I'm guilty of statutory rape."

"Yes, but you openly admitted it and brought it yourself to the D.A. I'm not a criminal defense guy, but I agree you're going to, at worst, get probation and community service."

"It's nothing to gloat over. It was a stupid mistake."

The court clerk had entered again and was taking her position to call the court to order.

"How is she, Mick?"

"Not good. She's still being held for psychiatric observation."

"Did you really pay for her criminal defense?"

He nodded. "Against some fifteen felony counts? Not even Ralph Lacombe could handle that. Chadwick and Noble and their insurance company want her head on a pike."

But the worst of it, Mick thought, was the stunned loss of a lifelong friendship which had predictably accompanied the destruction of Ralph's beloved daughter. And there was no way Mick Walker could excuse himself from his own culpability. She may have been a little girl with a crush, but he should have seen it. Physically loving her had been nothing less than a gross violation of trust.

"All rise!" the clerk called, continuing with the usual litany preceding the arrival of a member of the federal judiciary.

Dane put a hand on Mick's shoulder, speaking almost directly in his ear.

"Are you ready for the collective gasp we're going to hear?"

"Yes. Almost looking forward to it."

The opening rituals of calling the case and five minutes of routine matters before the court gave way at last to Dane Henry standing and waiting for the judge to acknowledge him.

"Mr. Henry?" the judge said.

"Your honor, may it please the court, the petitioner at this time wishes to file a supplementary declaration changing this action from one under Chapter 11 of the federal bankruptcy code, to a Chapter 7 liquidation."

"Continue."

"Your honor, Cascadia Resorts has reached a settlement in principle with Universal Underwriters, the insurance carrier for Chadwick and Noble. Under that agreement, Chadwick and Noble, because of the liability created by the actions of their employees, and one employee in particular, has agreed to take on all outstanding liabilities of Cascadia Island Resorts, Incorporated, agreed to refund on a dollar-for-dollar basis the capital of the corporation in return for assignment of the lease to Cascadia Island, and agreed to accept assignment in full of all liability to any third parties and former Cascadia employees as a result of the brief, catastrophic operation of the resort. In addition, they have agreed to remove all debris and other man-made items from the island and return it within five years to the status of a protected bird sanctuary."

The judge shook his head slightly. "I must say, Mr. Henry, this is a rather stunning turn of events. The court had the impression your client was fighting hard to rebuild."

"Yes, your honor, we were. But the reality is that Cascadia Island is unsafe, a reality Chadwick and Noble essentially knew and failed to communicate, and compensating all the damages still doesn't make the island safe. We will perhaps never know if the presence of Mr. Walker's wave-generating structure seismically triggered the swarm of earthquakes that led to the evacuation of the Washington and Oregon coasts that night, nor are we likely to ever know whether a few heroic actions authorized by Mr. Walker were the factor that ultimately prevented the massive, threatened quake from occurring. We do know two key things, however. Point one, Cascadia Resorts would have never built on that island if Chadwick and Noble had done their job and reported the extreme dangers; and point two, three hundred years of unrelieved seismic pressure is still locked beneath that island, and it's nothing to be trifled with."

Amid the quiet scramble of reporters leaving the courtroom and the declaration of a recess, Sherry Thomas materialized at Mick's side, smiling.

"What?" he asked, smiling back.

"May I say something very personal and off the record to the chairman?"

"Of course."

"I'm very proud of you, Mick."

He shook his head, the smile fading.

"That makes only one of us."

QUAALATCH, WASHINGTON

Marta Cartwright placed the fresh cup of herbal tea on the small coffee table and resumed her favorite chair across the tiny living room, smiling gently at the man sitting uncomfortably in a small, mismatched wicker chair.

"The hope that I had that my grandson would find the right path was almost destroyed. But now that hope is rescued through bravery, and, frankly, ending the association with those two fools."

"Bull and Jimmy?" he asked, sipping his tea.

She nodded. "No more contact is allowed by the judge, is that right?"

"Yes. Five-year suspended charges, then it all disappears if there's no new violation, and there's a list of people whom they can't contact. You included."

"With the name Lester at the top of the no-contact list?"

He nodded. "Yes."

"Very good." She sipped her own tea, her eyes wandering to the seascape beyond her window for a minute before speaking again.

"I did not read the signs correctly. I let my own feelings get in the way, my anger. It *was* the earth ready to rise up and cleanse these things that were wrong, but there was a solution short of annihilation, and I had not expected that. I did not expect to be here to see this, and I must tell you I'm grateful for the extra time, and to no longer see that hateful light flashing in my face."

There was a deep sigh from the other side of the table. "I'm so sorry I didn't sit down and listen to you a long time ago."

"It was easier to not listen. It was easier to let your ego rule you. There were voices all around you and you had your fingers in your ears like a little boy."

"That's about right."

"And now the island is to be restored, there is enough residual lease money to benefit everyone, the very legitimate charges for destroying other people's property have been dropped, and you have learned much that's valuable on this journey, including humility."

"You're right. There's no question I've changed along with that island. And it's high time I started listening to those voices and—how did you put it . . . let the universe bring me a few gifts for a change?"

She smiled and leaned forward. "How long a road it has been for you from Adelaide. Thank you for these gifts of hope, and for being brave enough to bring them to me in person, Mick."

Epilogue

Despite all her training and instincts as a helicopter pilot, Jennifer Lindstrom did the unthinkable and took her hands off the controls.

Yet the big commercial Chinook helicopter with twenty-six paying passengers aboard continued to fly straight and level, the overwhelmingly beautiful vista of the Caribbean and clouds and blue sky staying right where they should be in the windscreen. They were over an archipelago of beautiful islands baking far below in the tropical sun.

To compound the heresy, Jennifer also moved her feet off the pedals that controlled the yawing motion of the craft.

And still it flew on, steady as a rock.

Smiling, exhilarated, confident, and feeling decadent, she lifted her hands over her head and clasped them together, feeling free, losing herself like a kid riding no-hands on a bicycle—a gesture no sane rotary wing pilot would make at the controls.

The horizon remained steady.

She closed her eyes, feeling the smile grow, her eyelids fluttering open only when a small sideways motion caught her attention.

In an instant everything changed. Forces pulled at her the wrong way, shoving her to the right, and there were whitecaps and islands in the windscreen that moments before showed only blue skies. Her heart rate jumped to alarm level as she felt her body suddenly become lighter. Instead of flying straight and level, the big Chinook twisted to the left, its attitude dangerously nose-down, the airspeed rising.

But she was forcing herself to trust the machine despite its apparent betrayal. She folded her arms and made a supreme effort to relax, determined as never before to accept whatever happened and surrender control.

The surface of the ocean was rising fast as the helicopter spun inexorably downward, but still she sat and watched, willing the machine to do what it was designed to do, fly and recover.

And suddenly the nose was rising again, the side loads gone. The big chopper steadied out to level flight just as something hit her in the gut.

She looked down, confused, wondering how she'd come to be in a bikini all of a sudden and lying on a chaise lounge. She looked back up then to the sheepish grin of a young boy with ragged swim trunks.

Jamaican, she decided, with a lovely smile. He was pointing to her, half turning as if embarrassed to confront a pretty woman, and she dropped her gaze to find his Frisbee sitting on her stomach.

"Sorry, my lady!" he giggled, catching it adroitly as she spun it back to him with a flick of her left hand.

Her right hand was holding something and she looked in that direction, squinting against the delicious warmth and glare of the sun to see it was the hand of a well-tanned male dozing in the chaise next to her.

As she studied the detail of his body, Doug Lam stirred, smiling in his sleep, and she closed her eyes again to join him.

Author's Note

Someday, a great earthquake will begin shaking the U.S. Pacific Northwest from Northern California to Vancouver Island in British Columbia. The massive temblor will be a monster, lasting up to five minutes as it releases at least three hundred years of pent up tectonic energy and measures as high as M9.5 on the Moment Magnitude Scale. And, minutes after the shaking ends, the same coastal areas will face a massive tsunami, just as they did the last time.

Of course *Saving Cascadia* is a work of fiction, but I think it's important to know that the geophysical background of this story is mostly fact: there really *is* a Cascadia Subduction Zone, for instance, and it does run along a north-south axis from the coast of northern California through Oregon and Washington to the northern end of Vancouver Island. It's the area in which the westward-bound North American tectonic plate collides with and overrides an oceanic slab of rock known as the Juan de Fuca tectonic plate—the same continent-building process that produces mountain ranges and volcanoes—and one I wrote about extensively in a 1988 nonfiction book called *On Shaky Ground*.

There is a locked and dangerous section of the Cascadia Subduction Zone, and for the purposes of this high-speed tale, I've assigned it a fictional name: the "Quilieute Quiet Zone." It is, by whatever name, an area of locked rock in slow-motion collision some twenty kilometers beneath the coast, and as long as it remains locked, we remain spared from the next great subduction zone earthquake.

Similarly, my so-called "Theory of Resonant Amplification" concocted by the story's geophysicist, Doug Lam, is, in reality, nothing more than my own fictional leap from solid science to convenient speculation about what could trigger a catastrophic release of the pressure in the Quiet Zone. The theory, in brief, is this: That there are three spots along the Vancouver Island-Washington-Oregon coasts where any large, man-made vibrations or impacts on the ground (such as pile drivers or explosives) will be focused and amplified by the vertical shape of the strata below as the waves pass downward through the miles of rock, and that means that the resulting seis-

mic impacts—however puny in comparison with nature's normal forces—
would end up hammering away, squarely, at what is probably the hair-trigger of that future great quake. If the Cascadia Subduction Zone is already at
the breaking point (and it may well be), who knows whether something as
seemingly insignificant as that could serve as the proverbial "last straw."

Seismology is too new a science to have all the answers, yet what seismologists in particular have learned to do with seismographs is just short of
black magic: akin to someone placing a stethoscope against the side of the
Sears Tower in Chicago, tapping lightly on the wall, and redrawing the entire engineering schematic based on nothing more than interpretation of
the echoes. That "black magic"—accompanied by the brilliance and hard
work of our geologists and the U.S. Geological Survey—has put together a
clearer picture of the seismic hazards we face than we ever thought possible. For instance, we now know that the last great earthquake and massive
tsunami along the Pacific Northwest coast was not only in the year 1700,
but specifically around 9 P.M. on January 26, 1700, a fact uncovered by astounding scientific detective work spanning half the globe.

Come visit my Web site at www.JOHNJNANCE.com for more information and links to some fascinating Web sites dealing with these subjects.

Acknowledgments

First and foremost—and as always—this work was made possible by the the the professional efforts of my in-house editor and business partner, Patricia Davenport, BA, MA, as well as the steadfast support of my University Place staff, Gloria Gallegos and Lori Carr, and the extensive editorial help and ideas from Bunny Nance.

The writing of *Saving Cascadia* required the generous help of professionals in a host of disciplines, chief among them seismology, geology, medicine, aeronautics, nautical navigation, and engineering.

I especially want to single out and thank my old friend Dr. Brian Atwater of the USGS in Seattle, to whom this book is codedicated, along with Art Tiller, chief pilot for Airlift NW; Bob Yerex, veteran airevac and Coast Guard helicopter pilot; Clark Stahl, consummate helicopter pilot of Seattle's Chopper 7 (KIRO-TV) and another old friend (not too old); all of whom read the manuscript and assisted immeasurably by fine-tuning my presentation of both the massive seismic threat to the Pacific Northwest, and my presentation of the care and feeding of helicopters, especially those used to transport injured people. Brian Atwater was one of the bulwark contributors to my 1988 nonfiction work, *On Shaky Ground,* which covered the true threat of major earthquakes to the entire United States.

From the medical community there have been many friends and colleagues whose ideas and guidance have materially assisted me, including several from the National Patient Safety Foundation, Kathleen Bartholomew, BS, RN, nurse manager in Orthopedics at Seattle's Swedish Hospital; Dr. Paul Abson of the Everett Clinic and Dr. Diana Abson-Kraemer; and, even though he may not be aware of his contribution, friend and fellow author Dr. Alan Wyler.

In Laramie, Wyoming, Cindy Elrod of the University of Wyoming provided much appreciated reading and manuscript corrections.

I, of course, want to thank the members of my great publishing team at Simon & Schuster, starting with Executive Vice President and Publisher David Rosenthal; Publisher Carolyn Reidy; my wonderful Simon & Schuster senior editor, Marysue Rucci; and Marysue's frighteningly efficient and

eternally friendly assistant, Tara Parsons; along with copy editor Tom Pito-
niak; Elizabeth Hayes, associate director of Publicity; and my long-time
friend and mentor Adene Corns.

And my great appreciation, as well, to my agents at The Writer's House,
Amy Berkower and Simon Lipskar, whose advice and intellect guided this
project.

Ultimately, my eternal thanks to you for being a loyal fan and reader. The
Web site is for you, www.JOHNJNANCE.com, and my e-mail address is:
talktojohnnance@johnjnance.com. I love to hear from you, and that e-mail
address does in fact reach me in person.

About the Author

John J. Nance is the author of seventeen major books, five of them nonfiction. Two of his works, *Pandora's Clock* and *Medusa's Child*, aired as highly successful television miniseries. He is a decorated Air Force pilot, veteran of Vietnam and Operation Desert Storm, a veteran airline captain, ABC's aviation analyst, and a popular professional speaker on issues of safety, communications, and teamwork, especially to the medical profession. John welcomes communications from his readers and can be reached through www.johnjnance.com.